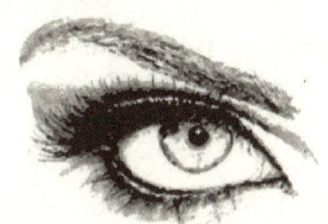
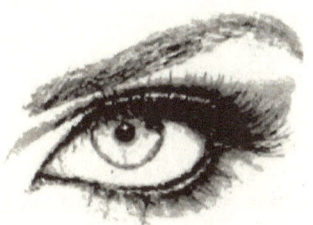

# RETRIBUTION

## A Novel By Stephanie Baldi

Published by Dancing Crows Press
306 Huntington Drive
Temple, GA 30179

ISBN: 13 978-0-9704420-2-4 – Print

ISBN 13-978-0-9704420-3-1– eBook

LCCN: 2019903411

Edited by Elyse Wheeler, PhD
Cover Design by Mary Rogers
Layout by Colin Wheeler

Printed in
The United States of America

# Dedication

To my Nick, for always being
there to encourage me.

And to my Mom, who knows I did it.

# Acknowledgments

Dr. Elyse Wheeler, my right hand, my guide, couldn't have done it without you. Claudia Rowe Kennedy, dear friend, for your continued support and encouragement. To all my Mexican Train gals at Fairfield, thank you once again for your love and inspiration.

My amazing family who never ceases to lift me up. To the Carrollton Writers Guild for continuing to make me a better writer. You are the best. To my Brooklyn girls, Marianne, Doreen, & Pat who are always close to my heart. And to my fantastic fans who inspire me to write the stories, I need to tell.

# CHAPTER 1
## Carmela

Carmela Santiago reveled in the power beneath her. With both her legs in a neutral position, she concentrated, applying equal pressure against Diablo's sides to increase her horse's speed. Hot wind swept past her face. The pounding of his hooves surrounded her, their rhythm a beating heart. She gripped the reins as they approached the first hurdle. Leaning forward, she held on, clearing the fence with ease. Her long, dark braid sailed out from under her riding cap. A smile spread across her lips. She patted Diablo's side in appreciation.

An hour later, with Mateo's help, she transferred the horse into the trailer. Diablo, given to her as a peace offering from one of the many drug cartels she dealt with, trained well. The world-class Arabian's stamina outdid Allegra's. But Allegra, a precious gift from her father, Ricardo, held a special place in her heart. While Allegra's performances at Dressage Competitions were outstanding, Diablo had neither the temperament nor patience to parade around a ring. He preferred the challenge of the jump, just like his master. Carmela rode both horses with pride.

She found it hard to believe almost six years had passed since Ricardo's death. The relentless ache inside her burned as she recalled how his life ended from a bullet to his brain, courtesy of Nicholas D'Angelo, the one-man Ricardo had trusted above all others. So much so, he'd wanted a marriage between Nick and his only child.

Carmela reflected on how her future might have gone if Nick hadn't betrayed them both. Her admiration developed from a child's crush into the cravings of a woman, but she never let her emotions show after discovering he wasn't in love with her. He'd fallen for someone else. Carrie Overton stole Nick away, turning him against her father.

She swallowed hard and chewed her lower lip. Carrie, now Mrs. D'Angelo, stood in the place belonging to her.

She'd found out, besides Carrie's son, Bobby, they had two children together, Isabelle, a five-year-old girl, and Michael, a two-year-old boy named in memory of Nick's deceased brother.

Thinking about those children set off thunderstorms in her mind. They were the children she should have borne him. Her teeth clenched, producing the familiar ache in her jaw. Taking several deep breaths, she tried to calm herself.

The past years had given her the freedom to continue to build her father's businesses into an empire fueled by a steady stream of drug money. She liked to think how proud he'd be to see how much she'd accomplished.

A silver Lincoln sedan drove up, and she climbed into the rear seat.

"You were amazing out there." His voice, smooth as silk, washed over her while his dark eyes caught hers in the rearview mirror.

*"Gracias,* Diego.*"* She sank into the soft leather and admired his jet-black hair dipping below his collar. Her desire rose. She smiled knowing soon they'd satisfy it.

Diego Silva, her most trusted bodyguard, had also become her lover. Not a wise choice, but running her drug business left little time for vetting suitors.

They drove to the stables behind the vineyards in Napa. The winery where her father died became the place to which she devoted most of her life. No one understood her attachment, but she stayed because she needed to keep the memory of his death close. Satisfaction would never come until she avenged his death.

Carmela followed Mateo to Diablo's stall while Diego leaned against the Lincoln. A musky scent emanating from the horses greeted her and mixed with the sweet-smelling hay. Hooks, hanging from the rough wooden walls in the tack area, held bridles, leads, curry combs, and other equipment.

She rubbed Diablo's muzzle before turning to Mateo. "Make certain you curry him before you brush him. Pick out his hooves. Check his eyes and nose—"

Mateo held up his hand. He tipped back his large black Cattleman's hat. The dark skin between his brows wrinkled. "*Señorita,* I will take good care of him...as always."

She shook her head and smiled. "I'm sorry, Mateo. I know you are as devoted to him as I am."

A loud whinny came from a stall behind her. Allegra pushed his head through the opening in the gate and whinnied again. She grabbed a carrot from a feedbag hanging outside the stall and presented it to Allegra. He chomped it down in two bites, then nuzzled her empty palm, his bristles tickling her skin.

"Mateo, turn Allegra out in the pasture. He seems restless."

"*Si, Señorita*

She left the stable, and Diego held the car door open. They drove, in silence, to the spacious mansion. She climbed the stone steps and hurried inside.

The Napa house, larger than the one in Miami and as well-appointed, boasted imported tile plus custom woodwork throughout. Massive windows framed grand views of the gardens and vineyards. Various rooms contained priceless art displayed according to their form, the collections here superior to the Miami artwork.

Her butler, Armando, greeted her in the marble foyer. Dressed impeccably in a white shirt with Windsor cut collar, grey tie, black jacket and trousers, he stretched out his arm.

*"Buenas tardes,"*

Employed by her family since her childhood, she was grateful when he agreed to stay on after her father's passing.

She removed her cap and coat and handed it to him. "Thank you, Armando."

He bowed and smiled. "Can I bring you anything, *Señorita?"*

"No, thank you. Maybe later."

With each step up the large winding staircase, her heart beat faster. Within minutes, Diego would climb these same stairs to her bedroom.

Carmela closed the door. She pulled off her riding boots and unbraided her hair, letting it fall in waves down her back, the ends dipping below her waist. Stripping off her clothes, she admired her caramel-colored skin in the full-length mirror.

The bedroom door opened. Diego rushed in. He removed his coat, then his shoulder holster, dropping them to the floor. Continuing to peel off his clothes, he shook his head. "My God, you make a grown man weak as a kitten."

The corners of her mouth edged up into a smile, her skin tingling at the sight of his naked body. "And you make a grown woman blush."

Diego pressed up against her, easing her onto the bed. He stroked her face and whispered, "Carmela, I love you. I have never felt like this before."

Her body went stiff, and she frowned. "Why do you have to spoil things?" She moved away and rose from the bed. Grabbing her robe from the pale blue tufted bench at the foot, she slipped it on. She didn't want to hear his foolish talk about love.

"Carmela, why do you act this way?" His voice held a twinge of anger. "Come back to bed."

She scowled at him. "Diego, we have gone over and over this a million times. I'm not looking for love. Not now, not ever."

Diego cursed under his breath. He jumped up and gathered his clothes. "What is this obsession you have? I'm warning you, if you pursue your crazy revenge, it will not end well. These things never do. You need to let it go, Carmela."

She crossed her arms and stuck out her chin. He could never imagine the scene she'd witnessed. Otherwise, he'd agree with her plans.

"This crazy revenge, as you call it, is not something I can let go. My father is dead!" A single tear erupted from her eye.

Diego moved closer. "I know how much you hurt," he soothed. "But this idea of yours may get you killed." He wiped the tear from her cheek.

Carmela brushed his hand away. She secured the sash on her robe. "You don't understand. It is my duty to make his assassin pay. My heart knows he will never rest in peace until I do." She rushed past him and ran downstairs to her study.

Turning the lock, she collapsed into the leather chair behind her desk. She removed a photograph from the drawer. Her pain still palpable, she studied the faces inside the frame. Nick stood beside her, his arm draped around her shoulder. They smiled into the camera. What a charade. Now, she could see right through his false smile, the too casual way his arm rested upon her. What she once perceived as love meant nothing more to him than a caring friendship. While his feelings floated above the surface, hers ran much deeper.

As an awkward young girl in middle school, she dreamt of a future with Nick. Something she had never admitted to anyone. If Nick had complied with her father's wishes to marry her, she wanted him to do it because he loved her and not out of obligation.

Those dreams of hers turned into a nightmare after Carrie stole Nick from her. Carmela's malice twisted itself around her gut, forming a deep chasm nothing could fill until the day she made Nick pay. The desire she once felt for him grew into a bitter hatred, encompassing all those he cared for.

Placing the photograph inside the drawer, she fingered a folder lying on her desk and flipped it open. She stared at still shots of Carrie D'Angelo and another man. She studied his features. His appearance proved him to be much older than her. Below the man's photo, written in her father's handwriting, she read the name, Travis Montgomery. Besides being the thief Nick executed for him, what was his connection to Carrie? The time to find the answer had come.

Sweeping the two photos aside, she picked up another one. She recognized the two men lying in pools of blood. Carlos and Eddie once worked for her father. Carrie Overton along with Travis Montgomery had shot them to death. Nick, given orders by Ricardo to find and kill them, deviated from his assignment by killing Travis and allowing Carrie to live.

In teaching her the business, her father had taken off the blinders, making it clear what kind of work Nick performed. He made sure she understood in the drug trade someone like Nick became a necessity.

Since her father's death, she acquired her own person of necessity, Miguel Medina. Whenever the need arose to eliminate someone, she called Miguel. Trustworthy and efficient, she relied on him to take care of the ugly side of the business. She could have ordered him to kill Nick and his family long ago, but she wanted more. They needed to feel her suffering.

She examined the photos again before sweeping them aside. Underneath them lay a newspaper clipping. Bobby D'Angelo's smiling face stared at her. The headline read, 'Young Art Dealer to Show Premier Collection at New York Gallery.'

Carmela pursed her lips and continued to stare at the newspaper. She reached for the phone.

"Bernardo, get my private jet ready. I need to fly to New York tomorrow." Carmela set the receiver down and closed the folder. She rose and wandered to the window.

"*Papi,*" she said. "I am listening to you. I hear you crying out from your grave. It has taken me a while, but I will make those words I said to Nick become a reality. I won't stop until he's dead. I won't stop until they are all dead."

# CHAPTER 2
## Bobby

Bobby D'Angelo stretched out his arms toward the woman lying next to him. Tracing the soft skin in between her shoulder blades, he buried his face in her hair and inhaled. Lavender tinged his nose. A low whimper escaped her mouth. She turned and nuzzled his neck.

"Good morning," she murmured, sleep still in her eyes.

Smiling, he gathered her close. "Sure is."

Her hand trailed across his chest. "What's buzzing around inside your mind?"

Bobby rolled onto his back. Out of habit, he swept away the lock of dark brown hair dipping over his right eye. Hands clasped behind his head, he relished the quiet morning and the woman beside him.

"Nothing too, much."

He'd been seeing Valerie Gold several times a week for the past two months. Late one night, her green eyes, the color of seagrass, and her long blond hair captured his attention in a club on the Upper East Side. Bobby couldn't imagine what this meant to her, but he understood what it meant to him. Lust, pure and simple. He couldn't afford to get tangled up in a relationship right now.

Bobby's career remained foremost in his mind. His passion for art had taken root not long after his mother's shooting in Lugano, Switzerland. During her hospital stay, with bodyguards put in place by Nick, he wandered the art galleries. From abstract to impressionism and contemporary, Bobby found art soothed him. While he studied the vast array of canvases, something sparked inside. He wanted others to feel and appreciate art the way he did. While his mother recovered, he switched majors and studied what he loved.

He attended gallery shows where he befriended wealthy collectors and gave them advice regarding their purchases. His reputation grew, and he became one of the most sought after, albeit the youngest, Art Dealer in the country, with a knack for finding up-and-coming artists.

To him, nothing topped living in New York City. Next to some galleries in Europe, no better place existed to take in the many art museums. He loved spending hours at a time at the Guggenheim, the Whitney, and the Metropolitan among others.

But right now, he wanted Valerie out of his condo. Set to premiere a young artist from Brooklyn at a gallery on Fifth Avenue in the evening, Bobby needed to get ready. His gut told him this artist's work would command a fortune one day.

He kissed Valerie's forehead and slipped out of bed.

She let out a moan. "What's the rush? Stay with me a little longer."

"Can't, babe. I have to go to the gallery and make sure everything is set for tonight."

"All right, but is there room in the shower for two?"

Bobby winked. "Always."

An hour later, with Valerie gone, and a towel wrapped around his waist, he stepped into his walk-in master closet. Oak shelving held sweaters on one side and shoes on the other. Jeans and several pairs of pants hung in a neat row beside numerous shirts, all this a far cry from his home in Laurel, Pennsylvania where, as an unhappy teenager, he had thrown his clothes inside his meager closet. Now a grown man, he took great care of his belongings and appreciated their value.

He dressed in jeans and a wine-colored cashmere sweater, always avoiding a suit. Unlike Nick, he hated the confines of one.

He crossed the grey carpeted living room leading to the modern kitchen. He stopped to straighten the striped throw pillows lining the contemporary beige sofa. Lightness filled his chest and he smiled. Last night, passionate kisses between Valerie and him had started here before they gravitated to his bedroom.

He glanced up at the canvas hanging above. The abstract painting by Carolyn O'Neill, an Australian artist, had been his first purchase of fine art. He fell in love with the piece at her art show and rejoiced knowing he could afford it. The striking mix of blues, greens, and oranges stirred his emotions, bringing him a sense of peace. A peace which had eluded him for so many years growing up in a household run by a monster.

Bobby grabbed the remote for the mounted flat screen and let the news drone on in the background while he brewed coffee. He sipped a quick cup and walked to the floor-to-ceiling windows.

Autumn exhilarated him. The trees, twenty stories below in Central Park, wore a montage of colors. He understood why Nick always longed to come here. But it wasn't safe. The people Bobby loved and cared for the most remained tucked away in a compound in Tuscany, Italy.

He couldn't live a secluded life, so he made a move to New York. Nick agreed to purchase the condo for him on the Upper West Side under the condition he teach Bobby how to protect himself. Shooting lessons and self-defense tactics became a priority before he left Italy for New York.

Grateful for everything Nick had done for him and his mother, each month he sent Nick a check, determined to repay him for the condo in full one day.

Bobby finished his coffee before putting on socks and a pair of loafers. He opened his top bureau drawer, lifted a pile of t-shirts, and searched for his Glock 40 Gen 4. He tucked it behind him underneath his sweater. Slipping into a light jacket, he headed out.

Down in the lobby, he waved at the uniformed doorman.

"Hey, Hank."

"Need a taxi?"

"Not today. Think I'll walk across the park."

"Enjoy." Hank tipped his cap, holding the door open, then retreated to his post.

Bobby trekked along Central Park West, oblivious to car horns and the wailing sirens in the distance. Exhaust fumes from the heavy traffic hung in the air. He traveled amidst the shadows of several tall buildings separated by narrow alleyways lined with stacks of empty wooden crates. A slight breeze carried the stench from the large trash containers overflowing with garbage. He joined the streams of pedestrians jockeying for their small bit of territory on the sidewalk.

Bobby zigzagged between cars and taxicabs, cutting over to the park entrance, winding his way toward Fifth Avenue. The din of the traffic noise receded, and the air turned crisp. A grin lit his face. This was his New York. He loved the contrast between the quiet park and the push and pull of the noisy city.

People strolled by, cell phones planted to their ears, speaking in unfamiliar tongues. To his left, several tossed a Frisbee back and forth. Dog walkers trudged along, pulled by fancy pedigree dogs attached to multiple leashes. A street musician strummed his guitar, its case lay open at his feet. The black velvet interior held a mixture of coins and one-dollar bills. Bobby drew a five-dollar bill from his wallet and dropped it into the case. The man dipped his head, smiled, and continued to play.

He exited the park onto Fifth Avenue, and the city noises boomed loud once again. Halfway up the block, he pushed open the gallery door. Near the entrance, a few signature pieces hung from the walls, encouraging people to explore. A sign read, 'Introducing the Artistry of Wesley Bell.'

He moved along the vast expanse of wall showing off Wesley's work. A blend of sweet grass, sage, and juniper permeated the air from diffusers placed around the gallery. Wealthy patrons became more inclined to buy with their senses heightened.

On the lookout for new talent, several friends urged Bobby to check out Wesley's paintings. From the moment he stepped into Wesley's small studio loft in Brooklyn, his instincts told him this artist's work needed an introduction to the art world. He was thrilled when one of his New York-based clients agreed to sponsor an exhibit.

Abstracts painted in striking hues, some soft, others bold, held their own against the stark white walls. Bobby stepped back a few times to ensure the lighting and placement highlighted each individual piece to its best advantage. He inspected each one for cards listing the artist's name, the title of the painting, and price below it.

"Hello, stranger," a female voice called.

A young woman with large red-framed glasses and brown hair cut in a bob came up to him. She wore a simple black sheath and black pumps.

"Lucy, how are you?" They kissed one another on the cheek. "I didn't realize you were still working here."

Lucy adjusted her frames and smiled. "I took a break. But I'm glad to see your fingers on the pulse as always. I love this artist's work. It's so vivid. So alive."

"Thanks. Let's hope my clients agree with you. How's the roster looking?"

"Everyone is confirmed. No cancellations. But …''

"But what?"

"There is one addition. She's flying in for the showing."

Bobby crossed his arms and frowned. His openings were exclusive and by invitation only to his wealthiest and most trusted clients.

"Lucy, you know how I feel about making exceptions for people."

Bright pink bloomed upon her cheeks. The corner of her mouth twitched. "I know, but she'd be a new client for you. She's purchased from this gallery before, just not through you."

He dropped his arms and shrugged. "Well, I guess it's too late to dis-invite her. But next time run it by me first, okay?"

Lucy's face relaxed. "Sure. It won't happen again."

A half-hour later, he managed the caterers while they set out silver bowls and platters containing black caviar, blue cheese stuffed olives, and marinated beef on skewers. He inspected the assortment of champagnes, wines, sparkling waters, and imported beers. Soft jazz music piped in from the hidden speakers played throughout the gallery.

Five minutes before his clients were due to arrive, Bobby retreated to the rear office and removed his jacket. He dropped it inside a cabinet in the corner of the room. Pulling out his Glock, he placed it underneath and pushed the drawer closed.

He hurried to the entrance to greet his guests. The elite of the city strolled in, men and women, with deep pockets and the desire to add to their collections.

Ready to mingle, Bobby hesitated as a white limo stopped at the curb. In his head, he had ticked off everyone on his client list. This must be the person Lucy added.

A uniformed chauffer hurried to open the rear door. Long, slender, bronzed legs emerged from the interior first. She moved with purpose, wasting nothing and came toward him. He observed the expensive sapphire blue dress, the beaded shawl draped over her shoulder. She held out her hand.

"Carmela Santiago." Her dark almond-shaped eyes locked on his for a moment.

His heart hammered as he shook the hand of the most stunning woman he had ever come across. "Bobby D'Angelo, it's a pleasure."

She slid her hand away and walked past him. Long hair, the color of maple syrup spilled down her back, making her as captivating from the rear. He caught the light scent of her perfume and fought the urge to breathe deep. She glanced over her shoulder and smiled before proceeding to a portrait by the far wall. His eyes followed each precise movement.

Inside, one of his clients stopped to chat. Glancing at her from across the room, Bobby fumbled for words. How could one woman have such an effect on him?

At the end of the gallery, Carmela plucked a glass of champagne from a silver tray held by a waiter before settling onto a bench by a painting.

Bobby tried to converse with several people before moving toward her. He caught her eye and smiled. "Like what you see?"

Her eyes traveled the length of his body before resting on his face. She patted the bench. "I like a lot of things. Come, sit, and tell me about this artist."

Bobby detected a slight accent. It made her speech even more alluring. He brushed away the hair falling over his right eye and sat beside her.

"His name is Wesley Bell—"

She wagged a red polished finger at him. "I know how to read, silly. Tell me how you discovered him." She took several sips from her glass and waited.

Warmth spread up his cheeks. He cleared his throat and explained how he first met Wesley. Her eyes focused on his, while her thick, dark lashes, fluttered seductively.

He glimpsed something behind those eyes though he couldn't quite decide what and sensed himself pulled. She was magnetic, as if she had a force field around her.

A sudden prickle in the pit of his stomach made him draw back. Unsure what it meant, he forced a smile and got to his feet. "Enjoy the rest of the evening."

He noted the bright red stickers on most of the title cards. "Let me know what interests you. It seems Wesley has almost sold out."

Before he could walk away, she pointed to the painting in front of her. "I think this one will do."

Bobby reflected on her choice. Bright fiery slashes of red mixed with brilliant blues lit the canvas. The most vivid work in the collection had drawn her. "I see you're attracted to saturation and intensity in art."

She smirked and opened her purse. "No, I simply know what I like," she said, holding out a card. "Here's my information. I will be in town for the next day or two. Call me tomorrow and let me know when it is ready."

She rose, handed him the empty champagne glass and made her way to the front of the gallery. His eyes lingered on her curves until she slipped out the door.

Bobby noticed a change in the air. He took a breath and studied the card, running his fingers over the embossed black lettering of her name printed on a white background with a phone number below it. A simple card. Too simple for a woman so complicated.

Bobby stuck the card in his pocket and tried to turn his attention on his clients. But the image of Carmela Santiago lingered and along with it the feeling his life was about to change.

# CHAPTER 3
## Carmela

Carmela slipped into her robe and settled herself at the table in the Presidential Suite of her hotel. She lifted the gold-domed lid before her and smiled with pleasure. Room service had done a good job. Perfectly cooked eggs benedict rested on the plate. Her appetite ravenous, she took a bite and let the creamy, lemon taste of the Hollandaise bathe her tongue.

Her mind drifted to the previous evening. She had taken a chance attending Bobby D'Angelo's show at the gallery, but her instincts served her well. He had no idea how much their pasts linked. Bound by murder and deception.

Nick would have kept names, dates, and places to himself. A good ghost would do everything to protect his family. The more they knew, the more it put their lives at risk. Biding her time was the right decision. Almost six long years should make Nick believe her threats were no longer of consequence to him or his loved ones.

She sipped her coffee and frowned. Bobby's rugged good looks unnerved her a little. Tall, with a square jaw, angular cheekbones, and full lips, he was one handsome man, but his ice-blue eyes and the way a patch of his thick dark hair drooped above his right eye caught her attention the most. She found these things particularly sexy.

She finished her coffee and reminded herself she couldn't let his good looks distract her. The focus must remain on avenging her father. He'd never rest if she allowed herself to detour from her mission.

With her plate empty, she pushed away from the table. There would be time enough to dwell upon those things once she had Bobby D'Angelo under her control. She showered and dressed, selecting tight-fitting black pants and a white silk blouse. She left her long hair loose and her feet bare. A pair of gold hoop earrings and a matching bracelet complemented the simple outfit. While she dabbed perfume behind her ears and at her wrists, her cell phone rang.

"This is Carmela."

"Hello, Ms. Santiago, it's Bobby D'Angelo. The piece you purchased last night is ready."

"Perfect." She detected a note of anxiety in his voice.

"I'll have it delivered to your hotel, or if you like, to your home."

"I am very particular about my art," she said. "I prefer you deliver it to my hotel." Silence greeted her. "Is there a problem?"

"Ah…no. I'll have someone bring it by."

Her free hand formed a fist at her side, her fingers clenched. "I'd appreciate it if you dropped it off to my suite."

"Sure. I can do that. See you in about two hours."

"Make it one. I'll be expecting you." She hung up without waiting for an answer and called room service. Within minutes, they arrived and removed her breakfast tray.

Opening her laptop, she busied herself checking on deliveries at the restaurants she owned by speaking with each manager. She wrote a check for Bobby, before going to the bar and pouring a glass of sparkling water. A soft buzz sounded.

Smoothing her hair, she hurried to the door, but caught herself, and stopped. She'd make him wait. Seconds ticked by before the buzzer rang again, and she opened it.

He wore a black tee shirt and black jeans. A dark grey, wool blazer set off a maroon-colored scarf draped around his neck. The artwork, professionally wrapped, stood against the wall behind him.

"I have your purchase, Ms. Santiago." He glanced over his shoulder at Diego stationed by the elevator.

"Why so formal?" she said. "Call me Carmela, please."

"Okay, Carmela." The flicker of a smile crossed his lips.

She stepped aside, and he entered carrying the heavy frame. She pointed to the far wall next to a tall window. "Set it down over there."

Bobby placed it against the wall while she drifted to the bar and put the glass of sparkling water down. Choosing a bottle of tequila, she held it up.

"Care for a drink?"

"Sorry, I haven't much time. I need to get to the gallery. Wesley did quite well last night."

"After such a big purchase, I don't think one drink will hurt." She spoke the words with firmness, making them more a command than a statement.

He hesitated a moment. "I guess I can stay for a drink."

She poured two shots and gestured toward the sofa. "Come, sit."

Bobby seated himself, and she handed him his glass. She slipped beside him, shifting her body, letting her knee brush up against his.

She raised her glass. "Here's to what I hope will be a long relationship."

They drank and set their empty glasses on the coffee table. "So, tell me," she said. "How did you become interested in art? And at such a young age."

He removed his scarf and swiped his hand through his hair. "It began while I lived in Europe. My ..." A shadow crossed his face.

"Is something wrong?" Carmela asked. His cheeks flushed. For a moment, she thought he might bolt from the room.

"No." He rubbed his palms down the front of his jeans. "I started going to the galleries and fell in love with what I saw. I studied art, built up a clientele, and here I am."

She fiddled with one of her earrings and smiled. "You make it sound so simple."

"Well, that's the short version, anyway."

She picked up a strange note in his voice. Her question made him uncomfortable. Not wanting to push things too far yet, she rose and grabbed the check from the table.

She stretched out her arm. "Here's the payment for the piece."

Bobby got up and reached for it. She drew her hand back and moved closer, her face now inches from his. The sharp scent of his cologne hung between them. He didn't look away. She studied his face, the slight curve of his mouth and the dark stubble along his jawline. With no sign of retreat, she slipped the check into his palm.

He folded it in half and placed it inside the pocket of his blazer.

"Thanks. I wish all my transactions were this easy."

"They can be."

"That's intriguing."

His stare matched hers in intensity. A hint of amusement played in his eyes. She sensed his self-confidence had returned causing her to feel bare, exposed. She took a step back to collect herself. Her insides calming, she said, "I wish to hire you as my personal Art Consultant."

"You mean, you'd like me to add you to my client list?"

"No. I would be your only client. I want you to help me build the most magnificent collection in the world." She waited, letting her words sink in, then added. "Your compensation would match your talent for art."

He backed away and shook his head. "That's tempting. But you can't expect me to abandon my clients."

She placed her hand on her hip. "It sounds so harsh when you say it like that."

He draped his scarf around his neck. "I would love to help you build your collection but not at their expense. I owe them my career."

Carmela gave him a small pout. "Okay. If you insist on keeping your other clients, I guess I have to live with that."

Bobby fished out his wallet. He placed a card in her palm. "Thank you again. When you're ready, give me a call." He adjusted his blazer and sailed past her to the door.

She glanced at the card and followed him. "Wait."

He tugged at his sleeve and checked his watch. "I need to get to the gallery."

"Well, will you at least come to California, look at my collection and give me your opinion?"

He gave a half-shrug. "Sure, I can do that. I'll check my schedule and let you know when I'm available."

She bit the inside of her cheek to curb her rising irritation. Who does Bobby D'Angelo think he is? She put on a fake smile. "I will send my private jet for you."

"That won't be necessary. I don't mind flying commercial. Helps with the frequent flyer miles." He gave her a quick wink.

Carmela's insides twisted at his words. He was making fun of her. "Once you fly private, your opinion will change," she shot back.

Bobby opened the door and stepped out into the hall. A cocky smirk planted on his face, he said, "What makes you think I haven't?"

She watched him saunter to the elevator. He nodded at Diego as the doors slid open and disappeared inside.

Diego walked toward her. Carmela shook her head. "No, I have work to do." Ignoring his hurt look, she closed the door.

She fingered Bobby's card before tossing it on the bar and pouring another shot of tequila. He had ruined her afternoon with his nonchalant attitude. One word from her to the right people and he'd no longer have a client list.

She swallowed the drink, and hurled the empty glass against the wall. It shattered, sending tiny shards across the carpet.

Disregarding the broken pieces, she walked to the window, and viewed the shadows playing against the tall skyscrapers. Later, those concrete giants would brighten the night, their lights glittering like jewels. Its inhabitants would come alive to dine at famous restaurants and take in the Broadway shows.

She had this entire great city at her feet, but still, melancholy engulfed her. A slow, steady breath escaped her lips.

Bobby D'Angelo was attracted to her. She glimpsed it in his eyes, sensed it in his body language. Her sour mood lifted and her mouth edged up into a smile. Bobby would come around. She'd gain control, and just like Diego, he'd be begging for more.

# CHAPTER 4
## Nick

Tuscan sunlight filtered through the umbrella pines and across the patio. Surrounded by flower boxes and hanging baskets bursting with color, Nick inhaled the sharp scents of rosemary and basil from the garden below. A wind chime swayed back and forth, its melodious tinkling flirted with the breeze.

Comfortable in his jeans and polo shirt, he settled into the cushions of the wrought-iron chair, he lifted his shirt and tucked his 9mm into his waistband behind him. His Hugo Boss suits, now idle, hung in the master closet upstairs. He peered over the top of his sunglasses. An easy grin lit his face. Isabelle and Michael ran across the lush expanse of grass beyond the patio toward Carrie, while their dog trotted behind.

Carrie's dark ponytail dipped below her shoulders. Her yellow flowered sundress showed off her deep rich tan. She laughed, bent, and gathered the children close, their tiny arms encircling her body.

Chino let out a series of joyful barks. Nick had rescued the white Akita years ago and gifted him to Ricardo Santiago. But Chino failed to obey Carmela's orders to attack him the day he shot Ricardo in the winery. She had scorned the poor dog, so Nick gladly took him home.

Behind Carrie and the children, rows of tall cypress trees towered above the stone wall encasing the yard. Stationed at the opposite end, a shoulder holster hidden underneath his light jacket, Marco Valletta caught Nick's eyes and dipped his head.

Nick watched Isabelle, Izzy, as they called her, pluck a flower from a clay pot. Smiling, she held it up to Marco. He thanked her and placed the flower in his shirt pocket. The red bloom peeked out and Izzy pointed her tiny finger and giggled. It saddened him to think he missed the birth of his first child, but under the circumstances, he left Carrie and did what he needed to do to stop the madness raining down on them.

He looked at his little boy, grateful he'd been there for Michael's birth, so far, the most unforgettable moment as he watched his beautiful son enter the world. They had named him Michael after the brother he'd never forget and still to this day missed. Created out of love, he treasured both his children.

It would have been hard for him to have imagined this life years ago. Time spent here, in their house in Tuscany, Italy became the happiest they'd known. He had a family of his own, and a woman he loved with every fiber of his being. One who accepted his past and all the hazards attached to it.

They had enjoyed lazy days roaming the surrounding countryside filled with vineyards and silvery olive groves. They explored the breathtaking cities of Florence, Siena, and Pisa along with countless other picturesque towns. Traveled past mountains covered with carpets of wildflowers in the spring. In warmer weather, they wound their way up the coast to Versilia where the children played in the sands of its golden beaches. And, for the first time, they had enjoyed spending several weeks with his sister and her family in Milan.

Nick wanted to believe they weren't in jeopardy anymore. The years had flown by without a single threat from Carmela. No ghosts appeared to harm them. But whenever he allowed himself to relax, he'd remember how he almost lost Carrie and

Izzy in Lugano, Switzerland and how Carmela's threats echoed against the vault in the winery the day, he shot Ricardo. Those threats remained as real as those of her dead father.

So many times, he questioned his decision to let Carmela live. Maybe, if he had pulled the trigger, his family would be safe, something he'd never know for sure, so they stayed in Tuscany. All, except for Bobby.

He refused to limit himself by living in the compound. Nick didn't like it, but he understood Bobby's youth and his need to explore the world. The best he could do was teach him how to protect himself.

Before he left Italy, Nick had taken the opportunity to instruct him to shoot, defend himself, pay attention, and listen to his intuition. It amazed him how proficient a shot Bobby became. Good enough to become a ghost, but Nick hoped that day would never come. He wouldn't wish a killer's life on anyone.

Bobby chose art as his vocation, and Nick encouraged him, gladly paying for his studies. He excelled and carved out a career and without fail, a check from Bobby arrived at the end of each month. But he wasn't aware that Nick deposited each one into a separate account where the money would remain in trust until he turned thirty years of age.

Nick eyed the whiskey bottle and two glasses he had set out earlier. He removed his sunglasses and placed them on the patio table. Dalton had called to tell him he'd flown in today with some urgent business…business he couldn't discuss over the phone.

He considered Dalton, his best friend. It was in Dalton's house in South Dakota where he fell in love with Carrie. It was also the place where she reconnected with Bobby. South Dakota would always hold special meaning in all their lives.

Maybe one day they could return to the United States and visit there once again.

Nick rose as Carrie moved through the trellis laden with thick green climbing vines and purple wisteria while Izzy and Michael trailed behind her. Strands of her dark hair had come undone from her ponytail, and her cheeks flushed a pale pink. No matter how many times he looked at her, Carrie's beauty always astonished him, as if he were seeing her for the first time.

Smiling, she grabbed his hand. "What are you doing sitting up here all by yourself?"

He pulled her close. "Watching you." He studied her eyes, glad fear no longer lived within them. After the shooting in Lugano, that fear had taken up residence for quite a few years until he'd made her feel secure again. He still blamed himself for almost losing her and Izzy.

Nick bent for a kiss. Tiny hands tugged at his pant leg.

"Daddy, Daddy, pick me up," Michael whined.

Nick sighed and let Carrie go.

Carrie burst out laughing. "They're all yours." She backed away and blew him a kiss. *"Ti amo,"* she said and slipped inside with Chino.

Nick grabbed Michael, held him up above his head, and spun him around. Michael's chubby cheeks grew red. He howled with laughter. His bright blue eyes crinkled at the corners.

"Faster, faster," he commanded. Within minutes, Izzy clamored for the same treatment. He set Michael on the patio and lifted her. Her face lit up, and her dark hair fanned out behind her while he spun her in his arms.

*"Come sei bella, Isabelle.* You're as pretty as your mother."

"Who would have thought I'd see a sight like this? Nicky D holding a little gal of his own." Dalton Burgess grinned, his white Stetson in his hand. His light blue denim shirt was tucked tight into his jeans. Brown scuffed cowboy boots dressed his feet. Grey peppered his thick head of hair and bushy mustache.

Michael scrambled toward him while Izzy clung to Nick.

"Uncle Dalton!" Michael shouted.

Dalton tossed his Stetson on the table and swept Michael up. "Are you behaving yourself?" He poked Michael's stomach, making him giggle.

Michael looked from Nick to Dalton. He wagged his head. "Yes. I'm being berry, berry good."

He set Michael down and gestured to Izzy. "And what about you, sweetheart? Are you keeping everybody in line?"

She bobbed her head.

"Well, then. I brought presents. They're on the kitchen table."

Izzy squirmed out of Nick's arms and the two children started for the door.

"Wait," Nick said. "What do you say?"

"Thank you," they called out in unison and ran inside.

With the children gone, they seated themselves.

"Drink?" Nick asked.

"Sure, make it neat. It may ease the pain of what I'm about to tell you." he settled into his chair.

Nick poured two glasses of whiskey. "Sounds serious."

"It is. We're being recruited. Or, should I say, ordered. And none too politely, I might add." Dalton raised his glass and swallowed the dark amber liquid.

"What the hell are you talking about? Who's recruiting us?" Dalton's words made him uncomfortable. He sipped his drink.

He eyed Nick. "The government wants our help."

"Government?"

"The good old United States Government."

Nick shifted in his seat. His eyes searched Dalton's face. "Are you serious? The government is—"

Dalton put up his hand. "Let me finish." He lowered his voice. "Look, I'm not sure how they found out about us. They know the type of work you used to do, and I still do, on occasion."

Nick's gut twisted. He studied his wrist and pretended to adjust his watchband. "They're guessing. They can't prove anything. Besides, why would they care about us killing some bad guys?"

Dalton gave him a somber look. "Because apparently, they want us to do it for them. What they can't prove, they'll falsify. You know as well as I do if the government wants to make something stick, make your life miserable, they will."

"Yeah, right," Nick said. "Anytime the government's involved, someone gets screwed. Listen, Dalton, I'm not about to get screwed."

A deep frown knotted Dalton's brow. "Just hold on for a moment. I mean, it's not a bad deal if you consider the alternative."

Nick shot him a look. "The alternative? I don't think I like where you're heading with this," he said, narrowing his eyes.

Dalton tugged on the end of his mustache. "Here's the bottom line, ugly as it is. We either go work for them, or they put us away. You know they have an extradition treaty with Italy." He pushed back from the table and stretched out his long legs. "They let me fly here today because I convinced them you would agree."

Nick jumped up, knocking his chair backward. "You did what? I gave up killing with one exception. To protect my family."

Dalton sighed. "Calm down, think about it logically. You don't have a choice, do you? Not unless you want to say goodbye for a long, long time to Carrie and those two beautiful kids of yours. Use your head, Nick. It's the only way out."

"Not for me. I'll find another way," Nick said, stunned at the news Dalton had given him.

"Look, I've never taken you for a foolish man. You've been running from Carmela for years, and now you want to try to run from the United States Government. What kind of life would that be for Carrie and the kids?"

Nick's head throbbed. Heat flushed through him at Dalton's words. Protecting his family from Carmela was one thing, but trying to evade the government for a lifetime would become an impossible way to live.

Dalton got to his feet. "Look, we've worked for some real, unscrupulous people in the past, but you have to admit, we rid the world of some bad criminals, albeit illegally. What's wrong with doing it for them?"

Nick blew out a breath in frustration. "I guess this means going back to the States?"

"I believe so. But, from what I hear, Carmela isn't a threat anymore. She runs the drug business along with the legitimate businesses and is involved with her horses. If she wanted to do something, I doubt she'd wait this long to do it. The woman is no dummy. She doesn't want to draw attention to herself. She's moved on and so should you."

"Maybe." Nick folded his arms. "But you know how these things go if we agree. Setting up a kill means I'd be away from home for weeks, or months at a time. I don't think I'm comfortable doing that."

Dalton jerked his thumb at Marco. "He's been with you long enough to have proven his loyalty. Your family's in capable hands."

"Even so, Carrie will have a hard time with this."

Dalton rubbed the stubble on his chin and fell silent a moment. "Ask her this then, would she rather be apart from you for a few weeks or months or twenty years or more? Simple mathematics."

He hated being backed into a corner. Forced to do something he promised himself and Carrie, he would never do again. Killing for the government or killing for a drug lord, neither one justified the end result. But thoughts of losing the family he had waited so long for became unbearable. Without a doubt, this situation proved to be black and white, there was no grey. If he had a choice, he'd choose his family every time.

Dalton stretched out his hand. "Can I tell them we have a deal?"

Nick hesitated before raising his own. The angst inside him rose, and underneath it, darkness lay waiting.

Their hands met in a firm grip. He couldn't help feeling besides his past allegiance to Ricardo, he had just made another deal with a new devil.

Only this devil could prove to become much more powerful. There would be no possibility of eliminating this one.

# CHAPTER 5
## Carrie

Following a tense lunch, Dalton excused himself and retreated to the guest room to make calls and rest before his flight home, leaving Nick and Carrie alone on the patio drinking the last of a bottle of Prosecco.

Nick eyed the baby monitor. "Michael asleep?"

"Almost," Carrie said. "He woke up early this morning, he'll nap for a good while."

She thought about Izzy in the house doing her lessons with her teacher. They started homeschooling her as a matter of safety. She looked forward to the day when she could enroll her children in public schools. She didn't want them living in a bubble their entire childhood.

She accepted Nick's need to protect his family after the shooting. But years had elapsed since then, and she wondered how much longer they would have to live their lives insulated from the outside world.

She missed Bobby, but she was proud he lived his life on his own terms. He refused to let fear control him, and she prayed he would stay safe.

Carrie sipped her Prosecco, savoring the taste of the light sparkling wine. She took a side-ways glance at Nick and sensed Dalton's visit meant more than just coming to see old friends.

Nick's body language and the way he drummed his fingers on the table all pointed to something bigger. She set her glass aside and drew her chair closer.

"So, what gives?" she asked. "You can't fool me. I know something's on your mind."

A pained look marred his face. "Is it that obvious?"

She tried to keep her voice light. "Dalton's visit came as a surprise. We always get a heads up when he's coming. This time, it was short notice."

Nick shifted in his chair. "You're right. I need to tell you something, and I'm not sure how you'll take it."

Alarm bells rang in her head. "Is Dalton sick?"

"No, no, nothing like that. Look, I'm just going to say it. We're moving to America."

Her mouth fell open. "I thought we couldn't go back."

"I'd always wished one day we would," Nick said. "Except, I wanted it to be on my terms, but it's not working out the way I planned."

Carrie listened while he told her the real reason for Dalton's visit. The wine in her stomach soured. Her pulse revved up at the prospect of Nick becoming a contract killer for the government. She understood what lay in his heart after he gave up being a ghost for her. Forcing him to return to that life could prove detrimental to the man he had become. The man who worked so hard at being a good husband and father, worked even harder at slaying those demons from his past sleeping deep within him. Killing again was sure to awaken them.

"But how can the government do this?" she asked. "This can't be legal."

"Legal?" Nick's brows drew together. "Do you think the government, any government, plays by the rules? They all have their own agenda, legal or not."

A cold tremor raked her body at his words. She fingered the stem of her wine glass before meeting his eyes.

"I know all this is hard to contend with," Nick said "But governments are powerful. What is and isn't legal slips under the wire."

Her hands crept together in her lap, and she gripped her fingers. "What will happen when *they* don't need you anymore?"

"I can't give you that answer because I don't know," he responded.

Carrie glimpsed the turmoil behind his eyes and wished she could erase it. Her mind scrambled. Thoughts of losing him spiked the buried fear lying inside her.

"If you refuse to cooperate, we'll face the consequences together. We can take the children and go somewhere else. The possibility of you being sent to prison scares me, but you can't go back to killing," she pleaded.

His expression turned dark. "Carrie, there is more than just my going to prison. They'll work with foreign governments to seize our assets. You and the children will have next to nothing. I can't live locked up and wondering how my family is surviving. Not even Dalton could help you. We're a package deal. They want both of us."

Nick got to his feet. He held out his hand. Carrie rose and his arms wrapped around her, holding her close. Close enough for her to feel the rapid beating of her heart against his chest. Her hands came up, and she pushed away from him.

"Why is this happening?" Tears clung to her dark lashes. "We tried so hard to leave the past behind and start a new life. We've lived in virtual seclusion, hiding from people who want us dead. What happens if we go back? What then?"

"Dalton believes the threat is over. He may be right; it's been almost six years. But I don't want you to worry. Marco will come with us. I'll make sure you and the children are safe whenever I'm away."

Carrie tilted her head up. "Nick, I'm scared. I'm afraid one day you'll leave, and you won't return." Her tears flowed, their salt stinging her lips.

He searched her face and his own softened. "I'll try my best not to let that happen. Especially, knowing what I have waiting for me at home." He held her close again.

"I see you've told her." Dalton came across the patio.

They broke their embrace, and she wiped at her eyes. "Yes, he told me. But it's hard to accept."

Dalton thrust his hands into his front pockets. He dipped his head and stared at the ground a moment. "I'm sure all this comes as a shock, Carrie. But we have little choice in the matter. Try to come to terms with it, and things will go much easier."

"Besides, Nick and I always look out for each other." He winked, and a slight grin creased his face. "And since you're my two favorite people in the world," he continued. "I want you to move into my guest house in South Dakota. It's the place where you fell in love. It should make you feel more comfortable about the whole thing."

"I don't know what to say," Nick said.

Carrie gave Dalton a half-smile. "Well, I do. I spent some of my happiest moments there. Since we have no other choice, and we have to go to America, I'd love to return to South Dakota."

Dalton's grin grew wider. "Good, it's settled. I need to fly home and prepare things. When you're ready, I'll send my plane for you." He kissed Carrie's cheek and left.

She picked up the empty wine glasses.

"Leave that for now," Nick said and stretched out his hand. "Let's take a walk." He motioned to Marco and pointed at the house. Marco crossed the garden and went inside.

She set the glasses on the table and slipped her hand into his. They stepped off the patio and strolled through the wrought-iron gate at the far end of the yard.

They moved along the stone path leading away from the patio toward the pasture below. Wildflowers played among the mixed grasses padding the surrounding ground, their bright plumes adding splashes of color. In the distance, sheep grazed while cows bellowed on a neighboring farm.

Fronds tickled Carrie's bare legs. She bent and plucked a flower. Inhaling its sweet fragrance, she smiled up at him. "I'm going to miss this place."

Nick nodded his head. "For sure. Lots of happy memories here."

He draped his arm around her shoulder. Their eyes focused on the scene before them. She wanted to remember the place where they began raising their children and where they celebrated the holidays together. It was her first real home.

High above, a mound of grey clouds scurried across the sky. The warm breeze turned cool sending a slight shiver through her body.

"Ready to go back?" he asked.

Carrie gave him a weak smile before taking his hand. She glanced up at the dark, angry clouds, their silhouette now blocking out the sun. The wind picked up and let out an echoing howl. Heavy rain charged across the pasture at them, pounding the fertile earth. They scurried up the path trying to outrun it, managing to reach the house and slip inside still dry.

Carrie stopped and peered out at the deluge drenching the pale patio stones, turning them a muddy, deep brown. She closed the door and pressed her back against it, not wanting the darkness to invade their lives again.

# CHAPTER 6
## Bobby

After a successful meeting in Paris, Bobby boarded the Air France jet to San Francisco in high spirits. Wesley Bell's paintings had almost sold out in New York, convincing Bobby to waste no time in introducing him to the elite in the City of Lights. He'd made arrangements to hold a private event at a small gallery off Rue Saint-Lazare to present some of Wesley's work to the wealthiest patrons in Paris. He was thrilled when they loved his work as much as he and their New York counterparts. One had agreed to sponsor a show at a larger, more popular gallery at a later date.

Bobby stowed his carry-on in the overhead and settled into his narrow window seat. He'd spoken the truth when he told Carmela he didn't mind flying coach. Although, he could well afford certain luxuries, traveling first class, or private made no difference to him. He had flown on his Uncle Dalton's jet several times with his mother and Nick, but they did so out of necessity.

Bobby's muscles tightened at the memory of how his anger surfaced again for a while after the dreadful shooting in Lugano. Almost losing his mother reignited his demons from childhood, and he had demanded Nick tell him the truth about what happened in America. Yet, as soon as his mother's condition stabilized, Nick had left without a word. Bobby understood with certainty he'd gone to find the person who shot his mom.

It was then that Marco Valletta, a good friend of Nick's came to protect them. To this day he remained a steady fixture in their lives.

When Nick came home, he moved them to the compound in Tuscany, then he sat Bobby down for a serious conversation.

'It's time you learned to protect yourself, 'Nick told him. I'll always do what I can to keep our family safe, but I need you to prepare yourself for what might come. I've got to know I taught you enough to improve your chances of survival.' So far, Bobby hadn't put those skills to use.

While his mother remained in the hospital, memories of growing up in Laurel, Pennsylvania returned. And with them, his longing for a life somewhere away from his small hometown to make him forget. Forget the beatings; forget spending hours locked in a dark closet under the basement stairs. A life without the constant panic setting in whenever Russ Medlow had walked into the room.

Bobby never regretted killing his adoptive father. His mother tried to convince him the gun had gone off by accident, but he knew better. He pulled the trigger to put an end to the beast he had feared for so long.

When his mother recovered, he broached the subject once again regarding his biological father. He could tell talking about him made her uncomfortable. Her answers were evasive, and he had gained little information. Not wanting to push things further and upset her he let it drop. His father died before his birth. What could he gain by digging into the man's past?

Bobby's attention turned to Carmela and the feeling in the pit of his stomach the day he delivered her painting. Nick warned him to listen to his intuition. Caution was necessary, but could he be trying to deny his attraction to her?

Living in New York and traveling abroad, he had met various, interesting, if not beautiful, women to pass the time with. If he wanted companionship, girls like Valerie Gold and others were always available.

Bobby lifted his cell and pressed the menu button. He scrolled through the text messages from Carmela. He had agreed to go to California to view her art collection. She could turn out to be a very profitable new client. He needed to keep his mind on business when in her company. Time would tell whether he'd made the right decision in taking her on.

Hours later, he glanced out the window as the plane descended. He would go to Napa, see Carmela, then fly home. Maybe take a little break and relax before returning to Paris for Wesley's show next month.

Bobby exited the terminal to find a limo driver holding up a sign with his name. He recognized him from the hallway in Carmela's hotel.

He nodded at Bobby and said, "I'm Diego. Ms. Santiago sent me."

He detected a sour note in the man's voice as he handed him his bag and eased into the dark interior. "Thanks."

Every so often, Diego glanced into the rearview mirror, his eyes fixed on Bobby. He never spoke, and Bobby chose to ignore him.

An hour and a half later, they pulled up a tree-lined road. Bobby slid the window down. Ornate wrought-iron gates parted beneath a sign reading 'Santiago Vineyards.'

His nostrils filled with the pungent scent of ripening fruit. Vines, tethered to wires and posts tamped into the hard-packed soil spread out for miles, their leaves abundant with plump red, purple, and green grapes.

On one side, vineyard workers were scattered among the older vines spaced too close for machinery. Wearing wide-brimmed hats, cutters in their hands, they snipped and harvested the grapes, designated for the flagship wine. On the opposite side, the hum of harvesting machines hung in the air as they rode up and down the rows extracting grapes.

Impressed, he became even more so when the car climbed up a paved drive and stopped in front an enormous estate nestled into the hillside. He stepped out and took in the panoramic views of the vineyards and valley below. Towering oaks cradled the front of the home. Lush gardens fanned out from either side, with stone pathways leading beyond the house. The sweet scent of blossoming flowers drifted past.

The door opened, and a gentleman, in full butler's attire, greeted him.

"*Señor* D'Angelo, it is good to have you here. My name is Armando."

Diego handed him Bobby's bag.

"Oh, that won't be necessary," Bobby said. "I have reservations at a hotel."

Armando bowed. "The *Señorita* insisted. She is down by the stables." He pointed to a pathway. Then, gripping Bobby's bag, he disappeared inside the house.

Bobby followed the path, walking through the elaborate gardens filled with varieties of sweet-smelling flowers. He came upon a clearing and noticed a paddock below. A flash of movement caught his eye. He continued to the fenced-in area and stopped.

She was electric. No other word could describe the scene in front of him while Carmela performed jump after jump. The horse's powerful body sailed up and over each hurdle, muscles straining underneath its magnificent shiny coat. Carmela's perfect form and breathtaking beauty matched that of her horse.

He approached the fence and hoisted himself up. Seated on the top rail, he was unable to come to grips with how much Carmela affected him. Something stirred inside him. Warmth spread across his chest, and an unfamiliar sense of weightlessness engulfed him.

Carmela spotted him and waved. She trotted over to him and removed her riding cap. One long braid trailed down her back. Her cheeks flushed a pale pink above her tanned skin.

"I see you made it." Her voice, low and mellow caused his ears to perk up while her dark eyes scanned his face. She gestured toward the horse. "This is Diablo. A gift from someone special."

Bobby eyed the magnificent animal, his deep chestnut coat, and white crest. "Some gift."

"Do you ride?"

"Not as well as you, but I've ridden a horse or two at my Uncle Dalton's ranch."

"Well, if you're up for it." She patted Diablo's rump.

Bobby hesitated. "If you don't mind, I prefer the front seat."

Carmela threw her head back and laughed. She tossed her cap on the ground and slid her body to the rear of the saddle.

Bobby climbed up and took the reins. Carmela's arms encircled his waist. He tugged the reins and gave a light squeeze with his legs on the horse's barrel. The horse moved at a slow trot.

"Open the gate, Mateo!" Carmela shouted.

A short, stocky man in a black cowboy hat approached the fence. He slid the latch and swung it open.

Bobby took the horse to a canter and headed across the paddock. Once on the trail, he increased to a gallop. The horse's hooves pounded the earth. She gripped his waist tighter. Her body pressed close to his, making him want to ride with her forever.

Later, he brought the horse to a canter again and rode to the paddock where Mateo waited. Bobby stopped by the gate in front of him. He jumped off and then held his arms up. She smiled at him as he helped her down. Mateo took the reins and led the horse to the stables.

Carmela wagged her finger at him. "I think you have ridden more than a horse or two."

"Still, I don't come close to your riding skills," Bobby said.

"Let's go up to the house."

He shoved his hands into the front pockets of his jeans. "About that. I booked a hotel room, so I won't be staying."

Carmela eyed him. "The least you can do is have something to eat before we talk business."

He fidgeted. His stomach muscles tightened. A multitude of emotions ran through him while they strolled up to the house. This woman affected him in so many ways.

The interior of Carmela's home proved to be just as stunning as the outside. A large entry foyer with inlaid marble and a crystal chandelier led to a living area with soaring ceilings and wall-to-wall windows that captured the astounding views. Hickory wood flooring spanned the entire space. A massive hand-carved fireplace anchored the room.

From visiting the homes of his clients, he could tell the furnishings were all imported and custom made. He followed Carmela to an enclosed patio off the huge double island kitchen. A table set for two stood in the center. The screened-in area overlooked an Olympic-size infinity edge swimming pool.

She pointed to a chair. "Sit, relax. You must be exhausted from your flight."

Bobby eased down while Armando placed a large bowl filled with various meats and another with rice on the table. He breathed in. "Smells delicious."

"It's *Arroz Atollado,* a native Columbian dish made with chicken, pork, and vegetables. I hope you enjoy it. Help yourself."

They made small talk while they ate. Bobby complimented her on the food although he was sure she hadn't prepared it.

They finished, and Armando cleared the table. He returned with a silver cart. Lifting a platter laden with various imported cheeses and fruits he set it between them. He performed a slight bow before placing an open bottle of red wine, a decanter and two glasses beside it.

Carmela smiled. "Now, for the best part."

With a practiced hand, he lit a candle, placed it on the table, and held the neck of the bottle over the candlelight. Careful not to spill a drop, he poured the wine into the crystal decanter, stopping when the sediment reached the neck.

Carmela smiled. "*Gracias*, Armando."

He dipped his head, put the empty bottle on the cart, and wheeled it out of the room.

Carmela poured two glasses. She handed one to Bobby. "This is our signature Cabernet. Let me know what you think."

Thankful for the circles he had traveled in the last few years, he swirled the glass, sniffed, and took a sip. He repeated the motions again and sipped. The best Cabernet he had ever tasted washed over his palette.

"Impressive," he said.

Over the next hour, Carmela spoke about her art collection in Napa and in her other home in Miami. Before long, they had finished the bottle. Feeling more and more relaxed, he studied Carmela's facial expressions, her fluid body language. All of it deliberate, almost practiced. Bobby liked what he saw.

She rose and reached for his hand. "Come, let me show you the reason I called."

Her soft skin pressed against his palm as he followed her along a corridor. She opened a door near the end. His chest heaved, and his jaw dropped. Before him lay a vast room, its walls filled with paintings. A doorway led to additional rooms beyond this one, all with countless displays.

He let go of her hand. Almost breathless, he wandered through her vast collection. Works by Monet, Renoir, and Cézanne covered the walls. A second held modern art by Pollock, Dali, Picasso, and O'Keeffe.

"I don't think you need my help at all," Bobby said.

"Oh, but you are wrong about that." Carmela took his hand, guiding him to another room. The walls were empty except for one. Wesley Bell's painting hung on a far wall. "This room will be dedicated to new and upcoming artists." She trailed her finger down the front of his shirt. "The ones *you* discover."

They were so close he could feel the heat from her body. Her dark eyes beckoned, and Bobby wrapped his arms around her. His tongue dipped between her lips. Her mouth opened, and her soft tongue collided with his. He ended the kiss, and she led him up the hallway to a winding staircase.

Bobby's head swam from the wine. He stopped at the top of the landing.

"Carmela, I don't think—"

She pressed her fingers to his lips, and they continued on to her bedroom. In one swift move, she undid her braid and let her long hair fall loose. In a hurry now, their desire for each other rising to new heights, they stripped and tumbled onto the bed, their hands exploring all the secret places of each other's bodies.

Carmela's fingers threaded through his hair. He ran his hands over her smooth skin and pressed his lips down her neck, leaving a trail of kisses. His lips found hers, and she kissed him with such passion, it astounded him. Every muscle and nerve in his body responded to her touch.

Bobby's mouth teased her nipples. She let out a moan while he trailed his hands along her belly and between her thighs. Carmela was more than ready when he eased himself on top of her.

His brain exploded as her hips rose to meet his and he slipped deeper inside her. Her fingers dug into the taut flesh on his shoulder blades while he drove harder.

Bobby brought himself to the edge, then held off, not wanting to end the pleasure sparking through him. He continued teasing until she cried out. Her back arched, and he let go as a shudder rocked his body.

He slipped beside her and attempted to hold her, but she moved away. Confused he dropped his arms. This woman made the walls he'd built around his emotions threaten to collapse and expose what he wanted to stay hidden. But he could tell she had walls of her own.

Exhausted, he drifted off. But sometime during the night he woke and found himself alone. He rubbed his eyes and tried to focus on the pale light streaming in from the hall. His heart hammered at the silhouette framed in the doorway. Carmela stood, silent, naked, and expressionless, the softness erased from her face. Unease washed over him like a cold wave and settled in his gut.

Unable to speak, he stared at the vision before him and wished for daylight. He needed the sun's rays to wash away the image and turn his life back to normal again.

# CHAPTER 7

## Carmela

Carmela leaned on her elbow and rested her chin in her hand. She pushed the covers away and studied Bobby's face in the moonlight. Sex with Bobby D'Angelo had surprised her. He appreciated a woman's body and how to satisfy her. She pictured his ice-blue eyes and how his lips had devoured hers with, deep, demanding kisses. How his hands explored all her soft curves, making her flesh come alive. His hips thrusting in a steady rhythm bringing her to the breaking point, then holding back.

Unlike Diego, Bobby's lovemaking, bold yet passionate, satisfied everything a woman with her appetite needed. But after they finished, she remembered her pain and pulled away.

In some ways he scared her, almost made her question her motives. Here Carrie's son lay sleeping beside her, unaware of her plans for him and the rest of his family. She'd never break her vow to her father. And she'd never break the promise she shouted at Nick long ago in the winery.

She slipped out of bed and grabbed her robe. Padding across the room she opened the door and went downstairs. Halfway down the hall, her heart jumped. A lone figure moved in the dim light. Diego appeared and her breath quieted.

"What are you doing?" she asked.

He stepped closer. "I might ask you the same question."

"What the hell are you talking about?"

He motioned toward the stairs. "He's still here, isn't he?"

Carmela shot him a look. "That is none of your damn business, Diego. And I don't appreciate your spying on me."

He placed his hand on her shoulder. "Carmela, you must stop this before it goes too far. All you need to do is send Miguel to eliminate Nick. Keep things professional. The rest is nonsense."

She pushed his hand away. Her insides burned. She could almost hear the blood rushing to her head. How dare he tell her what she should do. She had her mind set long before Diego came into her life.

"You call my father's death nonsense." Her voice rose in pitch as her fury grew. "Perhaps you have never had someone you love taken from you. Witnessed a bullet lodged in their forehead and their eyes wide open, staring into nothingness."

Looking sheepish, he stepped back. He spread out his hands. "Carmela, please I didn't mean…"

Her fists clenched at her side, she advanced. "I know exactly what you meant. Just remember you work for me. Don't think for a minute because I have let you into my bed you can tell me what to do."

Diego's cheeks flushed. "Why do you treat me this way? I have done nothing but love you. No one else will care for you like I do."

She swept her dark hair away from her shoulders and drew herself up. Her face inches from his, she said, "I am telling you this for the last time. Do not interfere in my business, Diego, or Miguel Medina just might pay *you* a visit. Now, go back to the carriage house where you belong."

Carmela pushed past him and into her study. She flicked the light switch before slamming the door behind her. Seething inside, she grabbed the crystal decanter from the bar and poured tequila. She downed the shot, stomped over to her desk and collapsed into the leather chair.

She made a huge mistake sleeping with Diego Silva. All his banter about love and how she should let Miguel handle things were getting under her skin. Her father would have been disappointed to learn his daughter had slept with someone so weak-minded.

Her threat regarding Miguel Medina was real. If Diego did anything to mess up her plans, she wouldn't hesitate to have him eliminated. His talk of love and caring played no part in her life. She'd waited too long for anybody to stand in her way.

Carmela glanced at the clock above the file cabinet. It read 2:00 a.m., 8:00 a.m., in Italy. She lifted the receiver on her desk, scrolled through her contacts, and punched in the numbers.

On the eighth ring, he picked up. "Marco? What news do you have for me?"

"Good news, I think. They are moving to America, to South Dakota."

"Will you be coming with them?"

"Yes, Nick has asked me to come."

Her sour mood lifted. The information Marco had given her couldn't be any better. With the whole family together in America, it would make things much simpler.

"Keep me informed?"

"Of course, *Señorita.*"

Carmela ended the call. Everyone had their price, and Marco Valletta was no exception. On her orders, he could have killed Nick and his entire family. But she didn't believe in easy. She wanted them to suffer.

Lifting the receiver again, she punched in another number. A male voice answered.

"Well, have you found out any information about this…Travis Montgomery?" she asked.

"Not yet."

"What is taking so long?"

There was a pause on the other end of the line. "The man is dead, Ms. Santiago. It makes things a little more difficult."

"I know he's dead," she said becoming irritated. "Don't you have anything new to tell me?"

"So far, I've traced him to a trailer park in Arizona. A place called Breezy Meadows. He lived there with some woman for a time."

Her curiosity peaked. "Does this woman have a name?"

"Well, she did."

"What do you mean? Get to the point."

"Her name was Helen Overton. Seems she's dead too. Murdered. Happened about six years ago."

Carmela took a breath. "Are you sure?"

"Positive. Read the police report myself. They never caught the person who did it."

"Find out everything you can about her. I'm paying you enough. I expect results. Call me when you have more."

Could this Helen Overton have been Carrie's mother? The last name appeared to be the same as her maiden name. If so, who killed her and why? Did Nick have a reason to do it? Somehow, Travis Montgomery had a connection to her.

Carmela's instincts told her she was edging closer to the truth about Carrie's past and her relationship to these two people. Soon, she'd have all the pieces to this puzzle, and find a way to use it to her advantage.

She left the study and went upstairs. Pausing in the bedroom doorway, she let her robe drop to the floor, she focused on Bobby asleep in her bed. Soft light streamed in from the hallway, and he stirred. His eyes opened. Thoughts of Nick and Carrie churned in her head. She smiled inside. Soon enough, she would turn their world upside down…along with Carrie's darling son.

# CHAPTER 8
# Marco

Marco Valletta closed his eyes and sank into the leather seat of Dalton Burgess' Gulfstream 550. The children had dropped off to sleep, and Chino lay sprawled at their feet.

Carmela Santiago made Marco's decision to accompany Nick and Carrie to America an easy one. Her promises of love, money, and a life of luxury making him see he could never attain those things if he remained a soldier for Nick.

In the beginning, he had derived satisfaction from protecting them. But as time passed, he grew envious of Nick's wealth and his perfect little family.

Then several years ago, on his day off, he took a drive to Rome. While sitting in a café on Piazza Navona, a tap on his shoulder caused him to jump. Having almost spilled his drink down the front of his shirt, he was ready to accost whoever dared approach him in such a rude manner. His eyes locked on the most beautiful woman he had ever encountered.

Carmela Santiago stood before him, a mischievous smile on her face. She apologized and asked if she could have a few moments of his time, those moments turning into a night of fierce lovemaking. When dawn broke, and they lay still, she told him about her father's unfortunate death at the hands of Nicholas D'Angelo.

Marco wasn't a fool. The drug trade was a dirty business, and he surmised that Ricardo Santiago had gotten what he deserved. Carmela wanted her revenge, and she wanted him to play a part in it. She had sought him out through her many European connections.

He expected her to ask him to kill Nick, but instead she asked him to spy. Someone to keep track of the family's movements until she decided to destroy Nick. In return, Carmela had promised him considerable sums of money and a life with her in America. Growing increasingly dissatisfied with his current situation, he weighed his options.

Until his meeting with her, his loyalty lay solely with Nick. They met a little over eight years ago while Nick was on a kill in Europe and in need of weapons. Through Nick's connections, he had come highly recommended as a dependable supplier. In the course of doing business, they struck up a friendship and Nick contacted him from time to time for supplies. Until one day, he approached Nick about becoming a ghost. Marco wanted in. He wanted to be a part of the underworld of hitmen.

Nick balked, explaining that being a killer for hire came with a hefty price. A burden he wasn't willing to put on Marco. Even though he agreed Marco had the potential to become a ghost, he refused to introduce him to the world's secret network of killers.

Along, with Nick's refusal went Marco's dreams of power and wealth. Having no other aspirations, he accepted Carmela's offer, envisioning a better future and a new, abundant life in America.

Marco opened his deep brown eyes and stretched his long, lean body. He stared out the window while the jet descended, landing on the tarmac in Rapid City, South Dakota. His fingers raked through his long hair dipping several inches below the collar of his jacket.

Carrie gathered up the children, and Marco helped them exit the plane. Nick supervised the unloading of their luggage, then they climbed into the limo for the drive to Dalton's guesthouse in the Black Hills. The United States Government had taken care of everything with Customs.

Izzy pumped Carrie with questions while she described their new home and how much fun they would have. Nick told them the story of their mother's first snowfall and how he watched her fall down from the window.

Izzy laughed. She pointed her finger at Carrie. "You fell on your butt. How come?"

"Because the snow was so deep, I lost my balance and tumbled backward."

"Daddy, did you pick Mommy up?"

Marco saw Carrie blush, and Nick's face soften.

"No, Izzy," Nick said. "I let her enjoy the snow. She got up all by herself."

Listening to them, Marco felt the pang of jealousy stinging inside him. Nick had everything he wanted.

Izzy directed her attention to Marco. "Are you excited to be going to our new home?"

He forced a smile. *"Sì,* I am very excited." No matter what his feelings were regarding Nick and Carrie, he loved Izzy and Michael and had been their protector from the day they were born.

Marco stole a quick glance at Carrie. Carmela, though beautiful enough, couldn't surpass Carrie's beauty. *Bellissima.* How much luck could one man like Nick have?

Sometimes he fantasized about making love to Carrie; confident he'd be better at it than Nick. So far, he hadn't overstepped his bounds. He made sure to remain respectful. It was a shame he'd never have the chance to…

"Marco, did you hear me?"

Nick stared at him. Marco shifted in his seat. "Sorry. My mind drifted."

"I was saying after we get settled, you and I will take two ATVs out for a drive so you can familiarize yourself with the property."

"*Sì,*" Marco said. "That will be good."

An hour later, Marco peered out the window as they drove up a paved driveway lined with huge pine trees and others with skinny white spotted trunks. They stopped in front of a massive stone and timber house with a wide porch running across it.

Marco followed them inside, trying hard to hide how impressed he was. To the left of the entryway a doorway led to a room with closets and a big wooden chest. Above the chest, a long shelf with coat hooks. He heard Carrie tell the children it was called a mudroom.

At the end of the hall, the house opened up to a huge formal great room. Wood beams ran across the length of the ceiling and polished wood floors gleamed. An immense stone fireplace was flanked on either side by brown leather sofas strewn with thick throws and fluffy pillows. A wall of glass let in views of the surrounding forest. Marco noticed how the trees, their leaves covered in orange, yellow, and red stood out from among the dark green pines. A ragged line of hills could be seen in the distance.

They passed into a beautiful kitchen with maple cabinets, black granite countertops and a large island anchored in the center of the room. Off the kitchen, a long table and chairs graced the middle of a dining room, with a hutch against the opposite wall. Sliders led to a patio with a massive outdoor fireplace.

He followed them to a second great room. A flat screen TV mounted above a stone fireplace, overlooked a burgundy sectional stationed in front of it. A pool table and bar sat at the other end. Another room held a fully equipped gym.

Nick showed him to a bedroom down the hall from the master and in between the children's rooms. All the furniture had been shipped ahead and was already in place. Under Nick's instruction, the limo driver had deposited all the luggage inside the bedrooms.

"This one is yours, Marco," he said. "Get settled. Then we'll take that ride."

Marco closed the door. The room, bright and airy, held a view from the front of the house to mountains in the distance. He took it all in, and the heaviness within him returned. How long before he would have a home like this?

He opened his suitcase and removed his coat to prepare for his ride with Nick before unpacking the rest of his things. He stuck his 9mm in his waistband, before pulling a grey wool sweater over his shirt. Downstairs, Nick waited for him in the kitchen.

"Dalton stocked the pantry, so we're good for a while," Nick said. "Do you want anything before we head out?"

"No, I'll eat when we return."

Fifteen minutes later, they drove ATVs along the trails. Nick told him he wanted him to ride out at least once a day. With a little over one hundred and twenty acres, it would take time for Marco to become accustomed to the property. They rode for the next several hours. It was early evening when they returned to the house.

Carrie led them to the dining room where she had set out a meal of roasted chicken, mashed potatoes, vegetables, a bottle of wine and two glasses. She had eaten dinner with the children earlier, and after the long day, went to settle them for the night. They ate in silence for a few moments before Nick spoke.

"Listen, Marco, I really appreciate your willingness to come to America with us."

Marco looked up from his plate. "I'm happy to be here."

"You're part of this family, I don't want you to think of yourself differently." Nick set his fork down and stared at him a moment. "Since I'll be away for weeks at a time, I take comfort knowing you'll be protecting everyone. Your loyalty these past years has meant more to me than you could ever imagine."

Marco averted his eyes and continued to eat.

"Is something wrong?" Nick asked.

Marco stopped eating and took a sip of his wine. "You know I want to become a ghost."

Nick pushed his plate aside. "We had this discussion already. You don't want to believe me, but I turned you down for a good reason. You have no idea how a life like mine has destroyed a part of me. A part I'll never get back."

Marco fingered the stem of his glass. He took another sip of wine before continuing. "And yet, you are getting ready to be a ghost again."

A flicker of irritation in his eyes, Nick said, "Look, I'm not doing this by choice. I've been forced into this life. A life I gave up a long time ago after I met Carrie. This is not something I want for my family or me. Count yourself lucky you never got into the game."

A shadow crossed Nick's face, and Marco's stomach clenched. He needed to be careful not to step over the line. He pushed his chair away from the table and threw up his hands.

"Okay, okay I know you are only trying to do for me what you think is right."

"No Marco, I don't think it's right, I know it's right. You're like a brother to me, and I only want what's best for you."

"What's that?" Marco asked.

"I don't want you to have those endless, sleepless nights. The constant rumble in your head while you try to push away the demons sleeping inside just so you can get through another day. If my life had turned out differently all those years ago, I wouldn't be sitting here talking to you about ghosts, and killing. Hell, I wouldn't be in this position at all. Put this idea to bed, Marco. For your own sake, put it to bed."

Marco shrugged and drained his glass. "I won't speak of it again."

"Good. All I need is your reassurance of my family's safety while I'm gone."

Marco feigned surprise. "How could you think otherwise? I would lay down my life for them."

Nick's face relaxed. "I don't doubt you would. Get some rest, and we'll go over some other things in the morning." Nick got up and left the room.

Marco poured himself another glass of wine and tried to quiet the frustration building inside him. Nick's words reassured him he'd made the right choice in siding with Carmela.

He pictured her face and longed to feel her skin, soft as butter beneath his hands. Since their initial tryst, they had met numerous times in Rome where he'd report on Nick's family. Afterward, they'd have sex and she would repeat her promise to him of a wonderful life in America with her.

Many months had passed since he last saw her. Hidden away on over one hundred acres, he doubted he would see her anytime soon.

He drained the rest of his wine and prepared to retreat upstairs to his room. Carrie walked in with Chino padding behind her. "All finished, Marco?"

Her long, ink-black hair hung loose. He observed her tight-fitting jeans. A turtleneck sweater fit snuggly over her breasts, the pale rose tint in stark contrast to her violet-blue eyes. Something stirred inside him and he forced himself to look away.

"So what do you think of our new home so far?" she asked.

"It is very nice," he answered. "The land is so rich with color, and the air smells sweet."

"Fall is one of the prettiest times of the year here. I don't know if he mentioned it, but Nick and I have a history with this place."

Marco forced a smile."Yes. He told me here is where you fell in love."

Her eyes brightened at his words, and she blushed. "That's right. It's hard to believe so much time has gone by. I hope you'll like living in America."

"I'm sure I will get used to it."

"I'd be sad if you missed Italy." She finished loading the dishwasher and dumped some table scraps into Chino's bowl. His tail wagged, and he licked it clean within a few minutes.

"Well, I'm beat. Think I'll go upstairs.

He gave her a slight smile. *"Buona notte."*

He waited a few moments before climbing the stairs to his room. Lying on the bed with his hands clasped behind his head, he pictured Carrie and Nick in their bedroom. His body ached for the feel of a woman of his own beneath him. He took several deep breaths and honed his mind on other things. Images of a wealthy, powerful life of his own here in America danced before him. He would have that life with Carmela Santiago.

Marco Valletta drifted off to sleep, content to dream about his future.

# CHAPTER 9

## Nick

Two weeks after settling into their new home, Nick received the call he dreaded but knew would come. While Carrie put the children to bed, he hauled a black duffel bag off the top shelf in the master closet and checked the contents.

Inside were two pairs of black leather gloves explicitly designed for firearm manipulation, thin for maximum dexterity with grip on the fingers for weapon control and touchscreen compatibility.

He packed personal necessities, plus three black turtlenecks, black jeans, and grabbed one of his Hugo Boss suits already hanging in a garment bag. He added black t-shirts to the duffel, dress shoes, and a pair of rubber-soled shoes. He'd purchase weapons at his final destination.

The previous week, Dalton flew to Virginia to meet their Washington contact. The rules of the game were made crystal clear by the Feds. A courier would pass a manila envelope at a location to be determined ahead of time. Inside were instructions for one or more hits.

If it contained a single file, he and Dalton could decide which one of them would do the job. Should anything go wrong, they were to abandon the exercise. Of course, the government would deny any involvement, including any knowledge of their operation or them. Last night, Dalton had picked up the first envelope.

He came out of the bathroom with his toiletry kit. Carrie, arms folded leaned in the bedroom doorway. "How long?" she asked.

Nick's heart dropped at the expression on her face. He wished he could give her the answer she wanted to hear.

"I can't tell you something I don't know," he said and finished packing. He set his duffel and garment bag by the bench at the foot of the bed.

Carrie closed the bedroom door and turned the lock. Nick drew her close, his eyes soaking in every small detail. He swept his hand through her long hair and planted a light kiss on her forehead. Lifting her chin with his fingertip, he said, "You know this is something I don't want to do. We talked about it. I have no other choice but to go." His voice threaded with pain.

Carrie put her arms around his neck. He studied her full lips, and he covered her mouth with his, their hot tongues thrusting and exploring. The warmth of her body engulfed him. He broke the kiss and led her to the bed.

Within minutes, they lay naked together, their bodies in tune. Hands traveled over familiar territory all of it suddenly feeling new again.

He traced the hollow of her neck with his tongue and teased her nipples with the tip. She moaned before his lips met hers again. His hand stroked the soft skin of her inner thigh, then dipped into the mound between her legs. Her breath caught, and she cried out, digging her fingers into his muscled back. He continued until she was ready to receive him.

Their hips moved in a steady rhythm. He drowned in the deep pools of violet-blue in her eyes. They clung to each other knowing this could be the last time they made love.

When they finished, he dropped beside her, and she melted into him. A sob escaped her lips. He stroked her cheek and fingered the tear trailing down her face.

"Please, babe, don't," he said gently. "It's hard enough for me to leave."

"I can't help it. Whenever I think about the possibility of you not coming back…if something happens to you, I'm not sure what I'll do."

"If something should happen to me, you'll go on because you have to for the sake of our children."

Carrie pushed herself up against the pillows. She cupped his face in her hands. "Don't forget how much *I need you.* Promise you'll come home to us."

"I wish I could make that promise. *Tu sei tutto per me,"* Nick whispered. "You are everything to me." His arms encircled her, and they fell into a restless sleep, both of them dreading the daylight that would arrive all too soon.


Early the next morning, Nick greeted Dalton on the tarmac. They climbed aboard Dalton's Gulfstream. They settled into their seats on either side of a small table before Nick asked, "Where we heading?"

Dalton removed his Stetson. "Bolivia."

He drew a manila envelope from his briefcase and emptied the contents. Photos of two men and a short dossier on each one lay before them. They were both known drug traffickers, heavy hitters in the export of illegal drugs to the United States.

"We can divide and conquer or work together," Dalton said. "Either way is fine with me."

Nick read the file and studied the photos. His mind drifted to Ricardo. These men, though not as well educated as Ricardo had been, were at the top of their own Bolivian Cartels. With many underlings to do their dirty work, they remained behind the scenes. To outsiders, they portrayed themselves as successful, wealthy business owners. Their legitimate businesses were a necessity. In order for them to survive, it was essential drug money be laundered, and government officials bribed.

"Neither one will be an easy kill," Nick said. He fingered a photo. A man in his mid-fifties, well fit, tan, and sporting an expensive suit stared back at him. Juan Carlos Oroza was printed beneath the picture. He laid the photo down and tapped it with his finger.

"I'll take him," he said.

Dalton grinned. "Guess Fredrico Molina is mine."

They discussed the logistics of the operation and their weapons connection in Bolivia before enjoying a meal prepared by the onboard chef. They finished eating, and Dalton retrieved a bottle of Johnnie Walker Blue Label Scotch Whiskey.

Nick's eyes lit up. "A man after my own heart. Make mine neat."

Dalton poured each a drink. He lifted his glass. "Here's to getting out of Bolivia alive."

Nick raised his own. "Hell, yeah."

They swallowed the smooth whiskey and Dalton poured two more shots. The men drank in silence for a moment.

Dalton tugged at his mustache. "How's Carrie?"

Nick drained his glass. "Not good. All of this is pretty tough on her. But she's proven she can be strong when it counts. If things don't work out, she'll survive."

"You got that right," Dalton said. "She walloped the hell out of Ricardo's man that night in South Dakota. The fireplace poker needed replacing afterward."

Nick smiled remembering how Carrie had almost beaten the poor guy to death while Bobby stayed locked inside the bathroom. "The stakes were high. You can never come between a momma bear and her cub. She did well. *Very* well."

"How is Bobby?" Dalton asked.

"I'm proud of him. He's living his life. Has a legitimate career in New York."

"With everything you've taught him, he'll be fine," Dalton added.

Nick shifted in his seat. "You're right, the rest is up to him."

They finished their whiskey and slept for the remainder of the flight.

Five hours later, the jet landed in El Alto, Bolivia. They breezed through Customs with forged passports and proceeded to a car rental counter. By the time the two men parted ways outside the terminal, it was early evening. Both of them carried separate files and burner cell phones.

Nick drove to the nearest five-star hotel. He ordered dinner in his room, spending the next few hours going over Juan Carlos Oroza's file. Little details were vital when setting up a kill.

He took note of Orozo's place of legitimate business, the restaurants, and clubs he frequented. Where his wife shopped, and his children went to school were equally important. A mark could change his routine and all these things could play into that.

He'd need to familiarize himself with Oroza's bodyguards…which ones always accompanied their boss, and how many guarded his home and family.

All of this could take several weeks, maybe over a month. Once he had full knowledge, he'd decide where and how the kill would go down.

Unlike his kills for Ricardo, there was no set timeline. So long as he completed the job, the government would be happy. He'd collect a nice check and wait for the next phone call. If they were lucky, he and Dalton might complete their kills around the same time.

After a few hours, his eyes straining, Nick put the file aside, his thoughts now drifting to Carrie and his children. Six years ago, he wouldn't have minded being away from home. He had nobody to go home to. Nothing to cherish. It still surprised him how his love for one woman had changed everything.

Murder had brought him to her, a common bond between the two of them and the reason they understood each other so well. No need to dissect and examine all of it again. The past couldn't be altered, and even if it was somehow possible, he dared not do it because, without her, his life was unimaginable.

Before Carrie, emptiness dug its claws inside of him refusing to let go. The loss of his brother, his parents, and his NYPD career as a detective had destroyed any hope for the future. Having nothing to lose, made it easy for him to slip into the role of a hired killer for Ricardo. Bitterness allowed him to ignore his conscience after each pull of the trigger.

Now, with everything on the line, he needed to make sure nothing went wrong. His life waited for him back in South Dakota, but his demons waited there for him, too. The demons he so far had managed to keep at bay no doubt would resurface and try to reclaim what was rightfully theirs. He'd need to undertake the painful task of forcing them down into the bowels of his soul where they belonged.

He pictured that day in the woods when he put two bullets in Travis's head. Only Ricardo's death had affected him more. Travis's pleading cries for mercy made no difference.

Nick refused to display even a drop of pity for a man who lived to deceive, abuse, and bed his own daughter.

A truth which also concerned Bobby. His childhood of horror with his adoptive family would be enough to make anyone go insane. But Bobby had survived all of it and gone on, reconnecting with Carrie and healing himself.

Nick couldn't imagine the repercussions if they found out Bobby was a child of incest and had convinced himself a long time ago, they must never know Travis Montgomery's true identity.

He needed to protect them from a truth bound to destroy them both. So, he'd always honor their pledge with one exception. His hidden lie concerning Travis.

Nick crossed to the window. He peered out at the traffic whizzing by below and asked himself when the time came to pull the trigger, would he feel his familiar adrenaline rush surge through his body? A rush so powerful, it made everything around him crystal clear. He used to call it his natural high.

What if it had gone away? Could he still pull the trigger? And if it hadn't, what did that say about him as a human being, a husband, and a father?

Bone tired, he rubbed his temples and forced himself to stop thinking. He showered and got into bed. If everything fell into place, he'd be lucky enough to return to Carrie and their life in South Dakota.

# CHAPTER 10
## Bobby

B obby hailed a cab and tossed his carry-on onto the back seat. He instructed the driver to take the Queensboro Bridge and settled in for the ride to Manhattan. His eagerness to see the city's skyline superseded the more accessible route through the Midtown Tunnel.

His flight from Paris had landed at Kennedy twenty minutes earlier. Glad to be home, his spirits rose in spite of his lingering jet lag. Wesley Bell's show had been a success. Once he completed his next collection, Bobby would arrange for shows in London, Milan, Denmark, and Germany making it his goal to display Wesley's paintings alongside works from his other clients. He pictured an art showcase where wealthy patrons would champion the artists and add to their collections at the same time.

The cabbie negotiated the mid-day traffic while Bobby reflected on Carmela.

After he left her home in Napa, he immersed himself getting ready for Wesley's show. He took pride in his work and wanted to ensure he did the best job he could for Wesley. It also gave him the space he needed to assess Carmela's true intentions. Just a client, or a client and a lover? He wasn't sure of either one.

Bobby never debated about sleeping with his clients. It was out of the question…until Carmela. He had broken his cardinal rule.

He heard little from her until his stay in Paris. She breezed into the gallery late one night and acted as if they had seen each other the previous day. In reality, it had been over a week.

Different from the women he was accustomed to, Carmela confused and yet excited him. Like a chameleon, she'd abruptly change, and break the connection building between them and become distant, not only physically but emotionally. So far, he hadn't confronted her about it, but he couldn't continue on this way too much longer. It made him uncomfortable, made him doubt himself at times.

They drove onto the bridge, and the New York skyline came into view. Exhilarated, he drew it all in. This was his city, his home, and no other place in the world compared. Away for two months, he delighted in the rush soaring through his body.

The cab inched its way up Central Park West. Flashes of red and green graced some shop windows decorated for the coming season. The holidays were fast approaching, and the city was dressing in the appropriate attire.

With Thanksgiving a mere two weeks away, he thought of South Dakota. His mother never questioned his independence, or pressured him to visit, but delighted when he appeared for special occasions. The Thanksgiving holiday was definitely one she anticipated having him spend with her.

He paid the cabbie and grabbed his carry-on. Hank, the brass buttons gleaming on his uniform in the afternoon light, tipped his cap and held the door open.

"Welcome home, Mr. D'Angelo."

"Thanks, Hank. All's well, I hope."

"Buildings still standing." Hank walked behind the lobby desk. "Got your mail right here." He handed Bobby a bundle of envelopes secured by a thick band.

Bobby reached into his pocket. "Thanks for taking care of that for me," he said, slipping him a fifty-dollar bill.

"No problem. Need help with your bag?"

He shook his head. "I can manage."

"By the way," Hank said. "A Miss. Santiago is waiting for you in the anteroom upstairs. I told her I couldn't confirm when you'd be arriving, but she insisted."

Bobby's shoulders tensed. "Thanks." He entered the elevator, his mail in one hand, carry-on in the other. He got off on his floor and checked the anteroom. Diego, seated in a chair, looked up from the newspaper in his hands. His forehead creased, a look of disdain washing over his face.

"The *Señorita* is waiting by your door."

Bobby refused to react to his surly mannerisms. Without a word, he strode out and rounded the corner to his apartment.

Carmela leaned against his door dressed in a belted white wool winter coat, her hair swept up in a chignon exposing her exquisitely long neck. The Diamond studs gracing her earlobes glittered in the hallway light.

"I don't understand your reluctance to fly on my jet." A hint of mockery laced her voice. She stepped aside while he inserted his key.

"I've told you before, Carmela. Flying private doesn't matter." He held the door open, and she brushed against him as she strutted past.

She eyed him, a mischievous grin lighting her face. "Oh yes, I forgot about those coveted frequent flyer miles." She glanced around the apartment. "Nice place."

Bobby ignored her comments and set his carry-on down. He tossed his mail onto the mahogany console. "You need to give me a heads up before you come. And by the way, why does Diego always have to be present?"

Carmela frowned. "Diego is a necessary part of my being a single, wealthy, businesswoman. You wouldn't want anything unfortunate to happen to me, would you?"

She removed her coat and held it out. The first three buttons of her peach-colored silk blouse were open revealing a hint of cleavage. Beige stilettos with gold detailing set off her wide-leg black wool trousers. Bobby snatched it from her and hung it in the hall closet. He didn't find her assertiveness endearing at all. In fact, he found it a little childish.

"Besides," Carmela said. "I could ask you why you always carry a weapon. Is there someone after you?"

He let out an exasperated breath. "You can never be too careful in this city, especially when you're dealing with valuable art."

Carmela's mouth formed a pout. "I thought you would be happy to see me."

"Of course, I'm glad to see you, but this habit of showing up whenever you feel like it is somewhat annoying." He removed his jacket and threw it onto the sofa. "Suppose I had plans. I guess you'd expect me to change them just for you."

She placed her hands on her hips and moved closer. "Do you?"

"Do I what?"

"Have plans?"

He crossed the room, his back to her, he stared out of the window. The trees in his beloved Central Park had lost their colors. Bare branches twisted in the wind, piles of dead leaves gathered around their trunks. Traffic snaked up the street below, the sound muted by the thick apartment walls.

Carmela's arms slid around his waist, her head pressed against his shoulder blades. "Let's not have a silly argument. I came because I missed you."

Her sympathetic tone caught him by surprise, a side of her he hadn't encountered before. He covered her hands with his own. "Look, I don't want to argue either. I'm frustrated because this thing, this arrangement between us has no foundation. I never know from one day to the next when I'm going to see you again."

Bobby turned and faced her. "I have to be honest with you, Carmela. I can't continue this unless I know for sure where it's heading. I'm beginning to have strong feelings for you. Before we go any further, I need to know whether or not you're all in."

Carmela wrapped her arms around his neck and drew him to her. She kissed his lips and swiped her hand through the strands of hair dipping above his right eye.

"Yes," she murmured. "I am all in."

Lost in her dark eyes, he traced his finger across her bottom lip. "I'm glad," he said before kissing her long and deep.

The next afternoon, after Carmela left to fly home to California, he picked up his cell phone and dialed.

"Bobby, I'm so happy you called," Carrie said. "We miss you."

"I miss all of you too. How are things? Is Nick back yet?" He detected a sigh on the other end.

"No, I'm afraid not. It's been over a month."

He heard the strain in her voice. "I know it's hard, but try not to worry. Nick can take care of himself." He didn't want his conversation with her to make matters worse, so he quickly changed the subject. "I'll be coming for Thanksgiving."

"Wonderful." Her tone lifted. "By the way, how did your show in Paris turn out?"

"It was a success. I'm planning a bigger show for later next year."

"I'm so proud of you. You've done well for yourself."

"Listen, I have something else I wanted to tell you," Bobby said. "I've met someone. It's been going on for a while. I may ask her to come for Thanksgiving."

"She must be special. You've never brought anyone home to meet us."

"Until now, there wasn't anyone worth bringing."

"Sounds serious," Carrie said.

He caught the amusement in her voice. "Mom, don't get ahead of yourself. I said I may ask her to come. It's not definite."

"I can hope, can't I?" she said, laughing.

Bobby laughed, too. "Love you lots. Talk to you soon."

He hung up and reflected on his mother's words. They hadn't met any of the women he'd dated casually at home and while in Europe. It never crossed his mind to bring anybody home to Tuscany or South Dakota to meet his family. Since meeting Carmela, he had broken things off with Valerie Gold, and no one else had caught his interest.

He grabbed his mail and sorted through it. He found it hard to concentrate. Last night and this morning with Carmela had been amazing. Maybe this was the beginning of something real for both of them.

A woman with many layers, Bobby felt the aloofness she sometimes portrayed wasn't part of her persona but a form of protection. Protection against what, he didn't know. She'd built a wall around her emotions. Bobby was determined to break through.

# CHAPTER 11

## Carmela

Carmela sunk into the chair and read the text message from Bobby. Would she like to spend Thanksgiving in South Dakota? Nothing fancy, it would be the two of them plus Carrie and the children since Nick, unfortunately, was away.

She drummed her fingers on the desk. If she did decide to go, the possibility Carrie might know all about her surfaced. But chances of that were slim at best. Nick would have protected her from names, places, and dates, just as her father had tried to protect her.

A trip to South Dakota could prove quite amusing. For the first time, she would be in the same room with Carrie D'Angelo, and she would have no idea how much she hated her. Of course, Marco would be there as well. But handling him wouldn't be difficult at all.

A knock interrupted her thoughts. *"Entrar,"* she called out, annoyed at the intrusion.

Diego, a wide grin planted on his face, seated himself on the leather sofa across from her. *"Hola,* Carmela."

Carmela cringed inside at his casual approach. She should have never allowed herself to be intimate with him. Since dating Bobby, she worked hard at keeping her distance. He didn't approve of her plans, and she tired of the same old arguments.

"What is it, Diego? I'm busy," she said. She folded her arms across her chest.

He shifted uncomfortably and cleared his throat. "Ever since you began seeing him, you have no time for me."

She sprang to her feet. "Must we go through this again and again? It is so exhausting, Diego. I know you'll never approve of my plans, but they are *my* plans, and I intend to see them through to the end."

Diego got up. "I realize nothing I say can stop this foolishness. Putting all of that aside, I miss being with you."

Carmela met his eyes, their dark wells filled with sadness. "Look, Diego, please understand we cannot be as we were before. I enjoyed our time together, but now I need to concentrate on the business among other things." She took his hand. "Those times were special to me whether you want to believe me or not. But you can't force emotions which are not there on both sides."

A frown darkened his face. "So, this is how it is." He drew his hand away. "I will abide by your wishes for now. But someday you may realize how much I care for you, and it will change your mind. Until then, I promised to protect you, and I will continue to do so." Without waiting for an answer, he walked out.

Carmela chewed her bottom lip and paced. She grabbed her cell phone and hit Bobby's number. "Yes," she said. "I'd love to go to South Dakota, under one condition. You agree to fly on my private jet. With the airports so busy for the holiday, it will make traveling easier." Her mouth curved into a smile. "Great, I'll text you all the details." She ended the call and placed another.

"Bernardo, prepare the plane for six o'clock Thursday morning. We will be flying to New York, then on to Rapid City, South Dakota."

She placed her cell phone aside and walked to the window. Peering out over the vineyards below, her mind focused on Carrie. Soon, they would meet face to face, and the woman who had caused her untold misery would find out what it's like to suffer and lose the things she loves the most in life.

Carmela picked Bobby up at JFK at noon. With the time difference, they arrived in Rapid City at two in the afternoon after an uneventful flight. While Diego loaded the luggage, they settled in the limo for the ride to the Black Hills.

"You'll love it here," Bobby said. He draped his arm around her shoulders and gathered her close. "They already have plenty of snow. We can ski or snowmobile. I've had some great times snowmobiling. With over a hundred and twenty acres, there are lots of trails."

Carmela rested her head on his shoulder. "I'm sure if you like it, I will too."

The excitement on his face and in his voice almost made her feel at ease, but her nerves refused to calm. If Carrie had any knowledge of her, all her efforts would be for nothing.

An hour later, Diego stopped at the wrought-iron gate where Bobby had him punch in a temporary code. Mounds of white drifts lined either side of the plowed drive. Ponderosa pine and aspen trees dipped their branches under the weight of the snow. They pulled in front of a massive stone and timber home. Carmela's anxiety peaked.

Taking a deep breath, she stepped out the limo. She walked to the rear of the car while Diego unloaded the luggage. He handed her a leather wine case and some flowers wrapped in cellophane before placing the suitcases on the porch.

"We will take it from here, Diego," she said. "You have your instructions. I will call you at the hotel when I need you to come."

Diego's face soured, but he nodded politely before slamming the trunk closed and driving away.

Bobby grabbed Carmela's hand and led her up the steps and across the wide front porch. She placed the wine next to the luggage and held onto the flowers. He opened the heavy door and ushered her inside.

"Mom!" he called out. "We're here."

She followed him to a huge great room. Two young children ran at them screaming Bobby's name. He bent and picked up the girl first.

Carmela's breath caught. She stared into the girl's green eyes. They were Nick's eyes and they reminded her that this child could have belonged to her.

"Izzy," Bobby said. "I want you to meet someone. This is Carmela."

Izzy gave her a big smile. "Hello. Are you Bobby's girlfriend?" She pressed her palm to her lips and giggled.

Bobby laughed and glanced at Carmela. "Maybe."

Carmela ignored the comment. "It's nice to meet you, Izzy,"

He set Izzy down and scooped up Michael. "Hey buddy, I've been missing you."

Carmela took in the boy's, dark hair, blue eyes and dimpled cheeks, a combination of his mother and father. She placed her hand upon his head, ruffling his hair. "Such a handsome little guy."

Michael squirmed out of his arms, and the two children scampered off. Carrie appeared with Chino trotting behind her.

"Bobby, I'm so happy you're here." She gave him a quick hug.

Carmela's pulse spiked. The air around her thinned. She clenched her fingers, nails digging into her palms while she tried to control her emotions. She studied Carrie's long, black hair, her perfectly sculpted lips, but most of all, her violet-blue eyes. Those eyes had bewitched Nick for sure. Blood rushed from her head, and she swayed. The flowers fell from her hands.

Chino slinked toward her, his head raised, and his ears erect. A low growl, then a whimper escaped his throat.

Bobby pointed his finger. "Chino, stop that."

Carrie grabbed the dog's collar, pulling him away. "Chino, sit," she commanded. The dog whimpered again but obeyed. "I don't know what's gotten into him. I'm so sorry. I've never seen him react this way to anyone."

"Carmela, are you okay?" Bobby asked. He took her arm and steered her to the sofa. "Come, sit down. You've gone pale."

Trying to quiet the roar in her ears, she eased down, aware she had underestimated her reaction to all of this. Every fiber of her being wanted to reach out and destroy this woman. Did Carrie have any idea of the destruction she had caused? Her father would be alive today were it not for Carrie D'Angelo.

"Here, drink this."

Carmela raised her head. Carrie, a look of concern on her face, held out a glass of water. "It's okay. I've put the dog in the mudroom."

Shaking her head to clear it, Carmela accepted the glass.

"Thank you," she said. She took several sips and set it on the coffee table. "I'm sorry. This is so embarrassing."

"No, don't apologize," Carrie said. "It's quite alright. Traveling can be tiring." She held out her hand. "By the way, I'm Carrie. It's so nice of you to spend the holiday with us."

Carmela hesitated. She could hardly stand to look at her without lashing out. Taking a breath, she shook Carrie's hand.

"Carmela Santiago. It was good of you to invite me."

Carrie scooped up the flowers. "Thank you, these are beautiful. Bobby, why don't you both get settled in the guest room. I think Carmela should rest before dinner."

Bobby helped her up and guided her upstairs. "Are you sure you're okay?" he asked.

She gave him a weak smile. He told her to relax while he retrieved the luggage. Moments later, he deposited their suitcases and the wine in the room.

Bobby bent and kissed her cheek. "You take it easy. I'll wake you when dinner's ready." He closed the door softly behind him.

Carmela berated herself for being so weak. Carrie must never see this side of her again. It was important, she maintain control at all times. She couldn't let on how much being in this house, with Nick's family, disturbed her.

She pictured the dog. How stupid of her to have forgotten about him. Another traitor once loyal to her father. The silly animal had disobeyed her order to attack Nick, and she had kicked his flank. Chino followed Nick out of the winery without looking back.

But of course, Chino would do that, she reasoned. Nick, had found and rescued the abused dog during one of his kills. After nursing him back to health, he presented Chino to Ricardo as a gift. Now, Chino's loyalty lay with this family. Carmela let out a sigh, thankful the dog couldn't talk. She'd just have to put up with him during her stay here.

Unable to sleep, she sat up. She glanced at the leather case containing the wine. It would play a big part in her visit here.

The bedroom door inched open, and Izzy peeked in.

"Mommy said you don't feel well."

Carmela beckoned. "No, I'm better now. You may come in."

Izzy came over and studied Carmela's face. "You're very pretty."

She smiled and patted Izzy's cheek. "So are you. I bet everyone tells you how beautiful you are."

Izzy's face lit up. "Yes, my daddy does. He says, *comes sei bella* to me all the time."

"I'm sure he does. "Where is your daddy?"

Izzy drew her arm up and pointed to the window. "He's far, far away on business."

"Do you miss him."

Izzy grew quiet. Her green eyes misted. "I miss him very much."

Carmela stared at the little girl's face. A feeling she couldn't describe or name welled up inside of her. Uncomfortable, she forced herself to look away.

"Come," she said to Izzy. "Let's go and wait for dinner." Izzy's hand slipped into hers, and they walked downstairs together.

Bobby and Carrie sat opposite each other at the large island. The sound of laughter carried across the room. The aroma of turkey baking permeated the air. It mingled with the scent of sweet potato casserole and a host of vegetables cooking on the stove.

Carmela let go of Izzy's hand and backed away. Her stomach sank, and she clasped her hand over her mouth. Turning, she ran up the stairs. At the top, she hesitated and gulped in air. After several deep breaths, her queasiness settled.

What was happening to her? Did meeting Carrie cause this physical reaction?

Before she could reason any further, someone blocked her path. She raised her head.

Marco Valetta smiled. "Carmela, it's so good to finally see you."

She gave him a half-smile and brushed past. "Not here, Marco. They can't know about us."

Before she could reach the bedroom door, he grabbed her arm. "I am not a fool," he said. "Do you think I would jeopardize all we have together?"

She glanced at his hand. "Let go, Marco."

He released her, but his eyes flashed as he took a step back. "How much longer is this going to take?"

"As long as it has to. This is not an easy thing. I am still gathering information. Now, I suggest you keep your distance while I am here."

Heat surged up her body. Some men were such silly creatures. Always thinking of themselves and what they want. Well, she would show them how one woman, if given a chance, could destroy them all.

Tomorrow, she would put her plan into place. She pictured Izzy's face and smiled. Carrie was about to get her first helping of heartache.

# CHAPTER 12

## Carrie

Later that evening, they all seated themselves in the dining room ready to enjoy Thanksgiving dinner. Fancy white-bone china with a blue-flowered border adorned the tablecloth. In the center a vase filled with the flowers Carmela had brought was flanked on either side by two tall lit white tapers. Steam rose from a bowl of vegetables set next to a pan of sweet potato casserole. Another held stuffing, and a third mashed potatoes. Cranberry sauce and freshly baked yeast rolls rounded out the sides.

Bobby surveyed the dinner. "Everything looks great. Thanks, Mom." He carved the turkey while Izzy and Michael clapped with enthusiasm. He finished, and Carrie set the platter in the center of the table along with the gravy bowl.

She beamed with pride. Contemplating for a brief moment all those Thanksgiving's she never had growing up, a spark of sadness lingered within her. In all their time together, holidays were something Travis had never bothered to celebrate, but thankful for all she had now, she focused on the present.

For the children's sake, Bobby said a short blessing. Carrie insisted Izzy start to learn to be grateful she had a good home and a family who loved her.

They started passing dishes and filling their plates. Carrie tried not to stare. She observed how Carmela picked at her food, taking only small bites. Something was off.

"Carmela, are you sure you're okay?" she asked. "If the food isn't agreeing with you, I won't be insulted. Please don't force yourself on my account."

"No, no," she protested. "It's delicious. I guess I'm not as hungry as I thought."

"Tastes wonderful," Bobby chimed in while he helped himself to the cranberry sauce, before pouring a generous amount of gravy over his mashed potatoes.

Carrie smiled at her son before directing her attention to the other end of the table. Marco's sullen expression made him look like he had just lost his best friend. She wondered if maybe he missed Italy, although to her knowledge he had no family there anymore.

She lifted her wine glass and sipped. "Carmela, this wine is wonderful. I can't imagine how much time and energy goes into running a winery."

"It's a lot of work, but I love it," she replied. "My wines have won several awards. I try to improve them each year."

Bobby drained his glass and poured a second. "I told Carmela, her wine's the best I've ever had." He smiled sheepishly.

Carrie could tell how entirely taken her son had become with this woman. She'd reserve her own judgment until she got to know her better.

While Izzy plied Carmela with a million questions, Carrie made sure Michael ate his food. She was glad Nick agreed to let Izzy enroll in a local private school. It gave her a sense of normalcy and the opportunity to socialize with other children. Apparently, she was trying her social skills out.

Carrie stared at the empty chair at the head of the table. A heaviness settled inside her chest. Nick should be here, enjoying the holiday with them. Instead, she had no idea where he might be or if he was alive.

She never imagined she could miss someone as much as she did Nick. She ached to feel his arms around her, see the smile in his green eyes, and hear the tenderness in his voice. They had never been apart this long. With each passing day, her angst grew.

"You remember all the fun we had," Bobby said, interrupting her thoughts. "Riding those snowmobiles up and down the trails."

"I sure do. Those were good times," Carrie answered. Taking another sip of wine, she pushed back the lump forming in her throat.

He must have noticed the look on her face. "I'm sorry. I know you're worried about him."

She tried to brush aside the emptiness in the pit of her stomach. "Yes, but I'm sure he's okay."

Carmela met Carrie's eyes. "Why are you worried? Bobby told me your husband is on a business trip."

Carrie shifted uncomfortably in her chair. "He is, but I expected him home for the holiday. Unfortunately, his business is keeping him away longer." She turned toward Michael again. "Oh, look at you. Turkey and mashed potatoes everywhere."

Starting to feel a buzz, she smiled at Carmela. "I'm sure he'll be home soon." Wanting nothing more than to change the subject, she asked Carmela about her house in Napa. Before long, she herself had downed another full glass.

They finished dinner and Bobby helped Carrie clear the table while Carmela took the children to the great room.

"So, what do you think?" he asked.

"She seems nice, but I've only just met her."

He loaded the last of the dishes into the dishwasher and leaned against the counter. "I know you better than that, Mom. You don't like her, do you?"

"Bobby, that's not fair," Carrie said as she finished putting the leftovers in the fridge. "I hardly know her. What's important is how you feel about her."

"Okay, we'll leave it alone for now. But I want you to understand I'm serious about her. I think she's someone I could have a long-term relationship with."

She studied his face for a moment. "If she makes you happy then I'm happy for you." She gave him a half-smile. "I'm exhausted. I had a little too much wine."

Bobby stretched and yawned. "Yeah, me, too."

"I'm going to get Izzy and Michael ready for bed. I think I'll make it an early night. I'll take Chino with me." She said goodnight to Carmela and headed upstairs with the children and the dog.

Sunlight streamed across the room. Carrie struggled to open her eyes. She looked at the clock on the nightstand and sat straight up. It was after eleven o'clock. Chino got up and pawed at the bedroom door. She threw on her robe and hurried to Michael's room where she discovered his empty crib.

Izzy's room was empty, too. Catching herself before panic rose, she remembered Bobby and Carmela were in the house. The children must be with them.

She found Michael downstairs with Marco in the great room watching cartoons.

"Marco, I'm sorry. I overslept. Two glasses of wine have never made me so sleepy before."

Marco smiled. "No problem. I gave him some cereal earlier."

She glanced around. "What about Izzy?"

"I think she must be with Bobby. She never came down this morning."

"Please let Chino out for a few moments, then secure him in the mudroom while I check."

She headed upstairs and tapped on Bobby's door. She knocked again and called his name. Her patience at an end, she pushed it open.

Fully clothed, Bobby lay face down on top of the comforter. There wasn't any sign of Izzy or Carmela. She rushed over and shook him. "Wake up, Bobby."

He rolled onto his back and rubbed his eyes. "What's going on?"

"Have you seen Izzy this morning?"

He shimmied up against the pillows. "No. I crashed last night. I hardly remember anything."

"Where's Carmela?"

Coming fully awake now, he surveyed the room. "Downstairs, I guess."

"No, she's not, and neither is Izzy."

Bobby swung his legs over the side of the bed. "Okay. There's no reason to get upset. They must be outside."

"I'll get dressed," Carrie said. "You go and see."

She threw on a pair of jeans and a heavy sweater and hurried downstairs, reaching the hallway leading to the front door as Bobby came in.

"I didn't find them, but I'm sure they probably just went for a walk. You know how Izzy likes to play in the woods. Let me get my cell and call Carmela."

Carrie brushed past him and into the mudroom. Izzy's jacket and boots were gone as were Carmela's. Pulling on her boots, a heavy coat, and gloves, she rushed out the door.

Calling Izzy's name, she made a trek around the entire outside of the house. The stillness of the surrounding woods increased her fears. A sudden bitter wind blew across the yard. She shivered as flurries erupted from steel-grey clouds. The front door opened. Bobby came out shaking his head.

"I don't understand any of this. Carmela's phone is upstairs."

"How could she do something like this?"

"Let's not jump to conclusions. You know how persuasive Izzy can be. She probably talked Carmela into going for a walk. They can't be far. Marco and I will take the snowmobiles and look for them."

"No, you come with me. Marco can stay with Michael," she insisted.

They mounted snowmobiles and drove out onto the trail leading into the woods. Carrie tried to fight the rising terror inside her. Memories flooded back of her mother and losing Bobby all those years ago.

She had no idea how long Carmela and Izzy had been gone. If they were lost, the freezing temperature would make matters worse. If anything happened to Izzy, she'd never be able to go on. How could she endure the loss of a child a second time?

Riding along each trail, they stopped periodically and called out. They rode for an hour against a biting wind. Bobby insisted they head back.

"We didn't see any tracks," he said. "Maybe we got this all wrong."

Carrie's stomach clenched at his words. "The flurries might have covered them. We need to keep looking."

"No, we 're going up to the house. If they're not home, I'll get Marco to ride out with me, and we'll call for more help."

By the time they rode up the trail toward the house, the snow fell hard and fast. Out of the swirling flakes, a black limo drove past them and along the drive toward the main gate. Bobby motioned, and they continued on.

They parked the snowmobiles and hurried inside. Carrie kicked off her boots and ran into the great room with Bobby. She spotted Izzy and Carmela sitting in front of the fire. Marco hovered over them holding Michael. Relief washed over her.

Izzy grinned at Carrie. "Mommy, look what Carmela bought for me." She held up a doll with long blond braids.

Carrie crossed the room, bent, and pulled her close. "Oh, Izzy, I was so worried."

Izzy pushed her away. "Mommy, look at my doll. Isn't she beautiful?"

Carrie eyed Carmela. "Yes, she's very pretty, but Mommy needs to talk to Carmela." She directed her attention to Marco. "Please take the children upstairs."

Marco stretched out his hand. "Come, Izzy. You can play in your room."

As soon as they left, she advanced toward Carmela. Hands gripped on her waist she said, "How dare you take my child out of this house without asking me first!"

Carmela rose, a slight smile crossed her lips. "I did not think you would mind. I had my chauffeur drive us into town. I am sorry we stayed so long, but Izzy insisted on going in and out of so many stores, I lost track of time."

Her panic gone, Carrie's temper exploded. She moved closer, her face inches from hers she shouted, "You could have let someone know, left a note or—"

"Mom, that's enough." Bobby rested his hand on Carrie's shoulder. "Carmela meant well. There's no harm done. Izzy is back."

Carrie shrugged his hand away and wheeled around. "Are you defending what she did?"

"No, I just don't want this to turn into a big thing. I'm sure she realizes now how upsetting all of this was."

Carmela lowered her eyes, a sorrowful look on her face, she said, "You are right, Mrs. D'Angelo, I should have asked you if I could take her with me. I thought you could use the break."

Caught in the middle, Carrie glanced from Carmela to Bobby. She had expected him to agree with her, but his facial expression, the tenderness in his eyes when he looked at Carmela, told her how much her son cared for this woman. Her uneasiness returned. If she forced the issue and he had to choose sides, what would he do? She had lost his love all those years ago and fought so hard to regain it. One incident wasn't worth taking the chance she'd lose it again.

She studied Carmela's face and wanted to believe her words were sincere. "Look, I know you meant well, but you can't just take off with someone's child without telling them."

Carmela blushed. "It will never happen again."

Bobby draped his arm around Carmela. "Maybe you and I can fix lunch, then do some snowmobiling together."

She smiled. "If you like."

Watching the two of them, Carrie had her answer. At this moment, right now, Bobby had chosen Carmela. She took a breath and forced herself to calm. "I'm going upstairs to see about the children." She stopped outside of Izzy's room and overheard Marco talking.

"That is a beautiful doll Carmela bought for you."

She leaned against the doorway. In light of what had transpired, she wondered about Marco. "Marco, why weren't you aware that Izzy left the house with Carmela?"

Marco raised an eyebrow. "I did not know this, because, like you, I had a little too much wine last night. They were gone when I woke."

"You need to be careful, Marco. I depend on you even more without Nick here."

Color rose in his cheeks. "Sorry, you are right. Wine has never had such an effect on me before. I will not drink so much again."

At his words, a chill skated down her spine. The wine appeared to be the common denominator in all of this. Carmela had barely taken a few sips at dinner. Speculation churned in Carrie's head. What would compel her to drug the wine? Bobby had drunk the same amount as she and Marco. It didn't make any sense.

Interrupted by the buzz of her cell phone, she removed it from her pocket. She stared at the unfamiliar number.

"Hello."

"Hi babe, I know it's a day late, but Happy Thanksgiving."

Her breath caught. She stepped out into the hall away from the children. "Nick, thank God, you're okay. I've been so worried. Why haven't you called before now?"

"If I could have, I would. Besides, stop worrying. I'm fine, except for missing you and the kids."

She gripped the phone as if doing so would bring him closer to her. "When are you coming home?"

"This job is taking a little longer than I expected."

"We all miss you so much." Not wanting to worry him, she brightened the tone of her voice. "Bobby's here."

"That's great. I'm glad you're getting to spend time with him."

She could almost feel him relax on the other end. "He brought someone with him."

"Must be serious."

"Yes, I think it is."

"Everything else good?" he asked.

Carrie recalled the day's events, but thought it best not to mention them. He had enough to deal with. "Yes. Izzy keeps asking for you."

"Give the kids a kiss for me."

"I will."

"You know how much I love you, don't you?"

"Yes, me too. Hurry home, Nick."

After the call ended, Carrie returned to Izzy's room. She stood in the doorway watching her children. While Izzy played with the doll, she pictured Nick's reaction to Carmela's antics, certain his anger would not have subsided as quickly as hers.

Wishing Bobby's attraction to Carmela wouldn't last, shame washed over her, but at the same time, she had no desire to rescind it. If only Carmela Santiago would break things off and leave her son alone.

She pictured Chino. His reaction still puzzled her, but animals were smart, sometimes smarter than humans. The dog sensed something. Maybe her assessment of this woman wasn't so far off.

She pressed her back against the frame and sighed. If only Nick were here to help her sort things out. Almost two months and only one phone call. Was this their life now? Nick coming and going at the government's whim. Her not knowing if he survived, or if she would hear from him. All she could do was hold on to the belief that he'd return and they might live like a normal family again.

# CHAPTER 13
## Nick

After a pounding rainstorm, early morning fog finally lifted from over La Paz. Nick crept along the inner wall of the flat rooftop. He reached the overhang facing the street below and scanned the area with his binoculars. Adjusting the lenses, he studied the entrance to the office building across the way. Juan Carlos Orozo conducted most of his daily business from there. Throngs of people trekked down sidewalks and in and out of various shops with vibrant red, blue, and green storefronts. Cars, taxis, and micro minibusses crawled along spewing black plumes of exhaust into the thin mountainous air.

These past few months, Nick had grown used to the altitude and landscape of the highest capital city in the world. But the sights, smells, and sounds of the busy town still jolted his senses. Open-air markets filled with fresh herbs and spices blended with the smell of urine from children relieving themselves in the gutter. But mixed in were also mouth-watering whiffs of street food from stalls with woman vendors called *cholitas* hawking their wares.

Coca leaves, legal to grow and sell in Bolivia, were part of the very fiber of Bolivian society and Nick could see why drug trafficking was so profitable here.

Orozo had proven to be one of the hardest men to kill. Smarter than the average criminal, his routine varied from day to day, which made it extremely difficult for Nick to set up a hit.

Four bodyguards accompanied and surrounded him at all times on his daily trips to his businesses, restaurants, and the family compound. Keeping close, hurrying him in and out of various destinations, making sure his exposure was minimal.

Even the weather failed to cooperate. Consisting of temperate valleys, highlands and humid jungles, Bolivia's rainy season ran from November right through April. Dealing with the almost daily deluge of rain could be daunting at times. Especially, when he needed to focus on his kill.

Unless he caught a break, Nick had come to the conclusion he would have to eliminate more than just Orozo, which lessened his chances of doing the hit and getting away without any hiccups.

For the past two months, he studied every move, every possible scenario in hopes of a clear shot, but not one single opportunity had shown itself to be safe for him to do so. Although patience needed to be the critical factor here, his started running short.

He ducked and slumped against the cement wall. Killing Orozo here in the city proved to be out of the question. Too many things could go wrong besides the fact there were innocent victims and witnesses to contend with. He hated the thought, but he would have to eliminate him closer to his home in the exclusive district of Achumani.

Experience had taught him to look for that one lapse in judgment Orozo, or his bodyguards were bound to make.

Nick left the rooftop and headed to Casa Grande. The hotel, only minutes from San Miguel was pleasant enough. At five stars, it boasted a spa, gym facilities, and a restaurant with a bar on-site. He'd been lucky to at least have a nice retreat all courtesy of the United States Government.

He showered, changed into fresh jeans and a T-shirt before going to the lobby restaurant. Settling into a dark booth in the corner, he ordered a whiskey neat. Frustrated this kill was taking so long, he sipped his drink and reflected on home. His call to Carrie the day after Thanksgiving had been short, but not too short to hear the worry in her voice. It pained him to know the fear he worked so hard to eliminate had taken root inside her once again.

Calling her was risky. He must leave nothing that could be traced to his family should he get caught. A powerful drug lord's reach was unlimited. He understood that all too well from his work with Ricardo Santiago.

Dalton, his kill complete, contacted him two weeks ago. He offered his help, but Nick declined. If this kill went south, he didn't want him in jeopardy too. After much haggling back and forth, Dalton relented but asked him to text a specific code to him when he finished the job so they could meet up and fly home together.

The waitress came, and he ordered a club soda and two *salteñas*. He'd gotten used to the local favorite, a savory pastry filled with beef or chicken in a sweet, slightly spicy sauce. He drained his glass and set it aside. No more alcohol. Tomorrow, he needed to be sharp and on point. He took his time finishing his meal before heading up to his room early. In anticipation of eliminating Orozo the next day, he slept soundly for the rest of the night.

At five o'clock on Saturday morning, dressed in a black tee shirt and black jeans, Nick packed his things. He checked out of the hotel and entered the deserted parking garage. He tossed his duffel inside the trunk of the rental car. Beside it lay a gun case containing an LR1000 long-range rifle.

Nick drove into the surrounding hills of Zona Sur, thankful the skies had not produced another downpour. He reached the outskirts of *Achumani* and pulled off the road straight into the brush. Tree limbs whacked the sides of the vehicle and battered the windshield, but he ignored them driving forward into the woods. Thick branches scraped, catching the undercarriage. With the car well hidden, he cut the ignition and popped the trunk.

Dawn broke as he lifted the duffel out and set it on the ground. Taking one last glance around, he removed the rifle, and started toward the road.

Procuring the weapon in Bolivia hadn't been easy. Although it had taken almost two weeks, his final contact had come through. Having used it numerous times before, he chose this particular rifle because of its low recoil, accuracy, and ability to shoot up to a thousand yards. Equipped with a suppressor to reduce noise and ground signature there was less chance of signaling his position.

Nick crossed the road and advanced along the opposite hillside until he found a spot approximately 600 yards away overlooking Orozo's U-shaped compound. He settled into the thick brush, lifted a pair of binoculars out of the duffel, and scanned the area.

The once elusive rising sun cast shafts of light across the red tile roof of the palatial estate below while creeping oxeye splashed yellow blooms along the tan stucco walls. A center courtyard held a fountain and a small garden. Several cushioned chairs gathered around a glass-topped wrought-iron table.

The surrounding streets were empty except for the occasional car traveling past. He took notice of the bodyguard by the front gate and another positioned on the roof, leaving two unaccounted for. Nick always trusted his gut, and his gut told him today was the day he'd eliminate Orozo.

An hour later, a middle-aged woman carried a tray into the courtyard and placed it on the table. Orozo, dressed in a robe and pajamas followed close behind.

Nick's pulse spiked. Orozo said a few words to the woman. She retreated inside while he sat down. He lifted a newspaper off the tray, setting it aside.

Nick watched him pour a cup of coffee. He took several sips before picking up the paper again. This was the break he'd waited for. The lapse in judgment by Orozo's bodyguards had shown itself. The surrounding walls cut off the view from the street, but from Nick's vantage point he could see the area clearly. The bodyguards should have accounted for the broad exposure from the hillside. One bodyguard atop the roof wasn't enough.

Unzipping the duffel, he put on his shooting gloves and ear protection. He lay in a prone position and rested his cheek against the stock comb. He adjusted the scope and zeroed in on the man on the rooftop. Within seconds, his familiar adrenaline rush swelled inside of him. The uneasiness of not knowing if it would return after all these years evaporated. It surged through him, made everything around him crystal clear. He scoped his target, aimed directly at the man's skull, and shot off one round.

The man staggered backward and collapsed onto the rooftop. At the sound, Orozo raised his head, coffee cup in his hand, glancing upward to where the man had been standing. Within seconds, Nick scoped his target and squeezed the trigger again. Orozo's body jolted back, the cup fell and shattered across the tiled courtyard floor just as the woman returned. She shielded her face and screamed.

Hearing the crash and the scream, the bodyguard at the door, attempted to run inside. His head jerked from Nick's bullet, and he collapsed onto the pavement.

Within seconds, a black sedan sped out the gate and headed toward the road leading to the hillside. Nick tossed his ear protection into the duffel and grabbed his rifle. He tore up the hill to the road, crossed over, and started his descent on the other side. He had reasoned Orozo's remaining bodyguards would jump in their vehicle and drive in the direction where they assumed the bullets had come from. By that time, he planned to be at the base of the opposite hill.

He continued until almost to the bottom. He stopped, threw the rifle into the brush, and removed his gloves. He opened the duffel, tossed them inside, and pulled out a light tan jacket. He slipped it on, zipped it up over his dark shirt, and grabbed the duffel. Within a few minutes, he stepped out onto the road leading to the center of town.

Moving quickly, he blended in with the throngs of pedestrians in the outdoor market. He took out his cell phone and sent a code to Dalton, then made his way to La Paz where he caught the bus for the five-hour trip to Puno, Peru. Once across the border, he traveled to the Inca Manco Cápac International Airport in Juliaca where Dalton waited for him. Entering the private airport lounge, he spotted him and smiled.

"Finally," Dalton said. He gave Nick a bear hug.

They seated themselves in a quiet corner. A waitress approached, and they ordered whiskey neat.

As she walked away, Dalton studied her from behind. "Not bad. She's got something going on."

Nick chuckled. "Why not? There's nothing holding you back."

"Well, maybe, maybe not."

"What do you mean?"

"There's been a certain redhead on my mind for a while now."

Nick raised an eyebrow. "Joann?"

"I've only met her a few times. Once at your wedding, and again after she came to Italy for Izzy's birthday last year, but she's kinda stuck in my head."

"Wow, and you never said a word."

A grin creased Dalton's face. "Nothing to tell yet. Maybe when we get home, I'll look into it."

The waitress returned with their drinks. She eyed the two men. "Anything else, gentleman?"

"Thanks, not at the moment," Dalton said. He raised his glass. "Here's to jobs well done."

They tipped their glasses and swallowed the smooth whiskey.

Dalton cocked his head. "I thought you were never getting out of Bolivia. Started to think maybe you decided to stay."

"Very funny," Nick shot back. He lowered his voice and said, "This job took longer than I expected. I couldn't get to the son of a bitch that easily. I'm more than ready to go home."

Dalton cleared his throat. "About that. We need to talk."

"We have nothing to talk about, Dalton. I'm flying home to my beautiful wife and kids."

"Look, I'm just going to lay it out for you. We got another envelope, and they want this one done right away. My plane is fueled and waiting."

Nick drained the rest of his whiskey. He stared at Dalton. "I guess you're flying alone. Count me out. I need to see my family."

"Listen, partner, I know how you must feel, missing Carrie, and those kids of yours, but we don't have a choice."

"Maybe you don't, but I do." He signaled for another drink. "I'm booking a flight and that's that."

Dalton sighed as the waitress cleared the empty glasses and placed two fresh drinks in front of them. When she was gone, he said, "We do this one together, a quick in and out, then we both fly home."

Nick's stomach knotted. He sipped his whiskey and said, "You're not hearing me. I'm flying home."

"Is this how it's going to be every time we have to do a job?" He pointed his finger at Nick. "You know how this works. We go home when they say we go home. Unfortunately, right now, we can't."

"No, *you* can't." Nick rose and walked to the large floor to ceiling window overlooking the runway, all the muscles in his body wound tight. Being a hostage of the government filled him with fury. He ached to see Carrie, look into those incredible eyes, and hold her in his arms. How long could he go on killing before their marriage suffered, before his children forgot about him?

A plane taxied down the runaway. Gathering speed, its engines roaring, it lifted up off the ground and took flight. *Freedom,* he thought. He lived in the land of the free, and yet his own freedom had been stripped away.

Dalton stood beside him. "Listen, after this job is done, no matter what, we'll head for home."

Nick let out a breath. "All I know is, we have to find a way out. First, I had to eliminate Ricardo to escape his wrath, and now I'm under the government's thumb. I can't continue to exist like this."

"I hear you, partner," Dalton said. "But I'm not sure it's even possible to get out."

Nick turned and caught the big man's eyes. "Oh, it's possible. It may take us a while, but we will find a way out. You can count on it."

# CHAPTER 14

## Carmela

Carmela stared at the plus sign in disbelief. She tossed the strip into the garbage, left the bathroom, and retreated to her study. She paced and clenched her fists.

Back in Napa from South Dakota for the past few weeks, she had refused to entertain the possibility even though symptoms presented themselves. She convinced herself they were all a reaction from meeting Carrie and the children. The tiredness, feeling faint over Thanksgiving, nausea, and her diminished appetite were all indicators pointing to pregnancy.

*"Es stúpido,"* she said under her breath. How could she have been so careless? Only once she hadn't used protection with Bobby. She'd run out of her birth control pills three months before and being busy, had put off renewing her prescription.

She pressed her palm to her stomach. A baby was not in her plans. Not now, and not in the foreseeable future. Especially, Bobby's child.

Only one solution came to mind. She'd get rid of it. There was no reason to tell Bobby. It would be over and done, and he would never know.

Carmela sat at her desk. She picked up her cell, scanned her contacts, and punched in a number.

A woman answered on the third ring. "Doctor Martin's office. How can I help you?"

"This is Carmela Santiago."

"Ms. Santiago. This is Bridgette. How are you?"

"May I have an appointment as soon as possible?"

"What's the nature of your complaint?"

She hesitated, finding it hard to say the words out loud. "I'm pregnant."

"Congratulations. How far along are you?"

"I'm not sure. But I would like to come in and talk to the doctor about my options."

"Oh, I see. Hold on, let me check her schedule."

Annoying elevator music came through the phone. Impatient, she drummed her red polished fingernails on the desk. She needed to take care of this situation right away. At dinner, a week ago, Bobby had questioned her lack of appetite. Just looking at her food had produced a wave of nausea. She decided to purchase a pregnancy test and had put off using it until today.

"Ms. Santiago?"

"Yes, I'm here."

"The doctor can see you tomorrow at two o'clock."

"That will work. Thank you, Bridgette."

Satisfied, she set her cell phone down. Tomorrow she would see the doctor, make arrangements to terminate the pregnancy and leave all of this behind her.

Managing to slip away without Diego, Carmela arrived at the doctor's office promptly at two o'clock. Although it was dangerous, she didn't want him in her personal business.

She flipped through a magazine for the next twenty minutes. Why did doctors always give you an appointment time but make you wait? She fidgeted, tapping her foot against the grey commercial carpet.

Fifteen minutes more went by before the nurse led her into an exam room. She took Carmela's vital signs and said the doctor would be with her shortly.

Carmela sat close to the edge of the exam table and studied the colorful pictures on the walls. One showed a women's anatomy. Another, a uterus with a baby nesting inside. She averted her eyes and stared at the floor.

A light tap on the door made her look up. Dr. Martin came in. Tall, with short cropped blond hair and a pleasant face, she greeted Carmela warmly.

"Carmela, it's good to see you. What brings you in?"

Carmela frowned and said. "Well, it seems I'm pregnant."

Dr. Martin studied her a moment. "Home pregnancy test?" she asked.

"Yes. I've been having certain symptoms, so I thought I should do one. It came out positive."

"Any idea how far along you are?"

She shrugged. "Eight weeks, maybe a little more."

"Let me do a sonogram to make sure the baby's in utero, and things are looking as they should."

"Is that really necessary?"

"Why yes. I need to see how you're progressing. We don't want any surprises if you're going to carry this baby to term safely."

Carmela shifted her body against the annoying paper sheet beneath her. "Dr. Martin, I am not sure about carrying to term."

Dr. Martin frowned. "I see, but I would have to refer you to someone else if that's your decision. I know a first pregnancy can be a bit scary, but you need to be positive termination is the right choice."

"Yes, for me, it is." Bobby's face flashed before her. If he knew what she planned, aborting their child might make him turn away for good. He mentioned a future between them with children someday. At the time, she had laughed it off, knowing she envisioned a future of heartache for him and the rest of his family.

"I would still like to do the sonogram to confirm things are in order."

"If you insist. You're the doctor."

A few minutes later, prepped and ready, Dr. Martin flipped the machine on and placed the transducer probe atop Carmela's abdomen.

Carmela turned away and stared at the ceiling. She didn't want to see the baby. The only child she had ever envisioned growing inside her body was Nick's.

"Ah, there we are," Dr. Martin said. "Everything looks fine. Let me adjust the volume."

Carmela raised her head "No, I don't..."

It was too late. The sound came through loud and clear. The baby's heartbeat filled the room. Fast, strong, galloping like a thoroughbred.

"It seems you're closer to ten weeks. If you change your mind, you're looking at a June baby." She followed Carmela's eyes, now fixed on the screen. She pointed and traced her finger along an outline. "See, he or she is resting comfortably."

Carmela's head swam. She stared at the image.

"Okay, all done," Dr. Martin said. "Would you like a picture?"

She shook her head yes without even realizing it.

The doctor smiled and wiped the gel off Carmela's abdomen. "You can get dressed now. I'll have Bridgette give you information for a colleague of mine who works at a well-known clinic. Although the circumstances aren't ideal, it was good to see you, Carmela." She set the picture on the counter and left.

Carmela dressed and stuck the picture in her purse. At the front desk, Bridgette handed her a card with the name of a doctor.

On the drive home, she played out several scenarios in her mind. Each one served to increase her anxiety. She could tell Bobby, but if he wanted the baby, then what? Having an abortion had been her initial reaction. Get rid of it and move ahead with her plans.

Carmela parked by the side of the road. She removed the sonogram picture from her purse. This wasn't only a part of Bobby; but a part of her too. What if there were no other pregnancies in her future? This child could be her first and only one.

She pictured Nick for a brief moment and almost smiled. Would he be willing to play the doting grandpa? The answer came as a resounding no, but he'd be forced to make a choice. Eliminate her and lose his stepson forever or allow her and the child to live, a constant reminder of the threat she still posed to all of them. Never knowing whether or not she intended to strike.

Having this baby could advance her scheme even further. If Bobby wanted this child, she'd become untouchable. Nick's walking away from the winery instead of shooting her served to convince her that he wouldn't dare kill a pregnant woman.

Carmela drove home with renewed determination, glad she'd be seeing Bobby later for dinner. Telling him about the pregnancy would set the stage for all her other plans.

They sat in a cozy curved booth in the far corner of *Buena Comida*, Carmela's Napa Valley restaurant. Bobby placed his hand on top of hers.

"As always, the food was excellent, although you haven't eaten much," he said.

"It should be," Carmela replied. "What we had wasn't even on the menu. My chef made it especially for us."

His eyes locked onto hers. "I've missed you."

"It's only been a week. I'm making sure you don't get tired of me."

Bobby squeezed her hand. "Tired of you? I can't imagine ever being tired of you. I think about you all the time."

She slid her hand out from under his. "I have something to tell you, and I'm not sure how you are going to take it."

A look of alarm crossed his face. "What do you mean? Are you sick? Are you breaking up with me?"

She shook her head. "Stop. No, silly. None of those things."

"What is it?" He moved closer and slid his arm around her. "You know you can tell me anything."

She gazed into his pale blue eyes and ran her hand along his cheek. "*Mi tesoro,*" she whispered, "I'm pregnant."

Bobby never lost a beat. He kissed her lips, and said. "I'm happy, if you are."

Carmela smiled. "Yes." Her desire for him rose up inside, and she longed to be lying naked with him in her bed. "Come, let's go."

They made love two times during the night before dawn broke, and the remainder of the darkness slipped away. While Bobby slept beside her, she studied his face. How naive he was with regard to bringing their child into the world. His eyes had glazed over at the sight of the sonogram picture. But she couldn't blame him. He wasn't aware of the history between her and Nick.

She thought of Carrie and her invitation for her and Bobby to return to South Dakota for the Christmas holiday. She'd decline and wait a little longer before returning. Maybe, Nick would be home by then. But the worried look on Carrie's face spoke volumes. Nick was up to his old killing tricks again.

The next time she set foot in that house, she wanted to be showing. No need to drug the wine again, her pregnancy would produce enough turmoil.

Carmela settled against the down-filled pillows and grinned. Yes, she certainly anticipated her future visit with the D'Angelos.

# CHAPTER 15
## Bobby

Bobby stared out the window at the night sky. The evening flight to New York felt like the longest of his life. Unable to concentrate on preparations for an upcoming art show, he closed his laptop.

He departed Napa without Carmela having any idea how much her pregnancy news disrupted his world. Suspicious since the incident at Thanksgiving and others, the possibility crossed his mind more than once.

In the past, when he joked about having a family one day, it had failed to amuse her. Could he trust her? She wasn't the type of woman to change her mind so easily. The sonogram picture made everything all too real. The prospect of becoming a father at this juncture of his life was daunting, but seeing the image of the baby growing inside her stirred something within him.

He pictured his mother and how she would react to the pregnancy news. She didn't care for Carmela, and he almost couldn't blame her after her bad first impression in South Dakota. Although what she did was wrong, her intentions were good. Once his mother got to know her better, her opinion would change.

At least he didn't need to worry about telling anyone. Carmela made him promise to keep the news to himself for now.

After landing at JFK, Bobby hailed a cab for the ride into the city. An hour later, he unpacked his bag, showered, and settled into bed.

Lying awake in the dark, it occurred to him that keeping Carmela's pregnancy a secret was going to be hard. He visualized Nick's reaction and chuckled to himself. He'd probably caution him on the responsibilities of fatherhood, but if he could be half the father Nick was, then his child would never doubt his love. No son or daughter of his would grow up in fear. No hours spent in locked closets, no beatings, and no stomach-churning panic.

It had taken Bobby time to deal with his childhood memories and to forgive his mother for what happened to him. He did blame his stepmother, Claudia, to some degree, but he also excused her failure to protect him, realizing she was as much of a victim.

His thoughts were interrupted by the buzz of his cell phone. He glanced at the clock. One o'clock in the morning in New York meant ten o'clock at night in Napa.

A grin spread across his face. "Hello," he said. "I'm missing you already."

Carmela's voice dripped honey. "Maybe not for long."

Bobby pushed the covers away and sat up. "What do you mean?"

"I was thinking about the Christmas holiday. How would you like it if we spent it together?"

"But you said you didn't want to come to South Dakota."

"I don't." Her tone had that finality he recognized so well.

"So, what are you thinking?"

"I think we should spend it in New York. I could come to your place, and we could do all those silly holiday tourist things. Go to Radio City Music Hall and Rockefeller Center to see the tree. Oh, and stroll along Fifth Avenue and stare into the windows, before ending the day at South Street Seaport for dinner."

Stunned, Bobby asked, "Why the sudden desire to spend Christmas here?" She hated coming to New York and usually insisted he fly to Napa or Miami.

"Don't you think, under the circumstances, we should spend the holidays together?" she said. "I mean, I know I've been difficult in the past concerning New York, but now I—"

"No need to explain," Bobby said quickly. "I'm happy you want to come here."

"Am I right in hearing a little reluctance in your voice, *mi tesoro?*"

He hesitated before answering. "It's just that my mother expects me to spend the holiday in South Dakota. That's one of the reasons she invited you for Christmas."

Her high-pitched laughter came through the phone. "Don't be silly. I refuse to go to there for the holiday. Your mother can't stand me. She only invited me out of courtesy."

"Carmela, that's not true. Yes, she was upset after you took Izzy without asking, but I know her better than you do and she is not the type to hold a grudge."

"If you say so."

Bobby got up and paced, cell phone held tight to his ear. Why did she have to use that condescending tone he hated so much? He took a breath before answering.

"Listen, I would love nothing more than for us to be together in New York for Christmas, but I also hate to disappoint my mother, especially since Nick is still away."

"But you wouldn't be spending it just with me. It would be the three of us."

Bobby's stomach churned. Guilt washed over him. He was going to be a father, and she presented him with his first test. Of course, he should be with the mother of his child for Christmas, but he dreaded calling home.

"Yes," he said softly. "You're right. The three of us should be together for Christmas."

"I knew you'd see things more clearly. It's why I care so much for you. I miss you terribly, and I can't wait to be with you."

"Me, too. Let me know when you'll be arriving."

"Sleep well. I will call you soon."

Bobby set his cell aside and lay back against the pillows. He folded his hands behind his head and stared at the shadows splayed across the far wall.

It creeped over him again. That strange feeling Carmela evoked that he found hard to shake at times. Never able to put his finger on what it was, he preferred to push it away, ignore it, but somehow, it always returned. Almost as if he perched upon the tip of some unknown precipice, unable to see what lay below. Was this blindness causing him to fail to recognize some hidden agenda?

Or maybe he was reading too much into things. They were about to become parents, he needed to trust her and be ready to welcome their child into his life. Try to build a future together as a family.

Bobby closed his eyes and drifted off into a restless sleep only to wake two hours later, drenched in sweat, from a nightmare.

His mind cleared, and he sat up against the pillows. He replayed the dream. Fog encompassed him while he tore through thick woods calling Carmela's name. The sound of a baby crying filled the dense air. He ran, unable to find the child or Carmela.

He came to a clearing, and the fog lifted. In the distance, Carmela stood at the edge of a cliff. She held a child in her arms. He moved closer. She faced him and laughed. Nothing but empty space behind her, she stepped back and fell off the edge as Bobby screamed.

# CHAPTER 16

## Carrie

Carrie admired the seven-foot Fraser Fir adjacent to the fireplace. The tree and a beautiful wreath had arrived several days ago from Dalton. Two of his men helped set things up.

Always so thoughtful, he had supplied boxes of lights, ornaments, and a gold star for the top. His card read, 'Just a little something to help you get through the holiday.'

No word concerning Nick or if either of them might be coming home soon. She hadn't spoken to Nick since the day after Thanksgiving, and although she understood his need to be careful, it hurt not to hear his voice and know he was safe.

Dalton's men stationed the tree upon a custom-made stand. Before departing, they hung the decorated wreath on the front door and strung lights across the porch railing.

The rich fir scent permeated the air as Carrie spent the afternoon decorating with Izzy and Michael. Chino lay close by while Marco threaded colorful lights through the branches. He helped her and the children hang ornaments, something she ached to do with Nick. For the children's sake, she tried hard not to let her disappointment show. But Izzy's constant questions regarding her father did even more to cement the loneliness surrounding her. With Christmas only a week away, the void he left grew wider with each passing day. Missing him and worrying zapped Carrie's excitement. The few bright spots she anticipated were Bobby's coming home and Joann and her children visiting. Of course, Aunt May would be flying in, too.

Carrie prepared to gather up the empty ornament boxes.

"Mommy, look," Izzy said. She held up a small red velvet box.

"Give that to me, Izzy." Carrie's hands shook as she lifted the lid. Her heartbeat quickened at the sight of the three stone drop Diamond Pendant. Tears clouded her vision. It meant he was alive.

Izzy tugged at Carrie's arm. "What's wrong? Let me see."

Carrie wiped her cheeks. "Nothing's wrong." She quickly closed the box. "I'll show you later. Now let's get things cleaned up."

They gathered the boxes, stacking them neatly by the staircase.

"Marco, please carry these upstairs to the hall closet while I put Michael down for his nap."

He grabbed the boxes and headed for the stairs. More sullen than ever before these past few weeks, he barely spoke to her unless it pertained to the children. Deciding to talk to him about it, she carried Michael upstairs while Izzy remained mesmerized by the tree.

With all the excitement, it didn't take long for Michael to fall asleep. She returned to the great room. Izzy sat at the foot of the tree. She pointed to the top.

"Mommy, look how pretty the star is."

Carrie went and sat beside her. "Yes, and we must remember to thank Uncle Dalton the next time we see him."

"When?" Izzy asked. "Can we go to his house and tell him?"

"No, I'm afraid not. Uncle Dalton is away. But I'm sure he'll be home soon."

Izzy studied Carrie's face. Her green eyes grew dark. "That's what you said about Daddy, and he's been gone a long, long time."

Carrie draped her arm around Izzy, pulling her closer. "I know, sweetheart. But grown-ups have to take care of important things. And sometimes, they don't have a choice. Trust me, your father would much rather be here with us. Unfortunately, he can't be home right now." With Izzy off from school the next two weeks, Carrie was sure the subject would come up again.

Izzy fell silent.

"How would you like some hot chocolate?"

"Can I drink it by the tree?" Izzy asked.

"Yes. Give me a few minutes. I need to talk to Marco."

Izzy smiled and nodded her head. Carrie's answer seemed to lighten her mood.

Carrie found Marco upstairs in the hallway, putting the last of the ornament boxes in the closet.

"Can we talk for a minute?"

He closed the door and took a step toward her. "Sure."

"First, I want to thank you for helping with the tree."

His eyes settled on hers. "I would do anything for you."

Her stomach gave a curious twist at his words, and she looked away.

"Is something wrong?" he asked.

She forced herself to look at him. "Actually, I was going to ask you the same thing."

"What is it?"

"You seem unhappy lately."

Marco frowned and shrugged his shoulders. "Sometimes, I miss Italy. But I no longer have family there so it would be pointless to return."

It struck her how hard it must be for him living in a new country. He cared deeply for the children, and it was apparent how much they both loved him and she had Nick, but Marco had no one of his own.

"You know, you're part of this family, and we would never want you to be unhappy. After Bobby gets here, I think you should take a few days off. Go and see some of the rest of the country. Everyone needs some time for themselves."

"Thank you for thinking of me. Maybe you are right." He squeezed her shoulder. A wide grin spread across his face. His teeth flashed against his dark skin.

Carrie's pulse spiked. She stepped away and gave him a weak smile. "Okay, we'll see after Bobby comes." She left him in the hallway and went downstairs to fix Izzy hot chocolate. Later, sitting by the tree, she found it difficult to shake off her anxiety concerning Marco.

Early the next morning, after starting a fire in the great room, Carrie made a cup of coffee and sat at the kitchen island. She relished the quiet before the children woke. A few moments later, her cell phone buzzed. Her face lit up.

"Bobby, it's so good to hear from you," she said. "When are you flying in?" Unexpected silence greeted her. "Bobby, are you there?"

"Yeah, I'm here."

His voice held a distant tone. It was so unlike him. "Is something wrong?"

"Well, I know you were looking forward to my coming for Christmas, but I've made other plans."

She paused and took a breath. Trying to keep her feelings in check, she asked, "Does it have to do with work?"

"No, nothing like that. Actually, Carmela and I are going to spend the holiday here in New York."

"But why? I invited both of you for Christmas. I don't understand."

"Please, don't be upset. I'll come afterward and stay for a week. Besides, if Joann is coming along with Veronica, Justin, and Aunt May, you'll have plenty of company.

"Bobby, it's not the same thing as having you home for the holiday, and with Nick gone, I really wanted you to be here. Not to mention you haven't seen Joann and her family for the last two years.

"I know, I know but—"

"What made you change your plans? Or should I say who?"

"Now, that's not fair. Carmela and I decided this together."

"Yeah, I bet you did." The fingers on Carrie's free hand curled. She tried to rein in the ire building inside of her.

"Maybe Carmela was right," Bobby said. "You didn't want her to come. You only invited her because of me," he lashed out.

"Is that what she said?"

"More or less."

Carrie chose her words carefully. "Listen, I always said I wouldn't lie to you. Yes, I wasn't thrilled with her last visit, but for your sake, I'm willing to give her another chance."

"Pretty big of you, Mom."

Carrie's spine tensed. He had never been disrespectful before. That woman was determined to get between them. But if she pushed Bobby further, he might become even more distant.

She softened her tone. "I can't force you to come, and I don't want to argue. So, enjoy your time in New York with Carmela and then come to South Dakota after."

"I don't want to argue either. But I will tell you there is a good reason why I need to spend Christmas with her. Please hug Izzy for me and tell her I'll see her soon. I love you."

Before she could answer, he ended the call. "I love you, too," she said into the dead air. Carrie picked up her cup and sat by the fire in the great room. Chino settled in at her feet. Hot tears welled up in her eyes, and she stroked his fur to comfort herself.

What was happening to their lives? First, Nick gone for so many months, forced into a life he tried to forget. Bobby so tangled up with a woman who may or may not have his best interests at heart. A woman who Carrie perceived as dangerous. Carmela could easily tear Bobby away from the family. She wondered what he meant by having a good reason for spending Christmas in New York.

She stared at the twinkling lights wrapped around the branches of the tree, then up at the gold star. The memory of sitting on Aunt May's front porch all those years ago reared up. How she had watched Bobby walk up the street not knowing he was her son. And all the time it took to build his trust once she found out.

No matter what lie ahead, she couldn't let Carmela break the bond between them.


Christmas day filled the house with shrieks of delight from Izzy and Michael while they sat by the tree and opened presents. Looking at the piles of wrapping paper strewn across the floor made Carrie realize she had gone a bit overboard with gifts.

But, she cherished the moments spent watching her children have a typical holiday, something she never experienced. Christmas meant little in Breezy Meadows and less to her mother. No decorated tree anywhere in the small trailer. With any luck, she received one gift, handed to her half-wrapped by her drunken, drug-addicted mother. Carrie wanted to make sure her children never suffered. She wanted them to always feel loved and secure.

The rest of Christmas week consisted of snowmobile and sleigh rides along with several silly snowball fights, tons of laughter around the dining room table and quiet moments reminiscing by the fire. Carrie marveled at how Veronica, at twenty-one, had become a stunning woman. Her long auburn hair fell past her shoulders and her green eyes were set into a heart-shaped face and she had a smile that lit up the room. And Justin, at nineteen had grown into a tall, good-looking young man with dark brown eyes and hair the same red color as Joann's. Both were disappointed Bobby hadn't come home for the holiday.

Aunt May stayed for five days before returning to Laurel. Her questions concerning Nick, and why he wasn't there unnerved Carrie, but she stuck to her story about his being away on business working for the government in Washington. A half-truth. May's sideways glance let Carrie know she wasn't buying it.

At the end of the week, Veronica and Justin left with May. Joann wasn't due to leave until late afternoon. Carrie, happy to have some time with her alone, studied her friend's new look. Gone were the red curls once piled high atop her head. Instead, she sported a shorter cut. The fringe of bangs replaced by gentle waves framing her face. She believed it suited her.

Memories of working at the Palisades Diner buzzed through her mind. It was hard to believe so much time had gone by since she lived and worked in Laurel.

While Izzy and Michael played with their new toys, she and Joann settled themselves at the kitchen island for coffee.

Carrie took out cups, spoons, and napkins while Joann grabbed the sugar and milk.

"So, how do you like living in South Dakota?" Joann asked.

Carrie lifted her cup and sipped before answering. "I like it well enough, and Izzy is doing great at her new school."

A flicker of irritation shone in Joann's eyes. "Okay hon, I've played this everything's fine game with you for most of this week. Tell me what's really going on."

Carrie set her cup down. "I should've known better. You could always tell when something's wrong."

A frown creased Joann's forehead. "You can trust me, Carrie. Now, spill it."

She debated, not sure how much she wanted to tell her. "Nick and Dalton have been gone for months."

Joann's eyebrow shot up. "Months? But to where?"

"I can't tell you, because I don't know. All I know is they're working for the government. I'm not at liberty to say more. As a matter of fact, it would put them at risk."

Joann's brow arched. "When was the last time you heard from Nick?"

"The day after Thanksgiving." Carrie fingered her diamond necklace, "I received this a week before Christmas. I feel in my heart he's safe and will come home soon."

Joann smiled. "Sure is beautiful. That man of yours has good taste."

"Thanks, I think so, too."

Joann studied her cup for a moment. "You mentioned Dalton."

"Yes, the two of them left together."

"That big lug kept calling me Red the last time I saw him."

Carrie laughed. "I think he's attracted to you."

"I don't know about that." She chuckled. "He is one handsome man. But enough about that. How is Izzy with missing her daddy?"

It's been hard because she feels he abandoned her."

Joann covered Carrie's hand with her own. "How can I help? What can I do to make you feel better?"

She met Joann's eyes. "I appreciate that. You've always been such a good friend to me, but there isn't anything you can do."

Joann slid her hand away. She lifted her cup and swallowed some coffee. "You mentioned Bobby's coming in a few days…that he couldn't make it for Christmas because of work. That doesn't sound like him. What's the real reason he didn't come?"

Bitterness stirred in the pit of Carrie's stomach. "There's something I haven't told you. The woman he's currently seeing came with him on his last visit."

She relayed the events surrounding Carmela's stay in South Dakota. All the while, her fingers remained clasped tight, her body tense at the memories.

Joann's mouth gaped. A line etched between her brows. "You think she drugged the wine?"

"It sounds crazy. But I can't find any other explanation for what happened. Then when she took Izzy out of the house without asking anyone I—"

"Carrie, hon, listen to me. You're under a lot of stress with Nick gone. Maybe you read too much into it."

"I understand it's hard for you to believe what I'm telling you, Joann. But something's not right. Bobby's changing because of her."

"Changing how?"

"He's distant, argumentative, and somewhat disrespectful at times. I know my son, and that's not like him at all."

"Well, I've never seen them together so maybe I'm overstepping when I say, for better or worse, Bobby's in love with her," Joann said. "His protecting her after the incident with Izzy and not spending Christmas with you says a lot."

Joann's assessment alarmed her. "If that's the case, what do I do?"

"Hon, you'll never be able to get in between a man and his woman. After Nick, you more than anyone should know that, so here's my advice. Take a step back and consider his feelings whether you agree with them or not. You'll only push him further away if you can't accept this relationship."

Carrie sighed. If Bobby loved Carmela, there was little she could do to change his mind. Joann was right, but her heart told her otherwise.

Later that evening, with Joann gone, and after putting the children to bed, Carrie grabbed her coat from the mudroom and stepped outside with Chino. Delighted to be running free in the moonlight, he pranced around the yard as she sat on the steps watching.

Overhead, the night sky filled with stars and a full golden yellow moon glowed. She could hardly stand this separation from Nick. Izzy and Michael were growing so fast. How much of their childhood would he miss?

That last night when they made love, she had wanted to hold on to him and beg him not to leave. But the anguish on his face spoke volumes, and she didn't want to make it worse.

She stared up at the stars and the moon. Nick was out there somewhere under the same sky. Was he thinking of her at this very moment?

A burst of wind whipped across the front porch. Chino came and sat beside her. She hugged his neck and buried her face in his warm fur. He let out a soft whimper.

Carrie raised her head and met his dark eyes. "I know Chino, I miss him, too." She looked up at the sky. Under her breath, she whispered, "Please bring Nick and Dalton home to us soon."

# CHAPTER 17
## Carmela

The sun descended, sweeping the sky with deep pinks and oranges before vanishing below the horizon. A sure sign, come morning, the Miami heat would return with a vengeance.

Carmela switched on the desk lamp and continued to study the computer screen. A yawn escaped her lips. Annoyed, she shook her head, forcing herself to stay awake. She found it hard to deal with the fatigue claiming her body since becoming pregnant, but thankful her bouts of nausea were gone.

Spending Christmas week in New York with Bobby caused her to fall behind with business, but she had no regrets. Carmela humored him by agreeing to observe all those silly holiday traditions. They went to Radio City Music Hall for the Christmas show and to see the tree at Rockefeller Center.

Bobby protested when she insisted on donning skates and gliding across the ice with him. She delighted in his worried expression. Afraid she might fall, he held onto her as they circled the rink. He panicked when she managed to free herself and skate away, the cold wind numbing her body and banishing malicious thoughts of revenge for a while.

They dined in exclusive restaurants and took in a Broadway show. She dragged him in and out of the shops along

Fifth Avenue where she purchased gifts for Bobby to take to South Dakota.

But she relished the nights the most when they returned to his apartment to have sex. The heat between them intensified by their pure lust for each other.

The landline rang, breaking into her musings. It was Luis calling from the front gate.

*"Señorita, Señor* Medina is here."

"Let him through, Luis."

*"Sí,* right away."

A few minutes later, there was a light tap on her study door. Armando appeared and performed a slight bow. *"Señor* Medina." He backed out of the room as Miguel stepped past him. The door slid closed.

Carmela rose. "Miguel, it's good to see you."

Miguel's arm muscles bulged underneath his grey suit jacket. He bent his six-foot-two frame and kissed her cheek. "The pleasure is mine, Carmela."

The dark stubble on his face brushed her delicate skin. She inhaled a hint of his cologne.

"Make yourself comfortable." She strolled to the bar and picked up a bottle of AsomBroso Tequila. "Drink?"

Miguel's hooded eyes relaxed. He swiped a hand through his thick black hair and unbuttoned his suit jacket. Taking the glass from her, he settled onto the soft leather sofa. *"Gracias."*

*"Salud,"* Carmela said, wishing she could have a drink of her own.

"None for you?" A smile flickered across the edge of his mouth.

"I had one just before you came," she lied.

He raised his glass and swallowed the amber liquid.

Carmela studied his handsome face, the full lips, and the cleft in his chin. She envisioned what it would be like to bed him. Only in this instance, it was better not to mix business with pleasure. Miguel was her ghost, her *sicario.*

As good a ghost as Nick, men like him were hard to find. But unlike Nick, she had never witnessed a soft spot in Miguel Medina. Cold, calculating, and determined, he followed orders without question. She depended on him and his loyalty to her just as her father had done with Nick.

Today, she had a different task for him, one she hoped wouldn't include killing this time. She sat behind her desk.

"So, I have a job for you. But this is not an ordinary request, and if you'd rather not take it, I will understand."

Miguel raised an eyebrow. He set his glass on the end table. "What is it, Carmela?"

"I need you to travel to a small town in Pennsylvania called Laurel. An old woman by the name of May Overton lives there. My sources tell me she is related to Nick's wife, Carrie."

Frowning, he asked, "Is this still about the business with Nick? When you did not give me orders to kill him after what he did to your father, I thought, perhaps you decided to let things lie. But of course, you know, I don't agree. People need to pay for their transgressions."

Carmela drew in a sharp breath. "Understand something, Miguel. It was never my intention to let things lie. I have thought of almost nothing else these past years. But I needed Nick and his family to believe I was finished. The time is drawing closer for them to feel my pain."

Miguel crossed his arms. "What do you want me to do in Pennsylvania?"

Opening a drawer, she drew out a manila envelope. "Everything I have found out so far is inside, but the man I hired has reached a dead end." She removed a picture and handed it to him.

"His name was Travis Montgomery."

"Was?"

"Yes, Nick eliminated him. I need to know what his relationship was to Carrie."

"And you think this May person will have the answer?"

"I believe so. Carrie resided with her after the robbery. In any case, who he was might prove useful to me."

"And if she won't talk?"

"Be discreet. Remember, at this point, I don't want anything getting back to Nick or Carrie. Try to fool the old lady. Make up a story. Pretend you're a friend looking for him. I'm not sure if she is aware of his death. I know it is unusual for a ghost to carry out an order this way." She gave him the manila folder. "You prefer to operate from a distance. Hopefully, killing this woman won't be necessary, but as always, handle it as you see fit."

She opened the drawer again and handed him a thick envelope. "Here is one hundred thousand and the address. If things prove tricky, I'll pay you an additional amount."

Miguel got up from the sofa. "Don't worry; I will get you the information you want."

She came around the desk and faced him. "I have faith in you. You have never failed me."

Standing so close, she could feel his raw power. She swore she glimpsed shadows moving deep within his coal-black eyes. Her flesh tingled. She sensed he knew what she was feeling, and she moved closer. Her body now inches from his; she lifted her head and parted her lips.

Miguel's eyes locked on hers. He kissed her cheek, and said, "We will speak again soon."

Her face grew hot. She watched him walk to the door. How foolish she was to think he'd respond to her advances. Miguel was a different type of man. But unlike Nick, he kept his emotions in check. It was a matter of survival. A ghost could not afford to let his guard slip.

"Rest easy, *Señorita,* you can always depend on me," Miguel said as he disappeared through the door.

She shut off the computer and went upstairs intending to nap before a late supper. But the fatigue she experienced earlier had vanished.

She eased onto the edge of the bed. A sudden movement inside her belly caused her to jump. Placing her hand on her stomach, she waited. Moments later, it happened again. A light flutter at first, then more pronounced. Bobby's child made its presence known.

It wouldn't be long before she'd begin to show. Soon a visit to South Dakota would be a priority once Nick was home. She'd use this baby against them, and any other means possible to further her own agenda.

Suddenly ravenous, she went downstairs. Armando greeted her in the kitchen. He stirred the *Sudado de Pollo,* the delicious chicken stew was one of her favorites.

Carmela seated herself at the table as he ladled the contents over a bed of white rice. The aroma of chicken, garlic, bell peppers, and cilantro filled the room. She lifted her fork and dug into the meal with a new sense of purpose.

In her heart, she was sure Miguel would bring her the information she waited for. Who was Travis Montgomery, and what did he mean to Carrie D'Angelo?

# CHAPTER 18
## Bobby

Landing in South Dakota, Bobby, stashed his two suitcases inside the trunk of the rental car and headed for the Black Hills. One bag contained his clothes, the other loaded with Christmas gifts.

At this point in time, he couldn't imagine revealing Carmela's pregnancy to his mother. Whether he liked it or not, that day would come soon enough. Nervous and excited regarding his impending fatherhood, he tried to picture his life with a son or a daughter. Children of his own were something he always imagined in the way distant future, but his feelings for Carmela had grown strong, and it made him glad she'd be the mother of his child.

Though he'd never spoken the words, I love you out loud, he knew with certainty he loved her. But his uneasiness regarding their relationship still surfaced now and again. He couldn't put his finger on why.

Other than her sudden moodiness over silly things, outbursts he attributed to pregnancy hormones, she'd been nothing but loving and kind to him.

His last conversation with his mother lay heavy on his mind when one hour later, he drove up to the gates and punched in the code. He proceeded up the long driveway past the tall, ponderosa pines, and skinny white birch trees. Patches of snow dotted the landscape.

He slid the window down and took a deep breath. Cool, crisp air filled his lungs. Determined to have a good time during this trip, he exhaled and forced his apprehension away. He'd redirect his focus on seeing Izzy and Michael again.

Bobby swung around the circular drive and stopped. Within seconds, the front door flew open. Izzy bolted down the steps, her long dark hair billowing out. Her green eyes grew wider with each step. Chino galloped close behind, his tail wagging. He let out a series of loud barks.

"Bobby, Bobby, you're here!"

He climbed out of the car and lifted her up. "I've missed you, little Bug."

Her skinny arms hugged his neck. "Me, too."

Setting her on the ground, he knelt and patted Chino's enormous head. "Missed you, too, buddy."

Bobby rose and opened the trunk to retrieve his bags. He turned and saw Carrie standing in the open doorway. Her eyes settled on his face. A slow grin spread across her mouth.

"Welcome home, stranger." She stepped aside as he lugged the suitcases into the house setting them in the hallway.

She held out her arms. "Can I at least get a hug?"

"Of course." Bobby kissed her cheek and gave her a gentle squeeze. "Where's Michael?"

"Napping," Carrie said. "He'll be up soon enough."

He turned to Izzy who danced from foot to foot. "I have some very special gifts for you."

Izzy's face lit up. She squealed, "Where, where, let me see!"

He hung his coat in the mudroom and grabbed one of the suitcases. "Let's go into the great room."

The crackle of the wood burning in the fireplace greeted him. But his mouth fell open at the sight of the magnificent tree. Among the branches, ornaments glowed against the colorful lights. The pleasing scent dominated the air. "Wow, that's a beauty."

"Yes, Dalton sent it."

"Dalton?"

"I know what you're thinking." She fingered her necklace. "Except for this, I haven't heard anything."

Bobby gave her a reassuring look. "Shows he's still okay."

They spent the next half-hour opening the presents he brought for Izzy. She tore at the wrapping paper, oohing, and aahing over a brand-new winter coat, clothes for her doll, and a delicate blue and white tea set.

He handed her the last one. "This is from, Carmela."

Izzy opened the small box and grinned. "Look, Mommy, a cell phone just like yours."

Bobby loved seeing her so happy. "Now, I programmed mine and Carmela's number in so you can call us whenever you want."

Carrie frowned. A flicker of irritation shone in her eyes. "Bobby, I don't think this is a good idea. She's much too young for a cell phone."

Izzy stomped her foot. "No, I'm not."

"Stop pouting or you'll be spending time in your room," Carrie said. "We will talk about this later, young lady. Why don't you try out some of those pretty new dresses on your doll?"

With a forlorn look at Bobby, Izzy grabbed the doll clothes and headed upstairs.

Bobby let out a sigh. "Mom, why did you have to make such a big deal? It's just a lousy cell phone." His body tensed. He could feel an argument coming.

"I'm not making a big deal. I think she's too young. She's barely six for God's sake."

"You can set limits for her. It's a good learning tool. There are educational games she can play."

"You're not going to change my mind, Bobby. Besides, if Nick were here, I know he'd agree with me. What was Carmela thinking giving her a cell phone?"

"Oh boy, here we go," Bobby snapped. "She tried to do something nice, and you jump all over it."

"I'm not jumping on anything. One day, when you have children of your own, you'll understand where I'm coming from. Parents have to make the rules, set limits. We both know firsthand how tough life can be. Izzy can't have everything she wants. She needs to learn the real world isn't like that."

Feeling guilty, he averted his eyes and stared at the tree. His mother had no idea of his impending parenthood. He knew next to nothing about raising a child. The cell phone might not have been the best gift, but Carmela's intentions were good.

"Look, if you don't want Izzy to have the phone, I'll respect your decision," he said. "Put it away for now. Give it to her when you feel the time is right."

"Thank you. I appreciate your saying that."

He grabbed a small box from the suitcase. "Here, this is for you from me and Carmela."

Carrie's face flushed pink. "You didn't have to buy—"

"I know we didn't. We wanted to, but you might not like it because Carmela picked it out."

Carrie rested her hand on his arm. "I'm sorry. I don't mean to ruin things." She took the box and settled onto the sofa.

Bobby softened his tone. "It's okay. Go ahead. Open it."

She lifted the lid and stared at the contents. A pair of sapphire and diamond earrings shone against the black velvet.

"We figured they'd look pretty on you. Especially, with your eye color."

"Thank you, they're beautiful."

Still frustrated, Bobby swiped a hand through his hair and sat beside her. "I know you don't care for Carmela, but all I am asking is for you to give her another chance. She's very important to me. As for the phone, it would be nice if Izzy could call us once in a while."

"I'll think about it," Carrie said. She rested her chin in her hands. "Veronica and Justin missed seeing you. Ronnie flew in from Stanford. College life agrees with her. She was lucky to get a full scholarship, and Justin is doing his freshman year at Penn State."

"I'm sure I'll catch up with them sooner or later."

"By the way, what did you mean when you said you had a good reason for spending the holiday in New York?"

It was on the tip of his tongue to tell her about the baby, but he and Carmela had agreed they would announce the pregnancy together.

Bobby sighed. "I need you to accept the fact I'm in love with Carmela. I know things between us have moved kind of fast, but she's the person I want to be with. Maybe, even for the rest of my life. And knowing your opinion of her, I wanted to spend the holiday with her alone."

"Look, Bobby, I told you once if Carmela is important to you then that's all that matters."

At her words, the tension eased from his body. "I appreciate that."

Carrie rose and dug out two big boxes from underneath the tree. "Here, these are for you. Merry Christmas."

Inside the first, lay a brown jacket. He ran his hand over the buttery soft leather. "Very nice, Mom." He slipped it on.

She smiled at him. "I'm so glad it fits."

He removed the jacket and opened the second box. He pulled out a navy cashmere sweater from beneath the white tissue paper. He grinned at Carrie. "Thanks."

He set the boxes aside. "By the way, where's Marco?"

She went to the fireplace, added a couple logs, and poked at the embers. "Please, don't be mad at me. Marco needed a break. He left early this morning."

"Left? For where? He doesn't know anyone else in the States."

"He hasn't been himself lately. I thought he might like to take a little vacation and see some other part of the country. He's been cooped up here with us since we arrived from Italy."

"Mom, you know Nick wouldn't agree with you."

"I know, but I wouldn't have told him to leave if you weren't going to be here."

With Marco away, Bobby acknowledged his need to be on guard. Nick would expect that of him. Things had remained quiet these past years, but it paid to stay vigilant. "Well, I'm not leaving until Marco comes back."

Carrie's face lit up. "That's more than fine with me."

Bobby wondered about Nick's return, a subject he didn't dare broach with his mother. Not with the possibility he might never come home. It hurt just to think about it.

The type of work he did for the government didn't matter to Bobby. If Nick had a choice, he'd be here and not out doing their bidding.

Later in the evening, after the children went to bed, Bobby and Carry retreated to the great room by the fire. Wine glasses in hand, they sat in silence until Carrie said, "I remember the first time we drove up to this house, all our futures so unsure. It almost doesn't seem real, now."

Bobby chuckled. "I'll tell you what was real, you beating the hell out of that guy upstairs in the bedroom." He moved to the edge of the sofa and faced her.

Her eyes misted over. "I didn't do a very good job before, but once I found you again, I was determined to keep you safe."

Bobby touched her shoulder. "Over these last years, you've gone above and beyond to make up for what happened. You must know by now, I've forgiven you, Mom. It's time you forgave yourself."

His heart swelled thinking how lucky they'd been to find each other. Her anguish at losing him must have been unbearable at times. He couldn't imagine her pain.

Thoughts of losing his and Carmela's child skated across his mind. A shiver ran through him, and he quickly pushed the image away.

But another thought nagged at him. He decided to put it out there. "I know you don't like to talk about my father. You told me he died in a car crash. I see the way you are with Nick. I mean…did you even love him?"

Her expression soured. "Bobby, I was so young. I didn't know what love was. He was gone, and you were all I needed."

"What about his family?"

"I didn't know them all too well. They moved away after he died."

"Oh," Bobby said. "So they didn't want to see me either."

"Please, don't do this to yourself. They weren't bad people, just wrapped up in their grief. People handle things in different ways."

Bobby saw she was visibly upset. "Sorry. I'll drop the subject."

"It's okay. I realize you have questions, but the answers aren't always what you'd like to hear. Anyway, I don't get to see you often. I'd much rather talk about good memories.

"Agreed." He didn't want to ruin his visit.

They began to reminisce about the first time they came to the Black Hills. Soon, there was easy laughter between them again. Bobby's spirits lifted. Their rift seemed to be healing.

# CHAPTER 19
## Marco

Marco paced his Miami hotel room and dialed Carmela's number. His restlessness had grown into full-blown fury. He hadn't spoken to her since his arrival three days ago. It was almost 3 o'clock in the afternoon and repeated calls to her remained unanswered.

Frustrated by her lack of response yesterday, he'd driven by her property several times. He observed the two armed men, who patrolled outside the large wrought-iron gates and decided not to approach. Causing a scene wouldn't lend itself to gaining entrance.

Carmela's visit to South Dakota and her outward disdain had left him wounded. All the promises she spoke of during their trysts in Europe appeared to be meaningless, empty gestures.

But those same promises convinced him to agree to come to America with Nick. Visions of a new, rich life with Carmela made it easy to leave Italy.

He threw his cell phone on the end table and sat on the bed. Shoulders slumped, hands in his lap, he stared at the grey carpet beneath his bare feet and contemplated his next move. His cell buzzed. He scooped it up and eyed the number.

"*Pronto*, I've been waiting in this lousy hotel for you to call me."

"Lousy?" Carmela barked at him. "Do you know how much your stay at the St. Regis Bal Harbour is costing me? An oceanfront room, two infinity pools, spa, and fitness center not to your liking, Marco?"

"I'm sure you can well afford it," he shot back. The cold silence on the other end almost made him regret his words. He wanted to see her. An argument would only serve to reduce his chances.

"I do appreciate the hotel, but you have failed to return my calls for three days."

"You do realize I am a very busy woman."

"I've flown a long way, Carmela. I think it's only fair you give me a little of your time." He rose from the bed, all the muscles in his body wound tight while he waited for her answer.

A heavy sigh came through the line. "Alright, alright, I will meet you in the bar downstairs in an hour."

"Why not come to my room?"

"The bar or nothing, Marco."

Her controlling ways irked him. Having little choice, he said, "One hour, then." He ended the call and prepared to leave. His mind set on convincing her to spend time with him in his room, he changed his clothes, splashed on some cologne, and headed for the elevator.

Downstairs, he entered and studied the bar. A gold and glass bar dominated the interior. The black marble top gleamed in the soft light. Several people perched on stools. The remainder of the place was empty.

Beige, velvet cushioned sofas and chairs stationed between small round tables added to the elegance. He ordered a Negroni and chose a quiet table in the corner. Unable to shake his somber mood, he took a few sips of the drink and tried to settle himself.

The kind of life he envisioned could slip through his fingers. All the luxuries he imagined, the fancy cars, the big house, unlimited amounts of money to go anywhere and buy whatever he wanted might dissolve if he couldn't convince her to keep her word.

Marco looked up from his drink, as Carmela approached. He had almost forgotten how beautiful she was. The white designer pantsuit graced her perfectly tanned skin. He glimpsed the laced edge of the pale blue silk camisole she wore underneath. Her long caramel-colored hair hung loose. Her strides sure and purposeful, her stilettos beat against the tiled floor.

She tossed her small clutch on the table and unbuttoned her suit jacket. The tops of her breasts rested just above the lace trim giving him ample view of her cleavage. She eased into the chair opposite him.

Carmela signaled the waiter and ordered a club soda with lime. She motioned at a tall, dark, gentleman stationed near the entrance. Marco understood the man must be her bodyguard.

The waiter set her drink down. Her eyes settled on Marco's face.

"Well, here I am. What is it you want from me, Marco?"

His pulse slammed inside his neck at her words. "What do you think I want? I want what you promised me."

She drummed her red polished fingernails on the tabletop. "And that is?"

"You know very well, Carmela. You asked me to spy for you. I delivered the information, and you said when I got to America, we would be together. Now, you won't answer my calls. I don't understand, after everything we meant to each other how can you treat me this way?"

Carmela's face soured. "Yes, and I told you to be patient. I must finish my end of things first. I warned you in South Dakota. We need to remain discreet. At this point, I'm not going to take chances. If anyone makes a connection between the two of us, it will ruin everything."

"How long?" Marco asked.

"However long it takes."

He reached across the table, his fingers encircling her wrist. "That is not an answer."

"Careful, Marco. Diego is very protective." She motioned in the direction of the man by the door. Through clenched teeth, she said, "Now, let go."

He glanced at Diego before removing his hand. "So, if I am patient, we will be together again?"

She relaxed into the tufted chair. Her expression softened. "Of course, we ill."

"What about right now?"

"Meaning?"

"Come up to my room. I want to hold you close. I've missed you, Carmela. A man can only take so much." His body throbbed with an aching need. "Please, just this once."

She raked her fingers through her hair. "Don't beg. I find it so unbecoming in a man. Try to enjoy your stay in Miami before you return to South Dakota."

His scalp prickled with shame. She reduced him to pleading. He gripped the arms of the chair. Heat traveled up his cheeks. "I see it is no use to ask again."

"I'm afraid not. You have to trust me and let things happen as they should. Soon, Nick and his family will regret their return to America."

He grew uncomfortable. "What do you mean by his family?"

"Are you becoming soft? What do you think I mean?"

"Not the children, Carmela. The children are innocent."

She cut her eyes at him. "That's for me to decide." She gathered her purse and rose. "Don't look so upset, Marco. You will see, it will all work out. Be patient. I promise when the time comes, I will take good care of you." Without looking back, she strolled away and out the door.

Marco finished his *Negroni* and ordered a second. He found it hard to believe her. Being patient was one thing, but being made a fool was quite another. He understood her taking out her revenge on Nick and Carrie, but she needed to leave the children out of it.

He gulped the rest of his drink. At the moment, there was little he could do to remedy his situation with Carmela. If he pushed her any further, he might not get what he wanted.

He thought about his return trip to the Black Hills. He pictured Carrie, and his body responded. Lust rose up inside him. What would it be like to bed a woman such as her?

With Nick gone these past months, her womanly desires needed tending to. He recalled those mesmerizing eyes and shapely figure, still so attractive even after bearing two children. All of it triggering his imagination.

His jaw grew tight. Why should Nick have everything?

Marco ordered a third, then a fourth drink. By the time he went up to his room, his mind swam with images of Carmela and Carrie. The first woman inaccessible, the second waiting back in South Dakota.

He undressed and crawled into bed. Within a few minutes, he fell into a drunken sleep. He woke around noon the next day, showered, and dressed. He'd take Carmela's advice and enjoy whatever Miami offered.

By the end of the week, Marco had swum in the ocean, drank his fill of liquor, danced at all the popular nightclubs, and visited with some of the local prostitutes. He was ready to fly to South Dakota where Carrie waited without her man.

He didn't need Carmela. He'd stare into those violet eyes and convince her he could make her pain go away and cure her loneliness. And after he finished, she wouldn't want Nick ever again.

# CHAPTER 20
## Miguel

Miguel Medina arrived in Laurel by late afternoon. The beauty of the snow-covered mountains surrounding the quaint town escaped him. He despised places of this nature. Small towns, contained small-minded people who had no idea of the real world and the perils it presented, a lesson he learned at a young age.

He recalled the night, threatened by paramilitaries, his parents took him and fled their home in Cali, Colombia along with thousands of others. They became part of Colombia's displaced persons' population seeking refuge in Soacha, a Borough of Bogota.

Growing up in one of Colombia's worst slums made Miguel never forget the stench of the raw sewage clinging to his clothes and seeping into his pores. The thirst and hunger gnawing at his belly while he scrounged for every meal. But Soacha had taught him, first and foremost, how to survive.

Running the streets, he learned that the same drugs and gangs killing the people were also his means to a better life. Before long he became a dealer and gang leader, murder and torture a familiar occurrence among him and his peers.

His opportunity for escape arrived when a cartel drug lord took a liking to him. Miguel gained his confidence and began earning serious cash, enough to move his parents to Bogotá. But knowing where Miguel's money came from, his father rejected his offer.

His mother refused to leave without her husband, and Miguel, helpless, watched her steady decline. She died a year later. He never forgave his father for his mother's suffering.

He pictured his father's face. A bitter taste filled his mouth. Juan Pablo Medina had been a weak man, with limited education and no desire to elevate his family above their meager existence. He deserved to stay in the slums of Soacha. Miguel left home cutting Juan Pablo out of his life for good.

A few years later, his connections led him to the United States. But he grew tired of battling the cartels with strongholds on the trade in America. His appetite for running drugs steadily decreased prompting him to seek a new career as a *sicario.*

He trained long and hard to become one of the best-hired killers. Soon, he joined part of a secret network of ghosts, eventually going to work for Carmela.

Working for her the past five years, he'd grown to admire the way she handled her business. Not many women survived the demands of trafficking drugs while also running legitimate enterprises.

In all fairness, she'd inherited her father's connections, both in the trade and in the government. That, along with her iron will, made her both respected and feared among those who dealt with her.

Miguel, well aware of her flirtatious nature with men, Carmela's attraction to him did not go unnoticed. As much as he would like to reciprocate, Carmela remained off limits. He was her *sicario.* To allow emotions to enter into their professional relationship would only serve to complicate things. He'd seen this happen many times before. Unlike Nick, he believed it better not to get personally involved with his employers or those he had orders to kill. This proved to be the wiser choice.

But when it came to Carmela, he had spies of his own. Armando feared Carmela's recklessness. He cared deeply for her and confided in Miguel regarding her latest conquest. Miguel asked Armando to keep him abreast of things. This situation would be solved if only she would give him orders to eliminate Nick.

He slid into a booth at the Palisades Diner. His mind refocused on the task at hand. He'd consume his meal, then locate the address of this Overton woman. Of course, he'd be careful not to draw unwanted attention. If he stood out, people might remember him in too much detail. He needed to give the impression of someone just passing through town.

Miguel smiled at the red-headed waitress who arrived to take his order. Making polite conversation with her was all part of that impression.

He took note of her nametag. "Joann. What a charming name."

Her pale cheeks blushed pink. It came easy for him to con a woman with a few compliments. Add a pleasant smile and good looks, and he'd have them trapped into thinking he was sincere.

"Why, thanks," Joann said. "But it's a pretty ordinary name."

Miguel gave her a quick wink. "Regardless, it suits a lovely woman like you." He pretended to study the menu. "Perhaps you can tell me what you would recommend?"

A grin spread across Joann's face. "Well, we have a really nice ribeye special."

"Ribeye it is then."

"How would you like that cooked?"

"Make it rare."

"Mashed potatoes okay for a side?"

Miguel smiled. "Excellent."

While waiting for his food, he glanced out the window. A burst of snowflakes spilled from a grey sky. Traffic along the main street remained at a minimum. An easy exit if he finished his assignment soon.

Joann brought his order. "Here you go. Is there anything else I can get you?"

"No, this is quite perfect, thank you."

Joann cocked her head toward the window. "Looks like lake effect snow again. Unless you're staying in town, I'd head out after you finish your meal. It can fool you. Piles up pretty fast."

"No, I won't be staying. I'm driving to New York to see family. But thanks for the advice."

"Love your accent, by the way. I can tell you're not a native New Yorker."

He laughed. "No. My family is from Venezuela. We've lived in this country for the last ten years."

Joann tore his check off her pad and placed it on the table. "Well, it was nice talking to you. You can pay up front at the cashier when you're ready."

"The pleasure was all mine."

He cut into his steak. A stream of blood ran across the plate framing the edges of his mashed potatoes. He savored each bite, dipping pieces of meat in and out of the bloody juice.

By the time he left the diner, the flurries had grown into a heavy squall obscuring the surface of the asphalt parking lot. He climbed into his black Lexus LS and cruised up Main Street.

Miguel turned onto Birch. The snowfall diminished as twilight filtered in. He cruised past number sixteen, a white house with green shutters. He rounded the end of the block and scanned the alley. Pulling in, he parked behind her house.

He pressed the glove box and pulled out a leather sheath. Silver snaps popped as he opened the case and drew out his custom made ten-inch hunting knife. The brass pins on the Red Micarta handle shone in the fading light. The Damascus steel blade boasted wide serrated edges along one side. He slipped the knife into the sheath and placed it in the deep inside breast pocket of his coat.

He rummaged around in the glove box again and fished out two large zip ties. Reaching under his seat, he withdrew a ski mask and a pair of black gloves.

Miguel scanned the deserted street and exited the car. He moved deliberately up the alleyway and scaled the fence leading to the rear of May Overton's house. He slipped on the ski mask and gloves. He crossed the yard to the back door, snow crunching beneath his shoes, and peeked through the unobstructed glass.

He pulled out a small leather case and unzipped it. He found the right pick and inserted it into the lock. Within seconds, it sprung free, and he stepped inside.

The house lay silent. He took the knife out of its sheath and stamped his feet on the small mat by the door to remove the snow from his shoes. Miguel moved through the rooms in the dim light to ensure they were empty before returning to the kitchen. He glanced around. Another doorway led to a small laundry room.

Miguel placed the knife into its sheath, then into his coat pocket. He sat at the table to wait while the remainder of daylight faded and darkness swallowed the kitchen.

Twenty minutes later, he heard the front door open and he slipped inside the laundry room. He wasn't going to play any of Carmela's games. The old lady could cooperate, or he'd make her. Neither way mattered to him at all. Because, in the end, he'd get Carmela the information she wanted.

# CHAPTER 21

# Nick

Nick settled into the Gulfstream G550 jet's reclining leather seat. Exhausted and homesick, he closed his eyes intending to take a break before landing in Medellin, Colombia. He was drifting off when a light tap on his shoulder made him open them.

Dalton peered down at him. "We might have a change in plans."

Nick yawned and rubbed his eyes. He moved the seatback upright. "What do you mean?"

"I need to bring you up to speed. Some new information came over the secure server regarding this kill." He sat across from Nick and frowned. "You're not going to like this."

"Humor me, before you judge."

Dalton slapped his palms on the table between them. "Listen, you haven't exactly been Mr. Wonderful these past few months. Half the time you're bitching and complaining and the other half you're sulking like a two-year-old."

Nick shrugged. "You knew from the beginning I didn't want any part of this. Volunteering is one thing, being coerced is another. I don't think I need to smile and do a happy dance every time I pull the trigger."

Dalton sighed and stroked his mustache. "Okay, smartass, I can see my telling you what a dick you're being is having little to no effect, so I'll get on with it."

"Please do. I'm all ears."

"I know we agreed you would carry out this next kill by yourself, but if my intel is right, it's got to be more than just you."

Nick perked up at his words. "Because …"

"Seems there's a small cartel convention going on in Medellin at a major hotel and your guy plus two others will be attending. If we can get a clear shot, we have an opportunity to take out some big players."

Nick gripped the arm of the chair. "A major hotel? Kinda ballsey, isn't it?"

"Of course, but with all the cops and government officials they have in their back pockets, they've become extremely bold."

Nick smiled. "They build a wall of corruption around them and start to believe they're well-protected from assassins."

"Exactly. But if we can create a little diversion, it just might be doable."

"Still, I imagine this is going to be pretty tricky."

"Let me ponder this a while," Dalton said. "See if I can come up with something."

Nick rose and stretched. "I'll do the same." He swiped two beers from the mini fridge and handed one to Dalton. Both men sipped their drinks in silence for a few moments.

Dalton's face grew serious. "Look, I'm sorry for what I said earlier."

"No worries." Nick sat across from him. "You were right to call me out on my shit."

"I don't have a wife and kids of my own, Nick. I'd be lying if I said I know how you felt."

"And I don't know how to explain it to you. When I started working for Ricardo, I made it a point to avoid attaching myself to anyone or anything. But, man oh man, the day Carrie came through the kitchen doors of that diner, I knew I wanted something more. I tried to convince myself otherwise. I had a job to do…I needed to stay on track."

Dalton grinned. "You sure jumped those tracks, buddy."

"No," Nick said. "I got derailed." They laughed, easing the tension between them. He studied his friend for a moment. "Carrie is the first thing I think of when I wake up in the morning and the last when I go to sleep at night."

"A good woman will do that to you," Dalton said.

"Five months is a long time to be away. I appreciate what you did, sending the tree and all. I hope they had a nice Christmas."

"Look, even though you couldn't be with her, I'm sure it helped Carrie to know you're okay after she got the necklace," Dalton said.

Nick took a draw on his beer. These last months had shown him just how alive his demons still were. Asleep for so long, old nightmares returned to haunt his dreams. Images of Ricardo and the shooting at the winery emerged more vivid than ever before.

If he was to be a better man, a better father who could look into his children's eyes without feeling the shame of his past, he needed to do everything in his power to ensure this was his last kill.

"Remember back at the airport in Peru when I told you I'd find a way out of this?"

Dalton cocked his eyebrow. "Can't forget it. You scared me a bit. I didn't think I'd get you on the plane that day."

"If we survive this next kill, we're going home, Dalton. Then after a little break, we'll take some action regarding our situation."

"What kind of action?"

"Leave that part to me. But I can guarantee, when we're done, you and I will no longer be employed by the United States Government."


A week after landing at *José María Córdova* International Airport, Nick relaxed by the rooftop pool of their five-star hotel. He'd spent the last few days canvassing the place so they could familiarize themselves with the layout. The cartel meeting was to take place later in the afternoon.

Dalton flopped down into the lounge chair next to him. "Only one good-sized elevator to the penthouse suite. Key card access only. The kid at the front desk is in. If all goes well, we shouldn't have any issues."

Nick peered over the top of his sunglasses. "Let's hope not."

They ate and took in some sun before returning to their rooms. Nick showered and changed into black jeans, black t-shirt, and grey sports coat. He picked up his Glock 18C, inserted the 33-round magazine, and slid the lever to fully automatic. Grabbing his duffel, he placed the gun inside. He checked the rest of the supplies, then removed his shooting gloves, stuffing them into his coat pockets. His cell buzzed.

"How's the lobby view?" he asked.

"They've just arrived, and all three are heading for the private elevator," Dalton said. "Two bodyguards apiece. I've paid the kid. He'll make the call. The car is parked out back. I'll meet you downstairs."

Nick grabbed the duffel and headed for the lobby. He crossed the white and gold veined marble floors gleaming beneath the enormous chandeliers. Exotic potted plants and flowers added to the elegant surroundings. People hurried in and out the main doors while others lined the check-in counter. Dalton sat in a far corner, a newspaper folded in his lap. He made eye contact with Nick. "Thirty minutes. Let them get settled in."

Nick sat across from him. He slipped the duffel bag underneath his chair and surveyed his surroundings. Minutes ticked by. He didn't have a good feeling about this hit. Something nagged at him, and he grew uncomfortable.

He just wanted to finish this job and go home. He pictured Carrie and the faces of his children and remembered they were his constant, his reason for living.

Dalton rose, his newspaper tucked securely under his arm. "See you in a few."

Nick watched him walk across the lobby and disappear down a hallway. Moments later, fire alarm bells rang out, their loud clang echoing. People glanced around, unsure; they hesitated before heading to the exit. Clerks emerged from behind the front desk. All except for a tall, slim young man. They ushered people out the lobby doors.

Nick slid the duffel from underneath the chair and made his way to the front desk. He nodded at the young man, who picked up the phone, punched in a number, and shouted, "*Esto es una emergencia. Debe salir immediatamente! Sí, prisa, prisa!*

Nick walked beyond the desk and down the same hallway as Dalton. Panicked people scrambled past him while the fire alarm continued ringing. He made an abrupt right through a set of double doors. Dalton waited in the deserted hallway in front of an elevator, his weapon pointed at the doors.

Nick dropped the duffel at his feet and slipped on his gloves and ear protection. He pulled out his Glock. Both men studied the lit numbers above the door as the elevator descended. A soft whoosh emanated when it reached their floor. Adrenaline roared through Nick's body. He gripped his weapon. The doors slid open.

Nick and Dalton opened fire releasing a barrage of bullets. The deafening sound of gunfire split the air. Bullets ripped into the flesh of the men standing inside. Bodies jerked with each hit. Horror swept over their faces. They collapsed into one another, toppling onto the floor. One man fell across the threshold. The elevator doors, unable to close, smacked up against the body.

They fired until their weapons were empty. Nick discarded his clip and reloaded. He moved closer and peered inside at the bullet-ridden bodies. He pulled the men over onto their backs in order to get a good look at the three drug lords. The air brimmed with gunpowder and the coppery scent of blood.

He counted five bodyguards. One was missing. He stepped back. His head jerked as the stairwell door flew open. He swung around. A man burst out firing several rounds into the corridor. Nick fired a round. The man fell against the stairwell door. Nick kicked the man's weapon away.

"Well, that should be the last son of a bitch," Nick said. "Let's get the hell out of here." He turned toward Dalton.

His heart drummed in his chest. Dalton's face grew pale. Blood seeped through the front of his shirt. He'd taken a hit.

# CHAPTER 22
# May

May, Overton fished her key out of her coat pocket and hurried up the brick walk. A bitter wind chased her along Main Street then followed her to Birch where it died out under the shelter of her front porch. She shifted the sack of groceries and opened the lock.

Grateful to be inside, she pushed the door shut and flipped the light switch. She went into the kitchen, setting the groceries on the counter. Placing her heavy wool coat and scarf across the arm of a chair, she smoothed the loose wind-blown strands of her short grey bob.

Adjusting the hem of her pale pink cashmere sweater, she broke out in a smile. She fingered the soft material, a Christmas gift from Carrie.

She pulled the first item from the grocery bag. A gloved hand came from behind and cupped her mouth. An arm went around her shoulders pinning her limbs. She kicked her legs as someone dragged her across the floor to the breakfast nook.

"Don't fight me or you will make things worse," a male voice said.

He tightened his grip. His threatening tone sent waves of fear through her body. She stopped kicking. Her heart battered against her ribcage.

"I am going to take my hand from your mouth. If you scream, I will kill you. Understand?"

His hot breath fanned the side of her face. May shook her head. His hand slipped away, leaving the taste of leather on her lips.

"Now, when I let you go, I want you to sit on the chair."

He relaxed his grip. Her legs shook as she eased down. He grabbed another and sat across from her.

May flinched at the sight of the hulking figure before her. Ebony eyes lurked behind a black mask. His full lips were set in a hard line. She took note of his slight accent.

"If it's money you need, I'll give you what I have. You can take it and go. I won't tell anyone you were here."

"Money?" His mouth curved into a smile. White teeth flashed against the dark wool. "I'm not here for your money, old lady."

A tremor ran through May's body. "Then, what do you want from me?"

"I need information. If you tell me all you know, you have nothing to fear."

May prayed he was telling the truth. She tried hard to concentrate, afraid her rising panic would get her killed. She planted the bottom of her feet against the wood floor to stop her legs from shaking. "Okay, if I can help you, I will. But please don't hurt me."

"That is entirely up to you." He pulled a knife from inside his coat.

May stifled a scream. Light from the overhead lamp glinted off the blade revealing its deadly serrated edge. The once comforting kitchen grew smaller while the man and his knife filled her vision.

"Now, what can you tell me about Travis Montgomery?"

His question startled her. Many years had passed since she'd heard that name. What did this man have to do with Travis?

May's stomach coiled. "How do you know Travis?"

He placed the tip of the knife against the soft flesh of her throat. The point pressed against her skin. Afraid to move, May held her breath.

"I'll ask the questions," he said. "Let's begin again." He withdrew the knife. "What can you tell me about Travis Montgomery?"

"I used to know him." Her voice shook. "That is…he lived with my sister a long time ago. But I haven't seen him in years."

"If he lived with your sister, you must have known him pretty well."

"Too well. He wasn't very nice to her or me. Travis has a temper. I blame him for my sister's drinking and drug habit."

"Where is this sister of yours now?"

May's breath caught in her throat. She pictured Helen's face as she lay on the stainless-steel gurney in the morgue in Arizona. Tears welled up, and she fought to hold them back.

"Dead," she choked. "Helen was murdered."

"Murdered? Who killed her?"

"I don't know. The police never arrested anyone."

"So, what happened with your sister and Travis Montgomery?"

"Travis was a low life. The kind of person who brings out the worst in people. He destroyed all the good in my sister before running out on them."

May sobbed at the memory of Helen. She stared into the man's cruel dark eyes.

"Enough, old lady." He pointed the knife at her again. "What did you mean by them?"

"Helen had a daughter, but Carrie never knew Travis, thank God." May pressed her fingers to her lips. How stupid! She'd given him Carrie's name. What if he intended to go after her next? A tremor moved through her body.

His eyes bore into hers. He ran his tongue over his lips like an animal ready to devour its prey. "Are you sure?"

"Yes, but she was too young to remember him. She knows nothing about him. Please, don't involve her in any of this."

May couldn't tell if he believed her or not. All she had to go on were his coal-black eyes peering out from behind the mask. She hated Travis more than ever and was positive his evil doings had brought this man to Laurel. To try to convince him she had answered honestly might be her only hope.

"Listen, I'm telling the truth. I haven't seen nor heard from him in years. I don't know if he's dead or alive and I don't care to know either. As for my niece, whatever it is he's done, she's innocent of any wrongdoing. Like I said, she didn't know him."

May studied his eyes, the powerful shape of his body and last, the knife. Was she going to die by the hand of a masked stranger all because of Travis?

He got up and pushed the chair back. "I believe you, old lady. Now, get up. We are going to take a little trip upstairs."

"Up… upstairs?" Her heart thumped against her chest. "What for?"

"I said if you told me the truth, I wouldn't hurt you and I will keep my word."

The knife still in his hand, they climbed the stairs and entered the first bedroom.

He flipped the light switch and pointed to the bed. "Lie down."

"But you said—"

"Don't argue, just do it," he snapped.

May did as he asked. She lay there waiting for him to plunge the knife into her. A moment later, he grabbed her hands and slipped a stiff plastic tie around them, pulling it tight, then did the same thing to her ankles. She watched him open the closet door. He rummaged inside and pulled out a scarf which he tied across her mouth.

"I am warning you. Do not move. I will be downstairs. I still have unfinished business. Don't make me have to break my word. Do you understand?"

She nodded her head. The sound of his footsteps retreated, and the trembling in her body ceased. Maybe she wasn't going to die.

Hours passed while she lay there afraid. She hadn't detected any noise from downstairs for quite some time. Pushing the last of her fear aside, she swung her legs over the edge of the bed and pushed herself up into a sitting position. She lifted her tied hands and pulled the scarf away from her mouth.

Deciding to take a chance, she hopped to the dresser. She grabbed the pull opening the top drawer and searched for the pair of scissors she kept inside. Lifting them out, she bent and snipped the tie on her legs. Unable to use them on her wrists, she set them aside and stepped out into the hallway.

Her heart quickened as she descended the stairs. Silence greeted her at the bottom. She advanced toward the kitchen. It was empty. She peered into the laundry room. Empty. She crossed to the back door, reached up with both hands, and turned the lock.

Relieved, she took a knife from the holder atop the counter and turning it upside down, worked the tie on her wrists until it snapped in two. May shook her hands letting the blood flow free again then picked up the wireless phone and dialed 911.

A woman's voice came through the line. "911, what's your emergency?"

May returned the receiver to its cradle, ending the call.

What could she say? A big man in a ski mask broke into her house, asked her questions regarding someone her sister once lived with, threatened her, and left. She didn't even have a clear description to give them. He certainly wasn't someone from Laurel and probably long gone by now.

But it nagged at her. Why questions about Travis? Did he owe this man money? It was apparent they had some kind of dealings. Just the type of person Travis would be involved with.

May thought about calling Carrie but decided against it. She had a good life, with a wonderful husband and two beautiful children. No need stirring up memories from the past. They'd had their discussion a long time ago when she first arrived in Laurel. She was thankful Carrie had never known Travis.

Besides, right now, she remained tucked away on a gated property with Marco Valletta keeping her safe until Nick returned.

May paced, her mind unsettled as to what to do. If she didn't call Carrie and something happened, it would be her fault. She grabbed the phone and dialed.

"Aunt May, how are you?" Carrie's voice came through light and cheerful. "I miss you. It was great having you here for the holi—"

"Carrie, I need to talk to you."

"What is it? Are you okay?"

"I am now. Please listen. There was a man here today."

"What man?"

"He was here in the house when I arrived home. He broke in."

"Oh, my God! Did he hurt you?"

"No, I'm all right. Let me finish. He wore a mask, so I never got a look at his face. He threatened me with a knife." May heard her gasp.

"Aunt May, you need to call the police. I'll catch the next flight out."

"No, no, you mustn't do that, Carrie. You're safer where you are. This man asked me questions about the past. Your mother never made good choices when it came to men, and it seems he had some kind of dealings with one of them. It was many, many years ago. I don't know if he is dead or alive."

"Someone my mother knew?"

"Yes, and unfortunately, I let your name slip. But I told him you were too young to know this man or anything about him. Carrie, I'm so sorry. I needed to let you know in case he attempted to contact you. Tell Marco to be extra careful. I couldn't live with myself if something happened to you or the children."

A few moments passed before Carrie spoke.

"I don't know what to say, Aunt May. I still think I should come to Laurel or you should come to us."

"No, I promise I'm okay. I don't think he'll be back since he seemed to believe me. There is no point in calling the police. I couldn't give them a description, and I'm sure he is long gone.

"I'll speak to Marco, but I don't like the idea of you being there all alone. It will make me feel better if you call Joann and have her come over."

To ease Carrie's concerns, she agreed. "All right, I'll call her. I love you. We'll talk again tomorrow."

"I love you too, Aunt May."

May set the receiver down. She took several deep breaths before checking all the windows and doors. Returning to the kitchen, she grabbed her address book and dialed Joann's number. Sleep wouldn't come so easy for her tonight…if at all.

# CHAPTER 23
## Carmela

Carmela viewed her naked body in the full-length mirror. She traced the soft mound of her belly with her palm. More prominent now, she studied the veins running along the sides of her breasts. The tips of her nipples were darker, and she'd gone up a cup size and the child inside her grew more active while she prepared to enter her sixth month. She'd no longer hide her condition with loose flowing tops. It was time to let the world learn of her pregnancy.

Other than Bobby, Armando, and Mateo, she'd taken care to keep the news from her many employees. She smiled at the memory of Armando's disapproving look when she told him. But his disappointment evaporated, leading him to spoil her by cooking all her favorite dishes and supplying her craving for *Natilla,* the Columbian sweet custard made with coconut milk and cinnamon usually served at Christmas time.

With each movement of the baby, Carmela reminded herself to stay focused on the reason she chose to give birth to Bobby's child. The baby could divide the D'Angelo's, something she could use to manipulate and control them.

With Bobby due to arrive in Napa later that afternoon she refocused her attention on getting dressed. She slipped into a light pink maternity top with a boat neck and scalloped lace across the bodice and the ends of each sleeve. Wide leg black pants completed her outfit.

She gathered her long hair, twisting it into a knot and securing it with a pearl hair pin. Opening her jewelry box, she lifted out the silver and diamond hoop earrings Bobby gave her for Christmas. She inserted them into her lobes and inspected herself in the mirror.

"Not too bad," she said, wondering if she'd feel the same at nine months. She grabbed a pair of black sandals before going to her study. At the bottom of the staircase, she ran into Diego.

His startled look spoke volumes. "I suspected, but I didn't think—"

"You didn't think what, Diego?"

He blushed and pointed to her stomach. "That you would be so foolish."

"What you see as foolish, I see as an advantage." She moved past him and down the hall.

He followed close behind. "Carmela, what is this craziness?"

She stopped and turned. "Craziness? You know nothing of my plans. I am prepared to carry out what I started. This child will help me do it."

He shook his head. "If your father were alive, I'm sure he wouldn't agree."

She clenched her hands, nails digging into her palm. She stepped closer to him. "You never knew my father, so you have no idea if he would agree."

"That is true." Diego folded his arms across his chest. His dark eyes lit with anger. "But in my opinion, I have no doubt he'd be ashamed of a daughter who would use a child in the act of revenge."

Her muscles tightened at his words. "You have no opinion in this matter, Diego. But going forward, your responsibilities will change."

"Change how?"

"You have vowed to protect me, and I count on your protection as will my child."

He dropped his arms. The storm in his eyes receded. He studied her face and covered her hand with his. "I will never break my promise to protect you. But I will never agree with your plan of revenge. I've seen too many of these things go wrong."

Carmela's irritation dissipated at the touch of his hand in hers. She recalled how they used to be with each other, and she raised her head to meet his eyes. "And the baby?"

"Of course," he said, his voice laden with emotion. "I only wish things could have worked out between us."

"I know, and I'm sorry I hurt you." She let go of his hand and hurried up the hall.

Once inside, she crossed to the cabinet and removed a folder. She sat at the desk and emptied its contents. Pictures of Bobby, Carrie, Nick, and Travis stared up at her. She fingered Bobby's picture.

Why did he have to be Carrie's son? If only things were different, maybe, she could fall in love with him. But she mustn't allow herself that luxury with so much at stake.

Her father taught her long ago about the consequences of making foolish decisions. In order to survive, she needed to be tough and not let her personal feelings interfere with her plans.

This was the only path for her. Ricardo's cruel death could not go unpunished.

The phone on her desk buzzed. Could Bobby be early?

"Yes, what is it, Luis?"

"*Señorita, Señor* Medina is here."

Carmela hesitated. Miguel had left for Pennsylvania a little over three weeks ago, and she had heard no news from him. "Let him through."

She swept up the photos returning them to the folder. She smoothed her hair and adjusted her blouse. In a few moments, she'd reveal her condition to him.

The study door opened, and Armando announced, "Señor Medina."

"Thank you," Carmela said.

Miguel moved through the doorway. No matter how many times she saw him, the power of his presence always caught her off guard. Today, he wore a black turtleneck. His muscular arms strained against the fabric.

She rose and came from behind the desk. He stopped, his eyes trained on her stomach. A frown washed over his face. He continued across the room.

"Carmela, it is good to see you." He kissed both her cheeks.

"It's good to see you, too."

For the first time, an awkward silence passed between them. She went to the bar and held up the tequila. "Drink?"

"*Sí,*" Miguel sat on the leather sofa. "I guess you won't be joining me."

She gave a nervous laugh while she poured the tequila. "No, I'm afraid not."

She handed him the drink. *"Salud."*

*"Salud."* He tipped the glass and swallowed the amber liquid.

She patted her stomach. "I know this comes as somewhat of a surprise."

Miguel raised an eyebrow and shrugged. "Yes, but it is none of my business."

Carmela sat at her desk. She forced a smile. "A baby wasn't in my plans, but as you can see, I've decided to adjust them a little."

"Would it be rude to ask who?"

Heat rose in her cheeks. She chewed her lower lip. It was pointless to lie.

"Bobby D'Angelo."

He raised an eyebrow. "Nick's son?"

"Stepson actually."

"I see." He let out a breath. "I hope you know what you are doing because what I'm about to tell you may alter your plans."

"Meaning?"

"I went to Laurel and spoke with the old lady."

Her pulse fluttered in her throat. "Is she still alive?"

"I can assure you she was when I left."

"So, what did she have to say about this Travis Montgomery?"

Miguel clasped his hands together. "It appears he was Carrie's father."

"Her father?" Carmela gripped the arms of her chair. "She was running around committing crimes with her father?"

Miguel's eyes locked on Carmela's face. "Only she had no knowledge of this."

She shook her head. "You're confusing me, Miguel. What do you mean she didn't know?"

"From what the old lady said, he left when Carrie was a baby, and she never knew him. Somehow, he came back into her life, but I don't think he ever told her who he was. She seemed pretty clear about that, afraid I would contact Carrie."

"This is incredible news, Miguel."

"There is much more to tell. I traveled to Arizona and did some checking regarding the information in the folder you gave me."

"I believe Arizona is where her mother lived," Carmela said.

"That is correct. Carrie grew up in a run-down trailer park called Breezy Meadows. According to an elderly neighbor, she lived with her mother, Helen Overton, and Travis Montgomery. The neighbor even recalled the day they brought Carrie home from the hospital after her birth. But Travis abandoned them."

"Carrie became pregnant at fifteen," he continued. "Not long after she bore the child, her mother sold the baby for drug money. Carrie ran off right after that, and the neighbor never saw her again. Her mother spent ten years in prison. After her release, she was murdered a few years later."

Carmela's head pounded. Could all of this be true? Did Carrie not know Travis Montgomery was her father? Was Bobby the baby her mother sold?

"What about her baby's father?" she asked. "Did anyone mention him?"

"No, that is the strange thing. They never saw Carrie with anybody. They had no idea who the father might be."

Her head swam. She tried to digest the news Miguel had given her. She pictured Bobby's face. Nausea grew in the pit of her stomach. Could he be a child of incest?

At this moment she wanted nothing more than to be alone. "You have done well." She tossed an envelope to him. "I have included a bonus."

Miguel rose from the sofa. "Are you okay? You've gone pale, *Señorita*."

She waved her hand at him and forced a smile. "Thank you for all your hard work. I will call if I need you."

He made no move to leave. "Carmela, it would kill me if something were to happen to you. Let me finish this thing with Nick. You stay out of it and take care of your child."

She raised her eyes to meet his. "I know you mean well, Miguel, but I have no choice. I must honor my father. He will never rest until I do."

"Then make it easy on yourself, Carmela. Give me the orders, and I will carry them out."

"That is not an option for me. This is extremely personal. I want to see their suffering with my own eyes."

He shook his head. "I can tell there is no changing your mind."

"I am afraid not."

"I will take my leave. If you need me, do not hesitate to call."

"Miguel, before you go there is one other thing I want to discuss with you."

His dark brows drew together. "What is it?"

"I am not one hundred percent sure yet, but I may have an issue with a man who works for Nick. His name is Marco Valletta."

"The bodyguard?"

"You know him?"

"I know of him."

She fiddled with her earring. A flush swept across her cheeks. "It seems he has the wrong impression."

"Could it be *you* gave him the wrong impression?"

She rose and came from behind the desk. "I might have pushed him too hard. He was spying for me… keeping me informed on the activities of Nick's family. Now he thinks I owe him more than I'm willing to give."

Miguel folded his arms. "Has he threatened you?"

"Not in so many words. But his patience may be running out."

He shot her a disapproving glance. "What is it that you want me to do, Carmela?"

"Nothing yet. He is still living in South Dakota with Nick's family. If he pressures me again, I will let you know."

"Very well. But be careful. I will leave you with a bit of advice. It's risky to play with a man's emotions, especially if he's in love with you."

She shuddered inside at his words. "Thank you. I will consider what you have said."

With Miguel gone, Carmela decided to visit with Allegra and Diablo. Bobby would be arriving soon. She must not let him see her in this state. He could tell when something had upset her.

Spending time with her horses always soothed her mind. Uncomfortable in the saddle, she hadn't ridden as often since becoming pregnant.

A soft nicker emanated from Allegra's stall. Mateo came toward her dragging a bale of hay.

He touched a hand to his black Cattleman's hat. *"Hola, Señorita. ¿Cómo estás?"*

Carmela smiled at him. *"Estoy bien."*

Allegra's nickering grew louder. Carmela grabbed a carrot from the feedbag. She opened the stall. "Okay, okay, my sweet boy. Here you go." Allegra stomped his front foot and bobbed his head in greeting. The carrot disappeared in two quick bites. She stroked the horse's wide nose. His warm breath swept across her fingers.

"Don't worry, we will ride again soon." She left the stall and continued to the second one where Diablo waited. Taking another carrot from the feedbag, she entered the stall.

Diablo's tail swished from side to side. His nostrils flared, and he stepped back.

"What's gotten into you?" Carmela held the carrot out. But Diablo refused to take it. Ears bent backward, he whinnied and stomped his foot.

Mateo approached the stall. "I think someone is angry with you." He motioned at the horse.

"Why would Diablo be angry with me?"

Mateo shook his head. "A horse with a wild streak must be ridden. He misses you, and he misses the jump."

"Are you sure you are letting him out to pasture enough?"

"*Sí,* but he's used to his mistress working and training with him."

She held out the carrot again and inched toward him.

Diablo reared back. His front hooves shot up. His powerful legs hovered over her head. Carmela froze. Mateo grabbed her, pulling her out of the stall and closing the latch.

Carmela wrapped her arms around her stomach and let out a shaky breath. Diablo's dark eyes peered out. She looked at Mateo who had gone pale.

"I've never seen him act this way," she said. Her heart battered inside her chest. If Mateo hadn't grabbed her, Diablo would have struck.

"Neither have I, *Señorita.*" Mateo pushed his hat back. He pulled a checkered cloth from his pocket and mopped his brow. "I think it is best if you do not enter the stall for now."

Still shaken by the horse's reaction, she said, "I agree. But it worries me. Please have the vet come out to check him all the same. I want to be sure there is nothing else wrong."

Carmela left the stables and made her way up to the house to wait for Bobby. Her mind drifted to Miguel and the news he'd given her. If Carrie didn't know Travis Montgomery was her father, that knowledge could break her. And if by some chance she did, was she keeping it a secret from Bobby and Nick?

This new information had emerged as an additional weapon she might use during her trip to South Dakota. Between her pregnancy and that, she'd be armed enough to face Nick.

When he returned home, she'd make her plans to visit. Once Carrie and Nick laid eyes on her growing belly, they would know she had the upper hand.

And when she shared her news about Travis Montgomery with Carrie and threatened to tell Bobby, she'd turn their perfect little world upside down. Then she'd sit back and watch it all play out.

# CHAPTER 24
## Bobby

B obby relaxed inside the rear of the limousine. Over two weeks had passed since the last time he and Carmela were together. Between setting up an art show for a new client and trying to keep up with his others left him little room to get away.

Months sped by and his excitement concerning the baby grew. Both of them agreed not to find out the sex. Boy or girl, so long as everything turned out alright was fine with him.

The limo drove through the gates and past the vineyards. Used to having Armando greet him, Bobby was surprised to see Carmela waiting at the top of the front steps. The sight of her took his breath away. Her pink lace blouse showed off the child growing inside of her. He swelled with pride.

He hurried up the steps. "Hello, gorgeous."

He wrapped his arms around her. His lips hovered close to hers before he claimed them. She melted into him and their kiss went deeper.

He ended the kiss and stepped back. He placed his hand on her stomach. "How are we doing?"

Carmela smiled up at him. "We are doing fine. Come, let's go inside. Armando has prepared a nice supper for us."

She led him to the enclosed patio at the rear of the house where a table was set with pale yellow china atop a navy-blue tablecloth. A crystal vase in the center held a bouquet of freshly cut flowers. Red and pink roses mixed with white freesia, their heady scents dancing around them. Two tall tapers graced each side of the vase.

They sat across from each other. Armando entered the room. He dipped his head at Bobby and proceeded to light the candles. "It is good to see you again, Mr. D'Angelo."

"Please call me Bobby, Armando."

"*Sí*, Mr. D'Angelo."

Carmela and Bobby looked at one another and burst out laughing.

"He'll get it after a while," Carmela said.

They dined on *Chuleta Valluna*, a pork Milanese with potatoes, plantains, and salad. During the meal, Bobby downed two glasses of red from Carmela's winery. It paired perfectly with the meat. They finished with the *Natilla* custard that had become part of her cravings.

Bobby pushed back from the table and patted his stomach. "Wow, I couldn't eat another bite. Everything was delicious." He winked at Carmela. "Since I'm getting used to all this Columbian food, you'll have to get used to Italian food. My stepdad cooks the best Italian food, and my mom has come a long way with her cooking, too."

"And you?"

Bobby chuckled. "Me? No, unfortunately, I haven't had the time to learn. But once you and I are living together, I'm sure I'll give it a try."

He watched the smile fade from her face. "Did I say something wrong?"

Carmela took a sip of water, before answering. "I am not thinking that far ahead."

He shifted in his chair. "Wouldn't you want the three of us to live together?"

"I think we need to focus on the birth. I'll decide what works best afterward."

The same meal that a few minutes ago rested easily inside his stomach soured. Once again, she surprised him with her answer. He had assumed at some point they would live together as a family. He wanted to be a fixture in his child's life, not someone who came and went whenever Carmela allowed him to.

"What are saying, you'll decide?"

"Well, I'm the one giving birth after all."

He flung his napkin onto the table and rose. "Don't you realize how important you and our baby are to me? I want us to set an example, be a family, so our child is secure and knows how much we love him or her. Something I never had growing up."

Carmela gave him a sullen look. "Why do you have to ruin a perfectly good evening? All I am saying is that you are jumping too far ahead. Can't we just enjoy our time together before making any major decisions?" She pointed to his chair. "Please, sit down."

Undecided, he hesitated. He didn't like her answer, but at the same time, upsetting her couldn't be good for her or the baby. He settled into his chair. "We don't have to discuss it anymore tonight. But it's important you know how I feel."

Carmela eyed him. "What did you mean when you said, something you never had growing up?"

Bobby looked away. He concentrated on one of the candles. The flicker of the orange and yellow flame conjured up memories he'd rather forget. Neither one had ever discussed their childhoods. It made him realize how little they knew about each other. If they were going to be a family, it might be time to remedy some of that.

Unable to meet her eyes, the shame still lingering inside, he said, "I was abused growing up. My father used to lock me in a closet under the basement stairs."

Carmela gasped. She gripped his hand. "How awful."

"When I got older, he used to hit me a lot."

"And your mother, Carrie, did nothing?"

Bobby forced himself to look at her. "No, no, she wasn't in my life then. I lived with my adoptive father. His wife died when I was pretty young, so I don't remember her. He married my stepmother not long after that."

"Didn't your stepmother try to protect you?"

"No, she couldn't. He used to hit her too. She was terrified of him."

"How long did this go on?"

Bobby took a breath. He rubbed the back of his neck and searched for the right words. Realizing there weren't any, he blurted out, "Until I killed him."

The color drained from her face. It wasn't the answer she expected. But he wouldn't lie to her. Not now, not ever.

"What happened? How did you…how did he die?"

"There was a struggle. The gun went off…" Bobby let go of her hand. His shoulders slumped. "I meant to kill him, I was, and still am glad he died that day." He searched her face, waiting for her response.

"You said your mother wasn't in your life at that time and you lived with adoptive parents. Why?" she asked.

He'd leave out nothing. "Her mother, my grandmother sold me for drug money. It happened while my mother went to the store for formula. When she got back home, I was gone, and the police never found me. They sentenced my grandmother to ten years in prison. If she hadn't been addicted to drugs, things might have turned out differently. To this day, the most I've ever done is smoke pot. Hard drugs can lead to all kinds of bad stuff happening."

He swept his hand through his hair and sighed. "I reconnected with my mother after she came to live in Laurel, Pennsylvania where I grew up." Bobby pushed up his shirt sleeve and pointed to the red star-shaped mark on his forearm. "I know you've seen this before, but I never told you the story behind it." He traced it with his fingertip. "It wasn't until we ended up in South Dakota and she saw this birthmark that she realized who I was."

"And your biological father?"

"My mother doesn't like to talk about him. He died in a car accident before I was born."

"*Mi tesoro,*" Carmela murmured. "I am so sorry that all those things happened to you. I understand you much better now."

"I'm glad I finally told you. No one else outside the family knows the whole story."

His muscles relaxed. He took her hand, curling his fingers around hers. "Now, how about you tell me a little something from your past?

Carmela shook her head. "My childhood was nothing as dramatic as yours. My father raised me alone after my mother died giving birth to me." Her eyes glistened. "I have no complaints. He was very good to me."

"Where is he now?"

She drew her hand away. Her face grew dark. "He died some years ago."

"I'm sorry," Bobby said. "How did he die?"

Her bottom lip trembled. "He became ill and died not long after that."

"You have no other family?"

"No, not here. There are a few relatives in Colombia, but I have not seen them in many years." Carmela pushed her chair back. "Let's not talk about the past anymore."

"Okay, we don't have to right now," Bobby said.

They left the patio and retreated upstairs to the bedroom. In the soft evening light, Carmela stripped off her clothes while he watched from the bed. His heartbeat accelerated at the sight of her naked body and swollen belly.

He stretched out his arms. "Come here."

She crawled in beside him and nestled against his chest.

"You're so damn beautiful."

"You think so now, but what about when I am in my eighth or ninth month? After I've grown fat and my feet swell, will you think so then?"

"Of course," he mumbled into the soft waves of her hair.

She moved away and onto her back. Taking his hand, she placed it on her stomach.

Bobby sprung up. "The baby?"

Carmela nodded. "Yes, he or she has been more active lately."

He gathered her close again and kissed her lips, his tongue thrusting deeper. She moaned, and her arms came up around his neck. He caressed her swollen breasts. His hand dipped into the softness between her legs.

His desire intensified, and all his nagging doubts drifted away. She eased onto her side, and he kissed the smooth curve of her upper back and squeezed her buttocks. His body pulsed as she curled her leg around his thigh urging him on. He entered her from behind, and she gasped.

Bobby moved against her in a steady rhythm. Short ragged breaths escaped her lips. They climbed higher together. All his nerve endings firing at once, he shuddered and let go inside of her while they climaxed together. He eased away, and she nestled against him, her warm breath fanning his neck before he fell into a satisfied sleep.

Bobby woke sometime later. Carmela lay next to him, naked, moonlight spilling over her dark skin. He slipped out of bed. A cool breeze blew the sheer curtains hanging above the open window. He peered out at the garden below.

Telling Carmela about his past lifted some of the weight he'd carried with him for most of his life. She'd made the wall he built around his emotions collapse and expose those things from childhood he chose to stay hidden. Having heard what he went through, Bobby was confident after the baby came, she would agree to live together.

For now, the next step would involve going home to South Dakota and showing off Carmela's pregnancy. He wasn't worried about Nick. He just wanted his mother to accept his relationship with Carmela.

Bobby left the window and got into bed. He pulled the covers over the two of them and pressed his body up against hers, content to be with the woman he was falling deeper in love with and looking forward to the future with her.

# CHAPTER 25

## Marco

Marco zipped his black leather jacket. Grabbing his helmet, he climbed onto the ATV, kicked it into neutral, and started the engine. He slipped into first gear and let out the clutch. Easing the throttle, he headed for the trail.

Riding through the winding paths of the property, he barreled past towering pines and deep woods. Changing gears, he rode up a steep rise to the top of a hill. He stopped at a clearing, cut the engine, and jumped off the vehicle.

He removed his helmet and walked to the edge, looking out across the valley. The iron-grey March sky, thick with clouds, matched his ugly mood. Since returning from Miami and his visit with Carmela months ago, his sour disposition refused to diminish. He no longer trusted her promises. Her poor treatment cemented his mistrust. She had rendered him powerless.

Unable to persuade her to set a time limit on her plans or convince her to come to his room, left him feeling weak, and less of a man.

Now, his physical desire for Carrie grew almost daily, and he found it difficult not to act upon his feelings. Last night at the dinner table, he swore her smile and polite conversation meant much more than she let on. Women always send out signals. It was up to the man to decipher their meaning. Nick had been gone a little over five months, and Marco wasn't sure he would ever return. She hadn't had her husband for a good while.

Marco pictured her face, her long, dark, hair, and mesmerizing eyes. He drew in a sharp breath feeling himself grow hard. The time had come to find out what it would be like to bed such a woman as her.

He strapped on his helmet and drove to the house. He emerged from the garage into a biting wind blowing across the front yard. Twilight touched the edges of the sky, a full moon rising with the fading light.

He took the porch steps two at a time, stopping before the great room's massive window. Through gaps in the icy frost covering the glass, he could see Izzy by the fire playing with Michael. He'd spent the last six years of his life looking after Nick's family. As much as he loved the children, he'd grown tired of taking orders.

He directed his gaze to the sofa where Carrie lay stretched out, holding a book in her hands. His hunger for her grew. Backing away from the window, he clenched his fists. He cursed under his breath. Crossing the porch, he went inside.

"Marco, is that you?" Carrie called out.

"Yes," he responded.

He removed his snow-covered boots and placed them by the front door.

Chino padded down the hall to greet him. Marco continued on, ignoring him. He stopped at the end of the hallway where Carrie stood smiling.

"I was a little worried, Marco. Where were you? You usually let me know when you're going out."

He moved closer. A vein throbbed in his head. She spoke to him as if he were a child. "Riding the property," he snapped.

Her face fell. "Sorry, if I upset you. I was concerned. I've left a plate for you in the kitchen. We've eaten already. I'm going to get the children ready for bed. Help yourself."

Marco's eyes traveled to the outline of her breasts beneath her sweater. He watched her walk away, fixated on her figure, his arousal growing.

Frustrated, he retreated to the kitchen. Ignoring the plate Carrie had prepared for him, he pulled a beer from the refrigerator. The cold frothy liquid hit the back of his throat jolting his senses. He finished the bottle, then grabbed another and paced.

"Is something bothering you, Marco?"

Startled, he looked up as Carrie approached. Her hair hung loose. The soft light accented her flawless complexion and made her violet-blue eyes stand out. Desire burned in the pit of his stomach.

"You look upset." Carrie eyed the dinner plate. "If you don't care for what I cooked, you can have something else."

Finding his voice, he said, "No, no it's fine."

"Okay. I think I'm going to turn in early. It's been a long day. Goodnight, Marco."

"*Buona Notte*, Carrie."

Marco's heart galloped. His palms grew damp. He swallowed the rest of the beer and set the empty bottle on the counter. His opportunity to be in control had come.

He waited a few moments before mounting the staircase. He heard her bedroom door close. He crept up the hallway and closed the children's bedroom doors as he went.

Light peeked out from under the master bedroom door. He pressed his ear to it and heard the rustle of clothes. Seconds later, the light went out.

Marco waited. Visions of Carrie naked flashed in his head. He grew dizzy with excitement. Every nerve in his body came alive with anticipation. He let ten more minutes go by before he switched off the hallway light.

Gripping the doorknob, he twisted it open and slipped inside. He closed the door. Pale light from the full moon filtered in the window and splayed out across the bed.

Carrie lay on her side facing toward the windows. Marco moved closer. There was no movement, only, the low rumble of her breath as she slept.

He removed his 9mm from his waistband and set it on the floor. He unbuttoned his shirt, tossed it on top, then unzipped his pants. Easing onto the bed, he lay beside her and pressed his body up against hers.

"Nick?" she gasped. She turned her head. "Marco? What are you doing!"

He grabbed her shoulder, forcing her onto her back. She cried out, struggling beneath him, arms flailing, her eyes wild in the moonlight.

He wrapped his hand around her wrists, pinning them above her head with one hand. He tore at her silk nightgown pulling it down. The warm mounds of her breasts pressed against his bare chest, fueling his lust.

"Stop, Marco! Please, stop," she cried.

He covered her mouth. "I will not hurt you. I've waited a long time for this." Terror filled her eyes. His pulse raced. He tightened his grip and pushed her against the mattress.

"Don't fight me, Carrie."

This was it. He would show her how a real man takes care of a woman. She belonged to him.

# CHAPTER 26
# Nick

Nick stared at the monitors next to Dalton's hospital bed. Sedated for a few days, Dalton slipped in and out of consciousness. Refusing to leave his bedside, Nick endured sleepless nights in an armchair. Both men were always aware they might not survive a hit. So far, Dalton had survived. He thought back to what had transpired right after the shooting.

With the lone gunman dead, he dropped his weapon and ripped open Dalton's shirt. The bullet had entered his lower abdomen. He rolled him onto his side and found no exit wound. Wherever it lodged, the bullet could continue to do damage.

He removed Dalton's shirt, opened his black duffel, and drew out two thick self- adhesive gauze pads. Applying pressure to the wound, he wrapped the shirt around his stomach tying it tight to stop the bleeding.

Dalton's breathing grew ragged. Nick feared he was losing him. His luck changed when the young front desk clerk appeared. He stared at the massacre before him. The color drained from his face. He backed away.

Nick beckoned to him. *"¿Como se llama?"*

He looked at Nick, his eyes blank.

*"¿Como se llama?"* Nick repeated.

*"T... Tomás, Señor,"*

He motioned at Dalton. "Help me get him up, Tomás.*"*

Tomás failed to move.

Desperate, Nick put his hands underneath Dalton's arms and said, *"Por favor."*

He nodded. *"Sí, Señor."*

Tomás grabbed Dalton's arm and together they got him to his feet. They stumbled to the back exit. Outside, they laid him across the rear seat of the rental car. Nick applied pressure to the wound again. He gestured at Tomás.

Tomas hesitated, then climbed in, replacing Nick's hands with his own.

*"Gracias,* Tomás."

Nick jumped behind the wheel, speeding to Dalton's plane. With help from the flight crew, he settled Dalton inside instructing the pilot to fly to Venezuela. He fished out his wallet and removed a wad of cash. He handed it to Tomás.

"No, no, *Señor."* He pushed it away and made a flying motion with his hand.

"Oh, hell," Nick said, realizing he wanted to go with them. He hesitated, then glanced over at Dalton sprawled out on the convertible bed.

An ashen-faced flight attendant, hands pressed against Dalton's wound, motioned with her head. "Let him come. We've no more time to waste. We need to do everything we can to save him."

With Dalton hanging by a thread, the hour and twenty-minute flight became the longest of Nick's life. But he had no other choice. Venezuela, where he still had connections, would be safest.

He gave Tomás clean clothes. When they landed, he agreed to accept the money Nick offered him earlier. He had relatives here and would go to them.

Nick thanked him then got to the business of getting Dalton taken care of.

Surgery had been tricky, leaving damage to Dalton's small intestine and one of his kidneys. His incision remained open to allow the swelling to decrease and surrounding tissues to heal. That part seemed to be going well, but Nick's angst wouldn't ease until he regained consciousness.

Nick rose to stand at the window. Traffic sped by below. Pedestrians hurried along oblivious to the carnage produced by men like Dalton and him.

He pictured Carrie and his children, safely tucked away in South Dakota. The familiar longing welled up inside making him want to scream in frustration. If things had turned out differently, they'd be flying home.

"Hey, what the heck is going on?"

Nick whirled around. Dalton's eyes were open.

"You're awake." He stared at his friend, the tension of the past few days easing. "You scared the crap out of me."

A weak smile spread across Dalton's face. "You know this has got to stop."

"What are you talking about?"

"You saving me all the damn time."

"I wouldn't have it any other way."

Dalton chuckled. "Yeah, I guess so." His eyes studied the room. "How long have I been in…in…where the hell are we?"

"Venezuela," Nick said. "The closest place I've connections."

"Oh, Venezuela. I knew a little gal here once I was real fond of. Wonder if she's still around?"

Nick's anxiety eased at his words. "You can find out for yourself as soon as you're well enough."

Dalton's face grew serious. "How bad?"

"Bullet's out, but there's tissue damage, and it nicked a kidney. Doc says you'll heal with time."

Dalton smirked. "Could have been worse, I guess. Thank goodness it didn't nick anything else, if you know what I mean." He broke out in laughter causing a full-blown coughing fit.

Nick filled a plastic cup with water and slipped in a straw.

"Serves you right." He helped him take a few sips.

Dalton leaned back against the pillows. "Listen, on a more serious note. I've been thinking about what you said about getting out of the business."

"And I meant every word. No more kills for me at the behest of the government or anyone else."

"After what happened in Colombia, I couldn't agree with you more. I think my killing days are over, too." He pointed downward. "I'm losing the stomach for it."

"Really? Still making jokes." Nick rolled his eyes.

"I can't help it. Just thought I'd slide that last one in."

"Right now, all you have to do is get well."

A frown clouded Dalton's face. "Look, you need to leave. I can stay and recuperate on my own. Take my jet and fly home. You've been away from your wife and kids too long."

"As tempting as that is, I'm not going without you. We came here together to do a job, and we're leaving together."

Dalton turned up his nose. "Stubborn as usual."

Nick laughed. "It's one of the things you love about me."

"Only this time you're going to listen," Dalton said. "You are leaving today. I have lots of pretty nurses to keep me company."

He stared at Nick. His eyes grew moist. "You're a true friend, and I'll always be grateful to you for saving my life." He held up two fingers. "Twice."

"You'd do the same for me," Nick said.

Nick sat in the chair and stretched out his legs. "Okay, enough. Don't ruin your tough-guy image by getting all sentimental on me."

"You'll have plenty of time to show me how appreciative you are when you get home. Like that one-hundred-year-old bottle of whiskey, you keep telling me about."

Dalton winked. "You more than earned it."

# CHAPTER 27

## Carrie

Carrie woke. A body pressed up against her. "Nick?" Unable to process what was happening, she inched away. Fingers dug into her shoulders forcing her onto her back. Her eyes flew open.

"Marco!"

Within seconds, he pounced on top of her. His hands encircled her wrists lifting her arms over her head.

"Stop, Marco! Please, stop." She struggled against him. His full weight bore down on her. The odor of beer from his breath fanned her face.

He ripped open her nightgown exposing her breasts. He tightened his grip. Her heart hammered in her chest. She cried out, and he covered her mouth with his other hand. The bulge between his legs dug into her inner thigh. His breathing grew heavier.

Dark eyes bore into hers. "I will not hurt you. I've waited a long time for this."

She twisted herself, trying to break free, but his powerful arms held fast.

"Don't fight me, Carrie," he hissed. "Just enjoy it."

He removed his hand and pressed his mouth against hers. Her lips parted, and she bit his thrusting tongue. His body jerked, and she broke away.

She rolled toward the edge of the bed. Marco grabbed her arm, dragging her back. He flung himself at her again.

*"Cagna!"* he shouted. "You bitch"

He held her wrists with one hand, slapping her across the face twice with his other.

Her head snapped from side to side. The coppery taste of blood flooded her mouth.

Hatred swam in his eyes. "Just like her, you think you're better than me."

Memories of her abuse at Travis's hands flashed in her mind. How could this be happening to her? She couldn't understand what had set Marco off. "Please, don't do this," she begged.

Color flamed his cheeks. He drew in a sharp breath. "You caused this. Leading me on these past months."

"That's not true, and you know it. I never made you think I wanted you in this way." She scrambled to find the right words, anything to make him stop. "You're a part of this family. We love you … the children love you. If you go through with this, you'll never be able to live with yourself."

"Living? Is that what I am doing? You and Nick have everything. All you do is use me for your own means. I have taken good care of all of you for so many years and when I asked for one thing in return, your husband denied me."

As he spoke, his hand relaxed. Carrie eyed the bedside lamp. "What did he deny you, Marco? Nick has always treated you fairly."

"Never mind," he spat. "If you weren't so proud, you would stop fighting me and enjoy what I am about to do."

It took all her strength to tear her arm free and grab the neck of the lamp. She gripped her fingers around it and swung the base at him. He drew back too late, and she struck him on the side of his head.

Marco cried out. His hands flew up. Carrie slid off the bed and onto the floor. She eyed the door. Adrenaline surged through her. She forced herself up. Her legs trembled as she took a step. His long fingers wrapped around her ankle. She lost her balance, falling onto her knees.

She kicked at his hand. It slipped away, and she crawled toward the door. Grabbing for the knob, she yanked it open.

Marco came at her again, slamming her body face down. He snatched a handful of her hair. His fingers raked her neck. He straddled her, then bent forward. His ragged breath blew against her temple. "I will have what I want from *you!*"

He pulled her torn nightgown up with one hand while the other pressed against her spine keeping her still. Carrie struggled. Her nails dug into the pale grey carpet. The room swam. He tried to penetrate her, and she cried out.

A low growl made her look up. Chino blocked the doorway. His lips curled. White teeth flashed in the moonlight. He stretched his massive body and charged. His thick tail flared straight out.

Marco rolled off her, landing on his back. He screamed as Chino dragged him away, jaws clamped on his arm.

Carrie sat up. She scooted backward, brushing her leg against something cold. Marco's 9mm lay on the floor beside his shirt. Grabbing the gun, she scrambled to her feet.

Marco shook his imprisoned arm, swinging at the dog with his other. He kicked at the dog's legs, but Chino refused to let go. He wailed as blood ran down his arm, trickling onto his bare chest.

He shouted at Carrie. "Tell him to stop! Please make him stop!"

The white fur around Chino's snout grew red. His dark eyes blazed. Chino tugged at the arm again. Marco continued to wail. The dog swung his massive head, shaking Marco's arm. A low growl erupted from his throat.

She aimed at Marco and yelled, "Chino, release!"

Chino's jaws opened. Marco's arm sprung free. Chino panted, his long tongue dipping out the side of his mouth. His hindquarters hit the carpet. Eyes locked on Carrie, he waited for his next command. In that brief moment, she was grateful to Nick for training the dog and keeping the code words between the two of them.

Marco cradled his bloody arm. His pale face fixed in agony, he looked from the dog to Carrie.

"Go ahead. Shoot. I am as good as dead when Nick finds out what I've done," he sobbed."

"Get up, Marco," she said through clenched teeth, pulling her torn gown over her bare breasts with one hand. "Pack your things and get out of this house. Take the keys to the spare car and drive away. If I ever see you around here again, I will kill you. Unless Nick gets to you first."

His eyes on Chino, he rose. Blood dripped onto the carpet. He gathered his shirt. An ugly knot formed on his head where the lamp struck. Sorrow mixed with pain marred his expression. "I did not mean to hurt you."

"Save it, Marco. Get the hell out before I let Chino at you, again!"

He peered over his shoulder at the dog then hurried out the door to his room. A few moments later he appeared with his suitcase.

She kept the gun aimed on Marco. "Leave your keys."

He fished in his pocket and tossed them onto the floor.

"Now, keep walking," she ordered. "After what you've done there is nothing left to say."

"Follow, Chino," she commanded. Chino stayed within easy nipping distance of his heels She scooped up the keys and followed them.

Marco swiped the car fob off the hook by the front door. He gestured toward her one last time. "I'm sorry. Please, forgive me." He pulled the door closed behind him.

Carrie hit the lock and set the alarm. Her knees went weak. She put her back against the wall and slid to the floor. Placing the gun beside her, she called, "Chino, come."

He padded over to her. She stroked his fur. Her tears came, and she wrapped her arms around his neck. "You saved me, boy."

Chino let out a soft whimper. He eased down and placed his head in her lap.

An hour later she climbed the stairs. She checked on the children before returning to the master bedroom.

Removing her torn nightgown, she showered, scrubbing her body almost raw, wanting to erase any trace of him. With a towel draped around her, she stepped to the full-length mirror. A red bruise marked the top front of her left shoulder, and several scratches ran along the right side of her neck. The inside of her bottom lip ached from where her teeth had cut it.

Thanks to Chino, things hadn't gotten as far as Marco had wanted. Still shaky, she threw on a pair of pajamas, stripped the sheets, and replaced them with clean ones.

Carrie cleaned the trail of blood from Marco's wound before calling out for Chino. He trotted into the bedroom. She patted the foot of the bed.

"Come, Chino." He leaped up and settled himself by the footboard.

Exhausted, she crawled into bed, and with Marco's 9mm tucked underneath her pillow, switched off the light.

"Mommy, wake up!"

Carrie opened her eyes. Izzy jumped up and down, her long dark hair fanned out with each movement. Every bounce of the mattress made Carrie's head pound. The bedside clock read a little after eight. She'd only had three hours sleep. Grateful for Saturday, she sunk back against the pillows. At least Izzy was off from school.

"Okay, enough," Carrie said. "I'm awake." She held out her arms and Izzy did a slow crawl up the comforter. Carrie drew her close. Breathing deep, she kissed the top of Izzy's head. The need to push the memory of last night away grew. She must focus on her children. They were her anchor. There was no time to fall apart.

"Where's your brother?" Carrie asked.

"Still sleeping. He's a lazy bones." Izzy giggled. "Where is Marco?"

Carrie's stomach twisted at the mention of his name. "He had to leave to take care of some business."

Izzy frowned. "You mean like Daddy?"

"Not exactly." Wanting to change the subject, she said, "Let's go to the kitchen for some breakfast. The alarm is set, and the motion detector in the downstairs hall is on. Let me punch in the code first."

"Okay." Izzy got off the bed and pulled her Minnie Mouse slippers on.

She entered the numbers into the upstairs panel, and Izzy raced out of the room. Carrie locked Marco's gun in the safe and grabbed her robe. She checked on Michael, then continued to the stairs.

Voices drifted up from below. Chino yelped, and her insides trembled. Had Marco come back?

Laughter came from the kitchen. She stopped. Her hands shook. She edged closer and heard his voice. Her tension changed to excitement, and she rushed downstairs.

Nick stepped through the doorway holding Izzy's hand. Chino trailed behind them, his tail wagging.

Izzy's face lit up. "Mommy, look, Daddy's home!"

Carrie's breath caught. Her eyes locked with his. They didn't need words. Here it was again, the unmistakable bond between them. Her heart swelled. She swallowed back the lump forming in her throat.

Nick let go of Izzy's hand. He held out his arms. "Come here." His voice, husky and warm brought immediate comfort.

Carrie ran and melted into him. He stroked her hair, bent, and buried his face against her neck. "God, how I missed you," he murmured, holding her tight.

Everything she needed was here now. He was home.

# CHAPTER 28

# Nick

Nick grabbed his duffle and climbed out of the limo. He held his cell to his ear.

Dalton's voice came through the line. "You know we still need to talk."

"Yes, and we will after I spend some time with my family first," Nick said.

"Take all the time you need. Meantime, if another call comes in, I'll stall until we figure things out."

Nick frowned. "Nothing is going to change my mind. Like I said before, I'm done."

"Okay, don't get your britches twisted. I heard you loud and clear. Give Carrie and the kids a hug from me. Talk to you soon."

He slipped his cell into his pocket and hurried up the porch steps. He opened the front door just in time to catch sight of Izzy crossing the end of the hallway. She disappeared into the kitchen without spotting him.

Chino galloped toward him, fur flying, tail wagging. He let out a yelp. Nick rubbed his head. "I know, I missed you too," he whispered and smiled.

He crept up the hall to the doorway. Izzy, her back to him, refrigerator door wide open, retrieved a container of milk and placed it on the counter. He ducked and waited, afraid she'd drop it if she spotted him.

He peeked in again as she set a box of cereal next to the milk.

"Any breakfast for me?"

Izzy squealed and ran to him. "Daddy, your home!"

Nick lifted her up into his arms. He pressed her close. "Yes, baby, I'm home."

Izzy's tiny hands hugged his neck. She tilted her head up. Her forehead wrinkled. "Where were you? Why did you stay away so long?"

"I'm sorry. It won't happen ever again."

"Do you promise, Daddy?"

"Cross my heart." He heard footsteps, set Izzy down, and took her by the hand. They walked out of the kitchen together.

"Mommy, look, Daddy's home!"

His eyes locked on Carrie and he let go of Izzy's hand. He held out his arms. "Come here." Drawing her close, he stroked her hair then buried his face against the soft skin of her neck. "God, how I missed you."

There was a slight tremor in her body. "Babe, it's okay, I'm here."

She raised her head. Tears spilled down her cheeks.

"Please don't cry."

"I…I can't help it. I'm just so happy to see you."

Izzy tugged at the bottom of Carrie's pajama top. "Mommy, what's wrong?"

"Let's go into the great room," Nick said.

He prepared a fire while Carrie settled on the sofa. She looked at her daughter. "Izzy, go check on your brother. He's sleeping an awfully long time."

She scrunched up her face. "But I want to stay with Daddy."

"Izzy, do as your mother says," Nick said. "You can come right back."

She glanced from Carrie to Nick, stomped her foot, and ran out of the room.

"When did that start?" he asked.

"A couple of months after you left. Your absence had a negative effect on her. But then again, she does have her father's stubborn streak." She gave him a half-smile.

"Who me?" He dropped beside her. He draped his arm over her shoulders. "By the way, where is Marco? Out checking the property?"

"Yes, I think so. He left right before you got home."

Izzy came bounding into the room, Michael running behind her. "See, Michael. Daddy's home."

Nick sized up his little boy. He held out his arms. Michael's face lit up, and he jumped into Nick's lap. He pulled his son close, and kissed his forehead. "I love you so much, Michael."

They spent the next hour together in front of the fire. The children couldn't get enough of him as he lay on the floor wrestling with them. Later, Carrie cooked breakfast, and when they finished eating, the children grabbed some of their toys.

"Come on, Daddy. Play with us," Izzy said.

Michael tugged at Nick's arm. "Come play."

"I'll be in soon. I promise. I need to talk to your mother for a bit. You two go ahead." He helped clear the dishes.

Carrie picked up a dish towel and grinned while he loaded the dishwasher. "Boy, I missed this."

"You have no idea how normal all this makes me feel," he said. "All I want now is to be home with my family."

"I'm so sorry, Nick. As much as your leaving was hard on all of us, I can't imagine how things must have been for you."

His eyes searched hers "I won't leave you ever again."

"What are you saying?"

"Dalton and I've talked. We're going to figure a way out of this."

"But I thought there wasn't any way out."

"Leave that to us. I don't want you to worry." He cradled her face in his hands and kissed her lightly on the lips. "We *will* work it out."

Her cell phone buzzed. "It's Bobby. Should I tell him you're home?"

"Sure, why not?"

"Hello, Bobby. Yes, everything is more than fine. Nick's back. Yes, early this morning."

Nick watched her smile dissolve.

"No, it's okay. We've been over this already. Just bring her with you. Okay, see you then." Carrie set the phone on the counter.

"What was that all about?"

"Bobby's coming for a visit. He'll fly in tomorrow afternoon. He's bringing his girlfriend with him."

"So, is that an issue?"

"Look, it wouldn't be fair if I caused you to pre-judge her. Let's just say I have some reservations. But I'll let you form your own opinion when you meet her. I have to remember to put Chino in the mudroom before they get here."

"Why?"

"He frightened her a little last time."

"Frightened her?"

She shrugged. "Some people are uncomfortable around dogs, and Chino's a pretty big guy."

Nick glanced at her. "Marco should be back by now."

She fidgeted with the dish towel. "About Marco. I couldn't talk in front of the children. Marco's gone. He left last night."

Nick narrowed his eyes. "What do you mean gone?"

"I don't think any of us realized how unhappy he was living here." She broke eye contact.

"Marco wouldn't just leave," he said. Especially, if I was still away. His job is to protect this family."

He took note of the strained look on her face. Something was off. He sensed it the moment he held her in his arms, the tremor in her body due to more than his coming home.

"Carrie, come clean. We agreed not to keep things from each other. Ever."

She threw the towel down and gripped the edge of the counter. "Okay, but you have to promise to remain calm."

"I'm not promising anything because I don't know what the hell is going on."

"Please, sit down."

His body tensed. Whatever news she had was bad. He drew out a stool by the island.

Carrie sat beside him, hands clasped together. "There was an incident between Marco and me last night."

"What kind of incident?"

Her face grew pale. He observed how tight her hands pressed against each other, the skin across her knuckles white.

"I'm still confused. This was so unlike him. I never had any reason to distrust him while you were away. But last night, he came into our bedroom while I slept and he…attacked me."

Nick jumped up. "Attacked you? How?"

Her face flushed a bright red. "He tried to rape me."

Her words hung in the air. The man he had trusted with his life and the lives of his family had attempted to rape his wife. His stomach went into spasms as if he had just received a punch to his gut.

For the first time, he noticed the slight bluish tint on the skin beneath her eyes. He sat and placed his hands on top of hers, trying hard to keep his anger in check. "Tell me everything."

Pain racking her face, she told him about the previous night's events.

Nick took in every word. His temples throbbed. She had gone through so much. This would never have happened had he been at home.

She hesitated for a moment. "There was one thing Marco said that confuses me."

"What's that?"

"Just like her, you think you're better than me. Do you know who he might have been talking about?"

Nick shook his head. He couldn't recall Marco ever having spoken about a woman rejecting him. Still, even if something of that nature had happened to him, it wasn't an excuse for trying to rape Carrie. What the hell had prompted Marco to attack her?

"No idea, unless it was someone he knew in Italy. I should have picked up on it. Saw the signs."

"No, I don't want you blaming yourself. He changed a couple of months after you left. I mistook it for homesickness. I never imagined for one minute he would come after me. The look in his eyes…it was as if someone else had taken over his body." Carrie rose and went to him.

Nick drew her close. "I'm so sorry that happened to you, but thankful Chino stopped him." He swept her hair away from the side of her neck. Ugly red scratches trailed along her skin. Ready to explode, he asked, "What else?"

"Just a bruise on my shoulder. I'm okay. Please, don't torture yourself over this. It could have been worse."

Nick held her, but his anger and hurt wouldn't subside. An attempted rape was sure to bring up the abuse she suffered from Travis. Once again, he had failed to protect her.

She raised her eyes to meet his. "There was something else odd that happened while you were gone."

"What?"

"Someone broke into Aunt May's house."

"Is she okay?"

"As far as I can tell. She insisted I not come to Laurel and she wouldn't fly here. I urged her to call Joann. The whole thing was so strange."

"Was it a robbery?"

"No, he asked her questions about some guy from my mother's past. He wanted to know where he was now. He threatened her, but he left after she convinced him she hadn't seen this man in years.

An uneasy feeling washed over him. "Did she report it to the police?"

"No, she didn't have any details. He wore a ski mask. She couldn't describe him."

"Maybe we should make a trip to Laurel."

"Joann says she's fine. Besides, Izzy has school. Since they pushed her ahead to first grade, she's playing catch up. I don't want to disrupt her routine. We'll wait until she has spring break. I trust Joann. She would tell me if I needed to come."

"If you're sure she's okay."

"Positive."

Nick didn't like what he had heard. Why would someone go to Laurel to ask May questions about a man from her sister's past? None of it made any sense. But then again, he didn't know much about Helen Overton or who else might have been in her life. He'd leave it alone until he talked to May in person.

As for Marco, he needed to pay. The thought of him attacking her enraged him. He'd make it his mission to have him found, and he'd settle things with Marco.

Moonlight streamed in as he lay in bed with Carrie nestled in the crook of his arm. He kissed the top of her head, her hair silk against his lips. After her ordeal he insisted they skip making love and go to sleep. Comforted by the sound of her steady breathing he tried to quiet his thoughts.

He stared out the window at the full moon. Did he have a right to be with his family after all the killing he did? The faces of the men he shot flashed across his mind, the tops of their heads blown off by the pull of his trigger. They were bad people, each and every one of them, but it still wasn't easy to justify.

His demons were restless again. He'd fought long and hard to keep them sleeping. Working for the government had shocked them awake, and if he let them win, all of this could slip away.

He pulled Carrie closer, and she moaned. Her eyes fluttered open. A gentle smile washed over her face. She traced his features with the tip of her finger.

"I'm so glad you're home," she whispered.

"Me, too." He kissed her. His body came alive at her touch.

Although they had agreed to wait, neither of them could.

There in the moonlight, their hunger for each other swelled until they came together, filling each other with the love that had lain sleeping for so long.

# CHAPTER 29

## Carmela

Carmela surveyed her closet. Deliberating a few moments, she fished out her black wool V-neck sweater dress with the long sleeves and slipped it on. It was still cold in South Dakota. She stuffed a pale, rose-colored nightgown and matching robe into her overnight bag.

Her anticipation grew at the prospect of her upcoming trip. Initially, Bobby had planned to go alone, but when he mentioned Nick's return, she said she'd had a change of heart.

She had no idea how much Carrie had told Nick about her, but she wasn't afraid to face him head-on. His reaction would be priceless. No doubt he'd wish he had shot her that day in the winery.

Grabbing her tall black leather boots with the three-inch heels, she perched on the edge of the bed and struggled to get her swollen feet into them. Cursing, she gave up and settled for a pair of Valentino flats. She threw on her trench coat and a paisley scarf. Stepping in front of the mirror, she grinned. This would do for her reveal.

There was a light tap on her door. *"Entrar,"* she called out.

Armando bowed. "Ready, *Señorita?"*

"*Sí.* Please take my things. Has Diego brought the car around?"

"He is waiting outside." He picked up the bag and followed her downstairs.

Outside, Carmela blinked at the early morning sunlight and climbed into the dark interior of the limo. She made eye contact with Diego in the rearview mirror. Things between the two were polite but tense. She raised the partition and prepared for the ride to the airport.

The car traveled through the wrought-iron gates, and her thoughts turned to Bobby. The information he revealed regarding his childhood came as a shock. She pictured him a poor little boy locked in a dark closet, scared and helpless. A tiny bit of sympathy tugged at her heart. How awful for him to have grown up in such a manner.

To know Carrie D'Angelo had played an enormous part in all of it made her hate the woman even more. How careless she'd been leaving her child alone with her alcoholic and drug-addicted mother. Any decent human being would have known better. This only validated what Miguel Medina had told her after his visit to Arizona.

Her childhood, filled with love and affection, stood in stark contrast to Bobby's. Her father often spoke kindly of her mother who died giving birth to her. Carmela was thankful he had shown no resentment toward her for the loss of his wife.

Her impending labor crossed her mind. The chance still remained she could perish the same way her mother had. She squeezed her eyes shut for a moment pushing away the image of dying in childbirth.

Opening them, she took a breath and placed a hand on her stomach. She needed to stay focused. Once she finished with

Bobby and his family, she'd raise a strong, independent son or daughter, one who would continue to run her empire.

The limo slowed to a stop. Carmela peered out the window. She slid the partition down. "Diego, we cannot be late. We are flying to New York to pick up Mr. D'Angelo, and from there to South Dakota." She shifted in the seat. As her pregnancy progressed, it became harder to get comfortable.

He caught her eye in the rearview mirror. "I am well aware of that. I have no control over the traffic, Carmela."

"Take a detour or something."

"There is no detour." His voice spiked. "Don't upset yourself. It is not good for you or the child. The world will not stop spinning if we are a bit late to pick up Mr. D'Angelo."

She watched his gloved hands grip the wheel. Not so long ago, those same hands caressed her body. But now, only Bobby's hands touched her in all those secret places. How odd her desire for Diego, once so necessary, had simply vanished.

Her cell buzzed. She picked it up and frowned. Marco Valletta was calling. So far, she had managed to keep him at bay. She raised the partition and settled into the seat. Her cell buzzed again. She resisted the urge to decline his call.

"Hello, Marco."

"Finally. I have been trying to reach you."

"What is it? I am on my way to the airport."

"I need your help. Something has happened. There was an incident...."

"Go on. What incident?"

"I've left South Dakota."

Carmela gripped the cell phone. What had the idiot done now? His leaving South Dakota could spell trouble for her. Her heartbeat quickened, and she took a breath. She must keep a clear head and deal with the situation.

"Why did you leave, Marco?"

"I need to see you. I'll explain then."

"Where are you?"

"Miami. I wasn't sure where to go."

"Listen carefully. I am booking a ticket for you to come to Napa. I will text you the information and let my people know you are coming. My butler, Armando will put you up in the guest house. You are not to roam about the property. If you do, I will have you shot. We will speak after I return."

Carmela ended the call and dialed the airlines. She booked a one-way ticket for Marco, sent the text, and then called Luis. Her final call was to Armando. There wasn't much she could do about Marco at the moment. Without knowing why he left, she couldn't afford to have him running loose. One call from him to Nick could spell disaster for her.

Crawling through rush hour traffic, they arrived at the airport. In a little over five hours, they would land at JFK and pick up Bobby.

Reclining in her private quarters aboard the jet, Carmela closed her eyes and tried to imagine how she'd react when she faced Nick after all this time. Her love for him had morphed into a burning hatred long ago. She was more than ready to step up her plans for revenge. When she was finished, this visit could prove to be the most memorable of all for the D'Angelos.

On the ground at JFK, Bernardo, Carmela's captain and the rest of the flight crew readied the jet for the remainder of the trip. Feeling refreshed after napping, Carmela touched up her make-up and ran a brush through her long hair. She dabbed perfume behind her ears and at her wrists. There was a light tap on the partition, and she smiled.

"Come in silly. You don't have to knock." Expecting to see Bobby, her body tensed at the sight of Diego

"Oh, what is it, Diego?"

"This is madness. Carmela, you must not go to South Dakota. When they see you like this…in your condition."

She got up and faced him. "That is the whole point. You would be wise to mind your own business. Stop trying to interfere in my affairs." Her insides knotted. She had tolerated him long enough.

"Diego, you have overstepped your position too many times. It is time for you to go. You will not be accompanying us to South Dakota. I will book a seat on a commercial flight for your return to Napa. After you arrive, you will pack your things and leave my home for good."

Storm clouds built behind Diego's eyes. "All I have ever done is love you, Carmela, and you have thrown it back in my face. I have dared to speak my mind because your blind hatred has eaten away all the love inside your heart." He pointed at her stomach. "The child you carry will suffer greatly. You are not bringing this baby into the world out of love. You know I am right."

Carmela's spine went stiff. She raked her eyes over him and balled her fists. Blood rushed to her head and thundered in her ears.

"I don't care what you think, Diego. I told you a long time ago you could never understand what I've been through. Now, get the hell off my plane."

His brow furrowed. "I see you for who you really are. A spoiled little girl filled with hatred over the death of a father who was nothing but an educated criminal who raised a daughter just like him."

Her pulse spiked. She lunged at him, raising her hand, but he caught her wrist. She tried to pull away. His fingers dug into her flesh. "Let go, Diego!"

"After all this time, you think you can toss me out like a sack of garbage?" His face twisted into an ugly scowl, and he released her. "You will regret this."

She stepped back and rubbed the red marks forming on her wrist. Through clenched teeth, she said, "I'm not going to tell you again. Get off my plane."

"Do as the lady said. Now!"

Carmela spun around. Bobby filled the doorway. His face lit with anger. How much had he heard?

Diego moved away and glared at him. "You have no idea what is going on here."

"Nor do I care. If Carmela wants you to leave, you'd better go." Bobby jerked his thumb toward the door. "I said leave now, Diego."

He locked eyes with Bobby. "You'll find out soon enough what a mistake you made falling for this woman." With a last glance over his shoulder, he stormed out.

Bobby wrapped his arms around her. "Are you okay?"

"Yes, I'm fine." She rested her head against his arm.

"I came in on the tail end. What the hell was that all about?"

"Just a disgruntled employee." Relieved he hadn't heard the full exchange between her and Diego, she relaxed. "He has been giving me trouble for some time now. He did not take kindly to being fired."

"I never liked that guy, anyway. Something about him was off. I'm glad he's gone."

Carmela raised her head. "You do realize I am going to have to replace him. Diego was not only my driver but my bodyguard."

Bobby sighed. "Do what you must. I wouldn't want anything to happen to you." He patted her stomach. "Or the baby."

She took him by the hand. "Come, sit. We should be taking off soon."

They settled into seats across from one another. As they taxied down the runway, Bobby's face grew serious. "Listen, you need to know, no matter how things go when we reach the house, I'm on your side."

"I am sure they will be shocked at first," she said. "But all that counts is how we feel about everything."

A smile tugged at the corner of his mouth. "I agree one hundred percent. We're going to be a family whether they like it or not."

They landed three hours later, and Bobby secured a limo ride to the house. The closer to the Black Hills, the more animated he became. Carmela half-listened to his musings. Her focus remained on the task at hand. It didn't matter anymore if Nick gave her identity away. To drive a wedge between Carrie and her son using her unborn child would come first. If need be, she'd confront her about Travis Montgomery and gauge her reaction. If the information Miguel had brought her was correct, it could prove to be the most damaging of all.

They drove through the gates. Bobby slid the window down and breathed in. "I love this place."

Carmela couldn't help but laugh. "Yes, I know." It wouldn't be long before he hated it.

They stopped in front of the house, and the limo driver unloaded the luggage. Bobby placed his hand beneath Carmela's elbow, guiding her up the steps. He pressed the bell and waited. A moment later, the lock sprung, and Carrie appeared.

"Hey, Mom, we're here!"

She gave him a hug. "Yes, I can see that." She smiled at Carmela. "It's good to see you again. Come in, it's too cold to stand out here."

She hesitated, unaware of Chino's whereabouts. "What about the dog?"

"Don't worry. I put him in the mudroom."

They stepped inside. "Let me take your coat, Carmela."

She removed her coat. Carrie's eyes grew large. She took a step back.

"I…"

"It's okay, Mom. We wanted to surprise you."

"I'm surprised alright. Why haven't you said anything before now?"

Carmela produced her warmest smile. "Please don't be angry, Mrs. D'Angelo. I asked Bobby not to tell you."

"But why? Why would you do that?"

"I just felt we should tell you when the time was right." She saw a shadow cross Carrie's face and spied the anger simmering below the surface.

"Right for whom?" Carrie eyed her stomach. "You must be due pretty soon."

"Yes, a little over two months to go."

Bobby took their coats and hung them on the hall tree, then he placed a protective arm around Carmela's shoulders. "Mom, please don't spoil things. This is the reason I didn't come home for Christmas. We came hoping you would be happy for us."

"I don't know what I am right now," Carrie said. "Come on, Bobby, you have to admit, this is a shock."

"Yes, I realize that. Can we at least talk about it?"

"Let's go into the great room."

They followed Carrie. Carmela's heart galloped as her eyes searched the room. As if reading her mind, Bobby asked, "Where's Nick?"

"He's picking Izzy up from school.

"I thought Marco did that."

Carrie placed fresh logs on the fire. "Not anymore. Marco's gone."

At her words, a cold wave washed over Carmela. She eased onto the sofa. *Why* wasn't Marco here?

"What do you mean gone?"

"Never mind him now. I'll explain later. A lot has happened since your last visit. Maybe if you came around more…you'd be up to date."

Color stormed into his cheeks. "Really? You're going to throw that at me. You know how hard I work, how much I travel."

Carrie gestured toward Carmela. "But it seems you found time for that."

Carmela stood. "I think it's best if we leave. We didn't come here to upset you, and I didn't come here to be insulted."

A flush swept across Carrie's face. "I'm sorry. Please sit. I didn't mean it the way it came out. I'm still in shock."

"Are you sure?" Carmela asked.

"Yes, please accept my apology. It's going to take a little time for me to adjust."

Carmela sat, and Bobby dropped down beside her. "Look, Mom, I'm sorry we didn't tell you sooner. But now that you know, it would make things easier if we got your blessing."

Carrie sat down opposite them. "I want you to be happy, but a baby is a big responsibility Bobby, and you're so young."

"You were fifteen when you had me. I'm a lot older than that. Besides, we both have good incomes. We're more than able to raise a child."

Carmela savored the turmoil behind Carrie's eyes. The impending birth had knocked the wind out of her. She had no love for the mother of Bobby's child, and the feeling was mutual. When the time came, she'd make sure Carrie never got to see her grandchild.

"Look, Carmela, I didn't mean to hurt your feelings. I just hope both of you know what you're getting into. A baby changes everything."

She shrugged and smiled. "I think we can handle it."

The slam of the front door interrupted their conversation. Footsteps sounded in the hall and Izzy came bounding into the room. She took one look at Bobby and Carmela and let out a yell, dropping her backpack on the floor.

He held out his arms. "Hey, Bug, it's good to see you." He lifted her onto his lap.

She hugged his neck. "I'm so happy you're here."

"Where's your father?" Carrie asked.

"Putting the car in the garage." She wiggled out of Bobby's lap and went over to Carmela.

"Hi, Carmela. Do you remember me?"

She laughed. "Of course, I do. You are too sweet and too pretty to forget."

Carrie rose. "Bobby, help me put some refreshments together. I'm sure you're both hungry." She pointed at Izzy. "Put your books away and change out of your school clothes."

Izzy frowned. "Do I have to?"

"Yes. Please don't argue."

"Don't worry, bug," Bobby said. "We're not going anywhere."

Smiling, she grabbed her backpack and scampered up the stairs.

He kissed Carmela's cheek. "Be right back. You relax."

Carmela rose and walked to the floor to ceiling windows overlooking the valley. So far, her plan was working. Carrie was visibly upset and probably giving Bobby more misery in the kitchen.

"Well, hello there."

At the sound of his voice, her knees grew weak. Her breath caught. The moment she waited for had arrived. She forced herself to turn around. Nick stood in the doorway, his smile fading.

"Carmela?" He came toward her. "What the hell are you doing here?" His eyes landed on her stomach, and he stopped in mid-stride.

She rubbed a hand across her belly. "Yes, I'm pregnant. Bobby and I are going to be parents."

The anguish marking his face made her heart soar. Now he would find out the kind of damage she could do. Enough to rip his little family apart. He moved closer and grabbed her arm. "How could you do this?"

"I might ask you the same question. How could you put a bullet in my father's head?" She snatched her arm away. "Careful, Nick, you must not let your temper get the best of you."

He narrowed his eyes. "I should've—"

"What?" she sneered. "Put a bullet in my head, too. Well, it's not too late. Be a man. Go and get your gun. It shouldn't bother you to shoot a pregnant woman, you've done enough killing."

Nick took a step back. "Your bitterness and taste for revenge have taken over your whole life. Tangling Bobby up in all of this makes you even more despicable. He never did anything to you."

"Correct. But Bobby is Carrie's son. My father would still be alive if it weren't for her. That bitch stole you away from me. We could have had a future together."

"What are you talking about, Carmela?"

"You know very well my father wanted a marriage between the two of us."

"So, you lied to me that day by the pasture when you said you understood I wasn't in love with you."

"Yes, and I would have dealt with my feelings for you, but when I found out about her and your disloyalty to my father, it changed everything. The final straw came when you killed him. The only person I had left in this world." Tears flooded her lids, and she pushed them back.

"Whether you believe me or not, I never wanted to kill him," Nick said. "After Carrie got shot, I had no choice."

"There is always a choice, Nick. You just happened to make the wrong one."

He glanced over his shoulder and lowered his voice. "Listen to me, Carmela. You need to stop right now. Break things off with Bobby and go away."

She met his eyes and gave a half-laugh. "I am carrying his child. A child he wants more than anything in this world. I have no intention of breaking things off."

"This is madness," he said through clenched teeth. "Do you think I'm going to let you stay close enough to my family to hurt them?"

She waved a dismissive hand at him. "Silly man. I could have done away with all of you a long time ago." She moved closer, her face inches from his, she said. "And if you push me, I may have to put that option back on the table."

A muscle in his jaw twitched. His lips drew back in a snarl. "I ought to let Chino out of the mudroom."

"Go on. Do it," Carmela hissed. "And I'll scream bloody murder."

"Do you think I'm going to let you get away with this?"

She patted her stomach. "Seems like I already have. But, enough talk about me. I have a question for you. How did it come about that Carrie ran around committing crimes with her father and shooting poor Carlos in the neck?"

The color drained from Nick's face. She had struck a nerve. Cupping her chin, she pretended to think. "Let me see, what was the man's name?"

His eyes narrowed. "Carmela, I'm warning you."

"Travis…something or other. Oh yes, Travis Montgomery." She delighted in his anger.

"Carmela, I swear to God, if you repeat any of this, you'll regret it." His hands formed fists at his side.

"I see you two have met." Bobby walked in carrying a tray of drinks and sandwiches. He placed it on the coffee table. "I know…it's a shock. I hope you're not going to react like Mom did."

She grinned. "We were having a lovely conversation. As a matter of fact, your stepfather congratulated me."

He slapped Nick's back. "I knew I could count on you."

Nick jammed his hands into the front pockets of his jeans. "Bobby, I'm not sure what to say."

Carmela stepped in between the two men. "He was just telling me how excited he is to be a grandfather to our baby." She spied the refreshments.

"Looks good." She patted her stomach. "I am so hungry." She strolled over and swiped a sandwich and a drink from the tray. She turned and met Nick's eyes.

"I am so happy to be visiting your lovely home. I can envision spending much more time with all of you in the near future. Bobby, please bring our luggage upstairs. Pregnancy is exhausting. I think I will eat in our room."

Reaching the doorway, Carmela paused. She smiled at Nick. "So glad I finally got to meet you."

# CHAPTER 30

## Carrie

Carrie tossed the packages of cold-cuts onto the counter. She reached into the refrigerator again for condiments while Bobby set out a loaf of bread before pulling glassware from the cabinets. Her mind spun with the news of Carmela's pregnancy. She snatched a tray from the dining room hutch and prepared sandwiches. After a while, she broke the silence between them.

"Look, Bobby, you have to understand where I'm coming from."

He folded his arms. "Oh, I know where you're coming from alright. That little remark you made about me finding time for—"

She held up her hand in protest. "Okay, okay, my bad, as they say. You could at least admit keeping this from us for so long wasn't fair. Carmela is practically due."

Bobby's forehead wrinkled. "And if I had told you sooner, would you have reacted any different?"

"Probably not. But that is not the point."

"Okay, so what *is* the point?" He swiped his hand through his hair. "You haven't said one nice thing to me or Carmela since we got here. Even if you don't agree with us having a baby, all your little snide remarks were totally uncalled for."

His statement was true, but she couldn't come to grips with the situation. Her opinion of Carmela hadn't changed since her last visit. Suspicions regarding the wine still lingered.

"Did she trick you?" Carrie asked, almost afraid to meet his eyes.

"What the hell do you mean by that?"

"I mean, was the pregnancy planned or—"

"Are you kidding me right now?" Bobby stepped away from the island, a hurt look on his face. "Do you remember saying all that matters to you is my happiness?"

"Yes, and I meant it."

"The hell you did." Bobby's face flushed. He rubbed the back of his neck and slumped onto a stool. "I am happy, Mom. Why can't you be happy for me...for us?"

Her heart broke. He'd had so much unhappiness in the past. She needed to put her feelings aside. Bobby was going to be a father, and if she didn't get on board, he might distance himself from them for good. His love for Carmela was proof enough she held the upper hand.

Carrie finished arranging the tray before she spoke. "You're right. I'm sorry. Your happiness does mean everything to me. If you feel you're ready to raise this child with Carmela, then I'll try and support you."

Bobby lifted the tray. "Why is it, somehow, I don't believe you, Mom?" He disappeared through the kitchen doorway.

Carrie's head throbbed. Her son could read her so well. Not wanting to go into the great room just yet, she grabbed a sponge and wiped the counter. In her heart, she did feel

Carmela had tricked Bobby. Carrie believed she was manipulating him. But for what purpose, she wasn't sure. Living all those awful years with Travis, one of the most devious people she had ever come across, had taught her to follow her intuition and it was telling her she was right about Carmela.

She looked up as Nick walked in. "Well, I guess you heard…no, correction…saw the news."

He sat at the island without answering, a strange look on his face. Carrie went over to him. "Don't you have anything to say about this whole situation?"

He raised his head and met her eyes. "What is there to say? She's pregnant, and Bobby is beside himself with joy."

She placed her hands on her hips. "That's it?"

"Look, I'm not exactly thrilled about it, either. But if we push, you know what will happen."

"I guess I need to go inside and play nice," Carrie said.

"No, they took sandwiches up to their room. Izzy is with them."

"As long as Bobby is with her. I don't want her left alone with that woman."

Nick grimaced. "That's going to be difficult since they are staying for the weekend. Besides, what could she possibly do to Izzy?"

She averted her eyes and grew silent. Having enough on his plate with Marco, she had made the decision not to tell him about the incident with Izzy and Carmela.

"Carrie, look at me. What do you mean as long as Bobby is with her?"

She tossed the sponge into the sink and plopped onto the stool across from him. "Something else happened while you were away. It concerns Carmela and Izzy. I'll tell you the whole story, then you can give me your opinion."

She left out nothing, including what she believed about the drugged wine. By the time she finished, Nick's face had turned dark. He folded his arms across his chest. His green eyes settled on hers. "Why didn't you tell me any of this before?"

"Like I said, it happened while you were away and I didn't want you to worry."

Nick jumped up from the stool. "You were wrong not to tell me."

His words stung. "If I had told you, what could you have done? You were miles from home."

"That's not the point, Carrie. I would have known a long time ago who she was and…"

Carrie's stomach twisted. "What do you mean, who she was?"

"I meant to say, what type of person she is. I could have interfered somehow. Bobby always listens to me. He wouldn't be in this predicament now if—"

"Are you blaming me for all of this?" It was her turn to be angry.

"I don't know. Maybe."

"That's just great, Nick." Her throbbing headache developed into a pounding one. "Between you and Bobby, I've had enough. I'm going upstairs to check on Michael."

She swept past him. At the top of the stairs, laughter came from the guest bedroom. Izzy's high-pitched squeal rang out.

Carrie understood how much Izzy loved her big brother. She didn't want anything or anyone ever coming between them.

She continued into Michael's room. Awake, he smiled at her approach. She gathered him into her arms and planted a kiss on his forehead.

"Your brother is here. He'll be so happy to see you."

Holding her son released a rush of emotions. Carmela would give birth to her grandchild. She didn't doubt what type of father Bobby would be. Like her, it was doubtful he'd repeat his history of abuse with his own child.

She wasn't so sure about Carmela's parenting skills. She brought so much dissension into their home. Bobby became angry at her for not accepting the woman he loved. She and Nick were at odds. They couldn't continue this way. The baby would become a part of this family. No matter what their opinion of Carmela was, Bobby seemed happy, and she needed to live up to her role as his mother.

Carrie left Michael's room. She started downstairs, but turned back. The best thing to do now would be to follow the old saying, keep your friends close and your enemies closer. She tapped on the guest room door, and Izzy appeared.

"It's Mommy and Michael" she called out, swinging it wide open.

Carmela and Bobby lounged on the bed. His arm draped over Carmela's shoulder.

Hesitant, Carrie said, "May we come in and join the fun?"

Bobby's face lit up. "Sure thing."

Carrie took a breath and stepped through the doorway

The only two people who were unaware of the tension at dinner that evening were Izzy and Michael. Carrie scanned the faces seated around her while they all made polite conversation.

"So, do you know what you're having?" Carrie asked.

Bobby grinned. "No, Mom. We decided to let it be a surprise. We don't care as long as the baby is healthy."

"Can I come and see the baby?" Izzy piped in.

"Sure, Bug." Bobby caught Carrie's eye. "We would love for all of you to come after the baby's born. Isn't that right Carmela?"

Carmela set her fork down and wiped her mouth. "Well, not at first. I think it's best to wait until I establish a routine."

Bobby frowned. "I don't see why they can't all fly in for the birth."

Carmela's nostrils flared. "That's ridiculous. I don't want a circus around me while giving birth?"

Carrie studied Carmela's face. Her temper was showing. One minute she was cool and the next hot. "I don't think Bobby meant we would attend the birth, but we'd wait at the hospital. We wouldn't want to intrude like that."

"That's exactly what I meant," Bobby said. "You're the grandparents. You should be there."

"What about your family, Carmela?" Carrie asked. "Do they live close by?"

Carmela hesitated. "My parents…are gone. The rest of my relatives are in Colombia."

She regretted asking. "I'm so sorry, Carmela. I didn't realize you're all alone."

"I don't consider myself alone." Her eyes searched Bobby's. "I have Bobby."

His face softened. He reached for her hand. "Of course, you do."

Carrie focused on Nick sitting at the head of the table. He hadn't contributed anything to their conversation. "What do you think?"

Nick cleared his throat. "I think we should end this whole discussion for now. It's a little premature."

"I agree," Carmela said.

Except for Izzy and Michael's chatter, they finished their meal in silence. Bobby and Carmela retreated upstairs. The children watched television and played with their toys in the great room while Nick and Carrie cleared the dishes. She loaded the last of them into the dishwasher.

Nick's sullen face and quiet demeanor driving her crazy, she said, "Look, I don't want to argue. I waited a long time for you to come home. These past months have been agonizing for me."

His brow knit. "This whole situation has us both on edge."

She studied his eyes. "Is there something you're not telling me?"

"Like what?"

"I don't know, Nick. Somethings off with you. I can tell."

"I find out Marco almost raped my wife, and Bobby's girlfriend is not only pregnant, but she may have drugged the wine on her last visit. I think I need time to digest all of this."

"I know all those things are overwhelming, but we can't let it divide us."

Nick sighed. "You're right." He gathered her in his arms. His hand traveled up her spine and moved across the back of her neck.

She lifted her chin, and he kissed her lips. Her arms came up and she pressed her body into his, making the kiss go deeper.

"Ugh!"

Startled, they both turned. Izzy, stationed in the doorway, wagged her finger at them. "That's disgusting."

Laughing, they broke their embrace. Carrie was relieved the tension between them had eased.

Nick pointed at Izzy. "Come over here you." She ran to him, and he scooped her up. "What would we do without you, Izzy?"

She hugged Nick's neck. "You don't have to worry, Daddy. I will be here forever and ever with you and Mommy."

Carrie smiled while he held their daughter. The special bond between a parent and child was nothing short of a miracle to her. Sometimes, she still ached inside when she pictured her mother. From the very beginning, her mother had severed the bond between them. She'd never understood why she hated her so much. Why couldn't she have loved her the way Carrie loved her own children?

She recalled how Carmela's anger had shown itself at the dinner table. A temper like that could be a dangerous thing. Bobby needed to pay attention to those signs. If not for his sake, then for the sake of his child.

If only she could see what the future might hold for her son. A shiver ran across her flesh. She focused on Nick and Izzy. The smiles warming their faces settled her anxiety. At least, for now.

# CHAPTER 31
## Bobby

B obby recalled the past weekend which had turned out just short of disastrous. His mother had not welcomed the news of Carmela's pregnancy, and Nick's reaction had been less than enthusiastic. Neither one of them would explain why Marco left leaving Bobby with an uneasy feeling. It didn't add up. Marco was like family.

To make matters worse, they hadn't spoken much on the plane ride home after which Carmela had agreed to accompany him to his apartment.

While she lay sleeping, he decided to order in. He dialed the number for Shun Lee West, one of their favorite Chinese restaurants. They'd have a relaxing dinner and try to put the events of their trip behind them.

Forty minutes later, he unpacked the food. Steamed pork dumplings, crispy orange flavored beef, and braised silky bean curd with mushrooms hung in the air. He set out plates, and two sets of chopsticks.

"Something smells good." Carmela drifted to the table clothed in one of Bobby's pale blue dress shirts, the hem of which, because of her protruding belly, ended just below the top of her thighs.

"Hope you're hungry," Bobby said.

"Famished." She slid onto a chair and filled her plate.

He poured water into two tumblers, then prepared food for himself. They ate in silence for a few moments before he spoke.

"Listen, I know this past weekend didn't go as planned but I want to tell you that it doesn't change how I feel about you or the baby."

Carmela's brow furrowed. She sipped some water and continued eating.

"Are you upset with me?" he asked.

She glanced up from her plate. "Of course not. But understand something. I don't care what your mother and Nick think about me or the pregnancy. I refuse to live my life trying to earn the approval of others." She pointed her chopsticks at him. "Including you."

Stunned, Bobby stopped eating. He frowned while she plucked a dumpling from her plate and inserted it into her mouth. Her expression remained neutral as if the statements she had made were just fine.

"I can't believe you just said that."

"Oh, there you go again. Spoiling a perfectly good evening."

Unease stirred in his stomach. He swallowed the bitter taste forming in his mouth. Her words wounded him to his core. All the doubts about her he had pushed away returned.

He rose from the table. "It's time for you to leave Carmela."

She set her chopsticks down. "Are you throwing me out?"

"No, but after what you said, I think you should go. Since you fired Diego, I'll escort you to the airport, but I'm not coming to Napa with you."

"Why are you so upset? Would you rather I lie about my feelings? I am only being honest."

Bobby took a breath, heat rushed through his body. "I get that you don't need to earn anyone's approval, even mine. But I do expect you to respect me and my family."

Carmela got to her feet. "When have I disrespected you?"

"Your attitude alone is disrespectful. If you care for me, then I think you would at least try to work things out where they're concerned. My mother did come around."

She crossed her arms. "And how am I supposed to do that?"

"By being a little understanding. Finding out about the pregnancy shocked them. They need time to process."

Carmela dropped her arms and grew silent. Her eyes settled on his. She gave him a mournful look. "These hormones are making me crazy at times." She hurried to the other side of the table. "I really am sorry for what I said. I'm willing to give them another chance if it makes you happy."

He doubted her sincerity, but her stubbornness had attracted him in the beginning. Her little fits of anger, although not endearing, he attributed to her spoiled upbringing. Should he believe hormones were causing her to say those things?

Bobby stared into the depths of her dark eyes. No matter his feelings this minute, he'd not abandon her or his child. He was determined to make the three of them a family.

He pulled her into his arms, and she rested her head against his shoulder.

"*Mi tesoro,*" she whispered, her warm breath touching his neck. "I want us to be happy. Let's not argue anymore."

He drew his hand through her long hair. "Okay, we'll leave it alone for now. Sit down, the foods getting cold.

They finished the meal then Carmela went to take a shower. While she was gone, he picked up his cell and called Nick.

"Bobby, everything good with you?"

"Yeah, fine. I wanted to give you a call to get your input about the weekend considering things didn't go so well."

"How did you expect them to go after you hit us with news like that?"

Bobby wandered to the windows overlooking the park. "I don't know, I guess—"

"You and I should talk about all of this," Nick cut in.

The tone in Nick's voice made the knot in Bobby's stomach return. "What do you mean?"

"There are some things concerning Carmela you're not fully aware of."

"Like what?"

"We need to meet in person."

"Look, Nick, just say what you have to say. I already know how you and Mom feel about her, but I'm telling you right now it won't change my standing by her. I love her, and we have a baby coming. If you want to be a part of our child's life, you have to accept how I feel."

A heavy sigh came through the line. "Becoming a father is a big deal in itself, Bobby. Establishing a family is another thing. You can still be a father without staying with Carmela."

Bobby's pulse throbbed. "You don't get it either. Carmela, me, and the baby *are* going to be together. As a matter of fact, she's willing to give you and Mom another chance."

"For Christ's sake, Bobby. Can't you see how fast all of this is moving? Baby or no baby, you need to take a step back and clear your head. You've barely turned twenty-four years old, and this woman is changing your whole life."

Bobby swept a hand through his hair and paced. "You know I have the utmost respect for you, Nick, but you're wrong about her."

"Who are you talking to?"

Bobby spun around. Carmela came into the living room dressed in a bathrobe, her long hair wrapped in a towel.

"Um, Nick," he said.

She rushed over to him. "Oh, give me the phone. Let me say hello."

"I don't think—"

She grabbed it from his hand. "Hello, Nick. I was telling Bobby earlier that I would love the chance to see all of you again. I feel we might have gotten off on the wrong foot as they say."

She grinned at Bobby. "I know you and your lovely wife were a bit shocked. To make it up to you, I'd like to invite you to my home in Napa." Carmela caught Bobby's eye and winked. "Oh, I see. Well, maybe Bobby can convince you. Hopefully, you'll change your mind and come." She handed the phone to Bobby.

"Yes, I know," Bobby said. "Would you at least think about her invitation? Me, too. I'll talk to you soon." He ended the call and placed his cell on the end table.

"There," Carmela grinned at him. "I have extended myself, now it's up to them."

"Thank you. I appreciate your inviting them. Nick said he'd run it by my Mom."

She took both his hands, pulling him into the bedroom, a smile on her face. "I leave for Napa in the morning. Let's not waste the rest of the night."

Hours later, he lay awake while she slept. He tried to dissect his conversation with Nick. Of course, he was upset at him becoming a father so early in his life but could there be more to it? Asking him to meet in person and saying there were things about Carmela he wasn't aware of, left him confused and curious.

He leaned on his elbow and rested his eyes on Carmela's face. Whatever Nick had to say, it still wouldn't change his mind about the woman sleeping beside him.

# CHAPTER 32
# Nick

Early Tuesday morning, Nick punched the gas pedal and sped through the open gates of the property. The hour-long drive to Dalton's ranch was torture. The shock of seeing Carmela dug up memories he'd much rather forget.

He gripped the wheel while images of the day he killed Ricardo surged up. Witnessing her father's death had turned a sweet, beautiful woman, into a demon out for revenge and he was to blame for all of it.

The question always loomed over him as to whether he should have shot Carmela. Her screams had echoed through the winery, forcing him to stop and turn around. He raised his gun. But for the first time, his hand shook, his adrenaline rush failed him and he couldn't bring himself to pull the trigger. Instead, he had walked away knowing it put his family in jeopardy.

With Bobby in her clutches and possessing damaging information concerning Travis Montgomery, Carmela held all the cards. Caution was the operative word that popped into his mind. If he made any rash decisions, he could lose Carrie and Bobby.

He'd guarded the identity of Travis these past years. If Carrie found out the truth, she'd never forgive him for keeping it secret. Their vow of honesty to each other would break in two.

Nick arrived as Dalton ambled up the path from the barn to the house. "It's good to see you, my friend." He slapped Nick on the back.

"You, too. Feeling better?"

"Much better, thanks. Almost all healed up." He smoothed his mustache and grinned. "You sounded urgent on the phone. Is everything okay?"

"I'm afraid not."

"Sounds serious. Come inside." He poured drinks, and they settled into the leather chairs by the fire in the living room. He studied Nick's face a moment. "You look awful. What the hell is going on?"

Nick sipped his whiskey. He looked at Dalton and took a breath. "You won't believe what I'm about to tell you."

"Try me."

"Bobby showed up with Carmela this past weekend."

Dalton rocked back in his chair. "Bobby brought Carmela to the house? When did that start?"

"Apparently while we were away. She was full of surprises." He proceeded to fill him in with regard to the events of the weekend, leaving the part about Travis for last.

Dalton swallowed the rest of his drink and got up. "After that story, I need another. How about you?"

"Sure, hit me again." He handed him his glass.

He poured two more drinks and sat down. "Listen, I know all about the guilt you've been carrying with regard to Carmela.

But the truth is, had it been me that day in the winery, I might have made a different choice."

Nick stared into the fire. "For the first time in my life, I'm not sure what to do."

"I don't envy you either. With a baby added to the mix, things are pretty twisted." Dalton set his glass on the end table. "Look, from what you've told me, Bobby is all wrapped up in Carmela. You need to be careful about your next move. She could easily turn him against you and Carrie."

A sudden chill swept through Nick's body. "Bobby's like a son to me. It took a long time for him to trust me and I don't want to lose that. And Carrie loves him almost more than life itself. She still beats herself up over all the years she lost with him."

The lines on Dalton's face creased. "I know full well how she feels about him. Then there's the other matter about this Travis, fella."

Nick rose and paced. "You can imagine how I felt that day in the woods. When the piece of scum revealed he was her father, putting two bullets in his head was an easy kill for me." He looked at Dalton and stopped.

"I might know how Carmela got her information regarding Travis," Nick said. "Carrie told me someone broke into May's house. Scared the hell out of her, asking questions about a guy from Carrie's mother's past."

"She get hurt?" Dalton asked.

"No. But he wore a mask so she couldn't describe him. She never called the police. I have a feeling Carmela is involved. As a matter of fact, we're supposed to visit May during Izzy's break. I'll know more when I see her."

"Look, Nick, I can only tell you what I think you should do at this point. But you make the final decision."

Nick's eyes locked on Dalton's. "Go on."

"For now, let nature take its course. We both know you're not going to kill Carmela while she's pregnant. For Bobby's sake, play along until the baby is born."

"But these threats of hers…"

"That's just what they are, threats. I doubt she'll do anything right now. And if there is an outside chance she does…we'll handle it."

"So, you don't think I should warn Bobby? Tell him about Ricardo and the whole mess."

"From what you're telling me, I'm not sure it would do any good. Bobby's in love with her. He's got blinders on, and you don't know what her intentions are. She might try to keep the child from him."

"Exactly what I'm afraid of," Nick said. He grabbed his glass and gulped the rest of his whiskey. "By the way, she had the nerve to invite us to Napa. Can you imagine? The place where I killed Ricardo is not somewhere I look forward to returning to. And I know it's all a front for Bobby."

Dalton rubbed the grey stubble beneath his chin. "I think you should go."

"What? Are you crazy?"

"Maybe, but play along. Make her feel comfortable. Besides, Carrie will get curious if you refuse."

His skull about to explode, Nick pressed his fingers to his temples. There were so many variables to consider. If he didn't go, she might well spill her information concerning Travis. If he did, the same thing could happen.

"I don't know, Dalton. My major concern right now is Carrie and Bobby. If it comes out about Travis, it will hurt both of them."

"I feel for you, Nick." He lifted his glass and sipped.

Nick dropped onto the chair and studied the fire. He bent his head and clasped his hands together. "There is one other thing I haven't told you."

"What's that?"

"Marco tried to rape Carrie."

Dalton slammed his glass on the table. His face flushed. He gripped the arms of his chair. "That son of a bitch! Is Carrie alright?"

"Fortunately, Chino saved the day, giving Carrie the upper hand. She forced him to leave. He took the spare car."

"That is so unlike Marco. What the hell got into him?"

Nick shrugged. "I have no idea."

"I'll put some of my men on it. See if they can track him down."

"I'd appreciate that. When he's found, I'll settle things."

"If you need a man at home, I can spare one of mine."

"Not necessary as long as I'm there and Chino has proved his worth. If I need someone, I'll let you know."

"On another note, there's been no word from the government. I've convinced them I'm still healing." Dalton winked.

"Good, that's one less worry for now," Nick said. "When you're a hundred percent, we'll talk about my plan. I have enough to deal with right now."

An hour later, Nick headed back to the Black Hills. Talking to Dalton hadn't eased his angst concerning Carmela. Being around her was like walking through a minefield. One false step and she'd tell Carrie and maybe even Bobby, everything.

Dalton's approach might be the best course of action for now. Play along, go to Napa, and hope the secret she kept didn't destroy his family.

# CHAPTER 33
## Carmela

Dawn broke over the horizon as Carmela, dressed in an oversized plaid shirt and stretch pants, grabbed her straw hat, then climbed aboard the Yamaha Viking Utility Vehicle. Her new bodyguard, Emilio Campos, sat behind the wheel. Not as handsome as Diego, he was tall, with a solid build and a plain face. He came highly recommended by Miguel Medina and boasted excellent credentials.

Spring proved to be a busy time at the winery. They drove out to the vineyard to ensure the soil her workers applied to protect the vines during winter was removed. Riding up and down the rows, she supervised the planting of new ones where necessary and the weeding and aerating of the current ones. The scent of the rich, dark earth comforted her. Row upon row of vines made ready for the growing season sent her heart soaring with pride.

Finished in the vineyard, they drove to the vault. Fermentation and oak aging over the winter completed, it was now time to blend, filter and bottle. She assembled her team of tasters. Satisfied the blends were to her high standards, she met with her Winemaker, Lab Manager, and Cellar Master for the next few hours. Her final meeting with her Operations Managers insured the oak barrels and tanks were cleaned and prepped for the fall harvest.

By early afternoon, exhausted, she showered and dressed in a pale, linen shift and sandals. With Emilio by her side, she drove the Yamaha to her guest quarters situated two acres away from the main house on a secluded section of the property. A mini version of the main house, it boasted five bedrooms, six bathrooms, a fully equipped kitchen, and a dining room. Not often used, she chose this place for Marco in lieu of the carriage house which lay much closer to the main house and was occupied by Emilio.

Her delay in meeting with Marco had been deliberate. Hidden away in her guest house with orders not to come out, he'd no idea of her return to Napa over a week ago. They stopped in front and she climbed up the stone steps.

Carmela turned to Emilio stationed at the bottom. "I won't be long."

She tapped on the door and called out, "Marco, open up, it's Carmela."

She heard a shuffle of feet and it opened. Marco peered out. Ashen faced, unshaven, his eyes bloodshot, this was not the Marco she knew.

She pushed past him. "Close the door." She surveyed the living room. Clothes were strewn about. Several empty beer bottles lined the coffee table.

"What's going on, Marco? Why did you leave South Dakota?"

His eyes fixed on her stomach. His mouth gaped open. "You're, you're…." he stammered.

"Yes, pregnant. I'm not here to talk about me. Why did you leave Nick's home?" She settled into one of the chairs and waited.

His shoulders slumped. He eased onto the sofa across from her. "I'm not sure what I was thinking. I was upset with your mistreatment. You refused to come up to my room in Miami."

"You're wasting time. Tell me something I don't already know," Carmela scoffed. Her patience running thin, she rose and paced. "Go on, speak!" she snapped.

He hung his head and stared at the floor. "I attacked Carrie."

She stopped pacing. "You did what?"

He swiped his hand through his hair. "You have to understand. I was lonely, and she came on to me. I tried to ignore her but she wouldn't stop. Now, Nick will kill me if he finds out where I am." He broke into tears, burying his face in the crook of his arm.

She stared at him. Could what he said be true? Carrie had led him on? Nick had been gone for quite some time. She paced again. "I want details, Marco. Quit bawling and tell me all of it."

He wiped his face across his sleeve. "She's been a flirt from the very beginning and even more so after Nick left. I couldn't help it after she invited me to her bedroom. We started kissing, but she pushed me away. By then my hunger for her was too great, and I forced myself on her."

Carmela gasped. "You raped her?"

"Almost." He stood and rolled up his left sleeve exposing a deep gash on his forearm, the surrounding skin swollen and bruised. "Chino attacked me. Carrie grabbed my gun. She made me leave the house."

She pursed her lips. "I'm not sure I believe you. Carrie doesn't strike me as the type of woman who would cheat on Nick. You have no reason to lie to me, do you?"

Marco averted his eyes. He rolled his sleeve down. "No, of course not."

"Well, you're right about one thing," she said. "Nick will kill you if he finds you. It's only a matter of time before he does. I can only protect you for so long. You need to leave the country."

"Leave America?"

"It would be the wise choice." She stopped herself from smiling. He had done her a favor by attacking Carrie.

Marco rubbed his forehead. He pointed at her stomach. "You promised me life in America with you, but I realize you lied to me. This thing with Carrie would never have happened if you kept your promises."

"Whether you believe me or not Marco, this pregnancy wasn't planned." She spied the mistrust in his eyes. "You can still have a life here, just not now. The first priority is your safety."

"How do I know I can trust you?"

She wagged her finger at him. "If I didn't care about you, Marco, you wouldn't be here in my guest house. Give me time to figure this out. I will make all the arrangements for your departure. Make sure you have more than enough money and a place to stay. When the situation calms down, I will send for you."

His expression wary, he said, "Remember, Carmela, I know things too."

"You're in no position to threaten me, Marco. Do as I ask and you will be rewarded in the end." She walked to the door. "Stay inside. Armando will see to your needs."

Satisfied she had dealt with him, they drove to the main house. She didn't believe half of Marco's story. He tried to rape

Carrie, and she resisted. But the truth didn't really matter, because between her plans for him and Nick the man was as good as dead.

Scheduled to meet with Miguel Medina, she retreated to the screened-in patio. Armando set the table for a late lunch.

Carmela sank into the cushions of the chaise overlooking the rear garden. She reflected on her visit to South Dakota. Seeing Nick again had stirred up so many memories, but it also confirmed the fact that she no longer loved him. How could she ever love the man who killed her father? He had no idea how hard she fought to control her anger throughout the entire weekend, letting it slip only once at the dinner table.

Carmela hoped he'd accept her invitation. Pulling them closer would only make them hurt that much more while she ripped Nick's family apart.

She rested her hands on her stomach. This little one would be hers and hers alone. No D'Angelo would intrude into its life. She'd make sure Bobby saw the baby once before she left. The memory of his child stamped in his mind forever. Her plans to disappear with the child were already set.

Technology allowed her to oversee her businesses from anywhere in the world. The drug shipments were running smoothly, and the news of the assassination of several prominent heads of cartels made her life a lot easier for now. Until new drug lords took their place, it meant she had less competition.

Armando stepped onto the patio. "*Señorita, Señor* Medina is here."

Carmela rose. "Show him in."

He returned a few minutes later with Miguel.

"You may serve lunch if it is ready, Armando."

He gave a slight bow and retreated.

She held out her hands. "Miguel, it is good to see you."

Dressed casually in dark jeans and a grey pullover shirt, he took her hands in his and kissed her cheek.

She pointed to a chair. "Please sit."

He settled across from her. "How have you been Carmela?"

"Well. And you?"

His eyes stayed fixed upon hers. "No complaints."

Armando appeared. He set two porcelain bowls containing *Ajiaco* in front of them. The hearty chicken soup made with guascas, potatoes, and corn on the cob had been one of her father's favorite Columbian dishes. In the center of the table, he placed a plate of crusty bread, slices of avocado and sour cream. Lastly, he had prepared *empanadas* with a corn masa crust, each one filled with beef, and spices.

Carmela smiled and lifted her spoon. "Thank you, Armando."

"This looks wonderful," Miguel said. "A taste of home."

She ate her soup and recalled the afternoon she sat with her father discussing his desire for her to marry Nick. Her smile faded and her eyes watered, blurring Miguel's image. Dabbing at her lids with a napkin, she resisted bursting into tears.

Miguel dipped a piece of bread into the soup. He glanced up. "Is something wrong?"

She waved her hand. "No, no. My father loved this dish. I remember eating it with him."

His face softened. "I'm sure it's still hard. The two of you were close."

They finished their *Ajiaco* in silence. Armando cleared their empty bowls away, and set down plates for the e*mpanadas*.

Carmela took one, and bit into it. The rich spices cloaked her tongue. She sighed. "A little taste of heaven in my mouth."

Miguel swallowed the last bit of his e*mpanada.* "I agree. *Delicioso*."

Armando returned with a bottle of Tequila and a shot glass. He set both in front of Miguel.

"Thank you, Armando," Carmela said. "Everything tasted wonderful. That will be all for now."

Miguel poured the tequila and settled back into his chair. "How is Emilio Campos working out?"

"I think he is adjusting well."

"So, did you ask me just for lunch, or is there something else on your mind?"

"I visited Nick's family in South Dakota recently."

Miguel's brow creased. He narrowed his eyes. "That was a dangerous thing to do Carmela."

"Yes, I know. But there was little Nick could do once he saw my condition."

He swallowed the tequila. "You're playing with fire. Nick may not do something now, but after the baby is born, who knows what his plans are."

"I've doubled the number of men stationed around the property. I have plans of my own, Miguel." She tossed her napkin aside. "When the time is right, I will set them in motion."

He poured another shot of tequila and downed it. "So, since you have this all figured out, why am I here today?" His voice dripped with sarcasm.

Carmela chose to ignore it. She'd been receiving threatening calls and text messages from Diego. No matter how she once thought of him, elimination became the only answer. "

I need you to locate Diego Silva. He has been threatening me."

"Yes, go on."

"Well, he's more than a little disgruntled since I fired him."

"And when I find him?"

"Do whatever you have to do to make him stop."

"Does that include eliminating him?"

Diego's face flashed across her mind causing her to hesitate. But his anger could ruin everything if he chose to expose her to Nick. "Like I said, whatever you have to do, Miguel."

He studied her for a moment. "What about Marco Valletta?"

"What about him?" His question caught her off guard.

"The last time we met you mentioned Marco might be a threat."

"Not anymore. I'm taking care of Marco myself."

He set his glass aside, a confused look on his face. "What do you mean? That's madness."

Heat rose in her cheeks. "It is fine, Miguel. It seems he is on the outs with Nick. Right now, he trusts me. He is under my protection."

"Your protection? He may trust you but how do you know you can trust him?" He shook his head. "This is unbelievable. I thought you were afraid of him."

"Not anymore." She took a sip of water. Her foot tapped the tile underneath the table. Had he forgotten his place?

"I warned you the last time I was here. You can't play with a man's emotions, Carmela. First, Diego and now, Marco."

She pushed her chair back and glared at him. "I don't need a lecture. Just do what I ask, Miguel." She rose.

His face flushed, and he got to his feet. "I think you know I will always do what you ask."

He inched closer, his commanding presence overwhelmed her. Her throat pulsed. A tingling sensation rushed through her body.

He cupped her chin in his hand. "I would do anything for you."

Carmela's knees turned to water. Her heartbeat quickened. "Miguel, I…."

He kissed her lips. She opened her mouth and made the kiss go deeper. But the image of Bobby's face swam in her mind, and she drew back. She saw the hurt in his eyes and stepped away.

"Miguel, you know this is not right."

His shoulders slumped, and he let out a breath. "I've wanted to do that for the longest time. Admit it, Carmela. You've sent certain signals."

"Yes, but since you are my *sicario,* it would be wrong to pursue them."

He shook his head. "I think you may have developed strong feelings for the father of your child, which you are choosing to ignore."

She refused to give credence to his words. "No, I am not in love with him. I have no time for such foolishness."

Miguel chuckled. "Okay, if you insist." He walked to the patio door. "I will find out where Diego Silva is. You decide what you want me to do with him."

Before she could answer, he was gone.

Carmela eased into her chair. She ran her fingers over her lips. So many times she had envisioned herself making love with Miguel. To think a simple kiss, caused her to question her feelings for Bobby.

She tried to regain her composure as she rose and wandered to the patio door. A clap of thunder sounded in the distance. Dark clouds swirled above a steel grey sky. Within minutes, it released a torrent of blinding rain. Uneasiness wrapped around her. This baby needed to come soon. She'd finish her plans, take her child, and leave all this madness behind her, including Bobby D'Angelo

# CHAPTER 34

## Carrie

Carrie chose a comfortable navy pantsuit and a pair of flats for the flight to Napa. She folded several pairs of jeans, placing them in her suitcase. Earlier in the day, she had gotten Izzy and Michael ready for the trip.

Apprehensive, she tried to convince herself the visit would go well. She wanted nothing more than for Bobby to be happy, and if going to Napa could help, she'd do it.

She finished packing as Nick entered the bedroom. His quiet demeanor these past two weeks disturbed her. Not sure what was at the root of it, she held back questioning him. Part of it likely due to Marco's attack, but her intuition told her it was more.

"All packed?" she asked.

He placed his toiletry kit into his suitcase. "Pretty much."

Carrie sat on the edge of the bed. "I appreciate your going along with this trip. Bobby is so excited we're coming. He's finishing up some business in New York and will meet us there tomorrow."

Nick zipped up his suitcase and sat beside her. He draped his arm around her. "Listen, whatever happens, while we're in

Napa, good or bad, remember how important our family is to me. You, Izzy, Michael, and Bobby are my world."

His words startled her. "Of course." She rested her head on his shoulder. "You're a wonderful husband and a great father. And I've always appreciated how you love Bobby as if he were your own."

She raised her head. "You haven't been yourself, lately. I know you blame yourself for Marco's attack, but I don't want you to feel responsible, because you're not. I'm past it. I just want to forget and move on."

"Facts are facts, Carrie. If I'd been home, it never would have happened."

She pressed her hand to his cheek. "Please, for my sake, let's put it behind us."

He gave a half-smile. "I can't promise, but I'll try."

She got to her feet. He rose and cradled her in his arms. His lips brushed the top of her head. She melted into the warmth of his body.

"Okay," she murmured. "Before we're sidetracked, let's round up the kids and get to the airport."

Nick laughed. "You got that right."


They arrived at Carmela's late Wednesday afternoon. The limo stopped in front of the mansion. Izzy hopped out. Her eyes grew large.

"Mommy, look how pretty the house is."

"Yes, it is." Carrie hated to admit how taken she herself was with the beauty of the place. The views of the vineyards and surrounding countryside below took her breath away. The driver unloaded their luggage while she held onto Michael who tried to wiggle himself free.

The front door opened, and a man dressed in butler's attire appeared. He hurried down the steps and performed a slight bow.

"Welcome. My name is Armando. If you will please follow me, the *Señorita* is waiting for you. I will have your things taken to your rooms."

Carrie thought it odd Armando nodded at Nick but didn't speak directly to him. They entered the foyer. She almost let out a gasp. The detail in the marble tile and woodwork amazed her.

Carmela sailed through the massive archway leading to the living room on their left. She wore a plain linen shift, her growing belly prominent underneath.

"It is so good to see you all again. Welcome to my home."

Izzy ran straight to her. "This house is so big," she squealed. "I bet it's the biggest house in the world."

Carmela laughed. "I'm so glad you like it, Izzy." She caught Carrie's eye. "Thank you for coming. I believe your visit here will serve to bring us all closer together."

"It's nice of you to have invited us," Carrie said.

Carmela turned toward Nick. "My guest house is for guests, and since we're going to be family, I thought it best if you stay here in the main house with me. Tomorrow, I will take you and Carrie down to see the vault in the winery. We are in the process of blending and bottling our wines. I believe you'll find it interesting."

"I'm sure," Nick said through tight lips.

Carmela took Izzy by the hand and stretched out her other one to Michael. "Come, let's go into the dining room. Armando has prepared some special snacks for you. After, we will walk down to the stables. You can meet my horses."

Izzy's face lit up. "You have horses?"

"Yes, my sweet girl," she said. "You can feed them some treats too."

Carrie hung back as Carmela disappeared with the children. She grabbed Nick's arm.

"You could be a little more cordial. If not for me, then for Bobby's sake."

Nick tugged his arm away. "Don't tell me how to act."

Stung by his response, she glared at him. "We are her guests, after all."

"I'm well aware of that." He moved ahead of her into the dining room.


An hour later, Carmela led them through the garden to the paddock. Carrie, still disturbed by Nick's sullen mood, tried to lighten her spirits by taking in the exquisite botanicals. Along the way, they passed white impatiens bordered by white and green caladiums, surrounded by Japanese Maples.

She inhaled the sweet smell of a variety of roses in reds, yellows, and pinks adorning another section. They crossed a floral bridge decorated on either side with petunias, mandevilla, and purple angelonia. Several Koi Ponds held water lilies. She found the gardens nothing short of astonishing.

They arrived at the stables, and Carmela turned to Nick and Carrie. "I will have Mateo bring the horses outside to the paddock and meet you there."

Nick took the children by the hand. He hoisted them up onto the top rail of the fence. Carrie stationed herself below Michael while he stood by Izzy.

A few moments later, Carrie spotted a stocky, dark-skinned man dressed in jeans and a cowboy hat, leading two horses. He opened the gate at the far end and led the first horse in. He removed the lead, stepped away, and closed the gate behind him.

Carmela approached with a feedbag in her hand. She signaled to him. "Mateo let Diablo into the paddock."

"Are you sure, *Señorita*?"

"Yes, let him loose."

Carmela greeted them by the railing. "The one on the left with the lighter coat and white crest is Allegra. The one with the darker coat is Diablo."

"They're beautiful," Carrie said.

Carmela made a clucking noise. The horses whinnied and trotted over to the fence. She dipped her hand into the feedbag and dug out two carrots. She handed a carrot to Izzy and one to Michael. Diablo bobbed his head at Izzy.

"Hold out the carrot, Izzy," Carmela said.

She shook her head. "What if he bites me?"

Carmela smiled. "As long as you're gentle with him, he will be gentle with you."

Izzy held the carrot toward Diablo, He whinnied and stomped his foot before chomping down on the carrot. He shuffled his powerful legs and stepped back.

"He doesn't seem that friendly," Nick said.

Carmela laughed. "Nonsense. He just needs to get used to new faces."

Over the next few minutes, the children delighted in feeding carrots to the horses. Izzy got up the courage to stroke Allegra's muzzle. She complained when it was time to return to the house.

"Can't we stay a little longer," she begged.

Nick lifted her down off the railing. "No, Izzy. It's been a long day."

Carrie grabbed Michael and held him in her arms. "You can see them, again. We'll be here for the next few days."

Carmela signaled to Mateo, and he prepared to take the horses back to the stables. She patted Izzy's cheek. "That's right. And if it is okay with your parents, maybe you can go for a little ride tomorrow."

Izzy clapped her hands and looked from Nick to Carrie. "Can I? Can I?"

"We'll see," Carrie said. She set Michael down. "For now, let's walk up to the house. We haven't even seen our rooms, yet."

Carmela smiled. "That's right. There is a special one for you and Michael. And, Armando has prepared something extraordinary for dinner."

Carmela walked ahead with the children. Izzy chatted away about the horses.

Carrie took Nick's hand. "Looks like you might be buying a horse one of these days."

Nick shrugged. "Maybe."

She stopped and let go of his hand. "What is going on with you? You've been in a mood all day."

"Nothing. I guess Bobby becoming a father so quick is not sitting well with me. He hardly knows her."

"Yes, those were my sentiments exactly."

"What do you mean?"

"After today, my opinion of Carmela is beginning to change. She seems more genuine. I can see why Bobby is attracted to her."

"Well, I'm not convinced."

"Let's see what the rest of our visit brings. Maybe we'll both change our minds."

They walked to the house in silence. Carrie debated about the incident with the wine. This Carmela was nothing like the one who came to South Dakota. Could this be her way of making amends?

Either way, so far things were going well. The next few days might be the beginning of a new relationship. Only time would tell.

# CHAPTER 35

## Nick

Nick woke just before dawn. He dressed and slipped out of the bedroom. Downstairs, the house lay in darkness except for light illuminating the hallway from the rear of the house. He entered the patio and found Bobby sitting at the table, a coffee cup in his hand.

Nick dropped onto the chair opposite him. "When did you get in?"

"A couple of hours ago. What are you doing up so early?"

"Couldn't sleep. Any more coffee?"

Bobby motioned to a pot stationed on a server against the wall. "Help yourself."

Nick prepared a cup and returned to the table. They sipped in silence for a few moments. He debated how he should start the conversation. Carmela was dangerous. Her remarks about the vault were enough to convince him to try to caution Bobby.

"Having a good visit so far?" Bobby asked.

"Sure, for now."

Bobby cut his eyes at him. "What is that supposed to mean?"

"I've been meaning to talk to you about a few things concerning Carmela."

"Taking cues from my mother?"

"In all the time you've known me, Bobby, have I ever steered you wrong?"

"No. What is this all about?" He crossed his arms and stared at Nick.

"Look, you need to be careful. In the past, I've come across women like Carmela. She's a certain type."

A cynical smile twisted Bobby's lip. "Oh, I see. Now we're breaking it all down. You know her better than I do. Exactly what type of woman is she?"

Nick shifted in his chair. "Controlling, manipulative. She needs to have all the power in a relationship."

Bobby locked eyes with him. "And you know all this about her because…."

Nick's gut tightened. He was treading on shaky ground. If he came on too strong, Bobby would shut him out.

"Just from what I've observed."

"Yeah, that makes sense. You've been around her, what, two times and you came to those conclusions?" He pushed his cup away and rose. "I'm starting to regret your coming here. I thought you would at least give her a chance."

Nick stood up. "Bobby, I'm only asking you to be careful. Carmela may not be the woman you think she is."

"You've got nerve," Bobby sneered. "A man who kills people for a living passing judgment on her."

Nick drew back, Bobby's words stinging him to the core. This wasn't the Bobby he knew. Carmela's handiwork was evident. "Look, I've never made any excuses for what I do. I know who I am."

Bobby scanned his face. "As far as I'm concerned you can stay or leave. But one thing I'm sure of, you will respect the mother of my child for as long as you're here in her home."

"I thought I heard voices." Carmela breezed in. She hurried over to Bobby. "*Mi Tesoro*, when did you arrive?"

Bobby's eyes lit up. "Several hours ago. I didn't want to wake you."

She took both his hands in hers. "You look tired."

"A little."

"You go rest. I will be up later."

Bobby kissed her forehead. "Don't be too long." He glared at Nick and left.

Carmela turned to Nick. "I'm curious as to what the two of you were talking about."

Nick frowned and shrugged his shoulders. "I'll leave that to your imagination."

She crept closer, her body inches from his. "If you've told him what a bad girl I am, I suggest you prepare yourself for the worst."

"Don't threaten me Carmela, or I just might tell him the whole truth."

"Now, who's threatening whom, Nick?" She moved away from him, her hands clenched into fists at her sides. "You had better keep certain things to yourself, or I'll be forced to tell your poor, little trailer-park trash-wife about Travis Montgomery."

Nick looked into her eyes. No remorse or pity lay within them. Blood rushed to his head. He grabbed her by her shoulders and shook.

"Listen to me, you bitch," he said through clenched teeth. "If you dare say anything to Carrie about him, you'll regret it."

Carmela twisted free, stepping back. "Good. Then we understand each other." She spun around and stalked off.

The sun crept over the horizon flooding the patio with pale pink light. Nick tried to calm his inner storm. He poured another cup of coffee and slumped into a chair. A slender thread held all Carmela's and his secrets together. Any wrong move could unravel it causing untold hurt and misery for Carrie and Bobby.

Two more days and they would be out of here. He hoped that thread would hold.


Later in the afternoon, Bobby agreed to watch Izzy and Michael while Carmela led Nick and Carrie to the vault. Not wanting to raise Carrie's suspicion Nick went along with the tour.

"I've always wondered what the process for winemaking was like," Carrie said. Dressed in jeans and a t-shirt, she walked beside Carmela. Nick followed behind.

Carmela grinned. "I'm sure you'll find it interesting."

She opened the door to the vault, and they stepped inside. The hair on the back of Nick's neck stiffened. He broke out in a sweat. He viewed the long rows of oak barrels, remembering the day he killed Ricardo.

Carmela pointed to them. "Medium intensity wines are aged in these barrels for eighteen months. Heavier wines age for thirty months."

"Wow, that's interesting, isn't it, Nick?" Carrie said

"Yes." He walked behind them, his stomach twisting into knots at the smell of the oak.

They moved to the processing room and she showed them the large stainless-steel vats. "Here is where fermentation takes place."

Carrie studied one of the gauges. "Looks complicated."

"Somewhat," Carmela said. "What do you think of all this Nick?"

Nick's eyes remained glued on the cement floor to the very spot where he had shot Ricardo. His mind flashed to Ricardo's face. He remembered the words that had passed between them and Carmela's screams. His heart lurched.

"Nick, what's wrong?" Carrie rushed over to him. "You've gone pale." She touched his forehead. "You're burning up."

He gave her a weak smile. "No, I'm fine."

"Are you sure?"

"Yes."

"We better move on," Carmela said. "You're not looking too well, Nick."

They stopped at the bottling machines. Wine flowed into bottles from spigots attached to a circular machine while numerous employees ensured the bottles were corked and labeled. They ended in the tasting room, where she offered them samples of her wine.

Nick's stomach settled, but his anger toward Carmela escalated. His visceral reaction to the vault came as no surprise. Ricardo wasn't just any kill. The two of them had formed a bond, almost like father and son. His insides boiled knowing she enjoyed his discomfort.

They spent the remainder of the day by the pasture where Izzy delighted in a ride on Allegra. Her arms encircled Bobby's waist. She laughed as they rode around the fenced in paddock. When they finished, Carrie took the children up to the house with Carmela.

Disturbed by their discussion earlier, Nick hung back with Bobby as he led Allegra to the stables. "Listen, Bobby, can we talk?"

"If it has anything to do with Carmela, then no." He lifted the saddle off Allegra and placed it on a stand. "I think you know how I feel." Clucking softly to the horse, he stroked its muzzle before securing him in his stall.

He looked at Nick. "I don't want to argue. I realize this whole thing between Carmela and me has moved pretty fast. Why can't you be more supportive?" He gave Nick a sorrowful look.

"Your mother and I want you to be happy."

"You both have a funny way of showing it."

He understood he needed to pull back. Bobby loved Carmela. No use trying to talk him out of it. "Forget what I said earlier. Just promise me you'll stay alert and listen to your gut. Your intuition could save your life one day."

"I know we still have to be careful," Bobby said. He gave Nick a sheepish grin. His cheeks flushed. "I'm sorry for calling you out. It was wrong."

Nick squeezed his shoulder. "Never mind. All is forgiven."

They walked to the doors of the stable. "Let's head up to the house," Bobby said. I'm sure Armando has cooked another one of his fabulous meals."

They made small talk, but distance had settled between the two and Nick recognized the cause. He looked up at the darkening sky and wished things could be as they were before Carmela came into their lives. Nick refused to continue to live under her threats.

After the baby was born, Carmela's time would be up. This whole situation needed to come to an end one way or the other.

# CHAPTER 36
## Bobby

Bobby stirred awake. Exhausted from completing a show in New York, then hopping a plane to Napa, he'd excused himself after dinner to retire early. He sat on the edge of the bed and stared at the clock. Two in the morning. Carmela lay sleeping beside him, her long hair trailed across the pillow and down the comforter.

His conversation with Nick earlier in the day hung heavy on his mind. He wanted Nick's approval more than anything. His mother tried, but Bobby wasn't sure if her efforts were genuine or made just to please him.

Nick had used the words, manipulative, and controlling to describe Carmela. But Nick didn't know her as well as he did. Yes, she could be difficult at times. He had never met her father but assumed since she was an only child, she probably got her way most of the time.

Thirsty, he rose and slipped on his jeans and t-shirt. He crept out of the bedroom and downstairs to the kitchen. Flicking on the light, he drew a bottle of water from the beverage drawer underneath the counter before grabbing a pear from a silver bowl filled with fruit.

He wandered to the patio. A full moon bathed the room in a pale glow. He stretched out on the chaise and twisted the cap off the water bottle. Taking two large swallows, he let the cool liquid slide past the back of his throat. About to take a bite of the pear, he stopped as the lights came on.

Carrie walked through the doorway. "Oh, I'm sorry. I can turn them off if you like."

Bobby blinked. "Yes, please. The moonlight is enough."

The room dimmed again. Dressed in blue silk pajamas, she padded over to him, the bottoms of her slippers tapping against the tile floor. "Can't sleep?"

"I think I went to bed a little too early."

"You've been busy. You needed your rest."

"And you?"

"Thirsty."

He pointed to the kitchen. "Help yourself. There's water in the small fridge underneath the counter."

Carrie returned a few moments later, a bottle of water in her hand. "Mind if I sit?"

Bobby shook his head.

She eased into a chair by the table. "Our trip is going well so far. The winery is fascinating, her gardens are amazing, and I understand she has several restaurants on top of all of this. I'm amazed at how she handles it all."

"Carmela is very good at managing things." Bobby bit into his pear. Its sweet juice spread across his tongue.

"Listen, Bobby. I know you and Nick had words earlier today."

"What did he tell you?"

"Just that he didn't mean to upset you."

Bobby was tired of the same old discussion. He continued to eat his pear.

Carrie took a few sips of her water and set the bottle down. "I've seen a different side of Carmela. I'm willing to admit I might have misjudged her."

"I appreciate that. Maybe you realize now why I care for her so much. I know everything came as a shock, but all I need is for you and Nick to support us. I'm determined to make me, Carmela, and the baby a family." He swung his legs over the side of the chaise and sat up.

Her eyes misted over. "You have to remember, I didn't have you with me for all those years. In the blink of an eye, you became a man and started a career."

Bobby chuckled. "Well, you couldn't keep me at home forever."

"Are you still being careful?"

"Always. You don't have to worry about me."

Carrie rose. "I'll try not to. But you'll see after the baby comes. Your life will change. Half of the time all you'll do is worry. Now, I'm going to go back to bed before Izzy and Michael wake up." She kissed his cheek. "Goodnight."

Bobby tossed the remainder of his pear into the trash and washed his hands. He climbed the stairs and crept into the bedroom. A breeze swept over him. The curtains by the open window fluttered. He crossed the room and peered out.

A sudden movement in the shadows on the stone path below caught his eye. He squinted and tried to focus. He forced the window further up and spotted a figure darting among the bushes in the garden. If it was one of Carmela's men, they would not have run. A shiver coursed through his body. He grabbed the sash and shut the window.

Bobby fumbled in the nightstand for his Glock, glad he kept one here and one in New York. He hurried out of the bedroom, ran downstairs, and out the rear patio door. His eyes searched the darkness. He aimed his weapon and crept down the path.

Moving further along to the garden, he called out, "There's no use hiding. You better come out now."

Silence greeted him. He continued past the rose bushes, over the flower bridge, and stopped on the other side. Whoever had been there was gone. Bobby headed to the carriage house where Emilio resided. He pounded his fist on the front door.

"Emilio, it's Bobby D'Angelo."

A light came on, and the door opened. A sleepy-eyed Emilio peered out. "*Sí?* What is going on?"

"Someone was creeping around outside the house. They ran into the garden. By the time I came out they were gone."

Fully awake now, Emilio beckoned him inside. "I will call security and have them search the property." He picked up his cell and barked orders into it. "If they are still here, the men will find whoever it is."

Two hours later, after Carmela's men had found nothing, Bobby returned to the house and placed his Glock in the nightstand drawer. He undressed and slipped into bed. Why would someone be creeping around the property this late? He'd be sure and talk to Carmela in the morning.

He slept little for the remainder of the night and finally fell asleep just before dawn. But it was a restless sleep. His dreams haunted by a dark figure in a garden.

# CHAPTER 37

## Carrie

Morning light streamed in the window. Carrie watched Nick toss his things into his suitcase. Thirty minutes before, he'd received a call from Dalton.

"Can't it wait?" she said. "We're leaving tomorrow, anyway."

He zipped the suitcase. "No. I wish it could. You and the kids can leave tomorrow as planned. There is no reason for you to fly out with me since I'm going directly to Dalton's."

Her skin prickled. "You won't leave until I get home, will you?"

"Don't worry, I meant what I said. I'm done with this job, and now I have to make sure it comes to an end."

"How?"

He took her hand. "That's for me and Dalton to work out. You need to trust me. Enjoy the rest of your stay, and I'll see you when you get back."

Nick kissed her. She clung to him, unsure of his words, the thought of him going away again unbearable. All the uncertainty of not knowing if he would return became real once again.

His arms fell away, and he wheeled his suitcase to the door. "Tell Carmela, I'm sorry I had to leave and kiss the kids for me. I shouldn't be more than a day or two." He brushed her cheek and left.

Carrie slumped onto the bed. Right now, she needed to believe the words he had said were true. There wasn't anything she could do except wait for his return.

With the children still asleep in adjoining rooms, she took the opportunity to shower and dress in peace. By the time she finished, she heard Michael calling for her. Izzy lay awake in the bed next to him with a book in her hands. She picked him up and sat on Izzy's bed.

"What are you reading?"

She giggled and held up the book. "Carmela gave it to me. It's a story about a princess."

"That was nice of her. You can finish it later. We need to eat breakfast."

"Mommy, do we have to go home tomorrow? I like it here."

"Yes, I'm afraid we do. I'm sure Chino is missing us."

She stuck her chin out. "Chino is fine at Uncle Dalton's house. I'm going to ask Daddy if we can stay longer."

Carrie sighed. "Daddy had to go see Uncle Dalton. He left this morning."

She put the book aside and sat up. "How come he didn't say goodbye?"

"You were still sleeping." She kissed Izzy's cheek. "That's from him."

She scrunched up her face and rubbed her cheek. "I don't want his kiss."

"Izzy! Why would you say such a thing?"

"Because he left me." Tears pooled in her eyes. "He said he wouldn't go away again."

Carrie's heart sank. "It's okay. He'll be home when we get there." She wiped Izzy's tears away.

Her green eyes still moist, Izzy asked, "You promise?"

"Yes. Don't worry." She watched her daughter's face brighten. "Let's get dressed and go downstairs. We can ask Carmela if she'll let you ride one of the horses again today."

A half hour later, Carrie, Bobby, and Carmela sat at the dining room table with the children.

"It's a shame Nick's departure was so sudden," Carmela said. She sipped her orange juice and glanced at Carrie.

"Yes. But he'll be home by the time we arrive tomorrow."

"You're sure of that?"

Carrie shifted uneasily in her chair. "Yes, he promised. My husband has always kept his promises."

"Is that so?" Carmela bit into a piece of toast. She looked at Bobby. "And what do you think?"

Bobby frowned at her. "Nick keeps his word. Why are you so interested anyway?"

A flush crept up Carmela's face. She waved her hand at him. "No reason. Just curious."

Izzy finished the last of her eggs before saying to Carmela. "Mommy said I could ride the horse again today."

Carrie caught her eye. "Izzy, I said we could ask."

Carmela chuckled. "Of course, you can. We will all go down to the stables after breakfast."

"Don't worry, Bug," Bobby said. "We'll ride him together."

They finished eating and went to the paddock where Mateo waited. Diablo, stood saddled and ready. Bobby took Izzy and led her to the horse.

"Carmela, are you sure she should be riding Diablo?" Carrie said. "He doesn't appear to be as gentle as Allegra."

Carmela smiled. "Don't worry, Diablo is fine."

Bobby climbed on, and Mateo lifted Izzy up and set her behind him. She waved at Carrie, then wrapped her little arms around Bobby's waist. Carrie held Michael while they watched them ride around the paddock.

Izzy's dark hair flew up with each gallop. Bobby's long, lean body relaxed in the saddle as if he were born to ride. Carrie's earlier tension eased, and she smiled.

Bobby brought the horse to a canter. Diablo whinnied and bucked, shaking his head from side to side, refusing to cooperate.

Carrie's heart raced. The horse was out of control.

Bobby pulled the reins to the right, forcing Diablo's head to pivot. He clucked and drew the reins back again. Diablo slowed and Bobby gained control again.

"Bobby, get Izzy off that horse!" Carrie shouted.

"It's okay, Mom. He settled down now." He continued around the paddock, Diablo following his commands.

Carmela came beside her. "Don't worry. Bobby knows what he's doing. He won't let anything happen to Izzy. He is so good with her."

Carrie's angst quieted, but she kept a close watch on them. "He loves his sister."

"As I understand it, she is his half-sister. Correct?"

"Yes, that's right."

"It's strange that your son hasn't told me much about his father."

Carrie's cheeks grew hot. The ease she felt evaporated. "Bobby never knew him. He died before he was born."

"You're sure about that?" Carmela asked. Her eyes held a wicked gleam.

"Of course, I'm sure. What are you getting at, Carmela?"

"Have you ever told him the truth about his father?" Carmela's face turned dark.

Carrie's stomach cinched. Her muscles curled as if clamped together in a vise. A sick feeling swelled up inside of her. She locked eyes with her.

"Whatever it is just spit it out." She held Michael tighter and glanced over her shoulder. Bobby trotted past with Izzy oblivious to the confrontation between them.

"I'm not so sure you want me to do that. I have done some digging, and found out a few things about you and your family. It must have been awful growing up in a trailer park."

Carrie stepped closer to her. Adrenaline surged through her body. She set Michael down but held onto his hand.

"It's no secret that I grew up in a trailer park. Is that all you've got?"

"Silly woman," she sneered. "When I dig, I dig deep. Have you told your son he's a child of incest, created between a father and daughter?"

Carrie's throat muscles tightened. "You don't know what you're talking about. True, his father was not a good man, and I've held that from Bobby because I love him."

Carmela clenched her fists. "Oh, how you tell lies with those devil eyes of yours! Travis Montgomery was your father. You lived all those years in sin with your father."

Carrie's breath caught. Blood rushed to her head. "You evil bitch! How could you say such a thing?"

"Because it's true. Travis Montgomery was your father and Bobby is his child."

She shook her fist inches from Carmela's face. "If you weren't pregnant, I would—"

"You'd what? Shoot me the way you shot Carlos in the throat."

Carrie drew back and almost lost her footing. How did Carmela know about Carlos? This whole thing was going sideways. "Who told you that?"

"That's an excellent question. Why don't you ask that husband of yours? The one who never breaks promises."

Carrie's stomach dropped. "What are you trying to say?"

"Nick may keep his promises, but he knows nothing about telling the truth."

"I'm not going to stand here and listen to this anymore." Carrie whirled around. She called out to Bobby. "Bring Izzy here. We're leaving."

A confused look on his face, he said, "Why? What's wrong?"

"Just do it, Bobby." A burning sensation rose up in her throat. Blood rushed to her head as she stared at Carmela. "If you repeat what you told me to Bobby, I swear, I will kill you."

"Should be easy for you, you've done it before," Carmela snapped. "Don't interfere in our relationship and I won't."

Bobby approached. He lifted Izzy off the horse and up over the fence. "Mom, what's wrong?"

"I'm not feeling well. I think we're going to leave early."

Izzy tugged at Carrie's pant leg. "But I want to stay."

Carrie picked up Michael and took Izzy by the hand. Without looking back, she headed for the house.

Forcing one foot in front of the other, her mind buzzed with the words Carmela had spoken. It couldn't be true. Where would she get such information? Travis, her father? Her stomach twisted so violently her breakfast threatened to surge up.

She packed and called for a car to the airport, her nerves frayed. Every time she thought about Carmela, her trepidation for her son rose. Whether it was true or not, Bobby would know she had lied about his father dying before his birth. He would never forgive her. She'd pegged Carmela right from the beginning. The woman was no good.

Nick's behavior these last few days, made sense now. He must have picked up on something. Her heart lurched. Did he know more than he let on about Carmela? Surely, if he did, he would have told her.

Bobby waited at the bottom of the stairs. "Mom, please tell me what happened?"

"Nothing happened. I'm just not feeling well. I want to go home."

He helped her take the luggage out to the waiting car. She settled the children inside while the driver loaded their belongings.

Bobby's sullen face broke her heart. What started out as a nice trip had ended in disaster.

She hugged his neck and whispered in his ear. "Please, be careful. Always remember how much I love you."

Bobby pulled back. "You're scaring me."

"I don't mean to," she said. "We'll talk soon." She kissed his cheek and climbed into the car.

Teary eyed, Izzy said, "Why do we have to leave?"

She stroked her daughters head. "It's time to go home."

The ride to the airport appeared twice as long. Carrie started to send Nick a text but stopped. She could only imagine Nick's reaction when she told him what Carmela had said. He would be furious, but he was the only one she trusted to make sense of all this. Talking to him in person would be the better choice.

Travis's face crossed her mind. All these years had gone by without her knowing what happened the day Nick took him back to the cabin. It was time for her to find out and deal with the consequences. Carmela's words opened up old wounds. Those wounds would never heal until she knew the truth.

# CHAPTER 38
# Nick

It was late afternoon by the time Nick arrived at Dalton's. The two men sipped beers on the front porch while Chino lay at Nick's feet. Dalton leaned up against a post stationed at the top of the steps while he sat on the railing.

"So, why the urgent call?" Nick asked.

"I held them off for as long as I could, but we have another pickup."

"When?"

"Day after tomorrow. The meets inVirginia."

"Looks like we're headed to Virginia." He took a draw on his beer.

Dalton raised an eyebrow. "We? They only want one person there. They pass the envelope and leave."

"Not this time. We're both going, but they won't know that."

"You have some kind of plan?"

"Sure do. One of us will go to the meet while the other stays close by."

"Would you mind explaining further?"

Nick set his empty bottle on the railing and stood. "We both know the person who makes the drop is not the one giving orders. So, we need to know where the orders are coming from. We may have to force this person's hand so to speak, but it's the only way we can determine who it is."

Dalton shook his head. "Even if they lead us to the top man, then what?"

"Look, I don't care who it is, but everyone has something to hide. We find that skeleton in their closet and it's our ticket out. They never give us a time limit on a kill. They just want the job done. Meanwhile, we put all our efforts into digging."

A slow smile creased Dalton's face. "A little blackmail to ensure our freedom."

"It's worth a try."

"Okay, I'll make sure the jet is ready."

Nick's cell buzzed. He looked at the number. "It's Bobby." Nick stepped away to take the call. "Hey, Bobby. What do you mean she left?" His heart drummed in his chest. "Did they have an argument? I agree. Something's not right. She would have called me to let me know. Okay, we'll talk soon."

"What's going on?" Dalton asked.

"It seems Carrie left Carmela's. She's coming home a day early. Should be there this evening. Bobby said Carmela insisted nothing happened between them, but he's not so sure." Nick ran his hands through his hair. "She never called me. That's not a good sign."

His jaw clenched. Carmela's threats loomed large again. Had she revealed the truth to Carrie? Or had some other altercation taken place, forcing her to leave? His mind spun in several directions.

"Dalton, I swear, if she told Carrie about Travis, she's done."

"Hold on, Nick. Now's the time to keep a level head. There's too much at stake for you to do something you'll regret."

He locked eyes with Dalton. "I'm already regretting what I didn't do that day in the winery." He went past him and down the porch steps. "I've got to get home. I need to be there when she arrives." He opened the car door. "Chino, come."

"Go on. We'll talk later," Dalton said. "Try to stay calm. If Carmela did tell Carrie, she's going to need you now more than ever."

He arrived home just as a limo drove out through the gates. He sped up the driveway and parked. Taking the steps two at a time, he hurried inside with Chino trotting behind him.

Luggage lined the hallway. He headed for the kitchen. It was empty. He moved on to the great room. Izzy came running. She patted Chino's head and giggled while he licked her face.

"Daddy, you're home!" She rushed at him. Nick swung her up into his arms. "Where's your mother?"

"Putting Michael to bed. He fell asleep in the car." She wrinkled her face. "Mommy made us come home early. I didn't want to leave, but she said we had to."

"I know baby. It's okay." He set her down and scanned the staircase. Unwilling to go upstairs, he decided to wait in the great room.

Minutes ticked by before he heard Carrie's footsteps. She entered. Her face was pale, her eyes puffy. He could tell something awful had happened.

"Izzy, go and get ready for bed," Carrie said.

She scrunched up her face and stomped her foot. "But I don't want to go to bed yet."

"Izzy, do as you're told," Nick said. "Don't give us an attitude every time we tell you to do something. Go get ready for bed, and we'll be up in a little while to tuck you in. You can read until then."

She burst into tears and ran upstairs. He hated to see her cry but her demeanor needed to change. Carrie was right about his absence affecting her.

"Babe, what happened?" he asked. "Bobby called. He told me you insisted on leaving early."

She collapsed onto the sofa. Her shoulders slumped. She peered up at him. "I'll tell you what happened. That awful woman said some horrible things to me. Unspeakable things."

Alarm bells sounded in his head. Apparently, it was worse than he thought. He sat beside her. "Tell me what she said."

She looked away. Her body shook and her breath heaved.

"Carrie, I want to help you. Please, what did Carmela say?"

"It's so disgusting. She rose and looked down at him. "Carmela claims that Travis …was my father."

"That's ridiculous." His gut wrenched. He couldn't meet her eyes.

"Is that all you have to say? You don't even seem surprised."

"You can't listen to that woman. She's just trying to upset you."

Carrie fell silent. Her eyes bore into him, and he looked away. The knot in his stomach grew tighter.

"Nick, why won't you look at me?"

He glanced up. "I'm looking at you."

"No, you turned away just then." She took a step back. "There were plenty of other things she said."

"Like what?"

"She knew I shot Carlos. How is that possible? Unless…." She raised a shaky hand to her chest.

Nick got up from the sofa. "I want to explain, and I need you to stay calm."

She glared at him. "Go on, start explaining."

"The man I used to work for was Carmela's father, Ricardo Santiago."

"The same man who you claimed saved you?"

"Yes, and that part remains true. Ricardo and I were close. He was more than my employer, and I've known Carmela since she was a young girl. Ricardo asked me to marry her. Wanted me to run his business. But I wasn't in love with her, and I had no intention of getting involved with drugs."

A frown creased her brow. "Did the two of you ever?"

"No, no. I thought of Carmela as a little sister." Nick took a breath. How could he explain everything and still make her pain go away?

"By the time Ricardo made that proposition, I was falling in love with you. I refused to marry her. Worst of all, I kept you alive, when he wanted you dead."

Carrie's eyes flashed. "You knew her all this time, and you didn't say anything?"

"I was going to tell you eventually but—"

"Oh, how big of you, Nick!"

He threw up his hands. "Okay, you have a right to be mad at me. I was just trying to protect you. Carmela has it in for me because I shot her father after he sent someone to kill us in Lugano. Unfortunately, she witnessed his death."

Carrie pressed her hand to her throat. "Oh my God!"

"I tried to talk to Bobby. But under the circumstances, I don't think it would have made a difference."

She studied him for a moment. "What about the drugs? Is Carmela still in the drug business?"

"As far as I know, yes. She took over from her father. She runs legitimate businesses in order to laundry drug money."

A flush stole up her cheeks. "Do you realize what could happen to Bobby if he gets tangled up in all of this?"

"Of course, I do," Nick snapped. "But with the baby coming, it made things more difficult."

She raked her hands through her hair and paced. He watched her anger build.

"Does Carmela have someone doing the kind of work you used to do for her father? Someone who…"

"More than likely. Running drugs is a dangerous business. Carrie, I'm sorry I didn't tell you sooner. She's not the same person she was before Ricardo died. I'm partly to blame for that."

Her face twisted into an ugly scowl. "Don't you make excuses for her. I still can't believe you kept all this from me. My son is in love with her, and you said nothing."

"Your right, I should have told you from the very beginning."

She studied him for a moment. "What happened after you took Travis up to the cabin?"

"Why are you bringing *that* up?"

"Your penchant for keeping secrets," Carrie spat. "Now, tell me what happened to Travis?"

His gut wrenched. "I think you know the answer."

"I want to hear it from you. He started to say something at May's house that night, before you took him away. What was he going to say?"

Nick spread his hands. "How should I know?"

Tears filled her eyes. "You look at me and tell me! No more lies, Nick."

"Carrie, please stop. None of that matters."

"It matters to me. Did Travis tell you he was my father?"

He looked at her, his whole world crashing down around him. It wouldn't do any good to lie. She could see right through him.

"Yes. He claimed he was your father."

"How could you keep something like that from me?"

"You'd gone through enough." He laid his hand on her trembling shoulder.

She pushed it away. "Don't touch me."

"I was only trying to protect you."

She backed away. "I had a right to know!"

"Carrie, please," he pleaded. The hurt he wanted to save her from engulfed them both.

Her hands clenched. "I want to know what happened after he told you. How did he die?"

"Why now?" Nick said. "It won't make things any better."

"Tell me what you did to him." The anguish in her voice cut through him.

"Carrie, you need to stop. You're making all of this worse."

"You brought this on yourself, by lying. Now, tell me!"

He'd known this day would come. Long held secrets always reveal themselves, and she wouldn't leave it alone until he said the words. Why couldn't they have put this to bed long ago?

His heart thumped. "After he told me, I...I...took him out into the woods and shot him."

Color drained from her face. She glared at him and backed further away. "See, doesn't that feel better now?" she mocked. "You got everything off your chest. Carmela was right. You're a liar! God only knows what else you've kept from me."

"I trusted you when you said there were no more secrets between us. You're not the man I thought you were." She ran from the room and tore up the stairs.

"Carrie, please wait. I'm so sorry."

Moments later, he heard the slam of the bedroom door.

Nick raced upstairs. He stood outside the door. Muffled sobs emanated from the other side. His heart broke into a million pieces. He tried the knob. The door was locked. He ached to comfort her, but he didn't know how.

Going down the hall to Izzy's room, he found her fast asleep in her pajamas on top of the covers. Their daughter slept peacefully, oblivious to the surrounding turmoil.

Nick lifted her up and slipped her underneath the comforter, tucking it around her. He kissed her forehead and then checked on Michael. One of his tiny legs stuck out from underneath the covers. He straightened the blankets and brushed back his dark hair.

His eyes watered. Nothing in the world was more important to him than Carrie, Bobby, and his children. Carmela was determined to destroy everything he loved. Those threats she shouted out long ago were coming true. There was no telling how far she'd go to rip his family apart.

She couldn't be trusted to do the right thing for Bobby or their child. But Bobby's feelings for her were blinding him.

Nick settled into the guest room for the night. Exhausted, he fell into a deep sleep only to wake late the next morning.

Down the hall, the master bedroom door lay open. It was empty. He checked the children's rooms, both were empty, too.

He descended the stairs. The dread inside him grew. He peered down the hallway. The stillness in the house consumed him.

Chino sat by the front door. He whimpered as Nick approached.

He stroked the dog's head. "I know, boy. I miss them already, too." Carrie and the children were gone and with them went his life.

# CHAPTER 39

## Carrie

Heartbroken, Carrie climbed the front steps. She held Michael in her arms. Izzy stood by her side. The driver deposited their suitcases on the porch and drove away. She glanced around.

Signs of spring had come to the mountains. A cloudless blue sky hovered above. Tiny buds waiting to be born dotted the tree limbs. Green shoots from the bulbs May had planted lined the yard. In a few weeks, daffodils and tulips bursting with color would appear. But none of it could lift her spirits.

She rang the bell. The door flew open, and May appeared.

She took in Carrie's ravaged face, and hers fell. "Oh, sweetheart, please come inside."

She set Michael down. "Izzy take your brother while I get the luggage."

With the children settled by the television, drinking milk and eating cookies, May put on a pot of coffee.

Carrie sat at the kitchen table and rested her chin in her hand. May placed two cups of coffee, creamer, and sugar down before sitting across from her. They prepared their cups and sat in silence for a few moments.

Carrie took a few sips. "Thanks, I didn't know where else to go."

"You're always welcome here." The lines around her eyes deepened. "What happened? Why did you leave home?"

Carrie's chest heaved. "We had an argument."

"But it couldn't be that serious. All couples fight."

"I'm afraid so." No way she'd tell her aunt what she found out about Travis. To think she had lain with him not knowing the truth. All those years she longed for the father she never met to save her meanwhile he was right there beside her.

She shuddered. Water could wash her body clean, but nothing could erase the memory of Travis, sick enough to abuse and sleep with her. Bitterness took hold inside of her. Her mother never loved her, and her father had deceived her.

"Do you want to talk about it?" May asked. Her brow creased with worry.

Carrie met her eyes. "I'd rather not." She thought about Bobby and her stomach coiled. If Carmela told him about Travis, their relationship, already tenuous would never be repaired.

Her panic rising, she said, "I need to call, Bobby." She grabbed her cell from her handbag. Her wounds raw and deep, she ignored the missed calls from Nick and refused to listen to her voicemail. She scanned his text messages full of apologies.

May poured a second cup of coffee. "You do whatever you have to. I'll go inside and stay with the children."

"Thanks." Carrie dialed Bobby's number. "Bobby, are you okay? I need to talk to you."

"Mom, why did you leave?" he asked."

"Where's Carmela?"

"She went to the winery."

"Bobby, listen. I want you to be careful."

"Now you sound like Nick."

"I love you and I…"

"I love you, too, but I don't understand. I thought you and Carmela were getting along."

She broke out in a cold sweat. How could she explain anything? "We are, I mean we did."

"You're not making sense."

"I want you to always remember how much I love you, Bobby."

"You're scaring me again." His voice rose a few notches. "Look, I'm coming to South Dakota so we can talk face to face."

"No. I'm not in South Dakota. I decided to visit Aunt May. Izzy and Michael are with me."

"What about Nick?"

"He had some things to take care of at home."

"Now, I know something's wrong. He'd never want you to travel there alone."

"Bobby, it's fine, really."

"I'm coming to Laurel as soon as I can get a flight. You're not going to change my mind."

Before she could say anything else, he hung up. She tossed her cell onto the kitchen table. Things were getting progressively worse.

May interrupted her thoughts. "How is Bobby?"

"Fine," she lied. "He's decided to fly in."

"Does he know what happened at home?"

Carrie was quick to reply. "No. Please don't say anything about Nick and me arguing."

"Of course, if you don't want me to."

That evening, with the children asleep, she called Joann and asked to meet her at the coffee house outside of town. She changed into a pair of black pants and a cream-colored sweater. Twenty minutes later, she drove into the lot.

The rich aroma of the diverse selection of coffees, made her pause inside the doorway. Across the room, a couple sat at the very table she shared with Nick all those years ago.

Nick's handsome face, and deep green eyes, swam before her along with her harrowing car ride to the cabin where she believed he'd kill her. And last, Travis's voice.

Now she knew for sure how Travis died. A shudder traveled down her spine. What must Nick have felt when he pulled the trigger?

She moved to the rear where chrome expresso machines lined the counter. The whir of a frothing machine sounded above the clerks calling out orders. A glass case held a selection of muffins and pastries. She ordered a coffee, hazelnut with extra sweetener, and sat at a small table against the far wall. People around her pecked on laptops while others stared at their phones. She sipped and tried to collect her thoughts.

"Hey, hon. I was surprised to get your call."

Joann approached carrying a cappuccino. Dressed in jeans and a light jacket, she kissed Carrie on the cheek, and sat in the chair across from her.

Carrie relaxed at the sight of her friend. "It's so good to see you."

"So, what gives? Why the sudden trip to Laurel?" she asked.

Her eyes watered. Joann's face blurred. She picked up her napkin and dabbed her lower lids. How much should she tell her?

"Nick and I had an argument. I needed to get away."

Her face full of questions, Joann said, "Must have been a hell of an argument for you to hop on a plane and come here."

Carrie tapped nervous fingers on the table. "It was. The worse we've ever had. Bobby's worried, and he's flying in."

"We'll lay it on me. It might make you feel better to talk about it. You know if I can help, I will."

She told her about Carmela's pregnancy. All she was willing to tell her for now.

"Wow, that is a shock, hon." Joann clasped her hands and rested them on the table. "Bobby, a father? It seems only yesterday he was coming into the Palisades with those silly friends of his for burgers and shakes."

"I know," Carrie said. "I'm still not crazy about Carmela. I'm not sure what kind of mother she's going to be."

"But we both know Bobby will be a good father," Joann said. "I don't think you have anything to worry about in that department." She patted Carrie's hand. "It'll work out, you'll see."

She wanted to tell Joann everything. Knowing who Travis was lay heavy inside of her. Ashamed, she couldn't bring herself to say it.

"So, what was this argument between you and Nick that made you run away from home?"

"We argued over the whole Carmela issue, and it escalated. We said hurtful things to one another. I just can't be around him right now."

Joann relaxed into the chair. "Sometimes it's good to have a little distance, get a better perspective on everything. But one thing I do know for sure is how much that man of yours loves you."

Carrie tried to keep the rest of the conversation light. She asked about Ronnie and Justin. They talked about the Palisades and even laughed over memories of old times. She was glad she had called Joann. Those few hours enabled her to forget the madness swirling in her head for a little while.

Later, she drove to May's house and fell into a restless sleep, her dreams invaded by Travis. Her monster had returned.

# CHAPTER 40
## Bobby

Bobby opened the door to the winery. The alarming call from his mother filled his mind with questions. If Carmela had done something to hurt her, he needed to know what and why.

Ever since they announced the news of her pregnancy, things were falling apart. He stepped inside the vault and spotted Carmela standing below the rows of oak barrels talking to one of her employees. She waved as he approached.

"I'm almost finished," she called out.

Bobby waited for the employee to leave through the doors of the tasting room at the other end before he spoke.

"Listen, I just got a call from my mother. She's quite upset."

She fiddled with her gold earring. "What did she say?"

"I think you need to come clean. You can be unpleasant at times."

"And what about her? How do you know she didn't start something with me?"

Bobby fought hard to keep his composure. "I know my mother, and if she did, something set her off. Now, what did you do to upset her?"

"Nothing much. We began talking about the baby again, and she insisted she wanted to be there for the birth. I refused to say yes, and it angered her."

She attempted to walk away. Bobby caught hold of her shoulders, holding her back.

"No, not this time. You're not getting off that easy."

"Let go of me." she struggled, pushing against him. Unable to free herself, she gave in. "How dare you take her side. I am about to be the mother of your child, and this is the way you treat me?"

"You're forcing my hand, Carmela. If you didn't do anything wrong, why are you getting so worked up?"

Her eyes blazed. "Okay, if you insist on knowing. I can see you're convinced that I am the bad one."

Every muscle in his body tensed. "Go on, spit it out."

"I asked her about your father. Who he was, what he was like."

His mouth fell open, cold seeped through his core. His heart raced. "What did she say?"

"She got quite upset and told me I should mind my own business." Carmela placed her hand on her stomach. "Don't you think it is only natural I would want to know more about him for our child's sake, if nothing else?"

Bobby dropped his hands and stepped back. "I told you about my father. He died in a car accident before I was born."

"I don't believe that is true."

"She wouldn't lie to me. Not about something like that."

"Then why did she react the way she did? I think she's keeping things from you."

"Well, I'm leaving for Laurel. I want to hear her side of things."

"Laurel? What is your mother doing in Laurel?"

"That's a good question. She went to my Great Aunt's without Nick. I need to find out what the hell is going on. Too many things aren't sitting right with me."

Carmela's face clouded over. "Suit yourself," she said and stormed out of the vault.

Confused, Bobby hung back. Could there be even the slightest chance Carmela was right? He remembered past discussions with his mother. Whenever he had pushed for more information, she gave half- answers. He'd always assumed the loss was too painful for her to talk about.

His cell buzzed, and he recognized the number. "Hey, Nick. I was thinking of calling you. What is my mother doing in Laurel without you?"

"So, you've heard from her?"

"Yes, she called a little while ago." He grew uncomfortable. "What's going on, Nick?"

"We…um…we had words, and I think she needed some space."

Bobby sighed. They must have had a serious argument for her to up and leave. "I'm going to see her."

"That's not such a good idea."

"I'm going, anyway."

"Listen, we need to talk. I've held some things concerning Carmela back from you that I shouldn't have."

Bobby tensed. Whatever Nick had to say couldn't be good. But his major concern was for his mother. "I'll meet up with you after I speak to her."

"I would appreciate your meeting with me first."

"Sorry, I'll call you from Laurel."

He ended the call and left the winery. He made a flight reservation and packed his overnight bag, his mind buzzing. Something awful happened between his mother and Carmela down by the paddock and he needed to hear his mother's side of things.

Nick taught him to listen to his intuition. With Carmela, he had failed miserably. He'd ignored all those warning signs, wanting only to believe in his love for her. The words 'be careful' crossed his mind.

"When are you coming back?" Carmela stood in the bedroom doorway. A forlorn look on her face.

He continued packing. "I don't know. I need to sort things out."

She reached for his hand. "*Mi Tesoro*. I am going to miss you."

He ignored the gesture and zipped up his bag. "I'll call you after I land." He hurried to the door.

"So, this is how you leave me? Not even a kiss goodbye."

"Like I said, I'll call you after I land."

The closer he got to Laurel, the more apprehensive he became. A laundry list of things swam through his mind. His mother had gone there without Nick. And neither would discuss the reason Marco left. To make matters worse, Carmela's questions about his father had touched a nerve.

From the time he was a teenager and until today, he wondered about his father. What kind of man was he? Did he love his mother? Did he really die in a car accident or did something more sinister happen? His determination to find out the truth grew stronger.

It was early afternoon when Bobby paid the driver and got out of the car. He surveyed Birch Street. Since his stepmother's death, any desire to visit the mountain town had vanished.

Images of Bruce and Kenny appeared. A smile crossed his lips at the recollection of Kenny's beat up Camaro, afternoons spent hanging out at the quarry, and his infatuation with a neighborhood girl named Darcy Grant. His stomach soured for a moment as Russ Medlow's face invaded his thoughts.

He swung open May's front gate and strolled down the brick path. All those times he'd come here not knowing they were related seemed surreal. He crossed the porch and rang the bell. His mother appeared. He noticed the dark skin beneath her lower lids, the whites within her beautiful eyes stained pink, proof she'd been crying.

"Bobby I'm glad you're here, but it wasn't necessary for you to come."

He stepped past her. "Yes, it was. I need to know everything."

Her face fell. She wrung her hands and looked up at him. "What do you mean?"

The dread living deep inside him pushed its way to the surface. His palms grew damp.

He'd come to Laurel for answers no matter how much it hurt and he wouldn't leave until he had them.

His eyes fixed on hers, he said, "I want to know the truth…about my father."

# CHAPTER 41

## Carmela

Waking from an afternoon nap, Carmela sat up in bed and read her text messages. More threats from Diego. She dialed Miguel's number.

"*Hola,* Carmela."

"Don't *hola* me, Miguel. What are you doing to find Diego Silva?"

"Everything." His voice hardened. "It is not easy to find someone who doesn't want to be found."

"Am I supposed to just sit here and wait for him to harm me?"

"*Tranquila,* Carmela, please. I am doing my best."

"Do not tell me to be calm when he is blowing up my phone. He is using burners, his messages come in under different numbers."

"I will let you know when I find him. Do not leave the property without Emilio."

"I wouldn't do anything so foolish. Let me know when you have him, Miguel."

Carmela ended the call. She ran her fingers through her hair and sank into the bed pillows. Bobby's leaving the way he did, upset her. And his going to Laurel for answers was fruitless. Carrie would never tell him the truth about his father. That knowledge still worked to her advantage.

She pondered Carrie being in Pennsylvania without Nick. His lies might have caught up with him. She wished she could have been there to witness the scene between them.

Diablo had almost played into her plans, but she hadn't counted on Bobby being able to control him so well. It was too bad that the horse failed to continue to buck with Izzy on the saddle.

Pulling off the covers, she surveyed her swollen ankles. Six weeks to go and she could start to get her figure back. In the meantime, she needed to repair things with Bobby. She wanted him there at the birth so he could lay eyes on their child before she disappeared.

She slipped out of bed and tugged on a pair of maternity pants and a light blouse. It was time to check on Marco. Armando had kept him well fed and seen to his laundry and cleaning.

She summoned Emilio, and they drove out. To her dismay, Marco sat on the porch. Frowning, she climbed up the steps.

"What are you doing out here?"

He made no move to rise. "Getting some much-needed air."

"It's dangerous for you to be seen. Nick and Carrie visited recently. If either one of them had noticed you…"

He put up his hand. "You can't expect me to stay locked up as if I am in prison. I don't like going out only at night. I'm not a vampire."

Carmela flung the front door open. "Come inside now, or Emilio will drag you in."

"Okay, don't get so worked up. There is no one around." He followed behind her.

She closed the door behind them. Hands on her hips, she said, "What do you mean you only go out at night?"

Marco's face flushed red. "I sometimes go for walks late at night."

"In the garden perhaps?" she asked.

He shrugged. "A few times."

"You fool. I am sure it was you Bobby saw the other night. Can you imagine what would have happened had he caught you?"

"He didn't catch me," Marco sneered. "I'm too quick for that boy."

"Boy? Did you say, boy? Bobby is no boy. He is a man … man enough to shoot you if he gets the chance."

He slumped onto the sofa. "And you believe he would do this?"

"Bobby told me Nick taught him how to protect himself."

He stuck out his chin. "I will always think of him as a boy."

"Trust me. That is a mistake, Marco." Searing pain ripped across the bottom of her back, her breath catching in her throat. She let out a gasp and sank onto the sofa.

He held out his hands. "What is it, Carmela?"

She pushed his hands away as the pain subsided into a dull ache. "Nothing. I am fine."

Marco settled into the cushions. "So, what plans have you made for me to leave here?"

"None as of now. I want to be sure to send you someplace where you won't be found too easily. I am certain Nick is already hunting for you."

He jumped up. "I have been thinking, Carmela, and I don't understand how things turned out between us. When we were together in Rome, you were so different. I came to America to live the life you promised me, only to find out you are with Bobby." He pointed to her stomach. "And now this."

"I told you before. Having this child wasn't in my plans, but ultimately, it works to my advantage. At this very moment, Nick's family is falling apart."

"All this trouble when I just could have shot Nick and Carrie in their sleep."

"That was too easy a solution. I want them to suffer." She eased up off the sofa, the ache in her back now fading away.

"I will have your arrangements made within the next few days, Marco."

"Will you be joining me after the baby is born?"

"Joining you?" Marco was becoming a thorn in her side.

Miguel Medina could make quick work of him if she gave the order. But better to have Nick come face to face with the man who tried to rape his wife, leaving the spoils to Miguel.

"When it's safe, I will send for you."

"I think you have no intention of ever being with me."

She pushed past him. "Stop all this nonsense. When I am done, we will be together."

He followed her to the door. "What about the children?"

"Oh yes, the precious children. What do you take me for, some kind of animal? Don't worry, I will not hurt then."

His eyes flashed. "I'm warning you, Carmela, don't be so foolish as to think I will quietly disappear after you're done with Nick."

She stepped outside. "And I am telling you for the last time, do not threaten me again, Marco. You will find yourself in deeper trouble than you can ever imagine. Now, go back inside."

She called to Emilio who helped her into the car. Driving, away, she glanced at the receding figure on the porch. Tempted to call Miguel and have Marco eliminated, her eagerness to bring Nick and him together outweighed that decision. A little more time was all she needed. Retribution was coming. When she finished, her father would finally rest in peace.

# CHAPTER 42

## Nick

Nick rubbed his temples. His head throbbed, and the knot in his stomach refused to unravel. Flying to Virginia with Dalton, he worried about Carrie's state of mind.

Drumming his fingers on the table, he glanced at his cell phone. She wouldn't take his calls or respond to his text messages. But he didn't blame her. He had lost her trust.

"What gives?" Dalton asked.

Nick hadn't told him about Carrie. He wanted to wait until they were finished with their business in Virginia. "Is it that obvious?"

"I've never known you to wear a poker face. I can always tell when something is eating away at you." He retrieved a bottle of whiskey from the bar and poured two shots. He handed one to Nick and sat.

"Thanks." Nick tipped his glass. He swallowed the dark amber liquid. Its warmth spread through his chest, easing the tightness a bit. He set his drink down and told him about Carrie leaving and the reason why.

Dalton shook his head. "I'm so sorry. I wish I'd never suggested you go to Napa. Maybe—"

"You're not to blame," Nick cut in. "We couldn't have avoided going there forever, and Carmela would have found a way to tell Carrie, regardless."

"Carrie must be hurting real bad." Dalton swallowed his shot.

"That's what worries me. I want to help her, but she won't take my calls. To make matters even worse, Bobby is on his way to see her."

Nick rubbed the back of his neck. He'd give anything to heal things between them. Losing Carrie would be like cutting off one of his limbs. His love for her had grown stronger with each passing year. She'd given him the life he'd always longed for but had never thought he could have.

"Look," Dalton said. "If you need to abort this whole thing and go to Laurel, then you do that. I'll handle this on my own."

"At this point, I don't think I should," Nick said. "She's going to have her hands full telling Bobby the truth. I better give her some space."

"Well, you let me know if you change your mind. If there is one thing I'm certain of, it's you, and Carrie belong together. She'll come around. Things will work out."

Nick rubbed his palms. "I hope you're right."


It was late afternoon when they landed in Virginia. Using false identification, they each rented a car then drove to Shenandoah National Park, an hour and a half from Washington, DC. They exited and surveyed their surroundings. The park, surrounded by the Blue Ridge Mountains, sat underneath an overcast sky. Cool temperatures lessened the usual springtime crowds.

Oblivious to the white trillium and pink lady slippers blooming all around them, they made their way to the nearest visitor's center.

Once inside, they split up. Their contact was to meet Dalton in twenty minutes. Nick leafed through the pamphlets stacked next to the information desk. Dalton grabbed a local newspaper and seated himself at the far end of the room.

At the appointed time, a young man strolled in heading straight for Dalton. They exchanged a few words. He passed a large manila envelope to him and left out of the side exit.

Nick nodded at Dalton and followed the young man out. He caught up to him in the parking lot. By this time, it was almost empty.

"Excuse me. Can you tell me the best way to US 340?"

The young man eyed him and smiled. "Sure. When you drive out of the lot…"

Tires screeched. Dalton roared toward them. The trunk flew open, the car grinding to a halt. Nick grabbed the man's arm and pulled out his 9mm, planting the barrel square in his back.

"Hey, what the hell are you doing?" he cried. He struggled, but was no match for Nick. Nick pushed him into the trunk, slamming it shut. Dalton hit the gas and sped out of the park.

Nick followed in his car. Thirty minutes later, they drove into a parking garage. Dalton found a spot on the nearly deserted top level. Nick parked beside him.

Dalton popped the trunk and Nick hauled the young man out. He shoved him into the backseat of Dalton's car and climbed in.

Nick took out his 9mm. The man's eyes bulged. He tore at the door handle.

"Save it," Nick replied. "I won't hurt you unless you force me. Do you understand?"

He nodded, his face ashen. "What do you want?" He pointed to Dalton. "I gave him the envelope."

"That's right," Nick said. "Hand over your wallet and cell phone."

His hands shaking, he pulled them from his pocket and handed them to Nick.

Nick flipped open the wallet and took out a driver's license. "Mitchell Richards." He stuffed the license and cell phone into his jacket pocket and tossed the wallet back to him. "Now, Mitchell, we need to know who gave you the envelope."

"I…I can't tell you that."

Nick motioned with his gun. "Then I'm afraid things aren't going to end well for you."

"Please, you don't understand. If I give you that information, I'm as good as dead."

"Not if no one knows you gave it to us. Look, all we need is a name."

His eyes watered. He glanced from Nick to Dalton. "If I give you his name, you'll let me go?"

Nick saw this kid was scared shitless. "For what it's worth, I give you my word. It's not you we want. He will never know you gave us his name because he'll have bigger problems to worry about."

Mitchell hesitated for a moment. "His name…his name is Adelson. Senator John Adelson. He represents New Mexico."

"See," Nick said. "That wasn't so hard. Now, as long as you told us the truth, and you don't mention this little meeting, you'll never see us again." He patted his pocket with the license and cell phone in it. "Do you understand?"

"Yes, I understand."

Nick locked eyes with him. "Here's how things are going to go Mitchell. I'm putting you back in the trunk, then we're going for a ride. When we're a safe distance away, I'll let you go. Does that sound good?"

Mitchell nodded. "Do I have to get back in the trunk? I won't yell or make any noise."

"I'm afraid so. Don't worry, you won't be in there long."

Nick helped a shaking Mitchell into the trunk. Dalton pulled out of the lot with Nick following behind. They drove along the Blue Ridge Parkway. It was dusk by the time they reached a secluded spot off the main road.

Dalton wiped down the interior and exterior of his vehicle while Nick hauled Mitchell out of the trunk.

"Where the hell are we?" Mitchell said.

"Mitchell, look at me," Nick said. "Pay attention because I'm only going to say this once. We're leaving you here but I want you to wait until dark." He pointed to Dalton's car. "Then you drive that car back to the city. The keys are inside."

Nick patted his jacket pocket again. "Remember, we know who you are and where you live. Don't worry about Senator Adelson. He'll never know we spoke."

They flew back to South Dakota satisfied things had gone well in Virginia. Dalton made arrangements to dig into Senator Adelson's background. Something was bound to come up they could use against him.

Nick stretched and settled into his seat. "You know, we're not at the top yet."

Dalton winked. "It's a start. My only worry is what do we do after we get there?"

"What goes up must come down," Nick said. "When we find out who the son of a bitch is that got us into the killing game again, they'll be sorry they ever laid eyes on us."

Dalton's cell buzzed. "What have you got for me?" He listened for a few moments, before hanging up, his expression somber.

"What's up," Nick asked.

"They found your other car at the Miami airport. Seems Marco boarded a flight to Miami."

"Miami?" Nick's pulse spiked. He'd been waiting for this news.

Dalton let out a breath. "But he didn't stay there long. His final destination was Napa."

# CHAPTER 43
## Carmela

Carmela stroked Allegra's muzzle. "You are so special to me," she whispered. The horse's ears tipped forward, and he let out a soft neigh. She retrieved his currycomb mitt and slipped it on. Using circular motions, she rubbed his neck, then his left flank. Loose hair fell in plumes to the floor as she worked her way to the rear and right side.

It was Mateo's job to groom the horses, but Carmela found her anxiety eased whenever she took the opportunity to do a little herself. She picked up the mane and tail brush and with long, smooth strokes, she passed it through his tail. Last she combed his mane. Mateo would finish the rest later.

She handed Allegra a carrot, before closing the stall. Diablo whinnied and she grabbed another, feeding it to him from outside his stall. His head bobbed in appreciation. Since her previous encounter with him, she deemed it best to avoid getting close until after the baby arrived.

Mateo appeared dragging a bale of hay behind him. "*Hola, Señorita.*"

"*Hola, Mateo.* Please take the horses down to the paddock. I would like them to have some extra exercise today."

He tipped his Cattleman's hat. "*Si,* right away."

Carmela left the stables and wandered over to the paddock. Acres of rolling green spread out around her. In the distance, sun filtered through the trees. The sky was clear except for a few cream-colored clouds floating by. She peered over the fence rail as Mateo released the horses. Diablo bucked, then raced across the paddock, his long black tail shooting out behind him. Allegra followed but at a slower pace.

The sight of the two horses lifted her spirits until she thought about Bobby. She hadn't heard from him since he left. His anger surprised her. She had always been able to control his moods.

Soon, he would know about some things she said to Carrie. But Carmela was certain Carrie would try to protect him from the awful truth about Travis Montgomery and the murder of Carlos.

She rubbed her swollen belly. Had she made the right choice in having Bobby's child? Her decision most certainly cemented their relationship. Without the impending birth, she wasn't so sure Bobby would have stayed with her.

A peculiar knot twisted inside her at the prospect of losing him. She shook her head and pushed her emotions back. Love must not enter into her life. There was too much at stake.

Carmela turned away from the paddock and walked toward the main house. It was time to get rid of Marco for good. She could summon Miguel and let him eliminate Marco, but another idea came to her.

She stopped halfway along the garden path and took out her cell phone. Searching her contacts, she retrieved Nick's number. How wise she had been to go through Bobby's phone while he slept knowing specific numbers would come in handy.

Easing onto a bench across from a riot of red and pink roses she punched in the numbers.

"What do you want Carmela? Haven't you caused enough trouble?"

His tone cut through her like a whip. She recalled how his voice, once so tender and warm, used to make her heart sing all those years ago.

"If you hadn't tried to interfere in my relationship with Bobby, I would have kept certain information to myself. I know you said bad things about me that evening on the patio."

"Look, I don't care what you think I did or didn't say. You're using Bobby. If I have any chance at all of protecting him from you, I intend to do so."

"And here I am ready to do you a favor, Nick."

"What can you possibly do for me?"

"I understand you're looking for Marco. Just so you don't think I am all bad. I will tell you where he is."

"I'm a step ahead of you, Carmela. I know Marco flew to Napa and that could only mean one thing. Somehow, he's involved with you."

A laugh escaped her lips. "You are the clever one, aren't you? So clever, I will be nice and hand him over to you. You can do whatever you want with him. He's here in my guest house. Come whenever you're ready. He won't know. I will tell my men to let you pass."

"After all you've done, you expect me to trust you?"

"I'm through with him. Either you come and do what needs to be done, or I will have Miguel Medina do it."

"You sure are a cold-hearted bitch. You took a good man and turned him into a monster."

"Don't be silly. How much power do you think I have? Marco has always known what he wanted out of life. You failed to give that to him, and Carrie suffered the consequences."

"Don't bring Carrie into this. I can't stand to hear her name pass through your lips."

"You have twenty-four hours. After that, either way, Marco is history."

"Do whatever you want with him, Carmela. I'm not coming to Napa."

She ended the call and retreated to the house. Upstairs in her bedroom, she considered her conversation with Nick. Knowing him the way she did, he wouldn't pass up an opportunity to take Marco out. Not after what he did to Carrie. Satisfied he would come, her anxiety eased. Marco would no longer be her problem. She dialed her phone and instructed her men to let Nick through then she called Miguel's number.

"What can I do for you, Carmela?"

"It is time to get rid of Marco Valletta."

"That is good news."

"I have informed Nick of Marco's whereabouts. I've given him twenty-four hours. But I can't guarantee he will come. If Nick has not gotten rid of him within that time, I am giving you orders to eliminate Marco."

"Are you sure?"

"Yes, I am afraid things with Bobby did not go as I planned. It is time to put an end to all of this. Let me know when it is done."

"If by chance Nick should show up, do I have your permission to eliminate him also?"

"Not quite yet my *sicario*. But that time is drawing near."

Satisfied, she ended the call. Marco's time was up. Eventually, Nick would suffer the same fate. Carrie will soon find out what it was like to be a widow.

She stripped and got into bed. Within minutes, she drifted off to sleep waking hours later to darkness. She switched on the bedside lamp. Hunger pains surfaced, and her stomach growled. Time to have Armando prepare a late supper.

Carmela rose and slipped on her robe. She reached the top of the staircase. A rustling noise behind her made her hesitate.

Hands pressed against the middle of her back. Her body pitched forward. She tried to grip the banister. Her hand slid along the smooth wood, failing to catch hold. Her feet flew out from underneath her.

She screamed as she plunged down the stairs.

# CHAPTER 44
# Miguel

Miguel stared at his cell phone in disbelief. Had Carmela finally taken his advice? The order to eliminate Nick drew closer.

He studied the woman lying beside him in his hotel room. She had come at a high price from an elite escort service. He never engaged in local prostitutes. They were too tacky for his taste. He preferred women with a bit more class. A woman like Carmela.

He eased out of bed, grabbed his clothes, and went to shower. Twenty minutes later, he emerged fully dressed. The young woman lay propped up against the pillows. Her dark hair splayed out on the pillow, her eyes fixed on Miguel.

"Leaving so soon?"

"I'm afraid so." He placed a roll of cash on the nightstand. "Order room service. Stay as long as you like."

She winked. "I just might do that."

Glad he wasn't far from Carmela's estate, he drove out of the parking garage and onto the highway. He left a message with Luis to text him if Nick arrived even though he didn't believe he'd be foolish enough to come to here after Marco.

In his profession, Nick was a legend. To become a ghost meant taking a lot of high-risk kills. Miquel admired a man like that. Nick had honed his craft to perfection. Miguel looked forward to eliminating him. Doing so would only serve to elevate his status among ghosts.

Darkness fell by the time he parked his black Lexus LS. He attached the silencer to his 9mm and wound his way through the garden and on to the guest house. Pale yellow light emanated through the front windows. He crept up the steps and peered into the window.

He tried the door. It was unlocked. He aimed his weapon and kicked it open. It crashed against the wall. Miguel stepped inside. He moved past the living room and down the hall, taking pains to check each area of the house. Except for some of Marco's clothes strewn about, the place was empty. He went outside and searched the perimeter. Satisfied, he lowered his weapon.

Miguel stared at the mansion in the distance. A cold chill ran through his body. He dashed back through the garden. Just as he rounded the front of the house, he heard a woman scream. He rushed up the steps. Armando tore the door open.

"Help, the *Señorita* has fallen."

Carmela lay sprawled at the foot of the stairs. He ran over to her. She was out cold. Blood seeped from between her legs. "Call an ambulance!" he shouted at Armando.

Emilio arrived moments later. A look of horror swept over his face.

The wail of a siren coming up the drive echoed across the valley. Miguel focused on getting Carmela to the hospital. If anything happened to her, he would never forgive himself.

Miguel directed the attendants. He watched helplessly as they secured a collar around Carmela's neck and lifted her onto a gurney. He insisted on riding with them while Emilio and Armando followed in his car.

They arrived at the hospital twenty minutes later and whisked Carmela inside. Miguel's stomach wrenched. His intuition told him she hadn't fallen. Marco must have made his way into the house. Miguel simmered. When he caught up with him, a bullet would be too easy. He'd take his knife, split him open, and watch him bleed to death.

He called Luis who informed him that there was no sign of Nick. He gave orders to search for Marco and detain him. If they found him, they were not to do anything until he got there.

Hours crawled by while he waited with Armando and Emilio for word of Carmela's condition. She remained unconscious, but they would have to deliver the baby.

Since Carmela was stable, he left and drove back to the estate. Luis greeted him at the front gate.

"Have you found him?" Miguel asked.

"Not a sign of him anywhere so far. But the darkness makes it harder."

Miguel gripped the steering wheel. "I don't want excuses, Luis. Have your men keep looking."

He shook his head. "*Sí Señor* Medina. How is the *Señorita?*"

"She will be okay. She is a strong woman." He slid the window up and continued down the drive. He parked in front of the house, grabbed his 9mm, and went inside.

He stared at the blood-stained tiles at the foot of the stairs. Heat flushed through his body. He climbed to the top of the staircase and studied the carpet. Flakes of mud led away and down the hall. He followed them until they dead-ended at the last bedroom.

Miguel raised his weapon and stepped inside. He checked the closet, underneath the bed and the bathroom. All were empty. He did the same with the remaining upstairs rooms. Downstairs, he searched each room until he was satisfied.

All of this was so unnecessary. If only Carmela had heeded his warnings. Now, she lay unconscious in a hospital.

He had feigned surprise at her pregnancy and the mention of Marco staying in the guest house. Armando had already informed him of both some time ago. His angst had grown at the news, but Carmela had been too stubborn to listen to reason.

With her and the child's life at stake, he was determined to keep her safe. Nothing would come between them again. Especially not Bobby or Nick D'Angelo.

# CHAPTER 45
## Bobby

Bobby sat at May's kitchen table with his mother. May had taken the children to the Palisades to see Joann. His stomach was almost as knotted as the day he had come here to confess about digging up the briefcase.

He scrutinized his mother's face while she placed coffee cups between them and sat. She lifted the creamer and stared into her cup for a moment.

The need deep within him to learn about his father grew with each passing minute. Would she tell him the truth this time? But first, he wanted to hear what happened in Napa. He stirred some sugar into his cup and sipped.

"Mom, I want to know what took place between you and Carmela."

A shadow crossed her face. "What has she told you?"

Bobby shrugged. "Nothing much. She said you got upset after she asked about my father."

Her brow creased. "It's none of her damn business."

"We're having a child together. Don't you think she had a right to ask you?"

"What does it matter? He's gone."

His body grew rigid. "It matters to me. The only thing you ever told me was he died in a car accident. You've never said what kind of man he was. If he loved you, or you him. What did he do for a living? What did he look like?

She pressed her fingertips to her temples. "Bobby, please, I don't...I don't like talking about him. It upsets me."

He gripped the tops of his thighs. His fingers dug in. He tried to remain calm. "I understand, but that's not fair to me. I've waited long enough. You either start talking, or I'll do some investigating on my own."

Carrie slammed her palms on the table. "Okay, you want to know about your dear departed father." She locked eyes with him. "His name was Travis Montgomery. He was a horrible man. I can't begin to explain how much I suffered. He beat me, threatened me, and one time, he almost choked me to death. I was terrified of him."

He drew back. His pulse raced. This was the last thing he expected to hear. His stomach twisted while his thoughts tumbled one on top of the other. "But you said he died before I was born and that the two of you weren't together that long. Did he even die in a car accident?"

Teary-eyed she said, "I lied to protect you. Once I found out what an animal, your adoptive father was, I couldn't bring myself to tell you the truth about your biological father."

"How...how long were you with him?"

She dabbed at her eyes with a napkin. "Quite a few years. After my mother sold you, I ran away with him. I blamed myself so much for losing you that I believed I deserved the life I had with him."

Bobby's throat went dry. His head swam. "So, what happened? Where is he now?"

"He died around the time I first came to Laurel." She clasped her trembling hands. "I was finally free."

He asked his final question about his father. "How did he die?"

A blank expression on her face, she remained silent. She sipped her coffee.

He pounded his fist on the table. He wanted answers. "I asked you how he died."

She cleared her throat, set her cup down, and dried the remainder of her tears. "You're going to find out sooner or later if not from me then from Nick."

"What the hell are you talking about?"

"Your father forced me to commit a robbery. Two men died as a result. Those men worked for the same man Nick told you about. That man...was Carmela's father."

Bobby reared back. He broke out in a cold sweat. "Nick worked for her father? But I thought his boss was some kind of drug lord?"

"Yes, he was, and the money your father and I stole belonged to him. He sent Nick to kill us. But somehow, and I know it sounds crazy, Nick, and I connected, and he fell for me. He refused to kill me. I had managed to run from your father, but he followed me to Laurel. He tried to kill Nick, but Nick got the better of him. When Carmela's father found out, your father was dead, but I was still alive, he sent people after us."

Bobby broke out in a cold sweat. Nick had killed his father, who according to his mother mistreated her terribly. He hadn't died in a car accident. He was an abuser and a criminal.

"So, the money in that briefcase belonged to Carmela's father?"

"Yes. Nick returned the money, but it wasn't good enough. Her father wanted both of us dead. He tried once in South Dakota and again in Lugano. Nick had no choice but to kill him. Unfortunately, Carmela witnessed the killing. Bobby, Carmela is using you to get back at us. I'm sure she drugged the wine when she came to South Dakota the first time. She took Izzy out of the house to scare me."

His head spun. All this time, Carmela was plotting and planning. It explained her foul moods and attitude toward his family. He believed his mother now, about the wine. It all made sense. The fear he pushed away all these months surfaced. "Why didn't you tell me all of this in the beginning?"

"Because I didn't know who she was. I only found out from Nick a few days ago. She's dangerous, Bobby. He held back because she's having your baby."

"Is that why you left South Dakota? Because Nick didn't tell you." He saw her hesitate.

"Yes. It was part of our argument but not all of it. I prefer to keep the rest between him and me."

"Do you think she's still involved in the drug business?" he asked.

"According to Nick, she is."

He tried to control his rising panic. This explained so many things. Especially Carmela's need for a constant bodyguard wherever she went.

"Mom, what am I going to do?"

"You mustn't let her know what I've told you. You have the baby to consider right now."

"Nick wanted to talk to me before I came here, but I blew him off. What did you mean when you said he held back?"

"Bobby, I won't lie to you. Nick will do almost anything to protect this family. There are no guarantees after the baby is born."

Bobby stared at her for a moment. "I want to ask you one other thing. Why did Marco leave?" He saw her face flush. Her hands trembled.

"It's only fair that I tell you the reason. You've known Marco for a long time." She drew closer and rested her eyes on him. "Marco tried to rape me while Nick was away. Neither of us understands why he did what he did. Lucky for me, Chino attacked him and I was able to force him to leave."

Bobby shook his head. He reached across the table and placed his hand on top of hers. "I'm so sorry. I can't imagine him doing something like that."

Bobby's cell phone buzzed. He didn't recognize the number. "Hello." Armando's voice boomed in his ear. "Where is she now? I'm leaving right away." He rose on legs threatening to give way. His heart battered against his chest.

Carrie got up. "Bobby, what is it?"

"I have to go. Carmela had an accident."

"An accident? Is she okay?"

"I don't know. Armando said I needed to come to the hospital in Napa."

Carrie snatched May's car keys off the hook by the back door. "Let me drive you to the airport."

· "No, give me the keys. I'll drive myself."

"But…"

"Gives me something to focus on. I'd rather go alone. I'll let you know where I leave May's car. You and Joann can pick it up later." He rushed out of the room and grabbed his suitcase. "I'll call you as soon as I can."

Bobby's flight to Napa seemed endless. All he could think about was Carmela and the baby. Regardless of her intentions, he needed to know they were both okay. Now that the truth had come out, he'd be able to deal with it head-on. He arrived at the hospital after midnight. Bobby entered the waiting room. Armando rushed at him, his face ashen.

"The *Señorita* is not good," Armando said. "She no wake up."

"What happened?"

"The *Señorita* fell down the stairs."

"Have you spoken to the doctor?"

Armando's face drooped. "Not since bringing the *Señorita* here."

Bobby went over to Emilio. "Are you sure that's all there is to this, her falling down the stairs?"

"*Sí*, Miguel Medina found her in the foyer at the bottom of the steps."

Bobby had never heard the name before. "Who is Miguel Medina?"

Emilio hesitated. "He works for the *Señorita*."

A tall woman with short cropped blond hair dressed in scrubs walked over to them. "Are you here for Carmela Santiago?"

"Yes," Bobby said. "I'm the father of her baby. Are you her doctor?"

"Yes. I'm Doctor Martin. I've been handling her pregnancy."

"How is she?"

"Carmela was unconscious when they brought her in. As far as we can tell she has a broken arm and is banged up pretty good. The fall caused her to go into labor. The baby's in the NICU."

"Is Carmela going to be okay?"

"Neurology has done a brain scan, and so far, there is no swelling or other damage we can see. But, like I said, she was unconscious when she came in. Hopefully, she will wake up soon."

"What about the baby?"

"Come, I'll take you to the NICU. The baby arrived early and needs special care." She motioned to Armando and Emilio. "Just the father for now."

Bobby went with Dr. Martin. She stopped in front of a large glass window.

"You'll need to wash your hands before you go in. The nurse will give you a paper gown."

He did as instructed then followed the nurse. She led him to an incubator labeled Santiago.

"Here she is," the nurse said.

He stared at the tiny figure, aghast at all the wires and equipment attached to her. "She's so tiny."

"We're taking good care of her. She's having a little trouble breathing right now, so we're helping her do that. You can reach in. Preemies need to be touched."

He slipped his hand inside. Amazed, he watched her tiny chest pump up and down. He placed his index finger into her palm. Slowly her fingers curled around it. A lump rose in his throat. Overwhelmed, tears stung the corners of his eyes. He'd never felt this much love for another human being.

"Hi," he whispered. "I'm your daddy."

# CHAPTER 46

## Miguel

Miguel left the house and drove back to the hospital. Armando and Emilio remained seated in the waiting room.

"Any news?" Miguel asked.

Armando's brow furrowed. "Nothing has changed."

"What is her room number?"

"Room 420." He pointed down the hall.

"Have you seen her?"

"No, we must wait. *Señor* D'Angelo is with her."

Miguel shot him a look. "Do you think I care about him?"

He took off towards Carmela's room. The door was closed. He pushed it open and stepped inside. Bobby perched on the edge of a chair by the bed.

Miguel's eyes swept over him. So, this was Nick's stepson and of course, the baby's father. He couldn't understand what Carmela saw in him. His face was handsome enough, but he lacked presence. He seemed a mere boy.

What she needed was a man. Someone to appreciate the strong, intelligent woman that she is. He might even have a chance since she had indicated her plans with Bobby had not worked out. Once she recovered, he would make her see how much he cared for her. One little polite kiss wasn't nearly enough for a woman such as her.

He moved to the opposite side of the bed. Carmela appeared almost child-like, her mocha-colored skin pale, IV lines trailing from her wrist. A purple bruise marked her cheek and trailed along her chin. Her arm was dressed in a cast.

Miquel bent and covered her hand with his own. "*Estoy aqui,* Carmela.

Bobby glanced up. "The doctor asked that we visit one at a time."

Miguel frowned. "What do doctors know? It is good for her to have those who love her close by." Miguel let go of Carmela's hand. He crossed his arms and peered down at Bobby.

"I don't think we've met," Bobby said.

"Miguel Medina. I work for Carmela."

"I don't recall her ever mentioning you."

He locked eyes with Bobby. "No, she wouldn't."

Bobby squinted at him. "Exactly what is it that you do for her?"

"Whatever she asks me to do."

"Oh, I see," Bobby said. "We're going to play that game."

Miguel laughed. "Games are for children. I think when she wakes up, she will be done playing with you." Warmth spread through Miguel's chest at the expression on his face.

Bobby rose. "I'm going to remain calm and ask you to please leave."

Miguel squared his shoulders. "And if I refuse?"

"I'll have you removed."

"I suggest you do as Bobby asked."

Both men turned. Bobby nodded at a tall, muscular fellow with dark hair.

"Nick, what are you doing here?" Bobby asked.

"I caught a flight after your mother called me."

Miguel's pulse spiked. Here stood the man he had heard about for so many years. Nicky D, the famous ghost. A smile spread across his lips. He observed Nick's body posture and the way his green eyes narrowed. One hand remained tucked in his jacket, and Miguel knew what lay inside.

He moved toward Nick and held out his hand.

"Miguel Medina."

Nick remained motionless. "I know who you are. Now, please leave. You can come back later. Bobby needs time alone with Carmela."

Miguel dropped his hand. "Oh, of course, the father of the baby must not be disturbed."

"Glad you see things my way," Nick said.

Miguel shook his head. "No, not really. I just think this is neither the time nor place for things to become...messy."

Nick's stony expression never changed. "I'm sure when we meet again things will become quite messy."

Miguel winked and strode out of the room. Outside the door his hands trembled. Rage built inside of him. As soon as her condition improved, he would carry out his own wishes. The great Nicky D would no longer walk this earth. And neither would Bobby D'Angelo.

# CHAPTER 47

## Carrie

Carrie stared at her cell phone. After speaking with Bobby, she'd given Nick a quick call to tell him about Carmela's accident and the baby. Unable to wrap her head around his failure to divulge Travis's true identity, though he tried, she refused to engage in any further conversation with him.

How many other things had he kept from her? Until now, trusting him was never an issue. His attempt to convince her he had her best interests at heart failed to change her mind.

He had no right to withhold such vital information. For years she had wondered about her father … who he was and why he had left. She shuddered to think he was by her side all that time. Not at all the father she pictured, but one who abused and lied to her. Travis claimed he loved her, but it was a sick love at best.

Her drug-addicted alcoholic mother had never shown her any kindness. No hugs, no words of comfort, no I love you. Tears welled up. A sob caught in her throat recalling the many beatings she endured at both her parents' hands.

Her love for Bobby, Izzy, and Michael was limitless. She'd never abuse them or let anyone else hurt them, but how to tell Bobby the last bit of truth she kept from him haunted her mind.

With Carmela in the hospital and the baby in the NICU, she'd need to hold off saying anything.

Aunt May gave her a break by taking the children over to the Palisades to see Joann and have some ice cream. About to go upstairs, she jumped when the doorbell rang. She hurried to answer it thinking maybe her aunt had forgotten her key. To her surprise, Dalton Burgess was on the other side.

"Dalton, what are you doing here?"

"Some greeting," he said and winked. "Mind if I come in?"

Carrie stepped away from the door. "Not at all."

He followed her into the living room. She sat on one of the overstuffed chairs adjacent to the fireplace. She pointed to the sofa. "Please sit. Can I get you anything?"

Dalton removed his Stetson and set it aside. He unbuttoned his denim jacket before sitting. "No, I'm fine."

A moment of panic rose up inside of her. "Is Nick okay?"

He shook his head. "You tell me."

"Look, I don't know how much he told you, but this thing between us is pretty serious."

"Then you won't mind my being blunt?"

"No, go on."

Dalton cleared his throat. "That man of yours is very special to me. He saved my life more than once. So, when I see him suffer, I need to try to do something about it."

Carrie sunk into the cushions. "You think he's the only one suffering?"

His eyes narrowed. "Of course not. But there needs to be a way to fix things. True, he broke his word, but for a good reason."

Her arms curled around her middle. Nick must have told him everything. Her face grew warm with shame. It took all her resolve not to run from the room.

Dalton's brows knit together. "I'm not here to make you feel worse than you already do, Carrie. What happened to you in the past is not your fault. Nick was only trying to protect you. It's in his nature."

She raised her head. "What about Carmela? He kept everything he knew about her to himself. Bobby's life could be in danger. No one knows what she intends to do after the baby is born."

"I've never been able to trust anyone until I fell in love with him," she said. "We promised each other there would be no more secrets between us. I trusted him…he broke that trust. First by not telling me about Travis, then second by not telling me about Carmela. It makes me wonder what else he hasn't told me."

"Do you really want to know everything?" Dalton said. "I never took you for someone that naïve. Nick wouldn't put that kind of burden on you. He has a hard enough time living with some of the things he's done and is being forced to do now."

His words cut her to the bone. Dalton was right. Nick had always shielded her from all the killing. If he hadn't, their marriage would never have survived.

"Tell me something," he said. "Have you told Bobby everything about his father?"

"No. I don't know how I'm ever going to do that."

"Because you're trying to protect him the same way Nick tried to protect you."

"I guess so."

He grabbed his Stetson and rose. "I hope you'll consider what I've said. That man loves you more than life itself. If he hadn't put an end to Travis, where would you be now? You owe it to him to try to work things out."

Carrie got up and faced him. "You've given me a lot to think about. I appreciate you're coming all this way."

For the first time, she saw Dalton blush. He dipped his head and averted his eyes. "Well, you were the main reason I came, but not the only one."

Surprised, she said, "Oh, what's the other reason?"

"I also wanted to pay a visit to a certain redhead. She still work at the Palisades?"

Carrie gave him a half-smile. "Yes. As a matter of fact, she should be there now."

She walked him to the door. He bent and kissed her cheek. "Thanks for hearing me out, Carrie."

With Dalton gone, she grabbed her jacket and sat on the front porch rocker. Who was she kidding? Regardless of what had happened between her and Nick, she could never live without him. He saved her from Travis and gave her a whole new life. She had a real home and two beautiful children to cherish. His love was her safe haven, her retreat from all the horrible things in her past.

Carrie rocked and closed her eyes. She pictured his face, and could almost feel his arms around her. Opening her eyes, she studied the passing clouds. She longed to be with him again. She'd made a foolish decision by taking the children and running away. They had always faced everything head-on together.

Her thoughts were interrupted when Izzy ran up the front walk. May and Michael trailed behind her.

"Mommy, we saw Aunt Joann and guess what?"

"What?"

"Uncle Dalton came while we were there."

"Yes, I saw him, too. He stopped by here first."

Izzy frowned. "When is Daddy coming?"

"Don't worry, we'll see him soon."

Michael climbed up the steps, and Carrie scooped him up in her arms.

A huge smile lit his face. "We had ice cream."

Carrie smiled at her aunt. "I hope they weren't too much trouble."

"No, I love spending time with them."

Carrie ushered the children inside, fed them supper, and then gave them baths. She was thankful it was their bedtime. She tucked them in, then headed to the living room to talk to May.

She had put a scenario in her head with regard to how Carmela got her information about Travis. She suspected the man who broke into her aunt's house had something to do with it.

May sat by the fire, blue yarn wrapped around her knitting needles. She looked up as Carrie walked into the room.

"Aunt May, I'm going to make arrangements to go home."

May's face lit up. "I'm so glad you made up."

"We haven't yet, but I'm sure we'll work things out." She sat on the sofa. "But there is something else I want to talk to you about."

"I don't like the sound of that," May said. She put her knitting aside.

"You never told me much about the man who broke into your house."

May frowned. "What is there to tell?"

"You said he asked about someone my mother knew a long time ago."

"That's right." She shifted in her chair. "But there is no need to bring up the past."

"Please tell me who. I need to know."

"Carrie, you're scaring me."

"I don't mean to scare you. This is a hard thing for me to say, so I'm just going to say it. Was the person this man wanted information about Travis Montgomery?"

May moved to the edge of her seat. "Travis? But how do you know about him?"

She forced the words out. "I left home with him after Bobby was gone. There was nothing for me in Breezy. I told you most of the story when I first came to Laurel. Leaving with Travis was the biggest mistake of my life."

"I can't believe I'm hearing that name again for the second time in weeks. Yes, it was Travis."

"But you said he asked about some man. You never said anything about my father."

May's brow shot up. "What are you talking about? Why would I mention your father?"

Carrie's pulse spiked. "Because Travis *is* my father."

May shook her head. "Whoever told you that? Travis is *not* your father."

Carrie bolted up from the chair. "But…" The room swayed. She tried to steady herself. Confused, she said, "He claimed that he was."

May waved a hand in disgust. "Of course, he would. Travis claimed a lot of things. None of them true, either. If you really want to know all about your father, I think you better sit down."

Carrie, her legs jelly beneath her, dropped onto the sofa. If Travis wasn't her father, then who was?

# CHAPTER 48
## Nick

Nick scowled at Miguel Medina walking out of Carmela's hospital room. He squeezed Bobby's shoulder. "I'm sorry about all this."

Bobby eyed him. "Let's step outside." He closed the door part of the way. "My mother told me the whole story, so I guess you're not really sorry."

"I'm sorry for you and for the baby. As for Carmela's father, that was unavoidable. I tried to make peace with him. Ricardo wasn't going to let things go. I did what I had to do to save us."

"And Carmela?"

Nick sighed. "Unfortunately, she had a lot of bad karma coming her way. I'm probably to blame for most of it."

"Because of her father?" Bobby asked.

"She wasn't always an evil person. Witnessing her father's death set off her endless need for revenge."

"Could you have killed her that day?"

Nick's stomach twisted. "Yes, but I gambled. I chose to walk away instead."

"Do you wish you hadn't?"

"That's a hard question to answer, Bobby. All I'll say is, regardless of what Carmela has done or will do, my main priority remains the safety of our family."

Bobby stared at the floor. "Carmela's in a coma, my daughter's in the NICU, and I don't know what to do."

"Bobby, look at me."

He raised his head. Dark shadows stained the skin beneath his eyes.

"I'm not sure how you feel about Carmela after all of this, but you're a father, now. Your daughter is the priority. What kind of life do you want for her?"

"I want her to be loved," Bobby said. "I want her to be safe. Most of all, I don't want her to be the daughter of a drug runner."

"Then, if you still love Carmela and want to build a life with her and your daughter, when she wakes up, you need to make that perfectly clear."

Bobby's eyes misted. "And if Carmela won't agree?"

"That's up to you."

"What would you do?"

A tightness swelled Nick's chest. He studied this young man who he'd grown to love, knowing his life was about to change forever just as his own had after Izzy was born.

"That's not a fair question, Bobby. What I would or wouldn't do should have no bearing on your decision. We're two different people. I've done many things in my life that I regret and others that I feel were justified. And after all of it, I think the important question is what are you willing to live with?"

Bobby shook his head. "I understand."

"Now, how about we go to the NICU so I can see my granddaughter?"

They walked down the hall together. Before they prepared to go inside, Bobby stopped. "That Miguel Medina, you know him?"

Nick frowned. "I know of him. Carmela uses him to do the things she can't do just like her father used me." He caught Bobby's eye. "Do you understand what I'm telling you?"

"Yes."

"He's as dangerous as they come." He hesitated a moment. "You need to keep me abreast of how things go with Carmela."

The color receded from Bobby's face. "Do you think…?

"I can't say for sure, but I wouldn't take it off the table."

Bobby swiped at his hair. "I won't confront Carmela until I know she and the baby are going to be okay."

"Call it as you see it," Nick said. "All of this is hard on you, but you have to be aware of how the game is played in that world. I'll always be there for you if you need me."

"Thanks." The two hugged. Bobby stepped back. A smile lit his face. "Come on, let's go and see her."


It was late afternoon by the time Nick left the hospital and flew to South Dakota. Dalton sent a limo to fetch him from the airport. He climbed into the dark interior and sank into the leather seat. Thoughts of Bobby and Carmela swirled in his head.

With his tiny granddaughter lying in the incubator, he hoped Carmela would come to her senses and let go of all her hatred, maybe even start a life with Bobby.

He wondered about Marco. Carmela wanting him to come to Napa to confront him. As much as he wanted to settle things with him, he wouldn't do it there. He'd be too vulnerable, besides the fact he didn't trust her. There would be time enough to deal with Marco…if he lived.

The car arrived at Dalton's house. Nick hurried inside. Dalton waited for him in the living room.

"Come sit. How did it go?" He poured two shots of whiskey and handed him one.

He eased into the leather chair. "As well as can be expected. Carmela hasn't woken up but they expect her to. The baby is holding her own."

"What about Bobby?"

"I wish I could make things easier for him. He'll have his hands full trying to convince Carmela to quit the drug business. My biggest fear is that she won't agree."

"And if she doesn't?"

Nick swallowed his whiskey. "She's still on my list."

Dalton smoothed his mustache and cleared his throat. "I've something to tell you, and I don't want you getting mad. You're going to find out sooner or later."

Nick studied his face. "You know I can't guarantee that. What is it?"

"I went to see Carrie."

"You did what!" He got up and looked down at his friend. "Why? What did you think you'd accomplish by doing that?

Now, Carrie knows I told you everything. She's hurt and embarrassed enough already."

"Calm down," Dalton said. He pointed to the chair. "Gee, you're such a hot head at times." After Nick sat, he continued to speak. "Listen, no two people in the world deserve to be together more than you two. I felt I needed to champion your cause, so to speak."

Nick swiped a hand through his hair. "And how did that go? Did she throw you out on your ass?"

Dalton chuckled. "No, on the contrary, she invited me in. I think I actually did some good. At least I gave her a way to look at things from a different perspective."

"You might have wasted a trip. I haven't heard from her since she called me about Carmela's accident."

"Wait and see. Give it a little time." Dalton's eyes twinkled. "Carrie's somewhat like you. Hard-headed and quick-tempered when things don't go her way."

"You're not very amusing, Dalton," Nick quipped. "You went all the way to Laurel for me?"

A flush crept up his friend's cheeks.

"Aha! I knew it."

"Aha, yourself," Dalton said. "I just figured it made sense to pay a visit to a certain someone who's been on my mind lately. Why make a separate trip?"

Nick smiled. "Might that certain someone work at the Palisades Diner?"

"You know damn well who I'm talking about."

"Well, if Carrie didn't throw you out on your ass, maybe Joann did."

"I'm keeping that bit of information to myself. Let's just say it wasn't a wasted trip."

Still a little upset about Dalton's conversation with Carrie, he couldn't deny it made him happy Dalton had seen Joann. He only went after something if he was serious about it. Apparently, she fit the bill.

"Now, on another note," Dalton said. "Our digging into Senator Adelson has been more than fruitful."

Nick perked up. "How fruitful?"

"Seems he's not the family man he portrays. For starters, he's got a pretty little piece on the side. They meet up once a week at her apartment outside of Washington."

"I like where this is going," Nick said.

"Wait, that's not all. A friend of mine in the Treasury Department works under the Financial Crimes Enforcement Division. He did some more checking for me. Senator Adelson's been using campaign funds to support his mistress's lifestyle. There are large deposits into her accounts from a New Mexico LLC by a registered agent he traced back to Adelson."

Nick took a deep breath. He slapped his hand on the arm of the chair. "That's better news than I expected."

"I agree. I'm waiting for the video from the hidden cameras I had one of my guys plant in her apartment," Dalton said. "With hard copy proof of his financial transactions and the video footage, we should be ready to meet up with the Senator."

"What's this costing you?"

Dalton grinned and said, "Don't worry about that. If this gives up the person holding us hostage as hired killers it will be well worth it."

"How long?" Nick asked.

"I should have everything by tomorrow afternoon, then we're going to take a little trip to Washington." Dalton poured two more shots. "Here's to our freedom."

Nick lifted his glass. "To our freedom."

# CHAPTER 49

## Carmela

Carmela blinked at the light pouring into the room. She ran her tongue over dry lips and pushed away the fuzziness in her head. Her vision blurred. She tried to focus on the image to her right. She blinked again. Her mind clearing, she smiled. Bobby, his head sagging to one side, slept in a chair next to her bed.

She touched her stomach. Her breath quickened. An ache hit the back of her throat. The baby! She pulled herself up. The IV needle pinched. Something weighed down her left arm. She stared at the stark white cast.

"Oh, thank God." Bobby took her hand. "I'll be right back. I need to tell them you're awake."

Carmela clutched his hand, refusing to let go. Her eyes searched his face.

"She came a little bit early, but so far, she's doing okay," Bobby soothed.

Her heart swelled at his words. She had a daughter. "I want to see her."

He shook his head. "She's in the NICU. I'll take you to her when you feel up to it."

Ignoring her pain, she eased herself up against the pillows. "Go get the doctor. I want to see her."

Bobby raced out of the room.

Emilio poked his head in the door. A smile lit his face. "Glad to see you are awake, *Señorita.* Such a terrible accident."

Carmela frowned. "Yes, but I did not fall, Emilio. I was pushed."

His brow creased. "Did you see anyone?"

She shook her head. "No. Please let Miguel know. We must find out who did this to me."

"I will let him know." He left the room just as Bobby returned.

Forty minutes later, with the doctor's okay, Bobby wheeled her past Emilio stationed outside the door and to the NICU. She glanced at the numerous incubators. Little babies lay inside hooked up to monitors, wires, and machines.

He stopped in front of an incubator. "There she is."

A sob caught in her throat. She reached through the porthole and cupped the baby's tiny hand and her eyes opened. Speechless, she stared with wonder at her daughter.

"She's so beautiful," Bobby said. "Just like her mother."

Carmela slowly drew her hand away. "Take me back to my room."

"But—"

"I said, take me to my room. Now, please."

Bobby wheeled her out of the NICU. He helped her to bed and pulled the sheet up around her.

"Carmela, what's wrong."

How could she explain something even she didn't understand? Holding her daughter's hand released emotions sleeping deep inside. Feelings she'd been unable to bring forth ever since her father died.

Bobby carried a chair to her bedside and sat. "Are you in pain?"

Carmela fixed her gaze on his handsome face, his ice-blue eyes full of worry, and she understood at that moment what she couldn't admit to herself before. She loved him, and she loved their daughter more than she ever thought possible.

How foolish she'd been to allow this to happen. Her love for Bobby and their child could never erase what Nick had done to her father. She mustn't let him deter her from her original plans.

When she was well enough, she would give Miguel his final orders to eliminate Nick, then she'd take her daughter and leave.

Bobby squeezed her hand. "Please, I need you to tell me what happened. Was it an accident?"

Carmela closed her eyes, remembering the hands on her back, how she tried to grip the handrail before crashing down the stairs. She had made lots of enemies these last few years. The question was who hated her enough they would push a pregnant woman down a flight of stairs?

"I don't remember," she lied. "It all happened so quickly. One minute I was at the top of the staircase and the next..." Tears welled up, and she swallowed hard.

"Okay, we don't have to talk about it now. I just want you to get well." He let go of her hand and got up. "I'm going to the NICU to spend some time with our daughter. By the way, we never discussed names. Do you have one in mind?"

She hesitated. "Natalia."

"Hmm," Bobby said. "Natalia. It's a pretty name. I like it. I'll be back in a little bit to check on you."

She waited for him to leave. The door shut behind him and she whispered, *"Natalia. It was my mother's name."*

# CHAPTER 50

## Carrie

Carrie gripped the sofa cushion to stop the tremor in her hands. She stared at her aunt. "Travis, is not my father?"

Aunt May shook her head. "Carrie, I don't understand. How do you even know Travis? You were a tiny baby when he left your mother."

Carrie winced. Heat flashed inside her chest. "He came to the trailer one day when my mother wasn't home. I didn't know what a bad person he was back then."

She stared at the floor. "After she sold Bobby, I couldn't bear to stay there any longer."

"Carrie, look at me," May said. "Please, look at me."

Carrie raised her head. Pain gripped her throat.

"Is Travis Bobby's father?" May asked.

She forced the word out. "Yes."

"That rotten animal!"

"But I'm partly to blame, Aunt May. He didn't force me to go with him. Things were okay in the beginning, before he started to change. But even then, I stayed with him because I believed he was what I deserved."

"How could you think such a thing?"

"Because I should have protected Bobby. He was gone, and it was my fault. I still feel that way at times." Salty tears stung her lips.

"You made a mistake. People make mistakes all the time. You need to stop blaming yourself. The two of you found each other again, and that's all that matters."

Carrie brushed at her tears. "Nick tells me the same thing. I try, I really do, but to know how much Bobby suffered still rips me apart."

May cleared her throat. "Carrie, you deserve to know the whole story regarding your mother."

May sat next to her. "I told you the truth when you first came to Laurel. She was never any good at picking out men. That included your father."

Pain lit inside Carrie's chest and she pushed against it. "Who…is he, Aunt May? Who is my father?"

"His name is Alexander Paterson. He comes from a very wealthy family. She met him when she left Laurel at eighteen. She never liked living here. Got it into her head to move to New York and start a new life."

"She'd only been gone six months when I went to visit her. I was astonished to find her living in a fancy apartment I knew she couldn't afford on a receptionist's salary. But I found out how after I forced the information out of her."

Carrie tried to picture her mother all those years ago. Her aunt's story was almost impossible to believe. Her drunken and drug-addicted mother living in a fancy apartment in New York?

"She met Alex at work," May continued. "They dated, but when things became serious, she discovered he was engaged. The girl came from some high society family. By that time, your mother found out she was pregnant, and she threatened to go to his parents. He wanted her to have an abortion but she wouldn't. I think she believed she could change his mind. They fought a lot. He refused to continue to pay for the apartment and wrote her a check instead."

"A check?"

"Yes, making her promise to leave. She saw him a few times after that, but all they did was argue. She ending up leaving and bought the trailer in Arizona. There wasn't much money left after that."

A sick feeling hit the pit of Carrie's stomach. "So, my father didn't want me either."

"I think it was more complicated than that, along with his fear of being disowned. Alex came to see your mother once after Travis left. You were a tiny baby then. She got her hopes up, thought he would take her back, but her drinking was worse by then and they argued constantly. He left Arizona within a few weeks. To the best of my knowledge, she never heard from him again."

"When did Travis come into my mother's life?"

"I'm not really sure. But she didn't waste any time trying to find someone else after she left New York. She thought a new man would solve her problems."

"They met when she was a little over two months pregnant with you. She confided in me, and I told her she needed to tell Travis the truth. But instead, she led him to believe you were his. She said she didn't want another man walking out on her like your father did. But after you were born, that's exactly what happened, anyway. She started drinking, and they fought a lot until Travis up and left."

"Travis believed he was your father because she put that idea into his head." May frowned. "You and I both know he wasn't that bright a man."

"Your mother really never got over Alex."

Carrie absorbed May's information. So many things made sense to her now, even her mother's misdirected anger. Every time she looked at her daughter, it reminded her of Alex and how he threw her away. For the first time, she felt sorry for her mother.

May's eyes fixed on her face. "How did your mother never know about you and Travis?"

Carrie's palms grew damp. "When I think of it now, it was quite odd. He literally appeared out of nowhere one day outside of Breezy. Even though he was so much older than me, we became friendly. He'd take me for rides in his car after school, and things progressed from there. He never came near the trailer and made me promise not to tell my mother about us."

May rubbed her chin. "That figures."

"When I got pregnant, he disappeared," Carrie said. "He didn't turn up again until after Bobby was gone. By that time, I was so distraught and angry at my mother that I accepted his offer to leave."

May's face fell. Her lips pressed into a fine line.

"What is it, Aunt May?"

"Don't you find it odd that he turned up *right* after Bobby's disappearance?"

"Are you saying he had something to do with my mother selling Bobby?" Carrie's stomach twisted.

"It's quite possible," May said. "I certainly wouldn't put it past him. Has he ever tried to contact you again?"

Carrie's heart drummed. She couldn't tell her aunt what happened to Travis. She'd never look at Nick the same way.

"No, he hasn't."

"And what have you told Bobby?"

"The truth about what kind of man his father was."

"Good. He needed to know." May sighed. "He's young. He'll settle with it."

"Now, you sound just like Nick."

May gave her a half-smile. "I knew there was something I liked about him."

Later that evening, Carrie retreated to the front porch to sort out her feelings. Out there somewhere, unaware of her life and all the tortuous things she had gone through was the father she'd never met. Her heart was telling her she couldn't let it go. The day would come when she'd seek out the man who abandoned them.

She sat on the rocker and gazed up at the ebony sky filled with stars. Here was another thing she and Bobby had in common. Travis never wanted him either. She shuddered to think he might have conspired with her mother to sell Bobby.

Tension eased from her body while she rocked and studied the sky. All the misery Travis caused her and Bobby condemned him to the death he deserved. The guilt she carried for so many years finally slipped away. Her aunt was right. It was time to forgive herself.

Tomorrow, she'd take her children and go home to South Dakota. Home to the man who loved her for who she was. From the very beginning, he never judged her past or the mistakes she had made. She loved Nick now more than ever before.

Her cell phone buzzed. She checked the screen and answered.

"Bobby, how are Carmela and the baby?"

"The baby is doing well. She may not have to stay in the incubator much longer."

She heard the weariness in his voice. "And Carmela?"

"She's awake. Banged up, but for the most part okay."

Carrie took a breath. "Do you need me to come?"

"No. Nick was here. We talked. I know I need to make some hard decisions."

"I'm so sorry, Bobby." She wished she could hug him and say everything would be fine. But in reality, she wasn't sure it would be. "You know that whatever you decide, we'll be here for you."

"Mom, I'm sorry, too. I doubted you. You saw what I couldn't."

Her heart fell. "Don't do that. You're not to blame for falling in love with someone who you had no idea was using you for her own selfish needs."

"I guess…"

"Listen, I was going home tomorrow, but I can change my plans. I'd like to get a look at my granddaughter."

"Really, you don't have to come."

"I know I don't have to, but I think I need to be there with you."

"What about Izzy and Michael?"

"They can stay with Aunt May, and I'll have Joann look in on them. I'll get a seat on the first flight out tomorrow morning."

"Text me the information, and I'll pick you up at the airport."

"Good. I'll see you then."

The flight from Allentown gave Carrie the opportunity to think about her son's predicament. He now had a daughter to consider and Carmela could make his life a living hell if she wanted to.

By the time she landed, she was determined not to let her angst show regarding Carmela. Overnight bag in hand, she met Bobby curbside. She tossed her bag in the rear and climbed in beside him. His lips brushed her cheek. Dark stubble covered his chin and cheeks. His face was drawn and pale. Bluish tint stained his lower lids. He must have noticed her shocked look.

"I'm okay. Just a little tired. Thanks for coming. I've been spending most of my time at the hospital."

"I understand, but you need to take care of yourself, too," she said. "You'll be no good to anyone if you don't."

They drove in silence. He parked in the hospital lot, and they hurried inside to the NICU. Bobby pointed to an incubator. "There she is."

Carrie moved closer. Her breath caught. She reached in and stroked her granddaughter's arm, then placed her index finger into her palm. Tiny fingers curled around hers in response.

Carrie smiled, managing to suppress her tears. "She's so beautiful. What's her name?"

"Natalia."

"I love it. Such a pretty name."

"She's been breathing on her own now, and the jaundice is all but gone," Bobby said. He draped his arm across Carrie's shoulders. "I'm so glad you're here."

They stayed a few more minutes, and then headed to Carmela's room. Carrie steeled herself for the worst. They stopped outside the closed door.

"Are you sure you want to see her after what happened in Napa?"

"I'm sure. There is no use hiding from each other. We both need to heal for Natalia's sake."

Bobby pushed the door open. "Carmela, someone is here to see you." He stepped aside and let Carrie pass. "I'll wait out here."

She lay propped up against the pillows. A dark purple bruise ran along the side of her face. One arm, wrapped in a cast, rested on top of the sheet.

"Carmela, I'm so sorry."

Color invaded Carmela's cheeks. Her brow lifted. "What are you doing here?"

Carrie studied her for a moment. Not sure how to proceed, she said, "I'm not going to lie to you. Things didn't end well with us. But you need to know I am truly sorry about your accident. I'm a mother after all, and I wouldn't wish that on anyone…let alone the person carrying my grandchild."

"We have this beautiful little girl between us now, Carmela. It's time we stopped trying to hurt each other. I would think you'd agree with me."

Carmela's dark eyes settled on hers. "I don't know what I want anymore. Nick must have told you by now what happened between him and my father."

"Yes, and I guess you feel I'm to blame for a part of it."

"A part? No. *You're* to blame for everything."

"Sorry, but I don't agree with you. Nick wanted out for a long time before he met me. Those orders from your father were going to be his last."

Carmela's face pinched. "And he failed to carry them out because of you."

"That may be true, but things would have come to a head sooner or later."

"Did you know that we were to be married?"

Carrie grew uncomfortable. She was trying hard not to upset her any further, but she could see Carmela pushing against any type of reconciliation. She moved closer and stood at the foot of the bed.

"I know your father wanted the marriage, but Nick did not."

Carmela wagged her finger. "Sure. That is what he probably told you. He lies a lot. He didn't tell you the truth about me from the beginning. Nick and I were in love until you came along."

Her patience exhausted, Carrie moved to the bedside. "Okay, Carmela, that's enough. I'm not here to debate the past nor what you deem to be the truth. None of that matters anymore. I'm sorry about your father. I can't imagine what you went through."

Carmela shot her a look. "Speaking of fathers, you ought to be ashamed. Have you told Bobby he is a child of incest?"

Carrie shrugged. "I'm afraid to disappoint you, but Travis was not my father. My aunt told me about my real father. I know who he is and what happened all those years ago."

"If you say so." Carmela yanked the sheet up around her.

Carrie could tell there was no getting through to her. This woman would rather continue to play games than to make amends.

"Carmela, you can believe me or not, but make no mistake, I will not tolerate you hurting my son, or the daughter the two of you brought into this world. Bobby loved you. He may still love you even after learning the truth, so, you either agree to put things to bed, or we will have a rough road ahead of us. Now, my question to you is, do you love my son?"

Carmela stared at the far wall, her free hand clutching the sheet. Silence enveloped the room.

Carrie moved closer and gripped the bedrail. "Well, do you? Do you love Bobby?"

Carmela turned her head. Tears coursed down her cheeks. "No," she whispered.

Carrie had hoped for a different response. "Then you better figure out how the two of you are going to raise your daughter amicably. Because I meant what I said. Don't hurt my son, or you'll live to regret it."

Carmela wiped at her tears. "I will regret nothing."

Carrie studied her for a moment. What did this woman hope to accomplish by continuing to torture them? It certainly wouldn't bring her father back.

"Well then, I see we understand each other." Carrie turned and left the room.

The plane ride from Laurel to South Dakota couldn't have come soon enough. It was early evening when Carrie ushered the children into the hired car.

Wanting to surprise him, she hadn't called Nick. There had been no communication between them since her call about Carmela.

They stopped in front of the house. Carrie climbed out of the car, her spirits lifting. She had the driver leave the luggage on the porch and hurried inside with the children.

She expected to see Chino come running toward them barking, his tail wagging wildly back and forth. But only silence greeted them.

Izzy ran up the hall. "Chino, we're home." She yelled at Carrie. "He's not here."

Holding Michael's hand, Carrie went into the great room. It was empty.

"Where is Daddy?" Izzy asked.

"Maybe he's upstairs, honey."

Izzy tore up the stairs only to return a few moments later. "Mommy, Daddy's not there."

Disappointed, Carrie dropped onto the sofa. Michael squirmed into her lap.

Izzy tugged at her arm. "Where is he, Mommy?"

"I don't know. I'm sure he'll be home soon." She removed her cell phone out of her jacket pocket and pressed Nick's number. It went straight to voicemail. She typed an I'm sorry text and let him know they were home. Wherever he was, it must be important.

Minutes ticked by with no response. She decided to fix a quick dinner for the children and get them settled.

Hours swept by with no word from Nick. Exhausted, she put the children to bed, and then drew a hot bath. She poured in her favorite lavender scented oil and slipped into the water.

Resting her head on the bath pillow, the image of Carmela lying in the hospital came to her mind. If she told the truth about not loving Bobby, things were going to get ugly for sure. Any inkling of trust she had for her vanished.

How sad Carmela pushed away love. Her father had taken that with him when he died. Carrie now understood Nick's torment and how much he blamed himself for the beautiful young woman who had become so hateful and bitter.

She sighed and dipped further under the bubbles. If there were no way to get Carmela to repent, then they would have to do everything possible to make sure Bobby and Natalia were safe. Her granddaughter would not grow up with a drug-running mother. Whatever the cost, between her and Nick, they would do it.

# CHAPTER 51

# Nick

Nick dabbed smoked chili cocktail sauce onto an oyster and slid it into his mouth. Across the table, Dalton mimicked Nick's actions.

"These sure are good," Nick said.

Dalton swallowed. A grin lit his face. "Couldn't agree with you more. But I can't wait to get out of this monkey suit."

Nick chuckled and touched the lapel of his grey Hugo Boss suit. "It's not too often we dress up lately." He made a sweeping gesture with his hand. "Besides, you know what they say, when in Rome."

Dalton shifted in his chair. "Otherwise we'd stick out like a sore thumb in this fancy place."

"Are you sure he's going to show?" Nick asked.

"My sources tell me the senator eats lunch here every Thursday afternoon without fail."

Nick settled back into the teal blue chenille chair. He noted the difference here in Charlie Palmer Steakhouse. Unlike other steakhouses filled with dark mahogany wood, this one offered sleek décor with prices to match. Pale yellow light filtered through the round drum pendants suspended from the trey ceiling. Across the room, a vast expanse of glass captured the view of Capitol Hill. He observed the mirror-topped bar where several patrons sipped expensive cocktails.

They finished the oysters just in time for the waiter to bring two bone-in ribeye's, and sides of potato gnocchi with truffle, pecorino, and chives.

The restaurant started to empty, and Nick began to doubt if the senator would show.

"Heads up," Dalton said. He motioned at a table in the far corner by the window where a middle-aged silver-haired gentleman in a dark blue suit took a seat.

Nick smiled. "Guess we won't have time for dessert."

Dalton signaled the waiter and paid their check. Before leaving, he handed Nick a manila envelope. Nick rose, strolled to the senator's table, and sat across from him.

The senator looked up from his menu and frowned. Watery blue eyes locked on Nick. "Do I know you?"

Nick clasped his hands on the table. "That's a good question, Senator Adelson. You should. After all, aren't you the reason I'm traveling half-way around the world doing your bidding?"

He stared at Nick for a moment. "Do I need to have you removed?"

Nick took out his cell phone. "That wouldn't be wise, Senator." He pulled up a video. "That wedding band on your finger tells me you might want to take a look at this." He cut the sound and placed the phone on the table, screen facing the senator.

He grabbed for the phone, but Nick was too quick for him. He stopped the video, putting the phone in his suit pocket. "There are plenty of those videos, Senator. You and your little side dish doing all kinds of kinky stuff."

Senator Adelson set his menu aside as the waiter appeared. He nodded at Nick. "Whiskey?"

"Why not."

They sat in silence until the waiter returned with their drinks. The senator lifted his glass. He gulped his drink, then signaled for another.

"Look, my wife is well aware of my relationship outside of our marriage, but I prefer those videos stay out of the public eye." He rubbed his palm across the sweat forming on his brow. "How much do you want?"

"Nick sipped his whiskey. "Money is not what I want, Senator. I want a name or the names of whoever is sending my partner and me out to extinguish certain people."

His face flushed. "I'd be putting my life in danger if I told you." He shook his head. "I'll give you money for the videos and whatever else you have on the two of us, but that's it."

Nick's heart thumped. It was time to pull out all the stops. "I'm afraid that's not it, Senator. There's the matter of your, shall we say, misuse of campaign funds."

"I don't know what the devil you're talking about." The waiter set a second glass on the table, and he consumed it as quickly as the first.

Nick smiled inside. Things were going well. He held out the envelope.

"What the hell is that?"

"I think you'll find the contents very interesting. Such a shame to end a career like yours. Wonder how many years you'll spend in prison."

Senator Adelson reached for the envelope, glanced around, and undid the clasp. He drew out several sheets of paper. Through clenched teeth, he said, "Where did you get this?"

"Where or from whom doesn't matter. But it's proof of just how corrupt you really are. Look, Senator, I have no love for politicians. They never follow through with their campaign promises. They sit here in Washington like kings on their thrones, while the people who put them in office wait for them to fulfill all those empty promises they made." Nick locked eyes with him and folded his arms. "Now, you either give me what I want or your career is over."

Senator Adelson slipped the documents back inside the folder. He drummed his fingers on the table and stared at Nick. "You meet me here tomorrow, same time, and I'll have the information for you."

Nick shook his head. "No, Senator. You have until six this evening by the Lincoln Memorial, and bring proof."

"How do I know after I give you what you want you won't release those files or the videos?"

Nick smiled. "You just have to trust I'll do the right thing. Isn't that what you politicians tell your constituents?" He got up. "Six, Senator. No later and no funny business or I guarantee those documents will see the light of day."

Nick and Dalton sat in the hotel bar and waited. Nick was sure the senator would show. They agreed Dalton would hang back near the monument to make certain nothing went wrong.

Dalton took a long draw on his beer. "Listen, you do know that even if he gives us a name or names, we may still be climbing the ladder so to speak?"

"I don't care. Each rung brings us closer to the top." A dull headache erupted behind Nick's brow. "I want out. I'm tired of doing someone else's dirty work."

"Agreed," Dalton said.

Nick pulled out his cell. He grinned at Dalton. "Carrie's back home with the kids."

"That's great news. I knew things would turn out okay."

"With a little help from you, my friend."

Dalton shrugged. "Maybe, maybe not. But either way, I'm glad she's home. Have you heard anything more from Bobby?"

"Carmela's awake. My granddaughter is holding her own, and that's the important thing."

"And Bobby?"

"We talked. Poor guy doesn't know what to do. He fell in love with Carmela and now that he knows the truth, he has some serious decisions to make."

"He's a smart kid. He'll do what's right."

He eyed his friend. "And what might that be?"

"Put his daughter first, of course. What the hell did you think I was going to say?"

Nick let out a chuckle. "Just checking." He glanced at his cell. "Time to go."


Upon arrival at the Lincoln Memorial, they surveyed the area. Throngs of people milled about, some busy taking pictures. Dalton disappeared into the crowd while he waited at the foot of the steps. A few minutes later, the senator hurried toward him.

"You're late, Senator," Nick said.

"But I'm here."

They walked to the reflecting pool and away from the crowd. The senator handed him a dark grey file folder secured with a clasp. "That's who you want to be looking at. I just pray they never find out I gave you the information."

Nick winked. "Don't worry, your secrets safe with me."

He wrung his hands. The furrows along his brow deepened. "What about…"

"Like I said. You're going to have to trust me. You have one thing in your favor Senator."

"What's that?"

"I'm not a politician. Unlike you, I keep my word." He placed the folder under his arm and walked away.

Nick and Dalton sat in the limo making light conversation. They had agreed not to view the contents of the folder until they were in the air. By the time they were settled for the flight home, the suspense was almost too much.

Nick undid the clasp. There were two pockets inside. He drew a sheet of paper from the first pocket. It listed the names of the leading drug kingpins and their cartels. Names were crossed out in red alongside the ones he and Dalton had eliminated. But there were many more left on the list.

Nick let out a low whistle. "This would have kept us busy for a long time." He handed the paper to Dalton.

Dalton's eyes raked over the list. "You sure got that right."

Nick pulled out two sheets from the second pocket. The first one was a typed message from the senator. He read it out loud.

'Here is the who you want. Keep in mind how dangerous this information is. This person is powerful with many friends in high places. Please leave my name out of this, or I'm a dead man.'

Nick set the sheet aside. He looked at the second one. His heart lurched. Carmela's face stared up at him. A nerve quickened in his throat. He handed the sheet to Dalton.

They looked at each other. Dalton pounded his fist on the table. "That bitch had us running around out there putting our lives on the line, just so she could run her drugs."

"I knew she was bad," Nick said. "But this…this tops everything." Heat flushed through his body. He gripped the armrests. Bile burned his throat, and he swallowed it back. Carmela didn't care how much destruction she caused. If he and Dalton were expendable so were Bobby, Carrie, and, possibly, his children. Her hatred for him consumed her.

Dalton retrieved a bottle of whiskey. He poured two double shots and handed one to Nick.

Nick drained the glass. The warmth of the whiskey spread across his chest.

As much as he blamed himself for Carmela's vengeful wrath, he would do everything he could to stop her from causing further damage. Whatever it took to keep his family intact and out of her reach, he'd do it.

He locked eyes with Dalton. "Carmela is finished. I'm going to do what I should have done a long time ago."

# CHAPTER 52
## Bobby

Bobby drove through the gates of the Santiago Vineyards. He slid the window down. The familiar scent of ripening fruit filling his lungs brought little comfort. Clusters of grapes hanging from the vines foretold the promise of an abundant harvest.

But what of his future and that of the tiny baby who learned to breathe on her own? Natalia was out of the incubator, bottle feeding but still in the NICU for observation. If all went well, she'd be discharged soon.

He'd held back confronting Carmela. But now that Natalia was out of the woods and Carmela home and mending, the time to face her had come. All the warning signs were there. His love for her had blinded him to the truth. His vision of a family torn apart all because of one woman's quest for revenge. He couldn't forgive the hurt she'd caused him and the people he loved.

He pictured Miguel Medina. The tall, olive-skinned, muscular man with the hooded eyes made his skin crawl. After what Nick said, he could only fathom what kind of work he did for Carmela. With her a constant target for the cartels, drug running demanded hiring men like Miguel. All the more reason he wouldn't allow his daughter to grow up in that environment

He steeled himself as he traveled along the stone drive and hurried up the front steps of the mansion.

Armando greeted him at the door. "*Señor* D'Angelo."

Bobby nodded. "Where is she?"

"The *Señorita* is on the rear patio."

He brushed past him. Carmela lay stretched out on the chaise lounge. She smiled up at him. "*Mi Tesoro,* I'm so happy you're here."

"Cut the crap, Carmela." He raked his fingers through his hair.

Her eyebrow arched. "What the hell is wrong with you?"

"I never said anything while you were in the hospital, but I know the truth. You lied to me about who you really are. As a matter of fact, you lied about everything."

She eased forward and swung her legs over the side of the chaise. "I figured they told you and I wondered why you didn't bring it up." She pushed up with her free hand and got to her feet. "I had hoped we could put all of it aside for our daughter's sake."

"Put it aside! Do you know how much damage you caused my family?"

"No more than they caused me," she said. A bitter note in her voice.

Bobby's heart twisted inside his chest. His jaw went stiff. He'd given her his love, and she failed to give him hers in return.

As if he was seeing her for the first time, her once beautiful face turned ugly before him. "Was it all a lie? Did you feel anything for me at all?"

She swept past him. Lifting a crystal pitcher, she poured some water. "Does it matter?" She raised the glass and sipped. "I can see how much I disgust you."

Every single muscle in his body burned. His fists clenched. "How could you be so callous and unfeeling? I loved you, Carmela. I wanted us to build a life together with Natalia."

She spun around. "How could I be so callous? I witnessed Nick put a bullet in my father's head then turn and walk away."

Bobby moved closer. "Oh yes, the same father who almost had my mother and Izzy killed. What did you expect Nick to do? We had to leave the country because of him. Always looking over our shoulders, never knowing when the next hit might come."

Her nostrils flared. She threw her head back and glared at him. "Your mother deserved that bullet. She was the cause of everything!"

A bitter taste stung his mouth at her words. He stared at the thunder behind her eyes. "You're an evil woman, Carmela. Your hatred toward my family will destroy you."

Her high-pitched laughter split the air between them. "You silly man, nothing will destroy me, but I have shown your family just how much damage I can do." She brushed her fingers along his cheek. "And will still do."

Bobby pushed her hand away. "You think you can break my family? We're stronger than you. Always have been and always will be. Because we have something, you'll never have."

"And what's that," she sneered, scowling at him.

"The love we have for each other binds us together. It's much more powerful than any hate-filled bitch's revenge."

Her face flushed. She stepped back and pointed her finger at him. "You will never win. By the time I am finished, you will wish we had never met."

Bobby folded his arms. "If it wasn't for Natalia, I would wish that right now. My daughter will grow up knowing she is loved and cared for by good people."

"Your daughter? Natalia is mine and mine alone."

"I'm afraid not. When the court learns how you're nothing but a low life drug runner, I think they'll side with me."

Carmela flung herself at him. He grabbed her free arm and spun her around as she tried to batter him with her cast. He wrapped one arm around her waist and the other across her chest.

"Let go of me!" she cried. But she was no match for him.

Bobby tightened his grip. "You will never raise our daughter. I'll do everything to keep that from happening."

The rack of a shotgun sounded. Bobby jerked his head up. Armando stood in the doorway. "Let the *Señorita* go."

He dropped his arms and moved back. "Don't worry, Armando. You can put the gun down. I was leaving anyway."

Armando stepped aside, the gun still trained on Bobby. "Go now, please."

Bobby turned to Carmela one last time. "You'll live to regret all the things you did to hurt my family. I can promise you that."

Bobby stormed out of the house. He climbed into his car and headed for the hospital. The only thing he wanted now was to be with his daughter. Nick's advice had proven itself. Natalia was his first priority. His confrontation with Carmela had left a black hole deep inside of him.

His dream of them raising a child together at an end. He could never trust her again. He'd been a pawn in her game of revenge and nothing more.

Tears stung his eyes. The road ahead blurred. He wiped his face with the back of his sleeve. He needed to be strong. His daughter depended on him. No matter how much he was hurting, he couldn't fail her.

Anxious to see Natalia, Bobby parked at the hospital and rushed inside. He'd spent the previous afternoon with her, overwhelmed when the nurse placed her in his arms for the first time. The tension evaporated from his body. Warmth spread through this chest as he pressed her close and kissed the top of her head. The love he felt for his daughter was like nothing he'd ever experienced before. He would protect her at all costs.

He rounded the hall to the NICU and prepared to go inside.

"Excuse me, Mr. D'Angelo." A tall blond-haired nurse dressed in blue scrubs approached him.

"Yes," Bobby said.

"I'm surprised to see you here."

"What do you mean? I came to see my daughter."

"Your daughter was discharged yesterday evening."

Bobby's chest heaved. His adrenaline spiked. "Discharged?"

"Yes, Ms. Santiago insisted on taking her home. The doctor okayed the order. The baby's weight had come up, and she was breathing and eating just fine. She's a strong little girl."

Bobby's limbs went weak. He planted his hand on the wall.

"Are you okay? Can I get you something?"

"No, no. I'm all right." He forced his legs to move and wandered up the hall in a daze. Fishing his cell out of his pocket, he punched in Carmela's number. It went straight to voicemail. Cursing, he dialed again.

"Nick, it's Bobby. I need your help. Carmela's taken Natalia."

# CHAPTER 53

## Carrie

Carrie stretched out on the sofa, a book in her hand. With the children asleep, she tried to focus on the words in front of her. She still had no word from Nick. Wherever he'd gone, he had either taken Chino with him or left him at Dalton's ranch. Unable to concentrate, she set the book aside.

Carmela caused this wedge between them. They couldn't let her have that much power. No matter what the future held, they needed to remain united.

She heard the front door open and sat up. Chino raced into the great room.

"Hello boy," she said, ruffling his fur. Carrie got up and her breath caught. Nick was standing in the doorway. She ran to him. Her arms encircled his neck.

"I'm sorry I left," she whispered.

"Please don't ever leave again." He pulled her close. "I'm so glad you're home." He took possession of her lips, kissing her long and deep.

She broke the kiss and studied his face. "I have so much to tell you."

"Me, too," Nick said.

They sat together on the sofa. Carrie proceeded to fill him in on what she had discovered about her biological father from May.

Nick's face relaxed. "That's good news. I guess if you hadn't gone to Laurel, you might never have found out the truth."

For the first time, she noticed the shadows beneath his eyes. "Where were you? I tried calling and texting. Why didn't you answer me?"

"Washington."

She bit her bottom lip. "Are you leaving again?"

"No. Dalton and I will not be going anywhere." He moved to the edge of the sofa and clasped his hands. "We found out who is behind this whole government thing," he said, his voice hard as steel. "It's all a sham, controlled by one person for their own needs."

She took in the pained expression on his face. "Who?"

Nick stood and paced. He rubbed the back of his neck. "Carmela. Carmela is behind it all. She had Dalton and me taking out these drug lords for her own gain."

Carrie jumped up from the sofa. "Are you sure?"

"Absolutely. We got the information from a good source."

She gripped her stomach. "That means she…"

"Yes. We could have died out there. For her to send us to do her bidding so she could run her drugs more freely tops everything."

"I went to see her at the hospital," Carrie said. "I thought maybe, just maybe, she'd come around. But it didn't go well."

"I'm not surprised."

A sudden chill swept through her body. "What are you going to do?"

He faced her and placed his hands on her shoulders. "I'm afraid things got a little more complicated."

"How complicated?"

"Bobby called."

"Is he all right?"

"Yes and no. He had words with Carmela. After he left her, he went up to the hospital. Natalia was gone. It seems Carmela took her the night before. She was probably at the house the whole time Bobby was there. He's on his way here now."

Carrie stepped back. "Oh my God, poor Bobby. I warned her, Nick. I told her if she hurt him or their daughter, she would regret it."

"And she will," Nick said. "Dalton and his guys are already on this. I know she won't stay at the Napa house much longer. She'll take Natalia someplace else. When we find out where, we'll get her back."

Carrie wrung her hands. "And Carmela?"

He looked into her eyes. "After what happened between us, I promised myself I would never lie to you. I'm going to do everything in my power to make sure she never hurts this family ever again."

It was close to midnight when Bobby arrived. Carrie greeted him at the front door. The drawn look on his face made her ache. How much more would he have to suffer because of Carmela?

"Mom, she took her." His eyes filled.

"I know." Her arms encircled him. His body shook. "It's going to be all right." She ushered him inside.

"Come and sit down? Can I get you anything?"

"Coffee, maybe?"

"Sure, let's go into the kitchen."

He settled at the island while Carrie prepared the coffee. When it was ready, she poured each a cup and sat with him.

"Where's Nick?" he asked.

"Right here," Nick said. He clapped Bobby on the back.

"When can we go get Natalia?"

"Slow down. We can't go to Napa. Too many variables. Besides, Carmela isn't going to stay there."

Panic lit Bobby's face. "What do you mean?"

"She'll take her somewhere she thinks is safe. Somewhere she'll assume we won't find her. But we will."

Bobby sipped his coffee. "What happens when we do?"

Unsure, Carrie looked at Nick. The burning in the pit of her stomach told her what Nick's intentions were, but she believed, in spite of everything, that her son still loved Carmela. "One thing at a time. Let's get her back first," she said.

Bobby's face fell. "You know Carmela will never let me have her." A frown crossed his lips. "I should never have threatened her with court."

"But remember," Nick said. "She took Natalia before the argument without telling you. Her plans were already set.

His shoulders slumped. He stared into his cup. "I don't understand how she could be so cruel. I loved her. To find out that it was all for nothing."

"Bobby, look at me," Carrie said.

He raised his head, his face full of shadows.

"You fell in love with someone whom you didn't really know. Sadly, Carmela's heart is so hardened she is either unable or refuses to feel the love you had for her." Carrie sipped her coffee and debated a moment. "I asked her at the hospital if she loved you."

"And?"

"She insisted she didn't, but I'm not so sure I believed her. I want to know if you still love her, because your answer will determine what happens when we find Natalia."

"I don't know what I feel. Right now, I just want my daughter with me."

"Okay," Nick said. "Natalia is our first priority." He squeezed Bobby's shoulder. "Don't worry, I'll get her back."

Bobby stood and faced him. "No. *We* will get her. I'm going with you."

# CHAPTER 54
## Carmela

Carmela attempted to pack her suitcase. Giving up, she cursed the cast on her arm and hollered for Armando. She glanced over at the bassinet where Natalia lay sleeping. With Bobby no longer in the picture, her daughter meant everything to her now.

At the hospital, she had refused to admit her true feelings to Carrie. Torn between her duty to avenge her father's death and the man she loved was too hard for her to handle. It would mean breaking her promise to her father.

Her hopes were dashed when Bobby came to Napa. She thought his love for her would outweigh everything, that their daughter would be a bridge between them.

But the hatred in his eyes told her it wasn't to be. She'd never feel the warmth of his body against her bare skin. The taste of his lips would become a distant memory. It was almost more than she could bear.

A sob rose in her throat. She took a deep breath to push it down and steady herself. There was no time to grieve for a love that had died.

After Bobby's tirade, taking Natalia from the hospital last night had proved to be the right decision. His threats about going to court were of no consequence. She had too many judges in her back pocket to worry about losing her daughter. If her drug-running came to light due to a custody hearing, friends in high places would protect her.

She called out for Armando again. What was taking him so long?

"Don't bother calling your lap dog. I took care of him and Emilio, too."

She looked up and froze. Marco Valletta stumbled through the doorway, with a bloody knife in his hand. His clothes were disheveled and dirty. A torn shirt sleeve revealed jagged red scratch marks along his arm. His hair hung in strands. Mud-stained shoes encased his feet.

She backed away. "What the hell are you doing here?"

Crazed eyes stared at her. "What do you think I'm doing here, Carmela? I've come to get what is rightfully mine." He moved closer.

Charging to the bassinet, she scooped up Natalia. "Don't come any nearer, Marco. I will give you whatever you want, but you mustn't do anything foolish."

He waved the knife. "Or what? How does it feel not to have the upper hand? Not so good, I bet."

"What do you want, Marco?"

He made a sweeping gesture with his arm. "Why all of this. Isn't that what you promised? A big house, fancy cars, clothes, the life you so easily live."

She tried to gather her composure. Her heart pummeled against her chest.

"Marco, listen to me. I must leave here tonight. I have taken the baby away from Bobby. Nick will be coming soon. Will you help me?"

She inched her way backward toward the nightstand where. Bobby's Glock lay inside. "I just need to pack some things."

"Help you," he hissed. "Who was helping me when you sent your men? They chased me through the vineyards like an animal." He shook his head. "But, sadly for them, I escaped."

Natalia let out a cry. Carmela rocked her, while her eyes remained trained on Marco. "Is that why you pushed me down the stairs? Even after I took you in and protected you from Nick? I didn't know you hated me that much."

"I have no idea what you're talking about Carmela. Why would I try to kill the person who is able to give me everything?"

She reached behind her.

"*Fermare!* Stop! Keep your hands where I can see them."

A figure flew through the doorway. Marco cried out as Miguel dug his fingers into his scalp and yanked his head back. In one swift movement he slit Marco's throat from ear to ear.

The knife fell from Marco's hand. Blood spurted from the open wound as he clutched his throat. Eyes bulging, he stared at Carmela. He staggered forward a few feet before falling face down into a pool of blood. His body convulsed, then went still.

Carmela's legs went weak. She eased onto the bed. "Miguel, thank God," she whispered.

He wiped his knife on Marco's shirt and returned it to its sheath. He crossed the room. "Are you okay Carmela?"

"Yes, I'm fine." She scanned his face, afraid to ask. "Armando?"

"I'm sorry."

Tears pooled beneath her lids. "Poor Armando. I'll never forgive myself."

He eyed her suitcase. "You were preparing to leave?"

"Nick and Bobby will come for Natalia soon."

"But you have your men stationed along the perimeter."

"So did my father. Nick is much more daring than you think."

Miguel touched her shoulder. "We will go together."

"I have already called Bernardo. The jet is ready."

"Planes can be traced. You have a destination in mind?"

"Yes. My plan to leave has been in place for a long time."

She let Miguel help her pack the rest of what she needed. She wrapped a blanket around the baby and followed him downstairs.

Her breath hitched at the sight of Emilio lying by the front door. Blood trailed from his body and across the tiled floor.

"There is nothing to be done for him," Miguel said. He rushed outside and loaded everything into his car, then stood in the doorway.

"Come, we need to hurry, Carmela."

"What about…the bodies?"

"Luis will take care of things."

She grabbed Miguel's arm. "Armando must be buried here on the property," she pleaded. "He had no other family except me."

"Do not worry, it will be done."

"I want to see him before we go."

"That is not wise."

"Please. I must." She handed Natalia to Miguel. He pointed toward the hallway.

She crept down the hall. Her palms grew damp. Armando lay sprawled on the kitchen floor, a death stare on his face.

Blood oozed from the knife wounds covering his body. She bent and stroked his cheek. "I'm so sorry, dear friend. May you find rest." She kissed his forehead.

She hurried back to Miguel. He handed Natalia to her. "We must go now."

Slipping out the front door, Carmela took one last look around. "I'm sorry, *Papi,*" she whispered. They drove out of the gates of the vineyard for the final time.

# CHAPTER 55

# Nick

Nick led Dalton into the great room. Soft, afternoon sunlight filtered in through the massive windows. Bobby, already seated, nodded to them. Carrie came in carrying three bottles of beer. She handed one to each of the men.

Dalton sat across from Bobby. "I'm so sorry, Bobby."

Bobby twisted the cap off his bottle. "What do we do now?"

"We're working on it," Dalton said. "We do know she took Natalia to the Napa house from the hospital."

"Why can't we go there?"

Nick leaned against the fireplace mantle. "It's not that simple. That place is well guarded."

"But you were able to do it once."

"Yes, but Ricardo wasn't expecting an assault. Carmela is prepared. She has twice as many men posted."

"So, we just sit and do nothing?" Bobby asked.

Nick eyed him a moment. "I learned a long time ago that patience plays a big part in a successful outcome. Things like this take planning. Natalia is not in any danger right now. We wait for Carmela's next move, then decide what the best course of action will be."

Carrie sat beside Bobby. "Listen to him. We'll do what needs to be done to bring your daughter safely home to you." She placed her hand on his arm. "But we both know Carmela will do everything she can to stop us."

Bobby sipped his beer and stared at the floor. "That's what I'm scared of." He looked up at Nick. "What happens when we do confront her?"

Nick fidgeted with his bottle. The question he asked was inevitable. "There is something else you need to know regarding Carmela."

"I'm almost afraid to hear it," Bobby said.

"She was the one sending Dalton and me after the cartel leaders. She also turned Marco against the family. He was holed up at her place. I'm sure he's probably dead by now."

Bobby set his beer down. He raked his fingers through his hair. "Is there anything she's not capable of?"

Dalton eased forward in his seat. "Bobby, you have no idea just how much power she yields. Ricardo left her not only his wealth but his many connections. Do you understand what I'm saying?"

He looked from Nick to Dalton. "It means no matter what I try to do legally, she'd still maintain custody of Natalia."

"I'm afraid so," Dalton said.

Nick wished they could have kept the truth from him, but he needed to hear it. Going after Natalia meant putting an end to Carmela if she wouldn't relent and give Bobby custody. Natalia's future lay on the line.

Knowing her, Nick figured out exactly what her intentions were. First, she lied to Bobby about who she really was. Her pregnancy, whether planned or not, drew him in further. She used her visits to South Dakota to complicate things between him and Carrie. She even managed to turn Marco against them.

His biggest fear was her endgame. Did she intend to continue to torture them in her own cruel way by using the baby or could she still have plans to eliminate him or other members of the family?

Carrie glanced at Nick and Dalton. "There is one thing I need to say. You have to be sure how far you want to go with all of this. Carmela is Natalia's mother, and I know first-hand she will do anything to protect her child."

"Are you saying what I'm doing is wrong?" Bobby got to his feet. "I'm Natalia's father, and I don't want her growing up with a mother who runs drugs, orders hits and who knows what else."

Carrie shook her head. "No, but you need to be prepared for the outcome. This is a dangerous situation. It could go either way."

His face clouded over. "I will do whatever is necessary to take my daughter away from Carmela. Even if it means I die trying."

Dalton's cell phone buzzed. "Yeah, go ahead. Stay on it. Let me know where they end up." He looked at the three of them. "Carmela is on the move."

"Is Natalia with her?" Bobby asked.

Dalton hesitated. "Seems so." He glanced up at Nick. "She left with Miguel Medina."

Bobby's face fell. "I met him at the hospital. What does all of this mean? Where do you think they're going?" He began to pace.

"Take it easy," Nick said. "Dalton's men will find out. The disturbing part is who she's with. Miguel is ruthless. He's loyal to Carmela, and I know he'll stop at nothing to protect her. If she's on the move this fast, she has a certain destination in mind. Her plans were already made. All we can do is wait."

Bobby sat next to Carrie. He placed his hand over hers. His eyes brimmed with tears. "Now, I understand."

"Understand what?" Carrie said.

"How you must have felt when you came home that day, and I was gone. You've tried to explain to me so many times, but as a father...I realize for the first time how much you suffered."

Carrie squeezed his hand. "There is no greater love than the love of a parent for their child, Bobby."

Nick listened to the exchange and was glad that Bobby finally understood Carrie's suffering. A hard lesson to learn under the circumstances but a necessary one. It would only serve to bond them all the more.

Bobby rose and faced Nick. "Thank you for always being there for me and for my mother." Then he turned to Dalton. "And that includes you, Uncle Dalton."

"I wouldn't have it any other way," Dalton said and winked.

Nick shoved his hands into the pockets of his jeans and wandered to the window. Bobby and Dalton continued to talk. He focused on the sky washed in watermelon reds and soft pinks, the sun slipping behind the green pines across the valley.

How would he feel after Carmela was gone? Would her demise enable him to put the past to rest? Or would she become another demon dwelling deep inside of him?

Carrie's arms came around his waist, and she pressed herself against his back. He clasped his hands over hers. The warmth of her body soothing him.

"I know how hard this is going to be for you and I'm sorry," she said. "Please stay safe and bring my son and granddaughter home."

Nick turned to her. A single tear slid down her cheek. He brushed it away with his fingertip and pulled her close. He wished he could tell her they'd be okay, but for the first time in his life, he wasn't sure. Eliminating Carmela just might destroy them and whatever remained of his soul.

# CHAPTER 56
# Bobby

Bobby walked the length of the gallery in SoHo. He stopped every so often to assess a painting. His excitement for opening nights in New York had vanished along with the loss of his daughter. Two months had gone by, and they were still no closer to finding Carmela. The constant ache inside of him increased each time he observed some stranger with a baby. He wanted to hold Natalia and reassure her that he hadn't abandoned her.

His biggest fears surfaced on the nights he couldn't sleep. He imagined never seeing Natalia again and her growing up without ever knowing him. Maybe Carmela would be with someone else, and she'd make her believe the new man was her father.

"Bobby."

"Hey, Lucy."

"Are you okay? You seem a little off."

What should his answer be? That he'd fallen in love with a drug runner who had taken his daughter away, and he was heartsick.

Her deep brown eyes peered out at him through her bright red frames.

"No, I'm fine," he lied.

"Your clients should be arriving soon. Can I help with anything else?"

"I think I've got things handled." His cell buzzed. It was Nick's number. "Excuse me a minute."

Could this be it or was Nick just checking in as was his habit of late. He appreciated his concern for him, but their conversations had become strained.

"Listen, Nick. Craig Sutter's Opening is about to start and I—"

"Bobby, we think we've found Carmela."

His pulse jolted, and his knees weakened. "Where?"

"It seems Ricardo had another home built a number of years ago."

Confused, Bobby said, "How did you not know that? You worked for him for over ten years."

"Look, Ricardo didn't tell me everything. Besides, he wasn't listed as the owner. He did it all under an assumed name. Probably a safe house, in case things went upside down with the cartels."

"So, you think that's where Carmela is?"

"It's a long shot, but it makes sense. There are no records of her jet leaving the country. Dalton's connections tell him she didn't use a private service either."

Bobby's adrenaline pumped. "She's in the states?"

"Now, keep in mind, we're in the process of trying to verify everything. But if this turns out to be solid information, then yes, she's still in the country."

"Where?" he asked. "When do we leave?"

"Lake Tahoe. But her being there doesn't make things easy. I'm certain the place is well guarded."

"When will you know for sure?"

"Within a few days. Finish your opening, then come to South Dakota."

He couldn't stop the pounding inside his chest. "Okay. And Nick?"

"Yeah."

"Thanks."

"Don't thank me, yet. We still have a lot ahead of us. We'll talk more when you get here."


It was late afternoon, the following day by the time he made it to South Dakota. Between the show in New York and Nick's news, he was mentally exhausted.

His mother greeted him at the door. She hugged his neck.

"You look terrible," she said.

"That bad, huh?"

"Come inside and relax."

They walked into the great room and sat. Bobby glanced around. "Where's Nick?"

"Dalton's house," Carrie said. "He'll be back soon enough. Are you hungry?"

"No, just anxious to talk to him."

It occurred to him that someone else was missing. "Izzy upstairs?"

"No, he took Izzy, Michael, *and* Chino with him. He wanted us to have a little time together."

"Wow, he's got his hands full."

Carrie laughed. "Well, yes and no."

"What do you mean?"

"Joann is there. I'm sure she'll keep them busy while the guys go over things."

"When did that happen?"

"I think it has been brewing for a bit. It took a while before Dalton mustered up the courage to make his feelings known."

Bobby chuckled. "It's hard to imagine Uncle Dalton having to muster up courage for anything."

The smile dissolved from Carrie's face. "Listen, I want to talk to you. Going after Carmela means putting all your lives in jeopardy. Make no mistake, Bobby, I'm having a hell of a time with this."

"Mom, I can't just let her have my daughter. Not under the circumstances. From the day I left her house in Napa, Carmela never answered my texts or calls. Since then, her number has changed. Natalia isn't safe because of Carmela's ties to the cartels."

"I didn't say you shouldn't try to get Natalia. I need you to understand what's at stake." Her eyes misted over. "Yours and Natalia's safety are a top priority. But things can go very wrong when you attempt something like this. Promise me, you'll stay focused and listen to whatever Nick says."

He squeezed her hand. "I know what you stand to lose."

"Do you?" She wiped at the tear escaping from her eye. "If I lost either of you…"

"Nick and I will be fine." He said the words more to convince himself than her. Bobby hoped they were true.

# CHAPTER 57
## Nick

Nick spread a map out on Dalton's long dining room table. Bobby, Dalton, and five of Dalton's men gathered around. The evening had started out with a light supper and easy talk among them until now.

Nick traced his finger along a line. "Here's where Carmela's property borders US Forest land. This will be the best approach. We'll work our way in from here. The bad thing is, we have no idea how many men she has posted, but I'm betting it's a good number. When we reach the house, we split and cover the front and rear."

"But shouldn't we spread ourselves around the perimeter?" Bobby asked.

Nick shook his head. "No. That may have worked in Napa, but since we don't have numbers or exact locations, we go in as a group and face what comes." He hesitated, looking at Bobby. "I'd feel more comfortable if you brought up the rear."

"Whatever you need me to do," Bobby said.

Nick was grateful for Bobby's level head. They had spent the last several days at target practice and acting out different scenarios. Bobby proved himself a willing participant and an expert shot. Even so, Nick needed to do everything he could to make sure Bobby survived. The look on Carrie's face when they left for the ranch spoke volumes.

He had wished he could reassure her that getting Natalia away from Carmela wouldn't be as difficult as she imagined, but he knew better. She would be a mother bear protecting her cub. There was nothing more dangerous.

Instead, he kissed his children goodbye, and held Carrie close before leaving with Bobby. He chose to ignore the trembling in her body and the fear in her eyes. His primary focus was to get Natalia and bring Bobby and her home safe.

"When we make it to the house, we'll have to determine the best way to enter." He spread out another sheet holding the house plans. There's a front and a rear entrance. If possible, we split up and cover both."

Dalton swept his palm over his mustache. "Weather looks good. That ought to help."

"Is all the equipment loaded in the van?" Nick asked.

"Almost," Dalton said. "We have vests, gloves, headgear, communication, and wound kits. Choice of weapons is up to you, Nick." Dalton grinned. "I'm well-equipped to supply whatever you need."

"Okay. Each man will carry an M4A1. It's lightweight, compact, shoots up to 600 meters and has an optic red dot sight." Nick said.

One of Dalton's men asked, "How many rounds?"

"Thirty rounds with a full auto setting. The M855 green tipped cartridges are capable of piercing body armor. We don't know what Carmela's men are equipped with, but this may give us an advantage."

Nick motioned at Dalton. "Sound suppressor kits?"

"You got it. Plus, you might like a new little ditty I picked up." Amusement glinted in Dalton's eyes.

"What's that?" Nick asked.

"The ENVG 3. Enhanced Night Vision Goggle. Restricted to the military...that is until now."

"Sweet," Nick said. "I've heard about them. Guess we'll have a chance to try them out."

"I've used night vision with Nick." Bobby chimed in. "He showed me several kinds when he was teaching me to shoot."

"Not like these," Dalton said. "You mount it to the rifle. The wireless capability summons up a picture in seconds and allows you to see in two directions at once. You can maintain cover and still target what's there without exposing yourself to hostile fire. The image updates as you move. It has a second thermal layer, fusing two kinds of vision into one and even outlines objects allowing you to peek and shoot around a corner."

Nick glanced at the men. "As a sidearm, we'll take the MK23. It's a good 45 caliber weapon with a 12-round magazine, sound suppressor and laser-aiming module. Let's gear up and practice, so everyone feels comfortable with all the equipment."

Dalton led his men outside. Nick held back. He placed his hand on Bobby's shoulder. "Bobby, are you sure you want to do this? You have Natalia to consider. There is no shame in opting out."

Bobby thrust his hands into his pockets. His blue eyes blazed. "Look, I know you and Mom are worried about me going, but what kind of father would I be if I didn't? No matter what happens, I have to be a part of saving my daughter."

Nick's pulse throbbed in his throat. He recognized Bobby's need to do what had to be done for the sake of his child. "I want you to know how proud I am of you." He stepped back, forcing a smile. "As for your mother, she would suit up and come with us if I let her."

Bobby laughed. "I can believe that. Now, we better get out there."

Nick worked with Bobby and the men to ensure familiarity with all the equipment including the illuminated compasses.

They would take the van, leaving at four in the morning for the twenty-hour drive to Lake Tahoe. Nick insisted Dalton's plane could be traced if there were spies at the airport who relayed information to Carmela. Where Ricardo had never dreamed of an assault on his winery, she was much more aware of the danger they represented to her.

They arrived in Tahoe at two the next morning, stopping only for food and fuel. They piled out of the van. Nick donned his vest and gathered his gear, then finished lacing up his hiking boots.

"Bobby, you stay in the rear. If things go south, you make it back to the van, and you leave. There's an extra set of keys under the mat."

A distant look washed over Bobby's face. "I understand."

Nick glanced up at the sky. Clouds raced past a full moon. Dalton and the men gathered around him beneath a semi-circle of Jeffrey Pines. The odor of vanilla from their bark lay heavy on the night air.

"We'll head south." Nick said. "There are coyotes, black bears, and mountain lions in this area so stay alert." He checked his compass, set his night vision, and moved forward into the thick woods.

Dalton followed on Nick's right, his men spread out behind them, and Bobby last. The superior night vision equipment enabled them to see almost crystal clear and kept time with each movement.

They followed a marked hiking trail for part of the way, but as they advanced closer to the house, the path ended, and thick brush rose up. They moved forward, stopping every few minutes checking for sound.

Nick spotted a figure to his left at the same time Dalton did. They raised their weapons and fired. The figure bounced and jerked falling backwards. A shout echoed from beyond the brush. Bullets whizzed overhead. Flashes of light zipped through the canopy of trees. The men returned fire, letting a hail of bullets rip into the woods ahead. Clips empty, they reloaded.

Nick motioned to Dalton. The two men separated, Nick going to the right and Dalton left of the oncoming gunfire. The rest of the men continued to fire straight ahead.

Nick's heart drummed in his chest. He scrambled among the tall pines. He cut farther to the right flank, while Carmela's men continued to return fire. His body hidden behind the trunk of a tree, he inched the barrel of his weapon forward, the enhanced night vision allowing him to see ahead and to the side beyond the trees. Three men came into view. His adrenaline rush hit full force. Crouching low, he let a barrage of bullets rip until all three fell to the ground.

A second round of fire went off to his left. He moved past the bodies determined to get to the house. The sound of gunfire continued to rain.

A sudden movement up ahead made Nick dive behind a bush and take aim. He emptied the rest of his clip. He inched his way forward. Just beyond the bushes, two more men lay face down.

Silence engulfed him. He waited. Dalton's familiar whistle signaled all was okay. He flipped his night vision monocular up and let out a breath. Dalton and Bobby came into view.

"That was some good old-fashioned fun," Dalton said, grinning.

"If this is your idea of fun, I don't think I'll be hanging around with you much longer," Nick said.

He chuckled. "Oh, come on, you love it as much as I do."

"Is everyone okay?" Nick asked.

"Three flesh wounds," Dalton responded. "My guys are headed back to the van. They'll be fine, but this leaves us short."

Nick shook his head. "We have no choice but to move forward and make it work," His eyes searched Bobby's ashen face. He placed a hand on his shoulder. "Are you good?"

"I think so. I just never thought…"

"I know. People lost their lives here. It's different when things become real. You'll never forget tonight, but no matter what happens you need to stay focused. Now, let's go get your daughter."

# CHAPTER 58

## Carmela

Comfortable in her blue and white silk pajamas Carmela looked out past the veranda running along the front of the house. Her eyes traveled to the jagged mountain range beyond the lake. Early evening shadows crept across their granite capped peaks. Thankful her cast was off she brushed at the dry patches of skin stubbornly clinging to her forearm. She wrapped her fingers around the stem of her wineglass, lifting it to her lips.

Her one-hundred-acre estate in the Lake Tahoe basin was a well-kept secret. Ricardo had the home built as an emergency refuge several years before he died. Shocked when he revealed the place to her, Carmela was grateful for the private haven.

Though smaller than her other homes, and consisting mostly of Western Cedar trucked in from Oregon, the timber and stone residence held five bedrooms, five baths, and an indoor lap pool. It boasted views of the lake from every room. The grounds contained a fully fenced horse pasture with a stable and fuel supply. Not sure how long they would stay she had not yet directed Mateo to transport the horses. All the fine art in Napa and Miami had been placed in climate-controlled storage.

Two months had gone by since she fled with Miguel and Natalia. Glad he had convinced her not to take the jet, sure it was a crucial factor in managing to keep them safe.

But, on quiet evenings like this, Bobby's face appeared before her. She remembered their nights of fierce lovemaking and more tender moments. The longing inside her for Bobby refused to ease, and, at times, she thought she'd never recover from his love.

There were so many ifs in her life. If Nick hadn't killed Ricardo, if Carrie hadn't stolen the life she had wanted, if Bobby might feel for her again the way he once did. But she needed to move forward for Natalia's sake.

Carmela felt his arm come around her waist. His lips brushed along her neck. "Nice evening, *mi amor*."

She smiled. "Yes, it is."

Two weeks after they arrived in Tahoe, her relationship with Miguel grew more affectionate. So far, they hadn't consummated what she knew was coming. Right now, there were only soft kisses, a gentle caress, and sweet words between them.

Without Armando, who she still mourned, Miguel showed a softer side by helping her learn to cook meals, and by paying attention to Natalia, especially when she cried. He'd scoop her up in his arms and soothe her while Carmela prepared a bottle.

Her businesses endured little interruption. She kept in communication with her employees by using burner phones and email. She tracked her drug shipments and laundered money as usual. Things ran pretty much the same except for a disturbing phone call she had received from Senator Adelson before leaving Napa. The stupid fool had given Nick her name. If he could break that easily, something needed to be done about him. As her father taught her, everyone has their price. Not long after, the poor senator suffered a fatal heart attack in his mistress's bed.

She could only imagine how Nick reacted when he found out she was the one orchestrating his hits. His hatred for her had surely grown by leaps and bounds.

A squeal came from the baby monitor perched on the railing. Carmela slipped past Miguel. "I'm going to check on Natalia." She moved through the vast living area with its coffered ceiling and a massive double-sided Montana River Rock fireplace.

In the master bedroom, she padded over to the bassinet. Natalia, eyes open, scrunched up her face and cried.

"Okay, *pequeño*. Hush, my little one," she soothed. Carmela lifted her and headed for the kitchen. White Carrera Marble ran the length of the island and countertops. Cherry wood cabinetry gleamed beneath the recessed lighting along with the glass tile backsplash in muted grays, creams, and beige tones.

Holding her daughter in one arm, she prepared a bottle, and settled on the grey sectional in the living room. Natalia sucked greedily, while Carmela, who never tired of looking at her daughter, studied her features. Caramel-colored hair capped her tiny head, and Bobby's full lips formed her mouth. But it was her eyes that fascinated Carmela. Natalia had her father's ice-blue eyes. She wondered if, in the coming months they would change.

If not, Natalia's eyes would always remind her of Bobby. The man, who without knowing, had broken through her hard exterior and made her feel something she'd never felt since the death of her father. Love for another human being. And now, Bobby's last gift, Natalia, forcing her to feel it again. Her love for her daughter needed to be enough to sustain life without him.

Natalia finished her bottle, and she placed her back in the bassinet. Within minutes, she was fast asleep, and Carmela returned to the living room where she found Miguel sitting on the sofa. She dropped beside him and smiled.

"If only it could be this peaceful all the time," she said, resting her head on his shoulder. "With Marco dead and Diego no longer sending threats, things may be settling."

Miguel sighed. "There is a good chance that you are correct. But right now, you must not believe all is well. They are searching for us, and eventually, that search will lead them here. It is time to make a long-range plan."

She lifted her head. "I know what you are saying is true, but I don't want to keep running. That is not a life for Natalia or me."

"And the solution is?"

"I think we should stay and take a stand. Let them find us. I will station additional men around the grounds. We need to eliminate Nick, once and for all."

Miguel raised an eyebrow. "And Bobby?"

"If he continues to challenge my custody of Natalia, I will have no other choice than to have you do what is necessary."

Miguel got to his feet. He walked to the wall of windows. His back to her, he said, "Somehow I find it hard to believe you would have me kill Natalia's father."

Carmela rose and went to him. "Why is that so hard to believe, Miguel?"

He turned. His dark eyes scanned her face. "Because you are still in love with him."

A quiver traveled through her body at his words. "Not anymore," she said. "I gave that up months ago and I will not let him take my daughter from me. He will die before that happens." Her palm caressed his cheek.

Miguel gathered her into his arms. His breath grew heavy. He kissed her lips.

Without wanting to, she succumbed to his kiss, pressing up against him. Making it go deeper.

She broke the kiss. He took her hand and led her to his room. They silently undressed and slipped beneath the covers. His hands traveled the length of her body, exploring. He kissed the hollow of her neck, then each breast.

"Carmela, I…I've waited so long for this. So long to tell you…" His eyes brimmed with desire.

She pressed her fingers to his lips. "Don't speak."

Wrapping her arms around his neck, she drew him to her. Their bodies met. Her breath caught as he entered her. Carmela closed her eyes and imagined it was Bobby, his arms holding her tight, and his lips she was kissing. She climbed higher and higher until her mind exploded. A wave of pleasure washed over her, and she stopped herself from calling out Bobby's name. Miguel shuddered and arched his back.

The wave receded. She opened her eyes. Miguel's handsome face hovered above her. He kissed her softly on the lips and slipped beside her. His arm draped around her as they fell into a satisfied sleep.

It was well after midnight, when Carmela eased up and got out of bed. She threw on her pajamas.

"Where are you going?" His voice was low and soothing.

"To check on Natalia. I will be right back." She ignored his moan of protest and stepped out into the hall. Natalia's soft cry made her hurry into the kitchen where she prepared a bottle.

Carmela fed her and placed her in the bassinet. She crossed the moonlit living room and walked out onto the veranda.

Her arms cinched her waist. Would Bobby intrude every time she slept with Miguel? She breathed in the night air trying to quiet her mind. Bursts of gunfire rang out from the surrounding woods. She hurried inside.

Within seconds Miguel appeared, bare-chested, dressed in only his jeans, a 9mm in his hand.

He searched her face. "I'm sure I heard gun shots."

Her heart lurched. "Yes, I heard them too."

Miguel pulled her further inside. He dug into his pocket for his cell. Squinting, he punched in a number. A moment later, he punched in another. His face hardened in the moonlight.

"Luis and the others are not answering. I will go and see what is happening."

Her pulse raced. She knew this time would come. Bobby and Nick were out there somewhere.

He emerged from the bedroom fully dressed. "Take the gun I left in your bedside drawer and stay by Natalia."

"But what if…"

"Don't worry. I will be careful. There is no other choice. I cannot sit here and do nothing."

Her panic rose. "Yes, yes, you can. Wait until daylight, Miguel."

"Carmela, please do as I ask. Go and stay with Natalia."

She ran to the master bedroom. Her hands shaking, she removed the .45 revolver from the bedside drawer and shut the light.

The words she spoke earlier came back at her. It was true she didn't want to spend her life running the way Nick and Carrie had. She'd never have any peace, but a chilling reality washed over her. In order for her to stay in Tahoe and keep Natalia, Nick *and* Bobby would have to die.

Gun in hand, she went to the window. She parted the curtain and peered out. A lone figure emerged from the woods and sprinted toward the house. Her pulse spiked. Carmela raised the gun. Her knees grew weak. She fingered the trigger. The figure crept across the veranda, moonlight lit his face. She gasped. The gun slipped from her hands. It was Bobby.

At that moment, she knew she didn't want him to die, couldn't stand the thought of him dying. But Miguel was out there. If he found Bobby, he would kill him.

Men's voices sounded, and she ran from the bedroom and to the front door. She could make things right again, make him love her the way he used to. Whatever he asked of her, she'd do. How foolish to think her heart would forget him.

Carmela tore open the door. She searched the darkness. Miguel must not kill Bobby. He was her life. Her everything. She turned just as Bobby crossed the veranda.

*"Mi tesoro,"* she called out.

Something white hot pierced her chest. Carmela cried out and stumbled back. She looked down at the red spot fanning out across the front of her silk pajamas.

Her head came up, and she met his eyes. "I'm sorry," she whispered and collapsed onto the veranda.

A weight was on her chest. She could hardly breathe. A cold wave swept over her. She reached up, trying desperately to touch Bobby's cheek. "You...must t...take care of Natalia." Her hand grew heavy and dropped. She focused beyond Bobby as Ricardo rose up behind him, his arms stretched out. A smile crossed her lips. "I am coming *Papi,* I am coming." The warmth of Ricardo's arms wrapped around her. She took one last look into Bobby's eyes then felt herself float away.

# CHAPTER 59

# Bobby

Diego Silva's voice split the night air. "I warned you, Carmela. I gave you all my love, for nothing. Better you had died the day I pushed you down the stairs."

He leapt onto the veranda. Bobby aimed. Gunfire ripped. Diego jerked. His eyes bulged. His gun slipped from his hand and he fell a few feet away.

Bobby dropped his weapon and cradled Carmela in his arms.

"No, no!" he cried. He rocked her body, oblivious to his surroundings. A chill swept over him as he stared into her lifeless eyes.

How could she be gone? Weeping, he buried his face in her hair.

Nick's voice battered his ear. A hand grabbed his shoulder.

"Get hold of yourself, Bobby," Nick said. "We have to find Natalia and go."

He grabbed Bobby's elbow, forcing him up. Carmela's body slipped from his arms onto the veranda.

Dalton waved his MK23 and nodded at Nick. "Sorry, I was too late to stop him."

"We need to move fast," Nick said. "I'm going to take the rear entrance." He looked at Bobby. You go in the front. Dalton will cover you. So far, there's no sign of Miguel Medina. Make sure the house is empty."

Bobby stared at his bloodstained clothes. Everything seemed surreal, unfocused like he had stepped into a bad dream. "But…"

"Just do it!" Nick ordered. He continued to the rear of the house.

Bobby took a breath and gathered his weapon. He pictured his daughter's face. She depended on him now. He pulled down his monocular night vision.

Nodding at Dalton, he moved forward and stepped inside the door. Guns at the ready, he and Dalton crept through the darkened living area and along the hallway checking each room.

The sweep finished and satisfied the house was empty of any threat, Bobby moved to the rear entrance while Dalton stationed himself at the front.

A commotion outside made Bobby's ears prick up. He bolted out the back door. A hundred yards away, near the woods, the image of two men locked in battle came into view. He ran closer. Nick's weapons were strewn about.

An arm came up. Something glinted in his night vision. A blood-curdling scream filled the air. A shot rang out. Nick staggered back, collapsing onto the ground. Bobby aimed and fired off a round as the man disappeared into the woods.

He hurried over to Nick. "Are you okay?"

He clutched his left arm beneath the shoulder. Blood seeped through his fingers. He nodded toward the woods.

"Medina," he said. "He jumped me. I took him down and managed to wrestle his knife away. Sliced his face pretty good, but he grabbed his weapon and got a round off."

Dalton rushed at them. "What the hell happened?"

"Medina," Nick said. He held out his hand. "Help me up, guys."

On his feet, he pressed his palm to his shoulder again. He jerked his head at the woods. "He's long gone by now. With all this carnage around us and daylight looming, I don't think it's wise to pursue him. We need to get Natalia and leave."

"I agree," Dalton said. "There's no way to explain any of this to the authorities. We'll find something to make you a tourniquet." He gathered the weapons strewn on the ground.

The three men hurried inside. Except for a muffled cry, the house was still. Bobby moved forward. Pointing his weapon into the bedroom, he spied the outline of a bassinet.

He slung his rifle back, and lifted Natalia up into his arms, covering her with a blanket. "Daddy's here," he whispered. "I got you, little girl."

He grabbed the diaper bag and threw in some diapers. He went into the kitchen. Opening the fridge, he placed two baby bottles in the bag. There was no time for anything else.

Nick and Dalton appeared. A torn piece of cloth wrapped around Nick's upper left arm.

"Bleeding control kit is in the van. This will do for now," Dalton said. "Let's get the hell out of here."

His weapon readied, Dalton went down the front steps first. "All clear."

Nick came out. Bobby followed behind carrying Natalia. His knees went weak at the sight of Carmela's body. His voice broke. We can't just…leave her there."

Nick and Dalton looked at each other. Dalton sprinted up the steps. "Bobby, after everything she's done to you… to all of us."

"I know, I know, but she's the mother of my child. Carmela has to have a proper burial."

"He's right," Nick said.

Dalton sighed. He went inside and returned a few moments later with a sheet. He handed his weapon to Nick, then wrapped Carmela's body, hoisting her over his shoulder.

"Looks like I'm going to have to call in a few favors to fly her home."

Five hours later, everyone was secured on Dalton's plane except for two of his men driving the van back to the ranch. After a feeding and diaper change, Natalia fell asleep. Carmela's body lay wrapped in the cargo hold.

Bobby, though overjoyed to have his little girl, couldn't erase the image of Carmela's face. He recalled the first time he saw her at the art gallery and when they rode Diablo together, her arms tight around his waist, her body pressed against his. Through it all there had been tender moments between them.

Nick sat in the seat across from him. "I'm really sorry for the way things turned out."

"You know, it was Diego who pushed Carmela down the stairs," Bobby said. "I'm glad it was me who killed him but, shooting someone up close like that wasn't a good feeling."

"It shouldn't be," Nick said.

Bobby chewed his bottom lip and stared out the window. "I still can't help wondering if I did the right thing. What if we could have worked things out between us?"

"Look, you protected your daughter from a life with a drug runner. Carmela was a criminal. You'll never know what might have been, but remember how she took Natalia and ran away."

Tears erupted and slid down Bobby's face. He hung his head. "I did love her, you know."

"And there is nothing wrong with that," Nick said. "We can't always help who we fall in love with, even if that person isn't right for us."

He lifted his head and met Nick's eyes. "But what will I tell Natalia when she asks about her mother?"

"You tell her the good things, Bobby. How much Carmela loved her and how much she loved you. Because I believe in her own way, Carmela did love you." Nick placed his hand on Bobby's knee. "Focus on Natalia now. Give her all of your love. I promise you, it will be enough."

Bobby wiped his face. He looked out at the early afternoon sky, the previous night almost like a dream, the memory of which he'd be doomed to repeat over and over again for the next few months. He thought his love for Carmela had vanished the day he left the vineyard for the last time. The stark reality showed itself when he held her dead body in his arms. He loved her then, and he loved her still.

Bobby held Natalia in his arms while the casket was lowered into the ground. Carmela's burial took place in the small graveyard behind the winery. Three other headstones sat beneath the tall oaks. It was only fitting that she rested beside Ricardo and her mother, Natalia. Armando occupied a grave alongside of them.

Nick, Carrie, Dalton, and Joann gathered close together while the priest said a few words. Carrie tucked her hand underneath Bobby's arm. Nick stood, silent, on her other side.

Bobby's eyes scanned past the small wrought iron fence encircling the graves and spied Mateo, his Cattleman's hat in his hands, his head bowed in respect.

The previous day, Bobby had gone through Carmela's things. She had drawn up a Will leaving everything to Natalia with him as Executor. His little girl was now the owner of a winery and several restaurants, not to mention two horses and three palatial homes. It was overwhelming.

Without Carmela to run her drug business, her routes, and contacts had fallen into the hands of the cartels which suited Bobby just fine. He didn't want any of it to touch his daughter.

He shook hands with the priest and took one last look at the grave before walking away with the others.

Carrie stretched out her arms. "Let me hold her for a little bit." He smiled and transferred the baby to her. Nick walked beside them.

"Have you thought about what you're going to do with all of this?" she asked.

"I've met with the employees of the winery and it will pretty much run okay until I get up to speed. The Miami house will go on the market as well as the one in Tahoe. I'll consolidate all the artwork and bring it here to Napa. Mateo has agreed to stay on and look after the horses. I'm going to have him move into the carriage house for now. I'm not sure what to do about the restaurants. They're doing quite well."

"Bobby, you know you can count on us for any help you need," Carrie said.

He laughed. "I just might have to take you up on that offer."

They walked further along the path to the house before she asked, "What about your clients? I know how much your career means to you."

"I haven't figured that out either, but I will. I don't want to give it up."

They reached the front steps. "Mind if I talk to Nick for a minute?"

"I'll take the baby inside. There's lunch waiting in the dining room."

Bobby waited until everyone was gone before turning to Nick. "I need to ask you something."

Nick grew visibly tense. "Go on."

"If Diego hadn't shot Carmela would you and Dalton have let her live?"

"I've never lied to you, Bobby, and I won't start now. I can't speak for Dalton, but I'd every intention of eliminating her." His face clouded over. He stared at the ground for a moment then met Bobby's eyes.

"I hate to admit I was lucky Diego got to her first. As much as I wanted her gone, I'm not sure it was something I could've lived with. But I'll always do what's necessary to keep our family safe."

"I appreciate your honesty. I know she caused all of us pain."

Nick put his arm around Bobby and squeezed his shoulder. "I'm proud of the way you handled yourself. It was a lot to take in. Coming inside?"

"In a minute."

Nick nodded and walked up the steps. Bobby looked out over the vineyards below. A slight fall breeze carried the pungent scent of ripened fruit. It mixed with the blossoming flowers from the garden reminding Bobby of the love between him and Carmela. It was exactly that. Pungent yet sweet all at the same time.

The memory of Carmela would always be with him. He sighed, and walked up the stone steps, wanting nothing more than to hold his daughter close.

# CHAPTER 60

## Carrie

Bright flames licked the wood in the fireplace. The soaring eight-foot tree held a dazzling array of ornaments and lights. After an early winter snowstorm, late afternoon sun broke through the clouds and streamed in through the tall windows.

Carrie surveyed the smiling faces gathered in the great room in South Dakota. All the people in the world she loved were here celebrating the Christmas holiday. Dalton and Joann relaxed together at the end of the long sectional sofa. Aunt May, parked in a chair by the fire, read a book to Izzy who sat at her feet while Michael dozed in her lap.

Bobby, Ronnie, and Justin, seated at a table across the room laughed and teased each other while they played poker. Natalia, slept peacefully upstairs. Bobby kept the baby monitor close by.

Five months had passed since Carmela's death. Bobby appeared to be healing, though Carrie was sure he had his moments. Little Natalia had become his primary focus. He doted on her and was learning to be a good father.

For the time being, she lived with her and Nick while Bobby flew back and forth trying to sort out not only Carmela's businesses, but his own.

Chino sat at Nick's feet, delighting in each rub on his huge head from his master.

Carrie worried about the faraway look in Nick's eyes at times. The past year had taken its toll by awakening some of his demons. She knew Carmela's death played a big part. He still blamed himself for what she became. Carrie hoped one day those demons would sleep again. She snuggled closer to him and rested her head on his shoulder.

"Happy?" he asked.

She smiled up at him. "More than happy."

"Good to hear, since I haven't given you your Christmas gift yet."

She placed her hand over his. "I already have everything I want. All of us here together is more than enough for me."

"That being said, would you mind taking a little ride with me?"

Carrie perked up. "A ride? Where?"

"I told you I haven't given you your present."

"But…"

Nick placed a gentle fingertip on her lips. "Hush. No more questions." He got up and winked at Dalton. "We'll be back in a bit."

Izzy jumped up. "Can I go with you?"

Nick shook his head. "Not this time."

She poked out her lower lip. "That's not fair."

He gave her a warning look, and she backed down.

"Okay," she said and went to bother the trio playing cards.

"How do you do that?" Carrie asked, laughing. "With me, it's always a ten-minute argument."

Nick shrugged. "Daddy's little girl, I guess."

In the mudroom, they slipped on heavy jackets and boots. Outside, they trudged through deep blankets of snow to the garage. Once inside, they put on helmets.

He grabbed a set of keys. "Ride with me?"

"Sure." Carrie winked. "Just like the first time."

They climbed on the snowmobile. Carrie wrapped her arms around his waist.

"Where are we going?"

"You'll know soon enough," Nick said.

He gunned the engine. They veered off the main road onto one of the many trails on the property. Rows of Ponderosa Pines flanked them on either side, their branches dipping under the weight of the heavy snow. The scent of wood smoke blended with the fresh pine. Cold, crisp air streamed at them head-on.

Nick rode up a steep hill and stopped on a rise. He cut the engine and hopped off. Carrie, bewildered, looked around before standing beside him. They removed their helmets. He grabbed her hand, and they walked to the edge.

The valley spread out below them, a mosaic of snow-covered pines and grasslands against the backdrop of the surrounding Black Hills.

"Pretty, huh?" Nick asked.

"It's much more than pretty. It's quite spectacular."

He made a sweeping gesture with his arms. "So, what do you think of all this?"

Carrie eyed him. "What are you getting at?"

His green eyes lit up, and he gathered her close. "Merry Christmas," he said.

Carrie gasped as she caught his meaning. Her heart swelled.

Nick placed his hand beneath her chin and stared into her eyes. "Here, in South Dakota, is where I fell in love with you. It's the place we belong, the place we will always call home and, on this piece of land we'll build our dream house."

"But how, when did you…?"

"I bought 60 acres from Dalton. Half of what he owns here."

Carrie put her arms around his neck. "All those years I suffered with Travis, I could never have dreamed of the life you've given me. I love you so much sometimes it scares me…a little."

"Same goes for me," Nick said. "I waited a long time for you. But it was sure worth the wait." His lips found hers, and he kissed her. They turned toward the valley. Carrie leaned against him, drinking in the view. They had their happy ending at last.

**S**tephanie Baldi grew up in the Brooklyn neighborhood of Gerritsen Beach. Her love of writing began during Saturday trips with her mother to the small local library where children gathered to hear a story read by the local Librarian. When the story ended, Stephanie would pick out a book to take home and read.

But it was not until years later after a career in Patient Accounting and a stint as a Licensed Realtor that her dreams of becoming a writer flourished with a move to the Pocono Mountains in Pennsylvania. It was there that her first novel, *Redemption* was conceived. But family trials and tribulations forced her to abandon the manuscript for a time until her move to Georgia to be closer to her family.

As a writer, Stephanie is dedicated to giving her reader's fast-paced, high stakes, page-turning stories that keep you on the edge of your seat and are full of surprising twists. She resides at her lake home in Villa Rica, Georgia with her husband and two cats. Stephanie is currently at work on the final installment of this trilogy titled *Reckoning* which is slated for release in 2020. She is thrilled to have been nominated for Georgia Author of the Year for *Redemption.*

You can find her online at www.stephaniebaldi2com. Or follow her on facebook.com/sbauthor7 and Twitter at sbauthor7

COMING 2020

THE FINAL INSTALLMENT

# RECKONING

# EXCERPT CHAPTER

# MIGUEL

Miguel Medina strode to the bathroom sink. Dipping his head, he twisted the tap and splashed cold water onto his face. Having spent the July morning outside in the searing Sedona, Arizona sun, he wished for a colder climate.

"Miguel, you mustn't run when it is so hot. You'll give yourself a heat stroke."

Bianca Flores came through the doorway. Her pale blue linen sundress showed off her rich tan. Her long black hair was swept away from her angular face. Silver hoop earrings dangled from each lobe. Her sandals tapped on the terracotta tile floor as she moved toward him.

The woman whom he had loved so deeply was gone. For a short time, Carmela Santiago had been his reason for living. With every rise and fall of his breath, he'd fallen more and more in love. But the woman standing before him was nothing more than a poor substitute. One who cared for him with an enormous amount of passion and understood the black hole lying in the depth of his soul.

He took Bianca's hand and pressed it to his lips. He kissed her palm. "You know I must stay fit. The work I do requires it."

"Yes, but you could just as well use our gym rather than suffering outside."

"Ah, but it's the suffering that makes me tough not an air-conditioned gym."

Bianca shook her head and laughed. "I give up. There is no changing your mind."

She traced the ugly scar running down his left cheek. A scar to remind them each day of his bitter past. That night they took Natalia turned out to be the longest of his life. He thought, somehow Carmela would survive, but a bullet put an end to her. They had destroyed the most beautiful thing in his world. He wasn't sure which one pulled the trigger, but each would pay the price.

Like a wounded animal he had run through the woods until he determined it was safe to return to the house. Miguel arrived and hid in time to see them leave with Natalia and carry Carmela's body away. He'd never forgive himself for not saving her.

Many men had died that night, and he was glad to find Diego Silva among them. With a blood-soaked rag to stem the bleeding from the deep gash on his cheek, he had taken his things and traveled just shy of the Mexican border where he managed to have it stitched before he crossed over into Mexico.

"Three years is a long time Miguel," Bianca said. "They have been out there living life while we hide away here in Sedona."

He took in the shadows behind her dark eyes. The same ones that beckoned him one night in a Mexican Cantina as she set a shot of tequila in front of him. Later, their lust for each other was spent in a local motel where he learned of her early widowhood and subsequent poverty. Miguel chose to lift her out of that poverty which resulted in her undying loyalty to him.

"They will pay, Bianca. If it is the last thing I do on this earth, *all will pay*."

"Remember, my love, it is for the best reason in the world," she said. "Natalia must be taken away from them."

A flash of adrenaline surged through his body. "And she will be. It's time to draw them to us and rid ourselves of them once and for all."

She sat on the edge of the claw-foot tub, her hands clasped together. "You need to let me help you."

"And you will. But first, we need to make several trips. My sources tell me Nick and his family still live in South Dakota. I may want you to become familiar with them."

"Familiar?"

Miguel leaned against the sink and folded his arms. "Yes, seems they are running Carmela's restaurants. A new branch in South Dakota and another in New York. As a matter of fact, they could be short a waitress in the very near future." He gave her a half-smile. "Do you happen to know anyone with experience?"

Bianca got up and faced him. He pulled her close. She moved against him and looked into his eyes. "I think I know someone with lots of experience."

Miguel's desire rose at her words. He led her to the bed. As they stripped off their clothes, he gazed at the tall red rocks in the distance. Their deep rich tone fueling the anger buried within him, an anger nothing could appease until the day he faced Nick and Bobby again.

www.ingramcontent.com/pod-product-compliance
Lightning Source LLC
Chambersburg PA
CBHW020650110726
47901CB00001B/121